Also by Nina Kiriki Hoffman

PERMEABLE
BORDERS

PERMEABLE BORDERS

NINA KIRIKI HOFFMAN

FAIRWOOD PRESS
Bonney Lake, WA

PERMEABLE BORDERS

A Fairwood Press Book
July 2012
Copyright © 2012 by Nina Kiriki Hoffman

Fairwood Press
21528 104th Street Court East
Bonney Lake, WA 98391
www.fairwoodpress.com

Front cover image by
Elena Vizerskaya
Book design by
Patrick Swenson

ISBN13: 978-1-933846-32-3
First Fairwood Press Edition: July 2012
Printed in the United States of America

To all the editors who bought my stories, in roughly chronological order, and I apologize for missing some: Jessica Amanda Salmonson, Algis Budrys, Damon Knight, George Scithers, Darrell Schweitzer, Cathleen Jordan, Kathy Ptacek, Damon Knight, Kit Kerr, Jo Clayton, Dean Wesley Smith, Karl Edward Wagner, David G. Hartwell, Mike Resnick, Cynthia Sternau, Barbara Hambly, Pete Crowther, Stefan Dziemianowicz, Robert Weinberg, Roger Zelazny, Norm Partridge, Josepha Sherman, Lawrence Schimel, Keith R. A. DeCandido, Laura Anne Gilman, Larry Segriff, Gordon Van Gelder, Patrick Nielsen Hayden, John Helfers, Kerrie Hughes, Denise Little, Whitley Strieber, Constance Ash, Elizabeth Ann Scarborough, Greg Ketter, Eileen Gunn, Margaret Weis, Alan Clark & Elizabeth Engstrom, Esther Friesner, Nancy Kilpatrick & Thomas Roche, Al Sarrantonio, Brittiany A. Koren, Jennifer Roberson, Charles G. Waugh, Claude Lalumière & Marty Halpern, Brian A. Hopkins, Brian M. Thomsen, Jay Lake & Deborah Layne, Gavin Grant & Kelly Link, Kim Mohan, Russell Davis, Steve Berman, Loren Coleman, Eric Marin, Rob St. Martin & Julie Czerneda, Daniel Hoyt, Lois Metzger, Melinda Metz, John O'Neill, Bill Fawcett, Patrick Swenson, Heather Shaw & Tim Pratt, Steve Savile, Jeanne Cavelos, Eric Flint, John Joseph Adams, Neil Clark, Mary Anne Mohanraj, Léa Silhol, Kevin J. Anderson, Jeremy Lassen, Paula Guran, and Jonathan & Michele at DAILY SF.

Most especially for people who bought multiple stories from me across the years: Charles L. Grant, Patrick Lucien Price, John Betancourt, Marty Greenberg, Kristine Kathryn Rusch, Bruce Coville, Shawna McCarthy, Ellen Datlow, Terri Windling, and Sharyn November.

Thank you all for helping me live a writer's life.

Publication History

"Key Signatures" first appeared in *F&SF* (April 1996)

"The Weight of Wishes" first appeared in *Children of Magic*, DAW (June 2006)

"How I Came to Marry a Herpetologist" first appeared in *Twice Upon a Time*, DAW (April 1999)

"Strikes of the Heart" first appeared in *Maiden Matron Crone*, DAW (2005)

"Switched" first appeared in *Rotten Relations*, DAW (December 2004)

"Sourheart" first appeared in *The Ultimate Witch*, Byron Preiss Visual Publications (October 1993)

"Inner Child" first appeared in *Otherwhere*, Ace Books (September 1996)

"Home for Christmas" first appeared in *F&SF* (January 1995)

"Anger Management" appears here for the first time

"Trees Perpetual of Sleep" first appeared in *Enchanted Forests*, DAW (December 1995)

"Hostile Takeover" first appeared in *Wizards, Inc.*, DAW (November 2007)

"Here We Come A-Wandering" first appeared in *F&SF* (January 1996)

"The Wisdom of Disaster" first appeared in *Amazing Stories* (January 2005)

"A Fault Against the Dead" first appeared in *Realms of Fantasy* (June 2003)

"The Trouble With the Truth" first appeared in *The Dimension Next Door*, DAW (July 2008)

"Gone to Heaven Shouting" first appeared in *F&SF* (January 1998)

CONTENTS

FINDING
HOME

KEY SIGNATURES

As far as the system was concerned, Zita Wilson came into existence one September morning at 8:56 a.m. when she was about two and a worker found her on the welcome mat at the Social Services Offices.

At eighteen, she got out from under the system's scrutiny, but she couldn't escape the sense that she needed more than the food, shelter, and the care, rough and tender but never permanent, that the system had given her.

Ten years and eight moves later, she arrived in Spores Ferry, Oregon.

Angus's workshop was a basement room with fiddles hanging on the walls, and a workbench holding a bunch of blue horsehair, vice grips, and scattered mysterious tools and bits of wood. The air smelled of oil, glue, and furniture polish. Angus, a hunched old man with a disarming chipped-tooth grin and black-framed glasses, pulled a battered fiddle from the constellation on the wall and handed it to Zita, then equipped her with a bow after tightening the hairs.

Zita had sung in choral groups at some of the high schools she had gone to. She could carry a tune. She had even taken piano lessons for a year at one foster home, paying for a half hour lesson a week with money she got from doing extra household chores. She had had a sense that music was waiting just beyond her ability to play, and it saddened her when she had to move on and lost her lessons and access to a piano.

Unlike the piano, the fiddle had an infinite capacity to sound horrible, the piano's capacity to sound bad being limited to how many keys she could push down at once. The fiddle sounded dreadful as soon as she touched bow to string.

Angus, who told her he had been playing sixty-two years—"Built my first fiddle from a cigar box when I was six," he said—picked up another fiddle and drew a bow across the strings, sounding a sweet, clear note. "Only difference between a fiddle and a violin is attitude," he said. "If you were playing a violin they'd tell you all these things about how to hold this and where to put that, but in my old time fiddle class I just want you to have fun. If you get a tune out of it, all the better." He grinned at her and made the bow dance across the strings. A wonderful bouncy tune jumped out, making her feet itch to jig.

She handed him a hundred dollars and became owner of the battered fiddle, a beat-up case lined with worn yellow fake fur, a bow, and a lump of rosin.

A week later, Zita went to her first class in the new community. The Old Time Fiddle by Ear class met seven to ten Thursday nights in the cafeteria of an area elementary school. Zita had walked into more than enough new situations; she didn't hesitate on the threshold, but strolled in and chose a seat in the circle of chairs set out on the institutional beige linoleum. Angus greeted her, calling her Rita, and introduced her to a man six and a half feet tall and more than sixty years old. "This is Bill," said Angus.

Bill was wearing a guitar, cowboy boots, jeans, and a western shirt with pearl snaps. He had a villain's mustache, and the portable atmosphere of a cigarette smoker. He also had flesh-colored hearing aids in each ear. He gave Zita a wide grin. "Always like to meet a nice young lady," he said.

"Bill's our accompaniment," Angus said.

Zita switched her case to her left hand and shook Bill's right.

Other people were wandering in, setting their fiddle cases on the tables and getting out instruments, tightening bows and tuning. Though this was the first meeting of the class, many seemed to know each other already. Zita smiled at Bill, then went over to set down her own case. She had practiced scraping the bow across the fiddle strings at home, and received angry calls from people in the upstairs apartment. She needed to find somewhere else to practice.

By the end of class she figured she had picked the wrong thing to take this time. She took different classes in each new community, searching for something she could belong to. Playing the fiddle was too hard; the weird position she had to twist into to hold the fiddle to her chin and get her hand around the fiddle's neck tired her, and she couldn't get a good sound out of the damned thing.

The next morning she got up to go to work and noticed aches and pains she had never had before. The next night, she practiced (her upstairs neighbors had gone to a movie) and finally got a real note from the fiddle.

She was hooked.

At the sixth class of the ten-week term, Bill came to her and said, "You're getting real good on that thing. You ought to come out to the grange Friday night."

She had heard people in class talking about granges—there was a grange dance every Friday, rotating between four granges monthly. She had heard, but hadn't listened. She wasn't ready to perform for anybody, even though every week in class she had to stand up and play when her turn came. It wasn't scary in class. Other people played along, helping her keep time and rhythm and, in the wildly hard tunes, notes. She felt like she knew everybody in class as well as she had known anybody in her life, and they were all friendly.

"Come on," Bill said. "Why, I'll pick you up and take you out there, bring you home whenever you say."

Her secret life began the next night.

Sitting at her window in the bank, she wondered what the other tellers would say if they knew of her secret life. Most of them went home to television and children and exhaustion; to Zita it felt odd how her present life was fragmenting within itself, her job in one fragment, her fiddle class in another, and the grange dances in a third, different sets of people in each fragment, though Bill and Angus and a few other fiddle students overlapped two.

The granges were miles out of town, and gathered dancers and musicians from their local populations; she never saw people in town that she had met at the granges, aside from fiddle class people. She felt like a superhero. She could put on a whole different set of clothes and assume another identity, flirting and dancing with the men, gossiping with the women, pretending she was a country girl when she had spent most of her life in metropolitan areas. They knew nothing about her, but they accepted her without question. At first she knew nothing about them. She gathered bits and snippets of information and took them home to warm her in the silence of her apartment. On her first night she had listened to the musicians and realized none of them would ever make a record. Some of the fiddlers were talented, and some were very untalented. After six three-hour classes she could play a tune as well as the worst of them, better than a few. The guitar players just played chords and kept time. An occasional bull fiddle, mandolin, harmonica, or banjo lent spice to some of the meetings, but even without them, the dances went fine. Some people sang, but their voices weren't the kind you heard on the radio; syllables got swallowed, pitch varied from true, and sometimes they forgot the words.

When she shook off her competitive edge she started listening in a different way. She heard the music saying something in a language she could almost understand. It had warmth in it, an invitation. Come. Here is home. Her heart wanted to open, but the scar tissue was too thick.

She got books of lyrics out of the library and studied the words to the tunes she had learned on the fiddle, "Take These Chains," "You Are My Sunshine," "Have I Told You Lately that I Love You," "The Wild Side of Life," "Wildwood Flower." Most of the songs had been written decades earlier. That made sense. Most of the musicians and dancers were upwards of sixty; one of the fiddlers was eighty-seven, another ninety-one.

Some of the other tunes had titles but no words, and those, she thought, were older, brought to this new world from over the sea, passed down through families, trailing history with them; some had probably originated in the mountains to the East. Most of the people at the granges came from out of state, Minnesota, Arkansas, Kentucky, Tennessee.

Travelers, like she was, ending up in Oregon, as she had. Jetsam, washed up on this particular beach.

The Thursday night after class had disbanded for the summer, Bill called Zita and asked her if she'd like to go play music in Kelly's garage. Zita had picked up a few tales from Kelly and Bill, though she couldn't always understand their accents or their habit of speaking almost too softly to hear. Kelly and Bill had driven taxis together in San Diego after they left the navy following World War II, and before that, they had both come from Arkansas, though they hadn't known each other when they were younger, had only met after they had gone around the world. They had both moved to Spores Ferry in the late fifties, raising their children as friends, their grandchildren as mutual.

Zita had met Kelly on one of his visits to the fiddle class, and she liked him. She and Kelly sometimes made faces at each other at the granges. Kelly, whose hair was thick and white, who wore silver tips on the points of his collar and sported a turquoise bolo tie, could roll his eyes faster than anybody else Zita had ever seen.

Waiting for Bill to pick her up and take her to Kelly's, Zita took her fiddle down from the wall (one of the first things Angus told his class was, "Hang your fiddle on the wall, where you can grab it and play any old time. Don't make it hard to get to.") and thought of her lives in other places, how she had made an effort to meet people but usually ended up spending all her nonwork time in her apartment, communing with the television and all the friends there who never answered when she spoke to them. In her various foster families there had been brief sparks of warmth—a gentle haircut from one woman, a secret alphabet with a foster sister so they could write coded notes to each other, a treasured doll for her eleventh Christmas—and brief sparks of violence, shock, disillusionment. And long stretches of sadness.

She nested the fiddle in its case and looked at its battered face. "Tell you what," Angus had said when he sold the fiddle to her, "this fiddle used to belong to Jack Green. I think he got it from his granddaddy. Saw him play it many a time. After his death his widow sold it to a pawn shop, and I found it there. You take good care of it and don't leave it where the sun can get it, specially not in a locked car, hear me?"

Her fiddle had a longer history than she did.

But then, most instruments probably outlasted their players.

The door bell rang, and she closed and picked up her fiddle case. Never before had she had a date to go to someone's garage. She opened the door and smiled at Bill, and he smiled back.

Kelly's house was just another small suburban house in a neighborhood full of such houses. She had lived in houses like that herself. Grinning, Kelly pushed the garage door up to let Zita and Bill duck under, and inside there were six chairs arranged in a circle, and three old men sitting with instruments on their laps.

"Hey, it's a girl," said the one in the cowboy hat and flowing white beard. His blue eyes gleamed behind his glasses.

"This here's Sid," Kelly said, pointing to the bearded man, "and that's Harve, and that's Walt. They came down from Angel Home." Kelly turned to the seated men. "This little gal's just started playing, and she's picking it up real fast."

Zita smiled at them. A foster mother's warning about being alone with men flashed through her head and vanished. Bill was one of the nicest people she had ever known, though she had been suspicious of so much kindness at first. He had been lavish with praise, and cheered her when she learned to return compliments, a skill she had to learn from him. "Hi," she said.

"Sit right down," said Kelly, gesturing at an unfolded metal chair. "Want coffee?" Its warm brown scent flavored the air. He poured a mugful for her from an industrial-sized thermos, handed it to her. Bill sat next to her. A butterfly waved wings in her chest. She had finally gotten up the nerve to play a tune at a grange dance last Friday, with Angus playing along beside her and covering up her mistakes with his own loud accuracy. The experience was amazing: people had danced, and she had played the tune they danced to. She had felt a queer sense of power that almost scared her.

There was less room here for her sound to be swallowed by someone else's. What if they expected her to be perfect?

She put a mute on the bridge of her fiddle. Even she couldn't hear herself play. After half an hour of her playing tiny tentative notes and hoping they fit the tunes the others were playing, Harve (large in overalls, and wearing a billed cap that bore the logo of a tractor rental company in Oklahoma) said, "Take that thing off. Better to make noise than silence."

"Your turn to play a tune, anyway, and you got to play it so we can hear," said Bill.

She glanced sideways at him. She wanted to try "Chinese Breakdown," but she didn't know it well enough yet. She chickened out and played "Wabash Cannonball," which was so simple she had locked it down by the third class.

"Shaping up to be a fine fiddler," Kelly said when she had done. She smiled at him, then looked at the cracked cement floor.

Bill sang an old Hank Williams song.

"Remember the first time I heard that," said Sid. "We used to have battery-operated radios—"

Zita, picturing the big garbage-can-sized radios she had seen in thirties movies, said, "Weren't they wired to plug in?"

"Sure, you could get them that way, but we didn't have electricity in the cabin," said Sid. "After the sun went down you could pull in the Grand Ole Opry. And those big old batteries would be running out of juice and we'd scootch over closer to the radio and listen harder and the sound would fade and we'd scootch closer, and . . ." He cupped his ear and grinned.

Walt said, "When I went to war I was in the Navy, and they broadcast updates from the ship I was on. I didn't know about it till later, but my mama said she figured as long as those broadcasts came through, I was okay."

"Hey, you wanna talk, save it for the telephone," said Kelly, and struck up a tune on his mandolin, "There's More Pretty Girls than One."

Zita played along, feeling her bow slide smoothly over the strings, not bumping and jumping and jiggling out dreadful screechy hiccuping sounds the way it had when she first started. She thought of Sid as a boy, inching closer to his radio to catch scratchy distant music, and suddenly a vision opened up inside her, a vision of a web the music made, stretching across time and space, entering the ears of a girl a hundred years ago, edging out her fingers for her children to hear eighty years ago, coming out in hums from those same children now grown fifty years ago, in the hearing of their own children and maybe the children of strangers, melting from one form into another, threads of tune catching up different beads of words, carrying them, dropping them, threading through others, transforming and traveling and yet carrying the original signatures of the first drums, the first lyres, the first flutes, the first voices.

Here was a heredity, handed out freely, gathering in sons and daughters, only asking to be learned and known and passed on. She looked at these five men, who had come from five different directions and ended up here in the garage with her, joining her in the instant family that shared tunes created.

She smiled wide at all of them, and they smiled back.
"Here's an oldie but a goodie," said Walt. "The Log Cabin Waltz."
"Teach me," said Zita.

THE WEIGHT OF WISHES

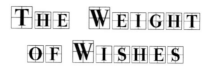

Beth and I played rock-paper-scissors to see which of us would have to take the Christmas stocking in to our daughter Lisa's room this year. As usual, Beth was paper, and I was rock. Dang! We knew each other well after twelve years of marriage, yet I always expected Beth to choose something new, so I stuck to the same strategy, and always lost.

Beth put a big candy cane into the red stocking and handed me the bulky thing. "Good luck, Will." She kissed me. She grabbed the green stocking, the one we'd put together for nine-year-old Tim.

Tim was our easy child.

I glanced around the master bedroom, which, on normal days, was a clash of Beth's and my versions of clutter amidst white-and-green bamboo print wallpaper. Tonight's clutter was clutter on top of clutter. Wrapping paper, ribbon, tape, and wrapped gifts lay scattered across the bed. The closet door gaped: there were still a few gifts on the upper shelves to wrap, but we needed a break.

I suspected Lisa had been in our room in the weeks leading up to Christmas, snooping through the closet, and nothing we had gotten her would surprise her. Had she wrecked Christmas for Tim? Had she told him what she had found? I considered. Lisa was in one of her hate-Tim phases. Was she Machiavellian enough to know that she could spoil Christmas by telling Tim about the bike, or was she petty enough to enjoy knowing without telling? I prayed for petty.

"Don't forget the costume," Beth said.

I wasn't fat enough to make a good Santa, and neither was Beth. We had an elf outfit that would fit either of us, though the red velvet pants only came down to my knees.

We'd had a theological argument about whether elves ever went on the sleigh to help Santa. Canon said No. Convenience and sense of being less ridiculous dressed as an elf than dressed as Santa said maybe. Beth had insisted we buy the costume after Halloween when there were tons of costumes for sale at half price, because last year, when I chose rock and had to take the stocking into Lisa's room, I had gone as myself, and Lisa had been awake. I hid the stocking behind my back before she saw it, and escaped by convincing her I was sleepwalking to the bathroom. Then I waited outside her door for two more hours, and finally went in while she slept. I spent Christmas in a state of unpleasant exhaustion, even though the kids were happy.

But Lisa was ten now, a whole year more sophisticated than she had been last year, and a year more powerful. The costume, Beth's brainstorm, was supposed to protect me from discovery; if Lisa saw me and thought "Santa's Helper," so what? I could place the stocking and get out, leaving us enough time to finish wrapping the presents and decorating the tree.

That was the plan, anyway.

I changed into the red velvet pants, pulled up red-and-white striped stockings, put on curl-toed slippers with bells at the toes, and donned the red velvet doublet. I finished up with the fur-trimmed red velvet cap with a white furry ball at the dangling end, which dropped halfway to my waist. I felt almost as stupid as I had in my sixth grade play, when I had to dress up as broccoli and deliver doggerel about the benefits of vegetables in a healthy diet.

"Come on, honey. Sit here. There's more to do." Beth made me sit at her vanity table. She got out spirit gum and a black beard and mustache. She smiled fiendishly while she stuck fake hair to my face. "You're devilishly cute," she said. "I'd kiss you, but I don't want to end up with the mustache."

I glanced in the mirror and saw a me I didn't recognize. "Ho, ho," I said. My voice lacked Santa authority; I was too unnerved by my transformation. I hadn't realized I could change so much without Lisa having anything to do with it.

"It ought to confuse her, anyway," said Beth. She kissed my cheek, while I tried not to scratch my face; the spirit gum made my upper lip itch.

I stood. "Okay, let's get this over with so we can get at least four hours' sleep."

Beth saluted and grabbed Tim's stocking. We left the master bedroom and headed our separate ways.

Lisa's room was toward the front of the house, a mistake whose magnitude we had only lately come to recognize. She looked out her window a lot, and if she saw things she didn't like, or saw things she liked too well, well. . . . It would have been safer if she had Tim's room, which looked out over the back yard, a region that belonged to us—but she was stubborn. She liked her room and didn't want to change it.

The bells on my toes were ringing. It irritated me. I had hoped Lisa would be asleep when I got there, a vain hope, I knew, but still a tiny hope. She was a light sleeper. The bells would wake her up for sure.

I eased her door open anyway, as if I were really a sneaky Christmas Elf. I crept across the carpet toward her bed, jingling softly. I hoped she hadn't redecorated the room since the afternoon; I didn't want to trip over anything. When she'd gone through her swamp phase, Tim had actually been bitten by a poisonous snake in here.

It was close to Christmas; Lisa had been acting Good for more than a week, a relief to everyone. If she'd changed her room around, it should still be friendly.

The bedside light snapped on. Lisa was sitting up, blankets bunched in both fists under her chin. She stared at me.

My daughter had the loveliest soft dark hair; it clouded around her head like glory. Her face was oval, her cheeks rosy, her dark eyes wide and brilliant. She sucked on her lower lip.

As my eyes adjusted to the onslaught of light, the first thing I felt was a rush of love for my daughter. The fear took a couple seconds to kick in.

"Wow," she said. "Wow! You—"

Her shifter power flooded through me. For the first time I realized what a dumb idea the costume had been.

"You're an elf!" cried my daughter.

Why did they call them elves when they were obviously dwarves? I wondered, as I dwindled down to the height of a five-year-old child. My ears pulled up into points, and my muscles bunched and tightened as my arms and legs and torso contracted. The outfit shrank with me. The beard and mustache rooted into my face, and my hair, usually short, sprouted into dark curls that tumbled down around my now-compacted shoulders.

The good thing about the change was that it was almost painless. Some previous shifts Lisa had put on me hurt. One or two of them were even life-threatening, but that turned out to be a good thing, though I didn't think so at the time. My being rushed to the hospital in an ambulance had convinced Lisa not to throw her power around carelessly.

"Yes," I said. My voice sounded different, deep and gruff. Dwarf, I thought. An elf's voice should sound like singing. Oh, well; my daughter and I were fishing different myth streams. I would find out firsthand what she thought of elves now.

My new shape didn't hurt, but there were warm spots in my chest and forehead I didn't understand. Was I going to sprout horns? My costume was now spangled with small gold balls. Were they real gold? Why did my tongue taste peppermint?

Something flowed into me, something warm and strong and scary. It flowed into the spots on my chest and forehead, then spread through me, rushing out to the tips of my fingers and toes, crackling like static in my new wealth of hair. Some of it flowed out of my hands and into the stocking I held. The bumps in the stocking shifted, some shrinking, some expanding. I remembered what Beth and I had put inside it, but I was pretty sure that wasn't what was in it now. This was the shiftiest shift Lisa had ever cast on me. "Yes," I repeated in my new voice. "I'm an elf. What are you doing awake, little girl? You're supposed to be asleep."

"I wanted to see magic," she said in a half-swallowed voice.

"Christmas magic happens while you're sleeping," I said. My voice reminded me of frog croaks.

A tear trickled down one of Lisa's flushed cheeks. "I know," she said. "The magic other people believe in happens while they're sleeping. I'm the only one magic happens to while I'm awake. I just thought. . . ."

"All right, all right. Now you've seen me." I walked to her bed and set the stocking down on the foot. Something moved inside the red velvet, squirmed toward the opening; the stocking looked longer, more ornate, with a gold-embroidered star on it; the white fur around the opening looked like rabbit fur. "You take a peek in here." I patted the squirming part of the stocking, wondering what kind of food we'd need to get for it. It had better be able to eat human food for at least a day. The pet stores would be closed on Christmas. "Take care of what needs care, but then close your eyes and settle down till morning. It'll take me a little while to prepare the rest of your Christmas, now that you've delayed me."

"I'm sorry, Mr. Elf." She sniffled.

"It's all right, honey." I patted her hand. "Oh, one more thing. You be nice to Tim today."

She nodded.

Jingling, I left the room. The door closed silently behind me before I had a chance to pull it shut, and my hands prickled.

The upstairs hall was lit by a nightlight so the kids could see their way to the bathroom, or sleep with their doors ajar for comfort. In that dim light, I stared at my new hands. Squat and sturdy and strange, different from the long-fingered hands I used to play guitar. Something prickled under the skin. I rubbed my hands together, trying to ease the itch. When I pulled them apart, sparkling flecks of light flew out, red and green, blue and lavender, danced in the air, then flattened in glowing snowflake patterns on the wall.

"Will?" Beth murmured. She stood just outside of Tim's room.

"What?"

I strode toward her. My head was waist height to her now. I grabbed her hand—so big!—and pulled her into our bedroom.

She dropped to her knees on the carpet by our bed, so our heads were level. "Oh, Will, I didn't know—"

"It's all right." I shrugged. "She wanted to see an elf, and the costume clinched it."

"What were those lights that came from your hands?"

"Good question." I looked at the chaos of our room, mid-wrap, and the heat in my chest burned hotter. "I'm a Christmas elf," I said. I pressed my new, short hand against my chest. The warmth still flowed into me, moved up my arms and buzzed in my fingers. "So I might as well use what she gave me—" I gestured, and the other presents wrapped themselves in paper we hadn't had before. Bows in red and gold foil frothed up from the tops of gifts. Things flew out of the closet and wrapped themselves before I could see what they were. Small, already wrapped gifts appeared out of the air. The presents stacked themselves on the bed, a lovely pile of loot. Brightly colored cards fluttered from nowhere to land like paper butterflies on the gifts.

Beth knelt beside me, her eyes wide. "Oh," she said. "Oh, no. Oh, wow."

"Now the tree."

She followed me downstairs. While I poured warmth toward the tree and watched the energy manifest as spun glass ornaments, filigrees of tinsel, gilded nuts, giant iridescent bubbles, Beth wandered into the kitchen. She came back with two mugs of cocoa with marshmallows; I could tell by the smell.

"Wow," she said.

I gestured, and the presents we had wrapped upstairs flocked down through the air and stacked themselves around the base of the tree.

I flicked a finger at the tree lights, and on they went, a blinking multitude of colors that sparkled through the clear ornaments and glittered reflections off the opaque ones.

I could get used to this, being able to remote-control everything by lifting a finger. I had had really good dreams like this.

I looked at my wife. She stood there with steaming mugs, her expression a mixture of pole-axed and irritated.

"What?" I said.

"I thought we were going to put the family ornaments on the tree. Together." She turned and sat on the couch facing the tree.

I went to the couch and climbed up next to Beth. She handed me a mug of cocoa. We sipped in silence.

"There's still room for our other ornaments," I said. I felt an edge of an ache in my chest that had nothing to do with Christmas elf magic. Beth was right. Our Christmas Eve preparations were something we had shared with each other since before the kids were born.

"Oh, come on. It's perfect. You don't want to add old junk to something that's perfect."

"Beth." I put my hand on her thigh. Warmth pooled under my palm. She was a big, solid presence beside me; she smelled like lilies and gingerbread, and she looked like the woman I had loved all my life, even before I met her.

Beth set down her mug and put her hand over mine on her leg. She leaned over. Her mouth tasted like cocoa.

Something passed between us, flavored with desperation and excitement. We went upstairs to bed.

Tim woke us in the morning by pounding on the locked door. "Hey!" he called through the wood. "It's Christmas! Come on!"

Beth's blonde head was resting on my chest, her arm across me.

Her brow furrowed, and she snorted. I raised my hand to stroke her hair and saw I'd gotten my guitar-playing fingers back.

Lisa's shifts could last an hour, a day, a week, or forever. I was glad this one had been short.

"Will?" Beth mumbled.

I sat up, gripping her shoulders so she wouldn't fall. "We'll be right there," I yelled to Tim, "after we shower and dress."

"Do it later!" he yelled back. "Santa came! We have to see what's here!"

"We sure do," Beth muttered to me. "Do you even know?"

"Lisa has a new pet. I don't know what kind."

"A new pet?" Beth frowned as I handed her a robe. "We decided against that six times, didn't we?"

"You and I did, but the elf—"

"Oh, come on, Will. That was you."

"Not entirely." As I spoke, I knew I was being ridiculous. Who else could the elf have been?

The contents of Lisa's stocking had changed in my stubby hands before I knew what I was capable of doing. Something had made decisions about what I was giving Lisa, and it hadn't felt like I was the one in charge.

Once, Lisa had changed me into Say Yes Dad. Whatever she asked me, I said yes. Yes, I would take her to the ice cream parlor and watch, smiling, as she ate the biggest sundae on the menu. Yes, I would buy her that expensive doll with huge wardrobe and dream house she'd been lusting after for two months. Yes, I would sit on the floor with her and play dolls. Thank goodness Beth came home before I said Yes to anything worse. Beth had talked Lisa into turning me back into myself.

One of Lisa's rules was that she could only experiment on one parent at a time, and she had to obey the other parent. When she'd started shifting us, about the time she was four, and we couldn't stop it from happening, we'd drummed that rule into her. She was going to break it, probably someday soon. The teen years were coming. All we knew how to do in advance was lay a groundwork of love, discipline, and hope.

While I was Say Yes Dad, I hadn't realized I was someone other than myself. Every Yes I said felt like the right choice. Maybe the elf had had elements of some Not-Will person in him. He had known how to do magical things, something with which I had no experience. What could we do now but go forward? "I'm sorry, Beth. Lisa has a new pet." I shook my head and tied the belt of my robe. Beth brushed her hair and sighed. "All right. Somehow we'll make it all right. We always have so far."

"An elf came last night," Lisa told us when we opened the bedroom door. Tim was already racing for the stairs.

"Really?" Beth asked.

"Really and truly. He brought my stocking. Look, Mom. He gave me a kitten."

"A kitten," Beth said. She glanced at me, her eyes narrowed.

"It's just what I always wanted," said Lisa.

The kitten was adorable, in a big-pawed, lavender-eyed, lilac-furred way, with darker points at nose, ears, and tail, like a designer version of a Siamese. Lavender eyes? Lilac fur? It rode Lisa's shoulder, and its eyes looked too intelligent. "His name's Singer," Lisa said. The kitten let out a musical meow.

"Lisa, you know you're not supposed to shift animals," Beth said.

"I didn't shift him, Mom, honest I didn't. This is what he looked like when he came out of my Christmas stocking. I know I'm not allowed to shift living things without permission."

I hooked my arm around Beth's neck, drew her close so I could whisper in her ear, "We did put a stuffed animal in the stocking, and it was those colors." Like a fool, I had thought maybe a plush animal would satisfy Lisa's eternal hunger for a kitten. In a way it had.

"Damned elf," muttered Beth.

I let her go and squatted in front of Lisa. "Well, Merry Christmas, honey. Hello, Singer. Welcome to our house." I held out my hand, and the kitten deigned to sniff it. He meowed a musical question and pressed his paw on my hand.

"Sorry," I said. "I don't speak song." I looked at Lisa, who shook her head.

"Mrrp," said Singer.

"Mom! Dad! Lisa!" Tim yelled from downstairs. "If you don't get down here right now, I'm going to open something without waiting for you!"

Beth hurried toward the stairs. I straightened. Lisa tugged me back down.

"Singer's the best present in the world," she whispered. "I don't care what else I get. I'm already happy, Daddy."

I lifted her in my arms, even though she was too big for that. I prayed I wouldn't throw my back out. She put her arms around my neck; Singer clung to both of us without breaking the skin, and I managed to walk downstairs carrying all three of us without tripping. I wanted to stretch any sweet moments Lisa offered as long as I could.

"Come on, Dad," Tim said. He jumped up and down by the tree. "Look at it! Look at it!"

I set Lisa down and sat on the couch beside Beth to stare at the tree. Had the ornaments lasted after I lost my power? They had. Beth and I had never gotten around to putting up the family ornaments. The tree was beautiful, almost unearthly—and unhinged from tradition. I took Beth's hand, and she squeezed mine.

"Oh, Daddy," Lisa whispered.

I swallowed. "Who wants to play Santa?"

"I'll do it!" Tim cried. That surprised me. Whoever played Santa had to hand a gift to everybody before he got to open his first one. We did the present opening in cycles. One gift for everybody, a wild ripping of wrapping paper, and everybody got to admire each other's gifts before we moved on to the next round. Tim had always been too impatient to play Santa.

Tim handed Beth a medium-sized present, me a small present I didn't recognize, and Lisa a medium present before rushing to the bike, which he had obviously scouted before he came upstairs to wake us. "Ready?" he cried. He tore paper before anyone else got a chance to answer. In seconds the green ten-speed stood revealed. "Oh, boy!" Tim cried. "Oh, boy! Oh, boy! I want to try it now!"

"Tim, calm down. You're not the only one who got a present," said Beth.

Tim hugged his bike, then turned to see what we had gotten. Beth held up a glazed clay handprint Tim had made her at school. I showed off my new red and purple tie from Lisa. Lisa held up a book by one of her favorite authors; I couldn't remember if Beth or I had gotten it for her. We all thanked each other and Santa. Singer watched from Lisa's shoulder.

"Next round," Beth said. Tim gave his bike another hug, then distributed more presents.

We had bought the kids more presents than we got for each other, so the distribution network broke down before the end of the present opening. Tim gave Beth and me small unfamiliar gifts wrapped in cellophane last, before he and Lisa plunged into an orgy of what-else-is-there.

Lisa's big present was art supplies—tubes of acrylic paint in many colors, with special emphasis on reds, oranges, and earth tones, her favorites; brushes with tips from broad to narrow; a palette, a fancy paint box with compartments for everything, and some pre-stretched canvases.

Beth and I had debated about the paints. Lisa had done some paintings at school with poster paint, and we both thought they were promising, but there was no guarantee she wanted to do more. Was she happy with the gift? I didn't know. We had given her a bike last year. There was no way for us to give the kids equal gifts, their interests were so different. Was she going to be mad that Tim got something more spectacular than she had this year? If she got mad, how would that manifest?

I saw Singer on Lisa's shoulder, remembered she had said that Singer was a good enough gift. She looked happy. Tim was still in bike heaven.

My final present had a note on it, one of the butterfly cards, and it was wrapped in red cellophane that crinkled as I untied the golden bow.

"Read the card, Will," Beth murmured.

I did. It said: "Don't try one until you're alone." It was signed ELF. Inside was a round brown tin the size of my palm with a red spot on the lid. I touched the spot. It felt hot. The lid popped up. An array of small ruby hard candies lay inside, glowing with light of their own. I lifted the box to sniff and smelled cinnamon and peppermint. A blue snowflake drifted out of the box and melted on my chest, and for a second I felt the return of elf energy. I closed the tin and tucked it in my pocket.

"Oh, boy!" Tim cried. He waved the card from a small gift wrapped in blue cellophane. "It's a spell, Dad! My first spell." He ripped off the cellophane, opened a jewelry box, took a silver ring out, slipped it onto his left middle finger. He held up his left hand, middle finger extended. The ring gleamed. "It's called Turnback. Just try anything on me now, Lisa. Just you try."

"What? I'm not allowed to shift you, Tim."

"Like that ever stops you. Come on. Turn me into a dog."

Lisa glanced at me. "Daddy?"

I looked at Beth.

"Turnback? A spell?" Beth asked.

I shrugged. "News to me."

"Special permission, Lisa," Beth said. "One small, short-term shift that doesn't hurt."

Lisa's smile was blinding. She set Singer on the couch, rubbed her hands, and sent shifter energy at Tim.

His new ring flared with blue light. He laughed as Lisa dwindled down into a chihuahua. Singer darted up the back of the couch, lavender eyes glowing as he watched the small dog. Lisa barked and raced around, trapping herself in wrapping paper. Her barks rose in pitch and frequency. She was scaring herself.

I lunged forward and caught her. "Hey, honey." I sat on the couch, cradling her in my arms. Her trembling rocked me. After a minute or two it slowed. She looked up at me with large black eyes and licked my nose.

"It works. It so works!" Tim cried. He hugged himself, then ran around the room flapping his elbows like chicken wings and crowing. "I am so gonna celebrate!"

Lisa shifted from dog to herself on my lap. I still had my arms around her. She sat with her back to my front, watching Tim. "Daddy," she whispered. She turned her head so I could see her profile.

"It will change things," I said, "but maybe that's better." We worked hard to keep her from mistreating Tim, but we couldn't watch them all the time. Something in her seemed to restrain her from doing things that would really hurt him; she had been fascinated by him when they were both babies, before her powers manifested, and perhaps that affection had transformed into a guardian mindset. Beth and I hoped so, anyway. We knew Tim's life was haunted by strange changes coming over him at odd times, and we weren't sure how to take care of him. We picked up the pieces after every shift we knew about and tried to sort them out. There weren't any manuals for this that we could find. Tim had friends, and spent a lot of time with them instead of Lisa. He was boisterous and happy most of the time. He seemed well adjusted, but who could tell?

The ring would definitely change the way he and Lisa related.

Lisa sighed. She had two friends of her own, but the need for secrecy about her skills meant she held a large part of herself back from her friendships. Tim was the one person close to her age who knew everything. She depended on him more than she knew.

Tim, crowing, raced up to us and waved his beringed finger in Lisa's face, then ran away again. I wished he'd put the ring on a different finger, but for all I knew, there were instructions included in the note that specified the middle finger; we'd probably have to apologize for him in public until we got him tamed down. "Mom, can I have some cookies?" Tim yelled.

"Not until you've had a normal breakfast," Beth said. "You're hyper enough as it is." She held a small yellow jewelry box in her hand, the orange cellophane it had been wrapped in folded neatly on her lap. She tucked the box in her bathrobe's pocket. Curiosity bit me. What had the elf given Beth for Christmas? For that matter, what had he given me? I guessed I'd have to wait to find out. Christmas morning was kids' time; parents would have the afternoon, while the kids broke or got tired of their presents.

"It's Christmas," Tim said. "Today, everything's different. I vote we have cookies for breakfast!"

"I vote we don't," Beth said. In our household, a grown-up's vote counted twice as much as a child's vote, one of the things Lisa kept trying to adjust before we convinced her to stop that. "Will? Lisa?"

"Cookies," Lisa said.

"Pancakes," I said. Everybody liked those, though not as much as cookies. The sugar-free syrup tasted okay and didn't make the kids quite so crazy.

"I change my vote to pancakes," said Beth.

"Awww," Tim said. He grabbed the handlebars of his bike, ready to push it outside for a try.

I set Lisa on the couch beside me and stood up. "I'll make the batter. Beth, you watch Tim try the bike, okay?"

"Can Singer go outside?" Lisa asked.

"Will he stay with you and not run away?"

Lisa reached up to the back of the couch, where Singer crouched. She stroked the kitten's head. "Will you stay with me? Not be a wild thing?"

Singer meowed a short snatch of melody. Lisa looked at me, and I shrugged. "I bet he'll be a wild thing no matter what. Just ask him to stay. I wish I knew what he eats. I hope we've got something we can feed him."

"Daddy, can I do a special-permission shift again?"

"What kind?" I asked. Beth, who was holding the front door open for Tim and his bike, paused before following him outside.

"I want to understand Singer."

I checked with Beth, who nodded. "Okay," I said. "Let's give it a shot. Don't make it permanent until you know you like it, though; maybe he's saying things you don't want to know. What if he's not really communicating at all? Put a provision in about not forcing you to understand if there's nothing there." Mental shifts were even trickier than physical ones; unexpected side effects abounded.

"Okay." Lisa sat with Singer in her lap, closed her eyes, frowned. She cocked her head. The furrow between her brows deepened, and then prickles of shifter energy needled my face and scalp.

"Hey!" I said.

Lisa opened her eyes. She rubbed her forehead and frowned.

"Did it work?" asked Singer.

Lisa and I stared at each other. We both nodded.

Beth said, "What did you do? Lisa, did you shift your father?"

"Yes," Lisa said in a small voice.

"What have we told you?"

"No shifting other people without asking. He said, 'let's give it a shot.'"

"Lisa. You know he didn't mean it that way."

"I know," Lisa whispered.

"One hour of alone time," Beth said, "but you don't have to pay until tomorrow." She went outside, letting the door slam behind her.

"What's that about?" Singer asked.

"That's my punishment for shifting Daddy without permission," Lisa said. "I hate being alone worse than anything."

"Let's go to the kitchen," I said.

"Is it okay if I carry you?" Lisa asked Singer.

"Better than okay, gifta," Singer said. "Let me up on your shoulder. I love your head. It's got woosa around it."

"What's woosa?" Lisa asked.

"Delicious," said Singer as we crossed the dining room. I held the kitchen door for Lisa, then followed her in.

"Singer, what are you?" I asked. I got out a bowl, ran water in it, and set it on the floor.

"What am I? You should know." The kitten blinked both lavender eyes.

Uh-oh. Don't go there. Maybe Lisa knew I had been the elf, and maybe she didn't. She usually knew when she shifted something or someone, though she had occasionally done a shift in her sleep before she got her powers under control. Fortunately, that was before she had the oomph she had now, and the shifts had usually been short-term and minor.

Shifting me into an elf was a big one, but she might have done it in a sleepy state, without noticing. She had really wanted to see an elf. She might have mistaken shifting for longing.

I didn't want to find out what the elf had done to bring the kitten to life, not until Lisa was out of the room.

"But I *don't* know." Whatever Singer was, I hoped he could take a hint. "Are you really a kitten?" I asked.

"I have the body for it." Singer broke into a melodic purr. "Woo!" he said above his own purring, "you should try this. It's like being massaged on the inside."

I got the feeling Singer wasn't really a kitten.

"What do you eat?" Lisa asked. I got out the Bisquick and a mixing bowl, milk, eggs, the eggbeater.

"I'm not sure," Singer said. "I think I'd like . . . meat. Any kind of meat."

Lisa went to the fridge, opened the door. "Daddy, can I give him some turkey?" We'd had a big feast over at my mother's house last night, and Mom sent us home with loads of leftovers. She made a giant turkey and gave us leftovers for almost every holiday, convinced that Beth was a terrible cook and nobody in our family got enough to eat. Beth didn't mind. Much. It was true Mom made excellent turkey, and Beth loved turkey as much as I did.

"Sure. Put some on a plate on the floor. Singer, whatever you are, you're going to have to act like an animal while you're in that body. You're odd enough already to give the neighbors things to talk about."

"We'll see," said Singer.

Lisa forked some turkey onto a plate and set it on the floor next to the water bowl. Singer jumped off her shoulder and stuck his nose into the turkey. "Heaven," he said, and ate.

I whipped up pancake batter and pondered the kitten. I had liked him better before I understood him. Now I didn't know who he was, or whether he was a safe companion for my daughter.

She knelt on the floor next to him and stroked his back, and he purred and ate—for the moment, a perfect picture, if you could get used to a purple kitten.

"If I take you outside, you won't run away, will you?" Lisa asked Singer.

"Are you kidding? Leave you, gifta? Never." He rubbed his head against her hip, then returned to the turkey.

Beth and Tim came in through the kitchen door, Tim hauling his bike right into the kitchen. I knew I had forgotten something: a bike lock. Well, the bike could live in the robbery-safe garage, but for now, Tim wasn't letting it out of his sight. Should make for an interesting bedtime.

"How'd it go?" I asked. I set the skillet on the stove and turned on a burner.

"This is the greatest bike in the world," Tim said. "I rode around the block and saw Ricky Davis on his new bike. Mine's much better. These racing stripes. And the Turnback ring. This is the best Christmas ever!"

"Glad you're enjoying it." I dolloped pancake batter into hot oil in my skillet. "Lisa? How you doing?"

She sat back on her heels and picked up the kitten, hugged him. "Thanks, Daddy. Thanks, Mama. It's my best Christmas, too."

Beth knelt and kissed Lisa's cheek. Lisa set Singer down and reached up to hug her mother.

I dished up pancakes, and we all ate. Afterward it was time to clean up all the wrapping paper. As the four of us wadded paper, threw the wads toward wastebaskets, and high fived if we scored, I found some purple cellophane near where Lisa had been sitting when she opened her gifts. The kids had already stacked their gifts and carried some up to their rooms. Under the tree, there were only a few presents left—for the grandparents and other relatives. "Lisa? Honey, what came in this wrapping paper?" I asked.

"It's a present I don't understand," she said. "I thought maybe it was a joke."

We all stopped cleanup and gathered to look at Lisa's mystery present, which she pulled out of the middle of her stack of books, art supplies, clothes, stuffed animals, and board games. MAGIC KIT, it said on the brightly colored tin box. AMAZE YOUR FRIENDS! CONFOUND YOUR ENEMIES! A magician in a turban waved a wand on the box top; a rabbit was emerging from a puff of smoke in front of him.

"Wow, is that ever a dumb present for you," Tim said. "Like you need stupid tricks! Who gave it to you?"

"What did the note say, honey?" Beth asked.

Lisa unstuck the note from the gift and handed it to her. "Use this to build your reputation as a magician," Beth read aloud. "Signed, Elf."

"I get it," I said. "I think I get it. You practice doing tricks from this box, Lisa. They'll look like other magicians' tricks. Everybody knows those are just tricks. You tell people you're studying magic, and show them some tricks, and then if they see you do other things they can't explain—"

"Oh, yeah," said Beth. "I love that elf!" She beamed.

"I tell people I'm a magician?" Lisa said slowly. "I tell people I'm a magician. But I'm not supposed to tell anybody anything."

"This would be okay to tell," I said. We'd had to change Lisa's school several times to cover up mistakes she'd made. These days I drove her six miles across town to Hillside Elementary, where she hadn't messed up yet. She'd only been going there since mid-October. If she decided to be a magician now, maybe she could stay all the way through sixth grade. "You have to teach yourself the tricks the hard way, though. No real magic, just imitation magic."

"That's weird, Daddy," she said.

"Can I try?" Tim asked.

"No!" Lisa said. She hugged the box.

"Why not? You don't want it."

"Yes, I do." She stared at the floor, her arms tight around the magic kit, then looked up at Tim and relaxed. "Okay. You can try. We'll both learn it."

"Yahoo!"

She opened the clasp and raised the lid. Inside was a manual with a magician on the cover. She lifted it out. Beneath it was a compartmentalized box with all kinds of tricks—a deck of cards; shell game shells; red and yellow juggling balls; steel rings; a traditional magic wand—black, with a white cap at either end; a bouquet of feather flowers; a collapsing top hat.

"*I* get to try them first. It's *my* kit," Lisa said.

"Well, hurry up and try something, so I can try it next," said Tim.

Beth and I rose, finished cleanup without any more scoring, and retreated to the kitchen.

"What was your elf present?" she asked.

"I don't know," I said. I showed her the candy tin and note. "What was yours?"

She got out the yellow jewelry box, handed me the note. "This ring's name is Bendshift. Love, Elf." She opened the box to display a slender silvery band nesting in yellow velvet. She took out the ring and slid it onto her ring finger, where it dropped into place above her wedding ring without being noticeable. "Bendshift," she said.

"Sounds promising." If she could bend Lisa's shift power, the way Tim could now turn it back—

We'd spent all of Lisa's life trying to get her to respect other people enough to leave them alone. If she wasn't such a good kid to start with, one of us would probably be dead by now. With the new ring powers, maybe everybody could relax.

"I love that elf," Beth said again. She gave me a kiss.

"I'm not—it wasn't—I didn't—I don't remember putting these gifts together," I said.

"Well, I love you more, Will, but I love the elf anyway. This is going to change things for all of us."

"I wonder if you can bend a shift that's already taken place," I said.

"Which one? Lisa's been so good today."

I took Beth's hand and led her to the kitchen table, where we sat facing each other. "I don't know about the kitten, Beth. He's not originally a kitten."

"She loves him. We can't take away something she loves." Her eyes looked hollow. We'd had some very difficult fights with Lisa in the past about things she loved that were bad for her. Lisa was better about such things now; she listened instead of throwing tantrums, and we didn't end up in the hospital after the fights. There were other kinds of scars, though.

"Not take him away," I said. "Understand him. She gave me the power to understand him; I wonder if you could extend that to you."

She consulted the note from her present, frowned. "It didn't come with instructions. I thought it would work like Tim's, protect me when she was shifting me. Let me see. Where did you feel the shift?"

"Face and the top of my head."

Beth laid her hands on my face; they felt warm. I smelled Christmas perfume I'd bought her on her wrists, something by Givenchy I'd noticed her trying more than once when we went to the department store. It carried a different kind of warmth, full-bodied and enticing. I wondered how soon we'd be able to get some real time alone. Probably not until after the kids went to bed.

"Oh," she said. "There's kind of a—" She moved her hands over my face, across my scalp. My skin prickled in the wake of her touch. "—a tingling. Ring, bend this shift so it touches me, too."

My face and scalp went pins and needles. Beth gasped. She sat back, her hands dropping from my head. Her face turned red; the color faded.

"Are you all right?" I grabbed her hands.

She took a deep breath, let it out, nodded. "That was just—so strange. Will. I did magic. I did magic. Oh, my, god."

"Let's see if it worked." We stood together and went back to the living room.

"Alakazam," Lisa said, and tapped the wand on one of the three yellow shells she had set on a table. "Your penny!" She lifted the shell and showed Tim a penny.

"Hey, how did you do that? It wasn't there a minute ago."

Lisa laughed and handed him the manual. He studied it, then turned the shell over, discovered the fake inside shell. "What a gyp!"

Singer was curled up on the couch beside Lisa, purring.

"Singer?" I said.

The kitten stretched, rolled over, looked up with half-lidded eyes. "Will?" he said.

"This is Beth."

"I know."

I checked with Beth, who nodded, her smile small. "He's kind of snotty," I told her.

"Oh," said Singer. "That was a formal introduction? Excuse me." He stood up and walked over to us, his fluffy tail hooked at the end. Beth stooped and held out a hand, and Singer smelled it. "I don't know why I feel compelled to do that. You smell very nice."

"Thanks," said Beth. She stroked his head, and he purred.

"Mom?" Lisa jumped up, scattering plate-sized steel rings and rubber balls. "Can you understand him? I didn't shift you, honest I didn't."

"I know, honey. I got a spell for Christmas, too. I can bend the shifts now. I bent Daddy's Singer-talk spell to me."

"Wow. Everybody got magic for Christmas? Wow! Daddy, what did you get?"

"I don't know yet."

"Everybody can understand the kitten but me?" Tim said. "That's not fair. Lisa, shift me too."

She looked at us. "May I?"

"You remember what you did last time?" I asked.

"Of course, Daddy."

I exchanged glances with Beth, something we did a lot of. "Well, Tim gave you permission, and we do too," Beth said.

Lisa closed her eyes and concentrated, then sent a shift at Tim. His ring flared blue and the shift bounced back, enveloping Lisa, who blinked in confusion.

"Oh, I forgot," Tim said. He pulled off his ring and set it on the table. "Do it again, Lisa. Please."

She rubbed her eyes, wrinkled her forehead, and focused again. She sent the shift.

"Ouch," said Tim. "Oh. Kitty, do you really talk?"

"Sure," said Singer. "Do you understand me now?"

"Oh. Yeah. Wild. Thanks, Lisa. Hey, can I try a card trick next?"

They started squabbling about things in the magic kit again. Beth nudged me toward the door. "Go try one of your elf presents," she whispered. "Find out what they do. I'll keep track of the kids."

I slipped out of the living room and went up to the master bedroom, shut the door, and locked it.

I sat on the bed and opened my tin of Christmas candies. They were small—I counted, and there were thirty of them. Maybe I should save them for emergencies. But heck, if I didn't even know what they did, how would I know which emergencies to use them for?

I took one out and put it in my mouth.

Flavor exploded across my tongue, peppermint, cinnamon, sugar, ozone. Heat wrapped around me. I felt again the flowing inrush of energy, and the contraction of my muscles and bones. My ears pinched and pulled, and my beard and mustache grew.

Hair pushed out of my head to tumble in dark curls around my shoulders.

I wasn't wearing the costume this time. My bathrobe didn't shrink; I was lost in its folds by the time the transformation finished. I fought my way free and did what I had been too busy to do the night before. I looked carefully at this alternate self in a mirror.

Stocky. Muscular. Small. My head was big in proportion to the rest of my body; my face looked nothing like the clean-shaven, taller Will. If I didn't know it was me inside, what would I think of this person?

I turned my head, pushed hair aside, revealed my ears. Foxy points. I leaned forward, stared into my eyes. When I was tall Will, my eyes were dark brown; as Elf, I had tawny eyes under heavy brow ridges.

"Why did I give myself this gift?" I asked out loud, my voice gruff.

I felt tides of power shift under my skin. "Remember," said my new voice.

We had always wondered where Lisa's powers came from, once we got over the shock of their appearance when she was about four. At first Beth and I had not been able to believe what was happening. Stuffed animals and cookies flew to her from across the room. Deal with it. Lock up anything Lisa shouldn't have, and if she shifted one of us through the air toward her, try to land without cracking a shinbone or breaking a finger. The awareness snuck up on us in increments, even as we learned all kinds of defenses. For a couple of years, we only showed her off to the relatives when she was asleep. Daycare was impossible; Beth and I adjusted our jobs so one of us would always be home with her. We didn't put her in school until first grade, and even then, we'd had home school discussions; it might come down to home school if she messed up at Hillside. Beth and I wondered why us, but we never got any answers.

"Remember," I said again.

I'd seen a face like the elf's before. Old Uncle Darius, a short-statured man, who had lived in the attic of the house where I grew up. He had his own staircase to the outside world, and kept to himself most of the time, but once in a while I climbed up on the roof and he came out too, and we watched the stars together, he smoking some fragrant tobacco in a small pipe. He wasn't a very conversational person. "There's hope for you, young Will," he told me once, "though the rest of the family has gone water weak." I never knew what he meant.

Uncle Darius died when I was fifteen; he had grown more taciturn as time went on. Now I couldn't ask him my questions.

My sister Vicki had seventeen volumes of our grandmother's journals from the nineteen twenties and thirties. She liked them because Grandmother had a taste for expensive gilded Florentine leather book bindings. I wondered if there were any family secrets inside. Maybe Grandmother wrote about the family before it went water weak. I didn't think Vicki had ever read them.

"Remember."

I closed my eyes and tapped into the power flowing through me. *Help me remember*, I thought, and then the answers came.

Not so long ago, powers ran through my family—not as strong as Lisa's, but a little in everyone. Something about the twentieth century had driven them all underground, as though someone had set a mimic curse on us to help us blend with the people around us. I remembered, though I didn't know how, that Beth's great-grandmother was from a different lineage of power, healers or harmers depending on their natures; shifters. Though neither Beth nor I had manifested any powers, they lay latent inside us. Lisa's elf-shift had finally forged a link from her invading power to my own source, opening gates that had been closed all my life.

"Do I have to shrink to use this knowledge?" I asked, and laughed, then realized that being short *did* put me closer to the source. Once I grew again, my powers would retreat to somewhere I couldn't touch them.

The elf had given me magic candy. How long did one hit last? I had fallen asleep last night before the shift ended, so it might be hours. On the other hand, with the powers I had in this form, I could shift myself back to tall Will right now. I would lose my powers, though.

A knock sounded on the door. "Will?" Beth called.

I was going to ask if she was alone, but my voice had changed. I didn't want the kids seeing me like this. I grabbed the robe and shrank it to fit me with a thought. I put my short-fingered hand against the door and felt outward through the house. The kids were in their rooms, putting away their presents.

I unlocked and opened the door.

"Oh," she said. She smiled, knelt, and hugged me.

Beth kicked the door shut behind her. "So this is what happens when you eat those candies?"

"Yes."

"Can you give magic presents now?"

"Do you need something?"

"No, I was just wondering."

"I get the feeling I could whip up a lot of mischief, yes."

Beth grinned. Then frowned. "Can you explain the cat to me?"

"Where did that cat come from?" I asked myself.

"He's a helpful spirit," the elf voice answered.

"What?" asked Beth.

"Lisa needs some extra help," said the elf. "That was everybody's Christmas wish. I brought my friend here—Singer—he's probably laughing about that name—to watch out for her. If Bendshift and Turnback don't work, Singer can help."

"But who is he?" asked Beth.

I waited for an answer. We both did. Finally I said, "I guess we'll find out by talking to him. Beth, I've got something else to tell you. I was asking myself questions before you got here, and I found a few answers. We both come from magical families. Your great-grandmother was a healer."

"Sure, Granny Nightshade. She died when I was ten. How did you know about her?"

"I don't know." I placed my hands on her shoulders, closed my eyes, and looked inside her for the hidden spring of her lineage. Barely a trickle, but there. I primed it with some of the magic I could draw in this form, strengthened it. "Do you feel that?"

"What? Oh. Yes." She stroked a hand down her front. "What is it, Will?"

"It's your power. I have some, too, but I can't get to it unless I'm in this form. Lisa got her magic from us."

She placed a palm on my chest. I felt a flow of warmth there that didn't come from me. "Will?" she said, fear and wonder in her voice. "Will?"

This didn't feel like Lisa's shifter power, a rain of pins and needles directed toward whatever part of me Lisa wanted to shift. It was more like a warm bath, being enveloped in pleasure. I closed my eyes. When I opened them, I had returned to my large self, the person Beth had married. She stared down at her open palm, then up at me. "Oh, Will," she said, and hugged me.

Christmas night, Beth and I took turns saying goodnight to the kids. While she was in with Tim, I sat on the edge of Lisa's bed, patting Singer, who, when he wasn't talking, did a passable imitation of a kitten. Lisa's art supplies covered a desk she had made larger to accommodate them. Some of the brushes stood upright in a jar of water, and some colors sat in three-dee oodles on the palette: red, blue, white, purple. She'd started painting on one of the canvases, outlined and half colored in a shape that might be a cat.

"You never told me what your elf gift was," Lisa said. "Did he give you magic, Daddy?"

"Yeah. Mine's different from Tim's and your mom's—it doesn't work all the time—but it's pretty good."

She sighed and snuggled deeper under her covers, her smile wide. "Now everybody has magic I can see in the daytime. This is the best Christmas."

I kissed her cheek.

FAIRY
TALES

How I Came to Marry a Herpetologist

When I first spoke in toads and snakes, I hated them and tried to kill them. They rendered me unfit for human company; I blamed them for everything.

But centuries passed, and I learned many things.

Above all, I learned to keep my own counsel.

Most of the people who knew me thought I could not speak. I worked in a library. When people asked me questions, I pointed.

I only let myself speak during my lunch break and at home. I took my sack lunch down to the riverfront park every day, so any amphibians I produced had somewhere safe to go.

On a day not so long ago, I sat on my favorite bench overlooking the river. The sky was pale blue with spring, and birds called in the quickening air. Light green flowers dangled from the branches of the maple trees. Paperwhites bloomed in shaded hollows.

I ate my yogurt and banana, then got out my list of unspoken words. I tried six. "Legume." A small brown toad with golden eyes. "Dobro." A spotted lizard with brown and white stripes across the back of its neck. "Protuberance." A tan serpent with a black head. "Spavin." A diamond-backed rattlesnake. "Upanishad." A fire-red salamander with black spots. "Concupiscence." A green-backed bullfrog.

The toad sat in my hand. The others raced, ran, or hopped away.

Sometimes I looked them up in books, but I usually couldn't identify them with certainty. A color would be different, size wrong, feature changed. Perhaps a function of magic.

I set my hand on the ground, and the toad, with one last long look into my eyes, hopped off.

And then a thing I dreaded happened for the first time in a long while.

With a rustle, a young man emerged from the bushes. (Later, I learned that he often observed wildlife from hiding.) He overflowed with questions, and became irate when I wouldn't answer.

He had seen me speak. He wanted me to do it again.

I packed my trash, glanced around to see that all my animals had disappeared, and walked away from him, not answering.

He saw my name tag, FANCHON BUFO, though, and from there derived my telephone number, and then he gave me no peace.

"How is it that each one is different?" the young man asked me.

Evening shut down the sky outside, and street lights drove back darkness. We sat at a table in a deserted coffee shop. My choice of meeting ground. Our reflections gradually displaced pieces of view where it was darkest outside. Steam rose from our coffee cups, possible prayers, doubled in the window's world.

After that one encounter, he had kept calling me and begging me to talk to him, and every "no" I gave him left me with another marine toad, the largest of all toads, and not so easy to care for, since it needs salt water. I had finally said "all right" (two small garter snakes), and picked a place to meet that wasn't home.

"It's a marvelous thing," he said, peering through his glasses at me. His brown hair was shaved short on the sides and left long enough on top to flop forward and obscure his vision. Through the lenses of his glasses, his eyes looked pale and strange.

I shook my head. I sipped coffee. He wouldn't call it marvelous if he had lived with it for four centuries.

"But each word, a different species," he said. "That it happens at all is amazing. That it happens with such variety is—is stupendous!" He reached across the table and touched my hand.

No one in all my life had looked at me with such longing and appreciation.

I am not by nature fair in any way. My countenance is, at best, pinched; my eyes are narrow, as are my lips; my form is thin and bony; my hair long, but not thick or wavy, a dull dark-brown color with no interesting words to describe it.

My best feature may be my hands, with their long, narrow fingers, or perhaps my long narrow feet and dexterous toes, though no one other than myself had seen my feet in an age.

Across the years I have done many things to change my appearance, sometimes wishing to render myself more attractive, sometimes less. I have cut my hair; grown it; dyed it; braided it; shaved half off and stiffened the other half with hair spray. Why not? I seem condemned to live forever; I may as well experiment.

I have had adventures as a result of some of these looks and my silence. The best I store, and the rest I forget.

I thought of my diamond-and-pearl-speaking sister, who married a prince. What a beauty she was. How could any man resist a woman who was beautiful and spat wealth with every word?

Did she ever know she was loved for her own self?

Did she even care?

Ah, well. That was *her* story.

Mine was different.

"Talk to me. *Please*," the young man begged, stroking the back of my hand.

I shook my head. I stared at him across the Formica-topped table. I glanced down to where his soft, pale fingers touched the back of my hand, and wondered what I felt. Not attracted, not repulsed; but a little less weary, perhaps.

"Say something," he whispered, "anything. Please."

A car drifted by in the street outside, headlights glaring, then gone.

"Something," I said. A small green treefrog plopped to the table top.

The young man caught his breath, held it behind his teeth.

"Riggit," said the frog, looking here and there.

My water glass was filled with ice. No safe haven there. I put out a hand to the tiny creature and it hopped up onto my palm. We were too far from a stream; I wouldn't have picked this place to meet if I had suspected I would speak. Maybe I should only use snake words. I couldn't always remember which words produced what.

The young man leapt up and went to the counter. He got a glass half full of tap water with no ice in it from the waitress, and floated a piece of toast on top. The treefrog was happy in the glass.

I smiled at this young man.

He smiled back. His face turned sweet. I saw something there I liked.

So our courtship began.

His name was Newton. He lived on an estate with his parents. Soon I went there to visit and found ponds and marshes and woodlands all looking as nature had left them, and inside the mansion, a wing of rooms where Newton studied cold-blooded animals without killing them. Those from other climates had comfortable terrariums full of the plants and soils and the temperature of their homelands.

All his life he had been fascinated by reptiles and amphibians, he told me.

He waited for my every word.

At home, with my orange tea-kettle, my slippers, my books, and my nineteen-inch television, I sat with my feet propped on the ottoman and considered options.

My sister had married a man who treasured the jewels she spoke. If I accepted Newton's proposal, would I not be doing the same cowardly thing?

When had I ever had such an opportunity before? Would there ever come another? Why not be loved, even if not for myself?

"My prince," I said to my room. Two brilliantly colored poison arrow frogs. "I love you." "I" was a snapping turtle; "you," a gila monster; "love," a giant cobra that raised its head, fanned its spectacle-marked hood, and hissed.

None of my creatures ever hurt me. It had been a while since I had produced so many poisonous ones at once, though. I called the zoo and they sent the usual handler over to pick up the animals. Because of the phone call, I had a good menagerie by the time Sheila arrived.

She shook her head the way she always did. She thought I bought exotic pets and didn't know how to care for them. I shrugged as I always did and appreciated her deft technique with the snake-catching stick. We nodded our farewells to each other.

I started a list of words that produced poisonous animals. I liked Newton and wanted him alive. If that changed, well, the list would still be a good thing to have.

When I had taken enough time to think it over, I said yes (a banded gecko) to his proposal.

"I do" produced a baby snapping turtle and a small pit viper which I caught before it woke to its surroundings. I put the snake in the pocket of my wedding gown before Newton slipped a gold band onto my ring finger. Newton caught the turtle and slipped it into a pocket of his tuxedo. It didn't even bite him. We both smiled, and I felt effervescent.

I moved to the estate and gave up my library job, and for a time Newton and I were very happy, each in our own way. I had never had someone appreciate my words before. Heady wine.

One day I sat on a stool in the room with the salt-water tanks in it. Newton had been pestering me to tell him a story. I was tired just then and kept shaking my head. Finally I yelled "No!" and a marine toad the size of a basketball plopped into my lap.

"Beautiful," breathed Newton. "That's the biggest one yet! I've got to get the camera." He dashed out.

I touched the toad's moist, mottled back. It gazed up at me with huge golden keyhole-pupiled eyes. It looked wise and strange and wild. I lifted it until I stared straight into its eyes. Its pale throat fluttered.

My biggest "no" ever, I thought, and kissed its wide mouth.

It changed, then.

In a moment between my legs stood a prince as beautiful as night, with eyes as dark as secrets and hair pale as sunlight. He was dressed all in burgundy velvet. He grasped my shoulders and kissed me again. I had never tasted anything so wicked or wonderful. "We've been waiting," he whispered, "all these years we've been waiting." He closed his arms around me. My nose bumped his chest. He smelled of violets. "Enchantments intersect," he said. "There aren't many doors into this world remaining, and for those of us trapped long ago and never loosed . . . we pray for you and await your every word."

The door slammed. "Who is this?" Newton demanded, behind me.

I felt a strange tightness in my chest. I thought of all the frogs, toads, snakes, lizards, efts, turtles, and crocodiles across the centuries. I remembered killing the first ones. How I had hated my mother for sending me to the well to meet the fairy who cursed me.

At first I killed them. Then my mother drove me from home, and everyone I met despised me and sent me anywhere so long as it was away from them.

When I had no one else left, I had learned to like my creatures, even as I learned not to make so many.

The prince's arms loosened and I pushed away. I stared up at his beautiful face, then glanced around the room, at tanks that hosted my words. I touched my lips. The prince smiled and nodded.

"Fanchon, who *is* this?" Newton asked me again.

I rose and went to a tank. An orange-eyed turtle stared at me through the glass. I lifted it from the tank and kissed its mouth, and it turned into a mermaid. She could not remain upright; she splashed and sprawled to the floor. Her tail fin spread wide and iridescent and damp across the cement. For a moment I stood, trapped in that resonance, the concrete and the fantastic.

She kissed my foot.

"Oh, man!" Newton started videotaping.

I wanted to tell him to stop that, but I wasn't ready to deal with another giant boa constrictor right now.

With the first prince at my shoulder, I went to each tank in the salt water room, lifted each creature, kissed it. Toads and sea turtles, a few snakes, and then a wolf eel, which didn't change when I kissed it. The first prince put it back in the tank. I glanced at Newton, who said, "I had that before I met you."

I went through all the rooms of the Reptile and Amphibian wing, trailing more and more people behind me, leaving empty terrariums and tanks in my wake.

Transformed, my creatures were people of different sizes, shapes, and colors, and they wore clothes from all over the world and all through time. Most were princes. Some were kings. A few were princesses, and there were sheikhs, pashas, caliphs, sultans, sultanas, queens, emperors. The one cobra I had spoken since Newton and I married turned into a rajah.

My lips were sore. There were so many glittering people they couldn't fit into our wing of the mansion, and they opened windows and doors and went outside. They spoke in murmurs to each other. All gazed at me as though I were their savior.

Newton kept taping.

At last I sat down on a bench in the garden and studied these fantastically beautiful people. (One of the larger princes carried the mermaid out and put her in the fountain.) In clothes like that, with looks like that, what could they do in this day and age? Walk out into the world and get mugged? Get jobs as supermodels? Actors? Prostitutes?

I thought of all the creatures I had sent to the zoo with Sheila.

All the ones I had let loose in the riverfront park while I worked at the library. All those who had lived out their aquatic or dirt-dwelling lives and died without ever being kissed.

My first prince sat beside me on the bench and stroked my cheek with the backs of his fingers.

How could I have known that locked inside my living words were such fabulous people?

"It's the nature of curses to crush things," he said. "We were all cursed, and you were too. Nested in your curse was the blessing of our freedom."

"I don't know whether to ever speak again," I said, then looked down at a lapful of squirming lizards, snakes, and toads. Wearily I lifted a small spadefoot toad and kissed its mouth. It turned into a very comely girl in scanty Arabian Nights-style garments. She went behind the bench and massaged my shoulders.

Newton put down the videocamera and seated himself at my other side. He leaned closer. "I liked them better before," he whispered in my ear.

If I kissed him, would he turn into a frog?

Of course not. I had kissed him on our wedding day, and since. He was the only stable person in sight.

We had a backyard full of strangers with no clear futures or destinations. Every word I spoke produced another stranger. What were we to do with them all?

I could lift their curses. Could they lift mine?

I kissed my last sentence from animals to people and leaned on my husband, who put his arm around my shoulder. "It's okay," he murmured. "It's okay. Better or worse, it's okay."

STRIKES
OF THE HEART

I had been a plantwife seven years when I noticed my grandmother's first stumbles. My grandmother's mind wandered now, and her magics followed.

Omara, my grandmother, the king's wizard and herbalist, was the mother of my heart. Laran, the mother of my body, was a warrior in the castle guards, often off on missions on behalf of the king, and rarely warm to me when she was home. She had never wanted a child. She had never named my father for me, either; perhaps she did not know which bed-friend of hers he was. Sometimes my mother gave me careless kindnesses, but more often she was unhappy to see me.

She called me Kishi, the line between sea and shore. Perhaps that was how she saw me, a place where two worlds fought, a barrier between her carefree life before and her life after I arrived.

When I was young and stupid enough to still seek her, I saw how she gambled and drank with the others, how the mother I sometimes knew as kind disappeared as the evening progressed and the drinks and games grew deeper. Someone else wore the face of my mother then, and this new person did not like me.

If I approached Mother in the midmorning, while she was still sorry for her excesses of the previous night but before she started drinking again, I could sometimes wile promises from her, such as permission to go with the guards to the forest when they went scouting for griffin spawn or dragon larva. When I went with the guards, I could go deeper into the forest than I could alone, and find plants my grandmother had not yet taught me.

Gran never went off on campaigns the way my mother did. She trained me in herb craft and stayed with me my whole childhood. We shared a room between the still room and the kitchen.

Gran taught me the doctrine of the signatures, how a plant would always show you what uses it had if you looked carefully enough.

Even an unfamiliar plant would reveal itself, if you could see the aura around it.

Many of Gran's magics were small and benign—you'd miss them if you didn't know where to look. An herb under a guest's pillow to keep dark dreams away; a sweet leaf halfway down the wick of a candle to quiet strife; butter mixed with cinders to settle a sour stomach. Gran's magics were the magics of smoothing lives.

Gran had other magics inside her, ones she did not unleash in these untroubled times. There were tales among the guards of the days long before my birth, when Gran was young and her hair was wild and red, flame that streamed out around her as she strode battlefields in her long black robe. I heard more than once how, when we were attacked by the nation to our north, Gran burned smokes and cast spells that laid whole regiments low: boils, flux, blinding headaches, rashes, the leaching of strength from muscles, magics that left battlefields choked with collapsed soldiers. Kinder than killing, some said, but the guards did not think magic made honorable battle tactics, even though it disabled soldiers, put the burden of caring for the fallen on the enemy, and eventually won our king the war.

Everyone was still afraid of Gran, though she hadn't cast such spells in years.

She taught me everything good I ever knew, except the lore I learned from my plant husband. When I was fifteen, I had a strange courtship with the Old Man in the Ground, wild cucumber. Gran and I came across the Old Man in one of our forays in the forest. Before I could stoop to study him, Gran dragged me back. In his signature, I saw the throbbing red of passion, but when Gran looked, she said she saw the dark purple of poison.

"Stay away from this one, Kishi," Gran told me. "There's no good in it."

But the red called to me. I was young and gawky then. None of the castle boys paid me any attention. I watched human auras as well as I could, but they were never as clear to me as plant auras. I knew passionate things happened in people all around me, and Gran talked to me about the ways of men and women, but nothing called to me as clearly as the signature of the Old Man.

Gran had never been wrong about a plant's signature before. Still, I woke in the middle of a moon night, and there was a scent on the air that drew me out of the castle, through the village, past the edges of where humans lived. Old Man in the Ground waited for me in the darkness. I searched out his signature from among the others. It glowed green and red in the darkness, promise and passion. I went to him and surrendered myself, and he accepted me.

What he planted inside me made me a more gifted herbalist than Gran could ever be. He strengthened my vision and gave me the power to hear plant voices, and even speak with those plants that lived swiftly enough to hear me. He taught me to see even more plant potentials; in our union, we learned how we could act on each other. I learned healing on a level below words.

My plant husband also made me unfit for a human husband, an outcome Gran had foreseen and feared.

Eventually Gran accepted my decision to be a plantwife, though it continued to trouble her. She loved the king, the queen, the three princes, and all the life of the castle. She wanted me to be her legacy to them. She had spent her life in service to this land, and she sensed that with the powers my husband had given me, I could go anywhere plants grew and find a life that would satisfy me. The ties of duty and love that bound her to King Eleks and the country did not grip me so hard. I was too odd to make friends easily, though I did count Maple, the cook, a friend, and Kian, the youngest of the three princes. Gran feared my solitary nature would make it easier for me to leave, robbing King Eleks and the country of my skills. I was the only apprentice Gran had.

She did her best to weave me into the tapestry of castle life. She linked me to others by work: she put me in charge of all the foods we got from the wild. I worked with Maple on menus and did much of the shopping for fruits and vegetables, once Maple trusted me to pick the best at the market. I led young men to the forest. They carried home whatever fruit, roots, seeds, herbs, and lichens I picked. I showed carpenters trees ready for harvest, and found downed wood for the woodcutters. At the castle, I held morning medical consultations with the ill, diagnosed ailments, mixed herbal remedies, and dispensed cures.

Everyone I worked with thought me odd, but they respected me. I suspected that none of them thought I was human; I didn't feel as though I were.

When I was seventeen, Gran wiled Prince Kian into desiring me. Gran thought that if Kian gave me a child, something my plant husband could not do, it would lock me to the life of the castle. There was no hope of a recognized union between me and the prince, for his future lay in political liaisons. Had I a child of his, though, I would be more valued.

My plant husband gave me the power to undo Gran's wile by changing my scent into one that disgusted the prince. He never consummated his attraction to me. Later, when Kian knew what had come over him, we spoke to each other and straightened out the tangle. We returned to being the friends we had been before, when we explored the forest together.

I thought no more about Kian's brief lust for me until Gran's troubles came, five years later.

At first only small things told of Gran's confusion. One washday, all the white laundry turned pink. Protection spells around the castle broke down and let in biting insects, and each bucket lowered into the well brought up frogs. One morning nothing the fireboy did could start a fire in the kitchen's stoves and hearths.

People complained to Gran about the troubles, which came thicker as time passed; sometimes Gran remembered problems long enough to correct them. When she didn't, people came to me.

I didn't notice connections between the problems in the beginning. I just figured out how to fix them. If they required wizarding only Gran could do, I reminded her to work on solutions until she found one; but I was surprised how many problems I could solve myself in consultation with my plant husband, who knew warding ways that did not work like straight magic. Insects could be repelled with scent; dyes could be altered, fixed, or washed out with a combination of crushed leaves and moon-silvered water; as for the frogs, they could be summoned out of a well with a certain scent, and set loose elsewhere. I spoke to dead wood and it woke to fire.

More and more small things claimed my attention every day. As I solved problems, I saw how much Gran had done in her full power to make life easier for everyone around her, and how much she was losing now.

On Seed Blessing Day in early spring, I woke before the sun. The force flowers I kept in pots on the stone windowsill, the ones that bloomed in response to my urgings instead of the seasons, had not yet opened for the day; their leaves were spread to the light, though, and the air smelled of sage and mint and lemon balm. Gran lay in her bed asleep, her face softened with dreams. I dressed quietly so I would not wake her. She needed more rest than she used to.

Today I would make enough mulled cider to serve everyone in the castle and the village. I had been collecting spices for months.

It was the day of the spring moon, when people brought their seeds to the temple for blessing. The king would walk the fields, giving each plot of earth a drink and a prayer for a fruitful season.

In the dark, cavernous kitchen, the fireboy was already at work. He had blown the embers on the big hearth awake, and fed them wood. The smoke was fragrant, whispering of wood dry and dead. As I came in, the fireboy stepped outside, headed to the wood shed to bring in the day's supply.

In the weak new flames of the morning fire, the bunches of dried herbs hanging from the rafters cast flickering shadows across the low ceiling. I lit the lamps and plucked leaves from various herb bundles for the morning tea, crushed those that needed crushing, roused the sharp, smoke-edged scents of Rise and Wake and Pay Attention. I stitched the leaves loosely into a linen bag and got out the big pot.

I went out in the cool morning to haul water for tea. The fireboy, his arms full of wood, halted when he saw me. He was large, taller than I was, and not clean. He was a new boy in the kitchen, probably in his late teens, got from the workhouse in the village after the previous fireboy had moved to the stables to take care of the horses. He slept among the ashes of the open hearth, near the source of his power. Black ash smeared his nose and chin, and his ginger hair was greasy with much rubbing to make it lie flat.

He stared at me as I walked past, then dropped his armful of logs and grasped my arm. My first thought was that something was on fire, and he was dragging me out of the way of disaster. I turned, and saw that the danger was his regard. The dark centers of his eyes flared wide. His grip tightened. He jerked the pot out of my hand and dropped it, then pulled me up against his sooty self. What a smell of smoke, grease, and stale sweat; I choked on it. He dragged me into the wood shed, then threw me down on the chilly floor among the scattered bark and slivers, and shoved my skirts up above my waist. He knelt over me, a shadow against the roof slats. I cried out as he fumbled for the ties at his crotch.

My grandmother was powerful in battle; she knew how to fight. I had grown up in peaceful times. It had never occurred to me I would need to know how to defend myself.

The wedding ring my husband had given me unwound from around my wrist, a live green band of vine that most times lay quiet as a tattoo against my skin. It twisted through the air between us and closed around the fireboy's throat. The fireboy did not respond right away, so busy was he readying himself to mount me. But after too long without air, he choked and fell forward on top of me. I lay panting and shuddering under his weight, trapped by fear and shock. My wedding ring dropped from the fireboy's throat and twined around my arm again, and from that, I took strength.

I shoved the fireboy off and scrambled to my feet, adjusted my skirts. I felt the pulse at his neck. His heart still beat. The small herb-harvesting knife at my belt came into my hand, and I thought how easy it would be to slit his throat, here in the wood shed where few people went.

Instead, I ran out through the castle gates, away from the gray stone walls that cradled the workings of government and all the servants who served those workings. I ran through the wattle-and-daub-and-thatched-roof village, past cultivated fields and fenced pastures, and on to the wilderness. I left the road and plunged into the woods, wending between sleepy plant auras and the deep greens of tree signatures. It was dark and cold under the trees, but I was warm in my run. I slowed, though; instead of trampling underbrush I pushed past ferns and young trees and bushes. They knew me and made room for my passage. The scent of waking forest calmed me, helped my heart slow.

I went to the clearing my husband had claimed, where his vines covered the ground, with their large, hand-shaped leaves, their thick, succulent vines, and the tendrils that spiraled from the stems at the leaves' bases to clasp anything that ventured near and stood still long enough. I waded in where the vines coiled thickest, and they rose to wrap around me. The hairs on the stems that pricked and stung others caressed me. The bitter scent of my husband's green soul surrounded me. My husband embraced and supported me. Tendrils wrapped around my arms and legs and belly and neck, wove over my face. Presently I calmed and told my husband what had happened.

The leaves in the clearing grew agitated. Some of the vines reached out to climb nearby trees. I felt my husband's anger, and I gloried in it.

He fed me the fruit he grew only for me.

He examined me, and found that there had been an alteration in my signature, an added fragrance that was not my own. He told me it cried out to male humans that I was ready to bear children and they should mate with me. It was similar to the fragrance Gran had set on me to attract the prince five years earlier, though less specific.

My husband studied the fragrance and disabled it.

Later, I rose from his embrace. He left more of his marks on me: scratches from our encounter, but also twists of tendrils around my arms and legs, waist and neck, augmenting my wedding band.

By this time the sun had risen, and I was two hours late for my morning duties.

Why had Gran laid a magic on me that would make the fireboy desire me?

The village was awake when I walked back. Vendors were already selling special festival cakes and apple ale. People wore ribbons and gathered for games.

The farmers had set up market in the village square, as they did twice a week, with canopies stretched above spaces where they would sell vegetables, fruits, and whatever they made at home. One or two greeted me, but many others ducked their heads when they saw me. Some knew I was a plantwife. Most were afraid of me. It didn't stop them from seeking me out when they needed healing or blessings. All sold their wares to me, though few met my eyes.

"Kishi?" said Marcola. She was a textile vendor. I sold her skins from some of the roots I collected, and lichens I harvested on the slopes of Higara Mountain. She used them for dyes. She had never feared me.

"Marcola. Do you need anything this season?"

"More of those little nuts that have no name. They make a butter brown that goes well in hunter pants. I'll take as many of those as you can get me."

"That's not so easy." I needed a warrior escort to get to the place where I had found the nuts. It was a day's ride, too close to our northern border for me to wander alone.

Every time I asked the guards to go with me somewhere, my mother made it plain that she resented my asking anything.

Marcola shrugged. "When you can. What happened to you, Kishi? Those green lines on your arms."

I glanced at my arms. The tendrils of my husband wove like lace up and down them, as though I wore an undershirt of green spider web. "It's my armor." I thought I was giving her a fanciful answer, but then recognized the truth in my words.

Marcola frowned. "Did something happen? Are we expecting an attack?"

"Not the country. Just me."

She touched my hand. "Are you all right?"

I turned my hand so that my palm was up, and she closed her hand around it. "I think I will be," I whispered, surprised by her care. No one at home ever asked these questions. Gran used to, but since I became a plantwife, she had put distance between us.

"Take care." Marcola released me.

"Thank you."

I went home. I hesitated at the kitchen door. What if the fireboy were there?

I slipped in. Cook was busy preparing breakfast for the royal family and the festival guests. She frowned at me. Someone else had made the morning tea, not even using the teabag I had prepared earlier, which still lay among herbs at my cutting board. I dipped up a mug and drank. It had very little flavor. I made a fresh pot.

The fireboy was not there.

I apologized to Maple for being late.

"Angry I should be," she said. "You gone, the fireboy run off. I had to lay my own stove fires, and it's been so long since I did it, I've almost lost the knack. How am I supposed to run a kitchen on a festival day without you?" She handed me a knit bag of tiny onions, armed me with a knife, and aimed me toward my cutting board. I dropped into the rhythm of helping with the meal preparation, made the morning blessings, then went to the treatment room, where the sick waited.

The fireboy was one of those waiting. He did not meet my gaze, but stared at the rush-matted floor. He kept his hand on his throat until I came to him after all my other patients had left, then let it drop so I saw the red stresses around his neck.

"Do you remember what you did?" I asked him.

He nodded, his gaze dropping.

"Are you sorry?"

He nodded. His brow furrowed in confusion. He waved his hands.

He opened his mouth, but no sound came out. My husband had hurt his voice.

"You couldn't help it," I said.

He nodded vigorously.

"I understand." The terror and anger I had felt when he threw me down flickered through me, but I let it seep away. If Gran had put a spell on me, how could this boy resist? He had no magic to fight it. "You won't do it again?"

He shook his head, covered his eyes with his hand.

I got out a healing ointment and massaged it into his neck, spoke words to wake its power. I finished and turned away. He touched my hand, and I glanced at him. He traced a finger up my arm, across the green loops and swirls of my husband's embrace, then met my gaze, a question in his eyes.

I willed the tendrils to rise up and wrap around his hand. He stood, trembling. I willed them back to my arm. "They won't hurt you unless you hurt me," I said.

He nodded. He touched his throat, mouthed "Thanks," and left.

Not until I was helping Cook and her workers prepare lunch did Gran come into the kitchen, and then she was sleepy and smiling. "What's the matter, Kishi? What happened to your arms? More of your—" she would not call my husband my husband; still she resisted my marriage—"wildcrafting work?"

I glanced at Cook, then tugged Gran back to our room. "You laid an attract spell on me, Gran. Why did you do that?"

"I didn't. I wouldn't. What are you talking about?"

"Gran! The fireboy attacked me this morning because of a spell you put on me! You made me into something he wanted without thought! He hurt me. Why? Am I being punished?"

"I wouldn't do that." She studied me with narrowed eyes. "There is no touch of such a spell on you, Kishi. Why are you telling me an untrue thing?"

I didn't know what to say. My husband was sensitive to all the flows of energies, natural and otherwise, and he had recognized the signature of Gran's spell. He had taken the taint off, but why wouldn't Gran remember she had put a spell on me? "Gran—"

"What were all those cauldrons doing on the hearth in the kitchen? Why are you making such a lot of spiced cider, Kishi?" Gran asked.

"It's Seed Blessing Day," I said.

"How could it—surely that's not for another month?"

"It's today, Gran. Look where the sun falls on the floor."

She glanced down, then up at me, her face confused.

I didn't want to see her confusion. "I have to address the mulling spices, Gran."

"What should I do?" Gran said.

A cold finger of fear touched my heart. Gran had never asked me that question before.

"Shouldn't you speak with King Eleks?" I couldn't remember a day when she didn't wake and consult with the king at breakfast about what they would do. But breakfast was long past.

"The king!" Gran turned and left the room.

The king would already be in the fields, pouring a blessing every fifty steps, from a jug of liquor I had made of strength and fertility from last year's fruits, mixed with tincture of wild plants that would help excite this year's crops into growing strong and wild and well.

Would Gran know to find King Eleks in the fields? I should have mentioned it. I had told her it was Seed Blessing Day, and she knew it was late morning; where else would she look for him?

How long would she remember what I had told her? She had trouble remembering all sorts of things. She did not always know if it were washday or market day or even a day on the lunar calendar when we harvested herbs. I had to tell her things more than once, sometimes more than five times.

Lunch would bring everyone back to the castle. If Gran didn't find the king in the fields, she would find him then.

A knock sounded at the open door. "Kishi?" Cook said.

"I'm sorry." Cook was in the midst of meal preparation, and I had left her. I followed Maple back to the kitchen. As she sliced a fragrant roast, I laid a blessing on it.

When the servants had taken the food to the great hall, Cook led me to the dark pantry and had me bless the new provisions that had arrived by wagon that morning, then gave me a length of festival red ribbon as thanks. "I hope you're all right," she said. "You are never gone when I need you. What happened this morning?"

"Gran put a spell on me," I muttered. I felt I shouldn't tell anyone about Gran's weaknesses, but Cook depended on me, and I had failed her.

"You, too?"

"What? What did she do to you?"

"You know those lemon tarts she loves? Two days ago I made two hundred of them. Supper was late because I couldn't stop making tarts. My apprentice made the meal. Is there some charm you can give me that will protect me from Omara's magic?"

"I wish there was," I said, "but I'm not sure I can protect myself from her yet." I took Cook's hand and pressed my wrist to hers, asked my green armor if it could protect Cook. It didn't move. I sighed. "I'll study this. I've never needed protection from Gran before."

By the time we returned to the kitchen, the dishes from the first course had come back, and the other two courses were waiting in their serving dishes. It was time for those of the house staff who were not serving to make their meal. We gathered around the servants' table and Cook gave us each dishes, then set communal bread and stew in the center. I said the blessing and everyone grabbed food. I sat between Cook and her apprentice. Gran's chair, between me and Cook, went empty.

I would have to find Gran.

Before we had finished with lunch, my mother came in. She wore her padded practice tunic, which was cut here and there from missteps in swordplay and knifework. The side lacings were undone. She clutched her stomach. Her hair had come loose of the greased braid in which she normally locked it. "Kishi," she moaned.

Everyone looked at me. I rose, nodded to Cook, and went to my mother. I led her to my room, settled her on my bed, and sat facing her. "What happened?"

"When I woke this morning and dressed for practice, my commander came into the room I share with the other women. He ordered them out, then took me. He did not ask. He threw me down and covered me. Owain, whom I have trusted with my life in battle! Only it was not he who did it. He was not home in his eyes. After he finished, my sword partner came and took me. Peter, my friend and right arm for eighteen years! I pleaded with him, but he was not inside himself either. He was like a sleeping person, except he countered every force I used to fight him. They are the only ones in my battalion stronger than I am. Nothing I did stopped them. How could they do that to me, the two men I respect most in the world? Afterward they were confused and ashamed, and then they forgot, though the whole battalion heard me cry out and fight. None came to help me. Now I am useless. No one will trust me in battle. Why did this happen to me? Have I displeased some god?"

I took her hands in mine. My husband's green lace reached across to wind around Mother's wrists. "Kishi!" she cried.

"It's all right, Mother. It is just my husband looking to see what happened to you." The tendrils took my mother's taste and measure, and told me what I feared: Gran had put an attract spell on her, the same one she had used on me. "Gran did this," I whispered.

My husband tested another thing, tasted my mother's blood, found that her body had already initiated the change.

Should I tell my mother she was pregnant? So early on, we could stop it without endangering her. I could concoct an arbortifacient with herbs I already had. I did not imagine she would want to keep the child.

The lace released my mother and wrapped itself around my arms. I squeezed my mother's hands and let go.

"Gran did this?" Mother repeated. "I know I've always been a disappointment to her, but why punish me so? I gave her you."

Mother had always been a disappointment to Gran? What did that mean? Mother was one of the king's best warriors. Perhaps that was a skill Gran didn't value.

"Mother, did you ever see Gran in battle?"

"Oh, yes. She was magnificent. She saved our country from invasion three times in my memory, Kishi, and several other times according to history. She put fear into our enemies. That's why the borders have been untroubled for so long. No other king has a mage with Omara's powers." Mother sat back. "But she hasn't done anything dangerous in years. Are you saying her spelling me has something to do with battle?"

"No." I hugged myself. "It is not an outward battle. Her mind is wandering, but she retains her powers."

"She did this to me without even knowing?"

"Sometimes she knows." I took my mother's hand. "She did a like thing to me this morning, but my husband protected me."

"Oh, Kishi." She gripped my hand harder than was comfortable.

"Mother, you are with child."

"At my age?"

"So says my husband. I think Gran did this to us because she wants more children of our line."

Mother stroked my hair. "Poor Omara," she murmured, then laughed, a harsh sound. "I gave her you, the perfect daughter, and you decided to end our line instead of having the children you were supposed to have. No wonder she's crazy."

Mother's words hurt like a blade to my belly. When had it ever been my job to have a child? Always, according to Gran. Never, according to my husband. My mother had not pressed me one way or another, but then, she had never shown any sign of caring what became of me. She was kind to me in a rough way; it was as though we were people of different stations who bumped into each other once in a while at the well and exchanged words about the weather.

Now Mother blamed Gran's ailment on me?

Mother turned away. "A child," she said. "By one of two strong men. I cannot return to my chosen work in this house. I'll need to leave this country and apprentice myself somewhere no one will know I was forced. I cannot abide the thought of staying in a place where everyone knows such a shameful thing about me."

"Doesn't the shame lie with the men who did this?"

"No." She pressed her hands to her belly. "The shame lies in being overcome. I can still be respected as a warrior if someone defeats me in battle, as long as I can defeat others; but this woman thing, to have someone force their way inside me, that is shameful. There is truly a baby started inside? How can you know this so soon?"

"It is one of my gifts."

She shook her head. "You have always been strange."

I hesitated, then said, "Mother, do you want to rid yourself of this child?"

She closed her eyes and sat silent for a moment. "I'll think about it. Thank you for the offer, in any case."

Just then Gran came into the room. Mother shrank from her.

"Laran! What are you doing here?" Gran asked.

"Omara, what did you do to me? Do you hate me so?" Mother said.

"What?" Gran, bewildered, looked at me.

"You laid the same spell on her you laid on me."

"Kishi, I did not spell you."

"You did. You spelled me and you spelled Mother. You made us hosts to men against our wills."

Gran pressed her hand to her forehead, then held out two fingers of her left hand and made the gesture for revealing the unseen. Red lines of a spell wrapped Mother round, and her stomach glowed orange. The lines bore the unmistakable signature of Gran's magic working, a certain shiver in the weft. Mother stared down at herself, then looked to me, startled. The red and orange faded, leaving my mother a pale ghost in her practice tunic.

"Oh!" Gran cried. She struck her chest with her fist. "Oh, I—" She sank onto her bed and covered her face with her hands.

"Kishi," she whispered presently. "I didn't do that to Laran."

I knew she had seen her own signature. Still, I asked, "Who did?"

"The other who lives in my head."

"Mother," said my mother.

"Half the time, I'm not awake," Gran whispered. "Someone else is, and she does things while I sleep. I wake in places I don't remember. People look at me with fear faces. They say I've done things I never did. Even the king fears me now. Kishi—"

I sat beside her. My grandmother, my guide all my life. The wisest person I knew. The only other time I had seen her afraid was when she learned I had lain with my plant husband. Then she thought I had been poisoned. In some ways, perhaps, I had.

"Kishi," Gran whispered. "It's time for you to stop me."

Everything inside me halted. The ice of a lost moment edged my fingers and toes.

"I'm awake now, but when I'm not—who else can stop me?"

"Will you let me stop you?" I asked, so afraid I had difficulty shaping words.

"If you do it now. The other Omara—"

Husband, I thought. *Help me.*

I took my grandmother's hands, and the green lace of my husband unknitted from my arms and wove a bridge to my grandmother. He wove around her body and sent tips under her surface to where her blood moved. She shuddered in his embrace. Our best calmers and soothers flowed into her.

Gran cried, "What are you doing to me?" She shivered, but did not pull away.

"Will soothing you stop your other self?"

"I don't know." Her eyes drooped shut.

Half the self my husband had gifted me with wound around Gran. It snapped its ties to the rest of him, which stayed with me. I felt afraid.

My husband and I worked well together, but when he did things on his own, I didn't always like them. Who would I prefer to have in control? Wild Gran, who tortured my mother and me for reasons we didn't understand, or my husband, who did not think like a human?

I eased Gran back onto her bed, lifted her feet, folded her hands on her chest, then glanced at Mother.

She wiped her face. "I never thought this would happen," she said. "She was supposed to be strong forever."

A knock sounded. King Eleks stood on the threshold. He stared at Gran. "Kishi?" he murmured.

I went to the door, and he led me down the hall into the still room. "What is it?" I asked.

"She came while I was blessing the last field," he said, "and there in front of all my people and the priestesses, Omara, my good right hand, defender of the kingdom, upholder of justice, exemplar of wisdom, and master of magery, laid a lust spell on me. It was only by grace that I was wearing the charm she made me last year to ward off spells. The charm protected me, mostly, but I had a difficult time keeping myself together until I finished the ceremony, and after that I was fortunate that the queen was waiting in our quarters. Kishi, I value Omara above many, but this is not the first time she has done something contrary to the country's best interests. What can you tell me?" he asked.

"Age." All my fear spoke, and still my voice came out a whisper. I did not want to believe that anything could harm my grandmother. An enemy had finally found her, and it came from within.

"As I feared. Is there nothing you can do to stop it?"

"I've put her to sleep for now. I don't know if there's anything I can do to halt what age is doing to her."

"If you cannot halt the process, can you do something to halt her? Omara has been my greatest treasure, the one who has made my rule fair and good. She has given us freedom from war and strength in peace. I owe her everything. But I also owe it to her not to lose everything she has gained for me because she is ill."

"I'm doing what I can."

He took a deep breath. "Kishi, with Omara impaired, I need another wizard."

"Majesty."

"Omara has been training you to be her assistant and replacement, though you have not come to court when she helped me with judgment."

I looked away from him. Ever since I chose my husband, Gran had left me more and more alone. I had been picking up the slack in all the domestic duties she used to do around the castle. But what of judgment? What of battle? I was not qualified for either of those things, not the way Gran had been.

"I'll help however I can, Majesty, but I am not my grandmother's equal."

"Omara has no equal. That's why we have been so prosperous these latter years. None of our neighbors has such a puissant wizard; they all fear Omara, and leave our borders alone. I hesitate to advertise for a new wizard; that will let the other rulers know we're vulnerable. Do you know any in the wizard community who would suit?"

I shook my head. Gran had taken me to wizard gatherings, but my skills were odd compared to most, and I had never made friends easily.

"I shall write to some trusted friends," he said. "Meanwhile, we must contrive. Sit at my right hand during judgment tomorrow."

"Majesty?"

"I need you." He left.

I went back to our rooms. Gran slept, her breathing soft and slow. Mother rose. "What did he want?"

"He wants a wizard, and may settle for me until he gets one."

"Kishi, you are a wizard."

I shook my head and herded my mother from the room.

She came with me as far as the kitchen, then paused with a hand on my sleeve. "I can't go back to barracks."

"You can stay with me and Gran."

She thought, then shook her head. "I'll go to the temple and talk to the priestesses. They'll help me think about what to do next."

The rest of the day was given over to the festivities of Seed Blessing Day. I served a lot of cider, blessed many meals, laid hands on women's stomachs and men's groins and recited charms for fertility. It gave me a strange pang to prepare others for an experience I never expected to have myself. I knew my charms were potent. Already there were babies born to those I had blessed last year and the year before.

Gran slept through everything. I went to our rooms between ceremonies and looked in on her. She always lay in the same position. After the evening feast, when all had gathered, servants, guests, and the royal family, in the great hall for Seed Blessing Day music and storytelling, King Eleks sought me out again. "See the castle seamstress tonight. Tell her to make you three white robes, the first by tomorrow. I need you to look like a wizard."

"But Majesty—"

"This will help, Kishi," he said. "When Omara sees you, she'll be reassured. Perhaps she won't lay any more spells on us." He left.

Prince Kian, his arms circled by green ribbons, approached me. "What did Father want?"

"He wants me to act as his wizard." I could leave. Tonight, before the king tied me here with bonds of duty and obligation like my husband's green lace. He was wiling me into place as surely as Gran could have.

Why did I want to leave? Here I had a place to sleep, food to eat, and the respect of the household. The king wanted to give me greater status, whether I was worthy of it or not. What more did I want?

"Good," said Kian.

"I'm not a wizard."

"Of course you are. Name one other person in the kingdom with your ability with plants. You're not the same sort of wizard your grandmother is, but you are a wizard."

I looked for his signature, and saw a faint flicker of blue and green around him. I didn't understand what these colors meant in people. In plants they meant health. They were clear colors, so they might mean he wasn't lying to me, but I wasn't sure.

Maybe I was a sort of wizard. No one else in the kingdom was a plantwife, or my husband would have told me, the way he sometimes passed on rumors of blight or fire or the fertilizer of blood shed in distant battlefields.

Kian touched my shoulder. The lace of my husband shifted on my upper arm, restless at the touch of another. "Think about it," Kian said. "Not many pay attention to you, but I know some of what you can do. You are a wizard, and you have strengths. Father can use your help." He gripped my shoulder and released me.

I sighed, and went to find the seamstress. I gave her the king's instructions about sewing me robes. She had drunk much cider and was the worse for it, but she grumbled and took my measure.

At the end of the day, I went back to the room I shared with Gran. Damp spring air came in the window and filled the room with cool and the scents of young plants and moist earth, over the wall in the fields beyond. Cats prowled the courtyard, yowling spring songs. The moon sent silver light through the window. It rested like gilt across Gran's face. She had not stirred since I had put her to sleep that afternoon.

I went to Gran's side and took her hand. "Let her wake," I told the green lace on Gran's arms. She frowned, stirred, and woke.

"Kishi?"

I wondered which Gran had awakened. "Gran."

"Why am I lying down, and why is it so late?" She turned to stare at the moon.

"Do you remember what you said before?"

"What I said before? When?"

"How there are two of you?"

"Two of me? You are not making sense, heart's daughter."

So this was the one who wasn't aware of the other. This was the one who cast hurtful spells. Or was it?

"Do you remember what you did to Mother?" I asked Gran.

"What I did—" She lifted her arms, stared at the lines of my husband's lace, dark in the silver light. Her eyes widened. "Kishi, what is this?"

Was this a third Gran, who couldn't remember any of her earlier selves?

"You set spells on me, on Mother, on Cook, on King Eleks. Perhaps others I don't know about. Spells that hurt us. My husband is protecting you from yourself."

"Take it off this instant, or I shall force it from me."

"Gran! Be the wise judge I know you are. Think. I am not one to attack you without reason."

"You're jealous of my position. You've always wanted my power. You want to unseat me and steal my place."

"Gran!" My stomach turned over, and there was a sour taste in my mouth.

"You're a serpent's child who has crept into my heart and waits to bite it."

"I'm not!"

"You have plotted my downfall ever since you met the Old Man in the Ground. Take these green lines off now or I will kill them, and poison the one who gave them to you." She raised her hands, and her fingers took spellcasting form.

"Gran!"

"Kishi, take this off me, *now*."

I held my hand out toward her, called to the tendrils wrapped around Gran's arms. They did not respond. Instead, tendril tips dived under her skin and pumped sleep into her. She screamed, a terrifying noise of rage and fear, the cry of a hunting hawk and a hunted animal. She collapsed on the bed.

A storm of weeping shook me. I lay on the cold stone floor and let sorrow cradle me. I knew how Gran had planned to use her hands. The spells that came from those finger positions spread hurt and harm. I had never seen Gran take such positions with an aim to using them; she had only ever shown them to me to teach me what to be wary of, if an enemy ever aimed spells at me.

Presently warmth seeped through me, nudged aside my despair. My husband had shifted the sea inside me, stilled the wild waves and weather. *It is time*, he said.

Time for what?

Time to make her fears come true.

Something pulled at my left arm. I opened my eyes and looked. In the moonlight, a dark rope of twisted strands led from my hand up over the edge of the bed to my grandmother. It tightened, pulling me toward her.

Up, Wife. It is time. A forest giant has fallen. Lightning has struck her, and she is no longer capable of good growth. Use what she has to nurture the next generation.

I can't do this.

You can and you must. You know who she used to be. It is what her well self would want.

I scrambled to my feet and sat on the edge of Gran's bed. My husband pulled my hand into Gran's, bound our hands together with a net of vine, my fingers interwoven with Gran's.

"Isn't there anything we can do to heal her?"

Look.

I saw/felt a vision of an ailing forest. The stream ran only in trickles, and many of the trees were dead or dying. Some of them had been struck by lightning, others eaten by insects or disease. A few trees still stood tall; light still fell on them and nourished them. Elsewhere the sky was dark and gloomy, though no rain fell.

She is like a wounded tree that sees its death ahead and spends all its last energy putting out seed. These were the spells she cast on you and your mother and the king: she craves children to carry her life on past her end.

Under the surface of Gran's soil, a tide of something not water flexed and flowed. I tasted it with the senses of who I was in the vision, something with roots and leaves and body, something that was all mouths of different kinds. The tide tasted of strange intoxicants. It geysered up one of the fire-twisted trees and shot out the top, flew to another part of the forest and struck a living tree, withered and wilted it. I heard a scream.

The magic has grown stronger than her control of it, said my husband. *Take it, Wife. You have the strength to contain it. I can help. It only hurts her now.*

Where had the tide come from? How could I take it?

My husband had shaped me as a tree in this landscape. I put down myriad roots, and Gran's magic flowed into me through them.

I tasted blood, grit, iron, bitter orange, decay, sour apple, vanilla, all riding on a stream of power rich and strange and frightening. I grew drunk as it invaded me. It flowed through me, opening walls and shifting rivers. At first I was stupid under its flood, and let it go where it willed, but then my husband spoke to me. *Control it, Wife. Cage it. Put it where you can use it, and don't let it change the parts of you you want to preserve. Watch and confine and direct it.*

I wasn't sure I knew how to do what he said. He held me in his embrace and helped me choose. *Hold it here,* he said, and showed me how to store the power in leaves and fruit and trunk, how to tame the tide, turn it from flood into potential.

More and more and more came. At first I felt overwhelmed. Then I learned to let the process of storing it click from thought into habit.

Don't take it all. Leave enough to sustain her, my husband said, much later.

I stopped pulling in power and glanced at the landscape of my grandmother's mind.

It looked cold and haunted now, the dark twisted shapes of dead trees everywhere, and yet, nearby, I saw a clearing. Seven healthy trees grew there, and the meadow was watered by the little power that still flowed. Flowers starred the grass.

I could not walk to the meadow in the shape I wore now, a thick-trunked tree heavy laden with fruit and rustling with lively leaves, but I could send a root to it. I tasted the undersurface of the clearing. Clean, strong like the smell of fresh, worm-aired earth, a comfort that reminded me of Gran as I had first known her, warm arms that hugged me when I cried, soft voice that eased my fears.

Go down, said my husband. I sent my roots below the soil of Gran's clearing. The power here tasted clear and sweet. I did not pull it into me, but pushed down deeper.

Far below, I reached bedrock. My rootlets stubbed themselves against a wall, moved over it through the soil until they found an opening into Otherwhere.

Build, said my husband.

I didn't understand him, but my muscles responded. The opening was too wide, and let through too much power. Some of it stained as it passed into the dirt of my grandmother's mind, darkened and flowed out to the places I had pulled it from before. I reached with my roots and grasped stones around me, built them into a rim that blocked the flow, shut it down to a small stream, just enough to nourish, not enough to storm through her mind and drown it again. I used some of the power I had gotten from her to strengthen the wall. I spelled it strong enough to abide, and to restrain the influx of power.

Afterward, my husband and I pulled up my new roots; I thinned my tree self and flowed along my husband's vines back into myself.

Fitting all I had taken from Gran into myself was a job I would not have been able to do alone. My husband helped me sort and store and reshape. He showed me how to claim new territory, space invisible and unattainable to my solo self. I had not known my own forest could grow in so many directions.

I found the river of my own power, the conduit to a different Otherwhere, and traced its flows, making sure they were open and clean, not blocked or filtered through fragile or dark places.

Another long, strange process. During it, I felt myself turn into someone new and terrifying.

I knew that I was my own forest, a host to my husband, even here, in the heart of the castle. I could leave, and carry everything with me. I could stay and be complete.

Only when we had finished our sorting and exploration did I notice someone shaking my shoulder.

"Kishi! Kishi! Wake up!"

I opened my eyes. How strange to be human-shaped again. How limiting. How different.

Stored inside me, great heaps of power fruit, blankets of bud, flower, seed, stem, and leaf. Some of the new leaves were the red of blood, some the purple of poison, but most the varying greens of hope and promise. The forest inside me had grown in many directions.

How had Gran ever lived a quiet life, with all of this power rustling inside her?

What was I going to do with it?

"What have you done?" cried Cook. Hers were the hands that gripped my shoulders.

I lay beside Gran on the bed, my fingers still meshed with hers.

Gran sighed. Her free hand rose, and she rubbed her eyes.

I lifted my free hand and rubbed my eyes, too. "Maple?" My voice tasted rusty.

"Kishi!" said Cook.

"What's wrong?"

"You two have been lying here twined together with green vines for three days now! What on Helnia's Hearth have you been doing?"

I worked my hand loose of Gran's. My fingers were stiff. Three days for me to go through my grandmother's mind and steal her power. I shook my head and pushed myself up.

"We've been trying and trying to wake you," Cook said. "The kitchen is in chaos. I never realized how many things you do to keep it in order. The king has been going mad as well. He hasn't held judgment since Seed Blessing Day. Are you truly awake now?"

My mouth tasted acrid. My stomach clenched like a fist. "I need porridge."

Cook hugged me, pressed my face against her floury front.

"Can't breathe," I told her eventually.

She released me. "We thought we had lost you."

"No," I said. "I have done a terrible thing."

"A terrible thing, Kishi?"

"I took away her wizard powers," I whispered.

Cook's brow furrowed. She glanced at Gran.

Gran sat up. She smiled at me and Cook. "Good morning."

"Lady Omara," Cook said. "How are you?"

Gran's stomach growled.

"Porridge for both of you, and pray Helnia I don't burn it. Kishi, do you do something to stop me from burning things? Never in all my born days have I burned so many things as these three days you've been asleep." Cook tugged me to my feet. "Bathe and put on other clothes, Kishi, my lady. You stink as though you'd been working in the sun." She bustled out.

I went to our wardrobe. Hanging beside Gran's white robes of peacetime wizard office were three new white robes, with longer hems, to fit my taller form. The seamstress had done the king's bidding. I hesitated, then lifted down one of the old and one of the new robes.

I led Gran toward the bath house.

Gran gazed around as though she had never seen the hall, the yard, the bath house before. She wore a smile that did not change, and her eyes were bright and shallow.

Powdery light came into the tub room from five long, narrow windows just under the roof. Between slants of light lay shadow. The water woman poured hot and cold water into a large tub and left us. Steam rose from the surface, blocks of it in the air where light touched it, invisible in the darkness.

I led Gran to the clothes hooks, hung our robes up beside the towels in one patch of light. "Take off your clothes, Gran."

She dropped her robe as though she had no modesty and stood before me, her aging flesh decorated with a loose green spiral of my husband's tendrils.

The Gran I used to know would not have abided my husband's touch.

I removed my tunic and skirts more slowly.

My husband's embrace of me was much more intense than the shadow self he had left on Gran; I wore a webwork of vines. Gran touched a junction of six lines that lay over my breastbone.

"Pretty," she said.

I felt the water with my hand, then stirred to mix the hot and cold. I tugged Gran into the water with me, and she sat, smiling, and let me wash her. I had never helped her wash before, though I remembered being a small child, the gentle roughness of the rag as she had scrubbed and soaped me, the pleasure as she poured warm rinse water over me. I stopped in midwash to hug Gran, and her arms met around me. Almost I could pretend she was her old self.

Afterward, she needed help with the fastenings of her robe.

The inside of my wizard's robe felt soft against my skin.

Gran took my hand. I looked at both of us, gowned in wizard white, and shivered.

I left our other clothes behind, with the dirt of the bath water. A different me had come out of the water, and a different Gran. I did not know either of us yet.

We went outside.

My mother waited by the bath house door, arms crossed over her chest, hands buried in her armpits. Her hair was trained back into its greased braid again, not a strand out of place; her face was pale, her shoulders hunched. She wore a heavy, quilted dress, clay red, with black ties lacing the sleeves and knitting the front together. The skirt was narrow, but so long I only saw the tips of her soft shoes below the hem. I could not remember the last time I had seen my mother in a dress.

I pulled Gran to a stop.

"Laran," Gran said. She smiled.

"Omara." My mother stared at the ground. She glanced up. "Kishi."

"Mother? How can I help you?"

Her arms loosened. Her hands dropped to grip her stomach. "I've seen the priestesses. I've consulted the oracle. Signs say I should stay here, stay the way I am. While I was at temple, Owain came to me. He spoke to the others in my battalion, discovered what he had done to me. He apologized. Everyone knows now it was a battle spell gone awry—" Mother glanced at Gran.

Gran looked confused. Mother turned to me.

"I don't know what she remembers," I said.

"Do you remember spelling me, Omara?"

Gran touched her forehead with the tips of her fingers. "I didn't sleep so well last night," she said. "Or, which night was it? I sat up after Kishi went to sleep, and my mind kept racing around and around. I knew there were things I'd left undone. It came to me that I could solve everything with a few spells. I sent them out to do good work, and then I could sleep."

"You're not going to do that again, are you?" Mother asked.

Gran frowned, pressed her forehead. "Nothing's here anymore."

Mother glanced at me. I nodded. She sighed, returned my nod. "Owain and I have talked. He said he will care for me as he would any warrior wounded in battle, that I will have time to heal, and then I can come back to work. If I bear the child, will you take it when it's born?"

"Oh, yes," I whispered, and then knew that in spite of my strange marriage, I too had had mother dreams. I stroked the green band at my wrist. My husband coiled a tendril around my fingers, released me. "Yes, Mother. Please."

"I'll see how the pregnancy treats me. If it's too much trouble, I may come to you for help in ending it."

"I know herbal cures to ease pain in pregnancy. Come to me if you need any kind of comfort."

She stepped forward, pressed a kiss to my forehead, then turned and left. Gran stared after her, brow furrowed.

"Come on, Gran." I took her hand. We went to the kitchen.

At the servants' table, Cook gave us porridge. As we ate, the king came to the kitchen. He knelt before Gran, his head bowed.

"Get up, Eleks," Gran said. "You look silly."

He raised his eyes to me. I felt a strange regard from him, something that stroked across the stolen powers in me. I realized he had his own measure of wizardry, one that looked deeper than normal people could.

He rose. "Please come to court, Lady Omara, Lady Kishi. We have many matters to sort out today."

"I haven't finished my porridge," Gran said.

He flushed and glanced at our bowls. "I beg your pardon." He stood and waited while we finished eating, then led us to the courtroom.

Two seats sat to the right of the king's throne where only Gran's had been before. The king seated me beside him, and then helped Gran to the second seat. She gazed out over the court with an unthinking smile.

I looked at the courtroom from the dais, a perspective I had never had before. The doors to the outer room stood open. A crowd pressed tight in the outer room, fidgeting, restless. The first three sets of petitioners waited in the courtroom, flanked by guards in case arguments grew heated, and advocates to help them state their cases.

"Let us hear the first matter," said the king.

The bailiff led two men forward, both claiming the same pig, one because it was born from his sow, and the other because it had fed from his garden.

When we had heard the arguments on both sides, the king turned to me.

This was not a dispute that required wizardry to resolve. I understood it was a test.

One of the new trees in my inner forest dropped a fruit into my mouth. I bit it. The taste of it murmured to the king: "Let them sell the pig. One fifth of the price goes to the man who provided the seed, and four fifths to the man who provided the fruit that built its body."

The voice that came from my mouth was Gran's, the words couched in my husband's idiom, the judgment mine. I closed my eyes, contemplating my internal mix. A touch on the back of my hand came from the king, who turned and spoke my judgment in a voice that could be heard by everyone in the room.

A touch on my other hand came from Gran. Her hand rested on mine, light and cool, without gripping, but without censure.

I opened my eyes and looked at my new future.

SWITCHED

I was ten when my father married my stepmother, and her daughter, Musette, was nine. My wicked stepmother, Habila, was cleverer than most wicked stepmothers; she had read the old tales before ever she married my father.

My father, on the other hand, was just like fathers in the old tales, too stupid to realize she only married him for money, and that she loved her own daughter and hated me.

My own mother had been a beauty and a saint, so lovely everyone adored her at first sight, so kind we had benches built in the garden for the beggars and the troubled who came by each day to ask her for aid and counsel. She was not as open-handed as she longed to be, for in those days Father still had some sense, and knew he had to maintain his wealth and not bankrupt himself if he wanted to sponsor Mother's charities for any length of time. He made her a daily allowance, and she had to decide carefully how to spend it to benefit the most people. This served her well; she did not give equally to the liars and the genuinely destitute: she learned to tell who told the truth.

In all her charitable work, she kept me by her side, and taught me, as she learned, how to deal with others, how to tell a schemer from a pauper, how to be kind and good and careful.

She had been dead only a year when my father married my stepmother.

My stepmother was a clever and accomplished woman. She had her own dark beauty. Her lips were redder than my mother's had been, and this, I think, owed more to her passionate nature than to any art. Unlike my mother's golden hair, my stepmother's hair was bog black, shimmering and iridescent as raven's feathers in the sun, and her eyes were a blue so deep they looked black in any light but daylight.

My stepsister Musette was as dark as her mother, but in some ways innocent. However, her mother loved her so much and catered so to her every whim that Musette believed everyone should defer to her. In this one area, my stepmother was at first blind to reality: she did not see that Musette offended those she considered her inferiors with her high-handed ways.

Soon after my father met Habila, he brought her home to dinner. I did not know what to think. She was beautiful and acted kind, and my father had been so melancholy since my mother died—as had I—that I was glad my father had found someone who gave him even a moment's comfort.

Habila took pains to charm me. "Oh," she said to my father, "Prudence is a lovely child. How sad you must be, dearest one, with no mother to care for you."

I was sad, so I took this for sense. I let her hug me, fool that I was, and took comfort in the warmth of her embrace. Father and I had not touched each other since the day of Mother's funeral. We had retreated into our own cold sadnesses. I had not known until Habila held me how hungry I had become for even the falsest of human comforts.

I had watched my mother learn to tell the deceiver from the honest person, had tried to continue in her traditions, seeing petitioners each day, with my father's blessing. But I was confused and could not always determine who to give alms to. Usually I gave a little to everyone.

Habila petted me and said what a good, kind child I was. She told Musette to be nice to me. Musette found this difficult; she had never had to be nice to anyone, but she tried. She let me touch her dolls, but she would not let me play with them.

My father's courtship of Habila lasted a month. Then they married, and Musette and Habila came to live with us.

"Oh, my Prudence, everyone loves you," Habila said to me the morning after her wedding. We were in the dining room, where Cook had set the breakfast buffet. Habila and I were the only two awake so early. She had come down before me, in time to watch Cook set the buffet. I came before Cook was finished, and Habila heard me thanking Cook for everything, as was my daily habit.

"Do they?" I said. I set toast and scrambled eggs on my plate and brought it to the table, set it at the place beside Habila's. I wondered when she would hug me again. She had embraced me at every meeting before she wed my father. I stood beside my chair, uncertain but hoping.

"How could they help it? You are all that is good and kind." She studied me, but she did not hold out her arms.

I wasn't sure how to respond, so I curtseyed.

Musette stumbled into the room in her slippers and robe then, her dark hair disarrayed, her cheeks flushed. "I want chocolate!" she cried after she had studied the buffet and discovered there was no cocoa there. She strode to the bellpull and tugged it hard. Cook came up three minutes later. "What took you so long?" cried Musette. "I want chocolate! Now!"

Cook nodded and fled.

"Oh, dear," said Habila. She touched my shoulder and said, "Sit, child. Eat. Your eggs are getting cold."

I seated myself beside her and ate. Musette filled a plate with pastries and climbed up onto the chair on the other side of her mother. When Cook brought her a cup and a pot of chocolate, she tasted it and threw the cup on the floor. "'Tis not sweet enough!" she cried. "Make it over, and this time flavor it correctly!"

Cook fled again.

"Oh, dear," said Habila.

She spent the morning baking, despite Cook's protests at the invasion of her space. By lunchtime, my stepmother had made her first spellcakes in my father's house.

At lunch she set a dark cake on my plate, and a white cake on Musette's. "From now on," she said, "you will each eat one of these with every meal. Eat it first, before you eat anything else. It is the only thing I ask of you."

My dark cake was sweet and rich. I thought it wouldn't be a hardship to live off such cake entirely.

Musette didn't like her cake so much. "'Tis too sickly sweet!" she cried.

"Eat it," said her mother. In that moment she looked different: her eyes held storm, her mouth shaped anger, and she grew until her wild dark hair brushed the ceiling.

Surely my eyes deceived me.

Nevertheless, Musette ate all of her cake, and never protested again.

At supper that night Father noticed our treats. "What is this?" he asked.

"Something to aid our daughters' complexions," said Stepmother.

"May I taste?" Father reached toward my plate.

I wanted to hide my plate in my lap. I didn't want to share my cake with Father! It was mine, mine alone.

"No!" cried Stepmother. "That is just for Prudence. Only girls get any benefit of it."

Father looked forlorn. Stepmother said, "Never mind, Louis. I'll make you your own special cake for breakfast tomorrow."

I ate the rest of my cake quickly, before anyone could take it from me.

Stepmother made Father a yellow cake that looked as delicious as the cakes she made for me and Musette. After he ate it, he became sleepy but contented. That was no good; she had to bake him something else for breakfast and lunch, or he became too stupid to do business, and Stepmother didn't want that; but she was delighted to have him sleepy and happy after supper, so he had yellow cake with every evening meal.

The week after I first started eating my special cake, I became too impatient to meet with petitioners any longer. I gave the housekeeper the day's alms to disburse, and granted her discretion over who to give them to. I discovered some time later that she had decided she and her husband, the butler, were more in need of alms than any of the beggars who no longer thronged our doors, but by that time I did not care; I was dipping into the alms myself. A woman needed ribbons and jewels, after all.

Two weeks later, I looked at the hair in my brush and noticed that it was darker than I expected. I studied myself in the mirror and saw that my curly blond hair was turning dark and straight, and my eyes, formerly sky blue, had gone lavender. At lunch that day I studied my stepsister as she ate her white cake and noticed that her midnight hair had streaks of blond in it now, leaving her odd-looking and piebald. Her dark eyes had flecks of green in them.

In the following month, my stepsister and I changed our coloring: she was fair, her hair a shining crown of wheat-blond curls, her formerly olive skin lightened to peachy pink, her dark eyes to a sea blue-green; my hair had gone to cave black, my eyes darkening to pansy-purple. Now when we went out shopping with Stepmother, strangers mistook me for her true daughter, and Musette for the adopted one. Musette no longer cried and cursed, either. She never sent anything back or complained of Cook's behavior or the laziness of the maids.

More things bothered me than formerly. My tongue's sensitivity to taste increased. Some flavors upset me so I couldn't finish my food. Meats tasted rotten; sweets were cloying, and when the bread was too dry, it felt like I was trying to swallow sawdust. I never got an apple but I found a worm in it.

The color of light changed, too; to me it always seemed stained with smoke, so that I saw no true sunlight any longer, and often there were scents in the air that made me sneeze.

Sometimes I complained.

Father always stared at me as though he couldn't believe the words that came from my lips. Stepmother smiled, and encouraged me to rage until I got my will. Musette, who had complained of the same things when she first moved into our house, grew increasingly quiet. She served herself the meat with the gristle, the burnt ends of bread, and left the choicer cuts to me. What I left, after Father and Stepmother had been served, Musette snuck to the dog under the table. If there was more, sometimes she took it outside to give to the poor.

Later, the housekeeper set tasks for Musette: clean out the fireplaces. Draw water from the well. Do the mending. Take the laundry from the line, iron and fold it.

Stepmother watched and did not interfere. She only smiled.

I watched, and thought: Musette deserves it. She's the interloper here. It is my house, after all, and she is just a latecomer. She *should* help.

One of Father's apprentices stopped by the house after a year-long sea voyage. He had not seen me since before my father's wedding, and he called Musette by my name, and asked for an introduction to me. I screamed at him, but it only confused him; he did not believe I had ever been Prudence. He never came to the house again.

I grew to enjoy my own reflection as my hair and eyes darkened. None of my old gowns suited my new colors, so I had to buy others, in ruby and sapphire and emerald. No longer would I dress in pastels. I gave my old clothes to Musette, until I realized how nice she looked in them. Then I made sure to shred them and put them in the donation box for the poor.

By then, Musette had learned how to mend, and sometimes, when her own clothes were worn to pieces, she rescued my old gowns from the box and mended them. I let her do that. I always knew where the mends were, and I took secret joy in the thought of her wearing what was flawed, even if it looked fine to others.

When Musette was sixteen and I was seventeen, an invitation to a ball came from the local prince. It was addressed to all eligible ladies of the household.

"Musette is not eligible," I said. "She has nothing suitable to wear. Besides, look at her hands. They are ugly." Laundry soaps, scrubbing, and scutwork had roughened Musette's skin, and her nails were short and ragged.

"Prudence is right," Stepmother said. "Musette will stay home while Prudence goes to the ball." And she helped me dress in my sapphire blue velvet gown. She bound up my black hair in a braid crown around my head, and sent me off in my father's best carriage to the ball.

The prince danced with every young lady who came to the ball, but I fancied he enjoyed my company the most. He danced twice with me, an honor he had not shared with any of the others. The floor was polished crystal, and the walls were lined with mirrors: when I saw us reflected as a couple, the prince in pale blue and I in dark sapphire, his hair gold as coins and mine dark as night, I thought: we are the perfect couple.

At ten, though, the doors opened to admit one more maiden.

The herald announced her as the Unknown Princess. She wore a ballgown of pink overlaid with silver net, and her hair was a cloud of pale gold around her head. Her neck was long and graceful, her face beautiful, her crystal slippers tiny as she stepped with small clicks down the stairs into the ballroom.

All music and speech stopped for her entrance. The prince, who held my right hand in his left, and rested his right hand at my waist, released me so suddenly I would have fallen, save I was prepared for this. He abandoned me and walked toward the new arrival.

I studied her face as she descended the stairs, and thought: I know her. Then: Who is she?

Then: Mother?

She was the image of my mother's portrait, taken just after my mother wed my father. The portrait hung in the front parlor over the fireplace. After Mother died, I had visited there every day, though we never used that room unless we had visitors. I had stared at my mother's face, longing for her to come back from the dead, praying that she would advise me as I tried to continue her charitable works. For a time it seemed I heard her voice as I listened to the petitioners, and I had thought my judgments sound.

I had abandoned all such work years earlier. This was not Mother as I had known her. This was Mother before I was born. This was the person I should be. This was Musette as she was now. The perfidy of my stepmother came clear to me in that moment.

As if pulled by strings, the prince advanced to the base of the stairs, and when Musette alighted, he took her hand in his. The music started then, a waltz, of course, and they glided over the floor in a space left bare by everyone else, who still stood, awestruck, staring at the prince and my stepsister. Musette was lovely, every step sure and floating. Her hands were concealed in elbow-length gloves. I had never noticed before what small feet she had.

"Miss Prudence?"

The man at my side wore a dark green velvet jacket and darker green unmentionables, and his figure was too slender and short for admiration. His face was clever rather than handsome, and his dark hair was thin on top. His dancing golden eyes protruded a little. I had known him for five years, as he was a business acquaintance of my father's, and often came to dine with us. He always wore some shade of green. He never left the house without me calling him "that frog" behind his back, which never failed to make my stepmother laugh, and my father protest that Mr. Baton was one of the best businessmen he knew, and I was not to make fun of him. Musette always shook her head, her eyes downcast.

Five minutes ago I would have said something cruel and sent him away, secure in my belief that the prince was mine. Now I said: "Mr. Baton?"

He held out a hand, and I took it. We danced. His steps were shorter than the prince's, of course, but he was energetic and lively, and his sense of rhythm was perfect. Unlike all the other men there, he did not spend the next ten minutes gawking at Musette.

Later in the evening, when I had danced with several other men, Mr. Baton claimed my hand again and led me to the chairs at the side of the room, seated me beside a little table, and went off to find me refreshments.

I looked around the room while Mr. Baton was gone, surveyed

all the young men who were here. My stepmother's years of planning had borne fruit tonight. Musette, the classic mistreated princess-in-hiding, would have the prince. I would be cast off. The love and tolerance Stepmother had shown me, encouraging me in her own image instead of in my mother's, would evaporate now, I was sure. It behooved me to make my own plans.

Mr. Baton was not as handsome as other men here who were not the prince. He was not as tall as most of them, and his shoulders were narrow. The lack of hair, would that bother me? He could always wear a wig, as many in society did.

Did I need height or strength or even hair in a husband? Mr. Baton was rich. Though not noble, he had interests in a number of businesses; he had a fleet of ships, three drygoods shops, part share in the lending library, an upcountry textile factory, and a fine house on a square not two blocks from my father's house.

His eyes were lively, and his hands were dry in mine, not moist and clammy like some of the younger men's. His breath was always fresh and sweet, not rank with rotten teeth like some, or ripe with the scent of onions and garlic, like others. I had seen appreciation in his eyes when he looked at me.

He brought me a plate of pastries and a flute of champagne. He seated himself beside me while I nibbled. I did not pout because the creampuff filling was too sweet, or complain that the champagne bubbles made me sneeze. I smiled at him.

"Miss Prudence," he said. "You regard me differently from the way you have in the past. Dare I hope?"

"What do you think of *l'Inconnue*?" I asked.

"Who?" He glanced around. "That creature in pink, the so-called Unknown Princess?" He lifted a quizzing glass and studied her as best he could between the men who thronged around her. "Pretty enough, I suppose, but she does not look as though she has much wit."

"What would you say if you learned she was kind and good-hearted and not at all stupid?"

"Good for her. Perhaps she'll make an adequate queen."

I set my half-eaten pastries on the table, placed my champagne glass beside them, and reached for his hand. He let me clasp it; indeed, he looked surprised and pleased at my forwardness.

Almost I heard my mother's voice again, though how that could be I did not know: I had eaten my regular portion of dark cake with my dinner that night. Perhaps enough hours had passed since then for the effect to lessen. I had a choice to make: I could entice this man into offering for me, and live with the security that would come of such a marriage, or I could tell him the truth about myself—if I even knew it—and let him make a more informed decision. My mother's voice advised me to tell the truth. "Mr. Baton? When I don't dye my hair, I fear I look much like the Unknown does."

"Impossible." He let the quizzing glass fall among the other fobs on his watch chain, and studied my face. He reached up and touched my hair just above my ear. Something in his eyes quickened then. "I spoke too soon," he murmured. "I see how it may be so." He cocked his head. "Do you plan to stop dying your hair?"

I looked away. "The choice may not be mine," I said. Now that Stepmother had her royal son-in-law, her happy daughter, would she ever make me spellcake again? Who would I be without its influence? I had forgotten who I was when my real mother died; I only knew who I was now. Once the effect of the cake wore off—

"Would you even consider my suit?" he asked.

"I would, of course. But you don't know whom you ask to marry. I don't know myself."

"I have detected a touch of sorcery around your father's investments," he muttered. "They are sometimes too successful."

"I've been under a spell as long as you've known me," I murmured, then wondered how I could admit such a thing.

"Is it a spell that enhances understanding? Do you anticipate it wearing off now?"

"Yes," I whispered. "No. I believe my understanding is my own, but everything else about me—"

"Ah," he said. He leaned back. His hand dropped to his thigh.

We sat silent beside each other. I gazed down at my sapphire velvet skirts with their insets of white satin. From the corner of my eye I watched as Mr. Baton surveyed the company, much as I had before. Was he searching for a better candidate for a wife? Most mothers and fathers would welcome him as a son-in-law, I suspected. He was successful and well-received.

By the prince's invitation, every eligible young woman of worth, and several worthless ones, should be here in the ballroom tonight. Perhaps Mr. Baton could not have his pick. But there were many he could choose, I was certain, girls who would be obedient to parents, who in turn would be obedient to economic pressure.

"Miss Prudence," he said at last, "thank you for favoring me with such relevant information, so prejudicial to your person. Given what you know and suspect of your own nature, if you should make a promise now, would your future self consider it binding?"

"Yes," I said. Suppose I lost my acquired selfish self. Surely the saintly self I used to be would never break a promise.

"I have already spoken to your father, though I feared I had no hope of winning you. He has given me permission to court you, but he says the final decision must rest with you."

"You prefer me to Musette?"

He lifted his glass and studied the Unknown again. "Musette," he said. "Ah. Of course. I much prefer you."

"I may be more like her tomorrow."

"And she?"

"I don't know. My stepmother planned this. After tonight—surely they will announce the betrothal tonight—she may have further plans. I don't know if she'll allow Musette to revert to her true self after she weds the prince, but I believe she will no longer care to keep me as I am."

"I believe I could love you either way. Could either of you love me?"

I smiled down at my skirts. "This is surely the oddest conversation I have ever had."

"It's not the oddest one I've had, but it is crucial to my future."

I glanced sideways at him. His golden eyes—so prominent—and yet, his mouth, so clever, with such a lovely, twisted, rueful smile on it. Why had I never appreciated him before? Perhaps it was so easy to see the flaws in him that the true heart lay hidden. I reached for his hand, and said, "I do believe I could love you either way."

"Miss Prudence, will you do me the honor of becoming my wife?"

Could I ever hope for more? Was I not lucky to be offered this much? I was fortunate indeed, no matter which self I became on the morrow. "Mr. Baton, I will."

He smiled. "Miss Prudence, would you care to take the air?"

Oh, dear, I thought. He means to kiss me.

Of course, you silly goose. He surely expects that in his wife.

"Gladly, Mr. Baton." I rose to my feet.

"Please. Call me Remy."

We went out through the tall French doors to the balcony that overlooked the gardens. Light from the myriad candles in the ballroom leaked through the many glassed, uncurtained doors to spill in rectangles of gold across the ground. Other couples stood there, leaned on the stone railing above the gardens, spoke in soft tones.

Remy led me past the others, down the staircase to the gravelled garden path that led past yew hedges and beyond the light. Tonight I almost enjoyed the air, as I had not since my stepmother moved into the house. Almost I could taste cool wet spring and fresh grass.

In a small alcove in the yew, Remy pulled me close. I was an inch taller than he was. I thought: how nice this is. Who would have thought it comfortable to dance with someone the same size? And yet, when I danced with those other men, none kept pace so well with me, or felt so comfortable with his arms around me, not even the prince. There is something to be said for being the same size as your husband.

He tipped my chin down, and I leaned forward to meet his lips, thinking of his crooked, clever smile.

He tasted of champagne and shyness. This is sweet, I thought. I will be able to put up with this the rest of my life. Indeed, perhaps I will enjoy it.

The kiss began as one thing and changed into quite another. What started with me leaning just the smallest bit forward, my hands gripping his head, ended with me tilted backward as he loomed above me, my hands having slid down over his shoulders to press against his chest. At first I was frightened, then terrified. He wrapped his arms around me to keep me from falling. "Prudence?" he asked. Even his voice had changed, deepened until I didn't recognize it.

Was this one last trick my stepmother played on me?

"Let me go."

Gently he released me, steadying my shoulders with his big hands so that I didn't collapse.

"Who are you?" I asked in a shaking voice when at last his hands stopped gripping my shoulders. In the starlight he was nothing but a shadow that blocked the sky. How tall was he, and how did he come to be in my arms?

"Your fiancé."

"Mr. Baton?"

"Prudence. You were not the only one under a spell. But I was forbidden to speak of it until you broke it for me. I apologize for wooing you under false pretenses."

"But—"

"I hope you can forgive me. I promise I'll make it up to you the rest of our lives."

"Remy. Who are you?"

"You know me, Prudence. Only the envelope has changed."

"Really?"

"Truly." One of his hands reached for mine, and I let my hand disappear into his, which was now big enough to enfold it completely, but he didn't; he left me room to slide my thumb over his and grip him back. "I anticipate some trouble when I go back to the firm. It may be that I'll have to present myself as my own son or brother. I'm sure I can work it out, though. I have all the knowledge I need; I'll be able to convince them."

We walked back toward the palace, Remy a large presence beside me, his hand warm and dry around mine. At least that hadn't changed; but that made me wonder about all the other things that might have happened. Would I still be able to dance with him? He was taller than anyone else at the ball, I could tell that even in the dark, just from where the sound of his breathing came from.

Only the envelope had changed.

I couldn't promise him I would stay the same inside when the spell on me was broken, and he had accepted me even so. Who was I to complain?

We climbed the stairs to the balcony, where light waited, and I looked up. And up, and up. He was not quite a giant, but almost. His shoulders were broad, his face more handsome than the prince's, his hair thick and dark and no longer disappearing. In fact, he had a respectable amount tied in a tail at the back of his neck now. His neck was a whole subject in itself, thick and mighty as a young tree. He still wore shades of green, but his clothes had grown with him.

He paused in the light and looked at me. "Will I do?" he asked.

"Oh, Remy." I couldn't keep the irritation out of my voice. I had just convinced myself of all the advantages of a short paramour, and now here I was, stuck with a giant one.

He laughed and leaned to press his forehead to my hair. "My love, your dismay does my heart good," he said.

"I expect I'll get used to you," I muttered.

"Excellent."

The clock struck midnight as we went back inside, and Musette pushed away from the prince and ran off into the night, leaving behind a crystal slipper on the stair. Anxiety swept the crowd, and gossip, people wondering who the mysterious princess in pink had been; plainly the prince was smitten. He made his foolish declaration from the stairs, that he would marry the woman whose foot fit the slipper. By then Remy and I had regained our seats, and I had given him the rest of my pastries. He vowed he was hungry, and I wasn't surprised. There was a lot of him to maintain now.

He saw me home not too much later, riding with me in my father's best carriage, but he walked off after he had kissed me goodnight, much to the outrage of the housekeeper who answered the door. "I'll call on your father tomorrow," he said.

I went to get a cup of water in the kitchen. Musette sat by the hearth, back in her rags again.

"You should have been there," I told her, feeling it was required of me. "I was sure the prince was mine, but then, very late, a vision in pink appeared out of nowhere, and the prince spent all the rest of the evening dancing with her, until she ran off at midnight, leaving behind only a glass slipper. No one knows who she is."

"Oh, Prudence," Musette said. "I know you knew me."

"You do?"

"I saw you staring. I saw you blink when you recognized me. I saw you dance with the frog! How could you, Prudence, after all the times you've teased him?"

"Oh, well," I said. "I'm going to marry him. The prince vows he'll marry the one who fits in your slipper, so your future is assured."

"You'll marry the frog?" she cried. She leapt up and came to me. "You don't have to do that, Prue. I'll marry the prince, and then you can come live with me in the palace. We'll find you a much better husband."

"No, no. I am content."

We went upstairs together, and bade each other good night; for once, we both meant it.

In the middle of the night I woke and stared at the ceiling. My fiancé. Who was he, really? Who had cast a spell on him, and how long ago? Would he ever tell me?

In the morning, I found a piece of chocolate spellcake on my plate, the same as every morning. I looked at Stepmother.

"What?" she asked.

"Is this any longer necessary?"

"Don't you like it?"

I was salivating as I stared at it. But I was confused, too. Remy and I would wed, whoever I happened to be. He had liked me better than Musette, but he had only known us as each other. If I could stay the way I was now—would he be happier?

Maybe Stepmother would give me the recipe.

I said, "Last night I became engaged, and I'm sure Musette will be, as soon as the prince knocks on our door with her slipper. Need we maintain this masquerade any longer?"

Stepmother smiled. She came around the table and kissed my forehead. Musette wandered in, yawning against the back of her hand, and Stepmother set a plate with white cake in front of her as she sat.

"Children," she said. "Eat."

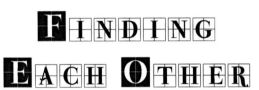

FINDING
EACH OTHER

SOURHEART

Edmund parked the rattletrap Volvo station wagon beside a narrow road in the Sierra Nevada foothills and turned off the engine. Westering sun reddened the iron-pink earth of the road cut, and the air out his open window smelled of pine.

Something up the slope among the evergreens had tugged at the place near his heart he thought of as his listening spot. In recent years, he had attained what he thought of as the third stage in his witchhood. The first stage, when he became a witch suddenly at sixteen, had been denial and disbelief; during the second stage, which set in soon afterwards and lasted for years, he had asked, how can I use this? In the third stage, he asked, how can this use me?

The answer he had found lay in listening. When he listened to the fainter cues beyond his own desires, he heard promptings. Following them led him in strange directions.

He touched the cloudy quartz globe on the dashboard, felt a faint warm vibration in his fingertips. He held out his hand above the seed pods, dried leaves, pine needles, and feathers that made his dashboard into an altar. An owl feather drifted up to touch his palm, then settled down among the others, crow, towhee, duck, jay, eagle, goose, some illegal to own, all gifts the ground had offered him as he walked through wildernesses.

Owl. Night energy, hunting energy. What he had wanted was green energy, a place to connect with Earth, cleanse the stains of contact with too many people and too many dark thoughts. Cities made him edgy, but sometimes the trail led him there. This time he had gone for his own reasons, to touch bases with his younger sister Abby, her husband, and her three children. They lived in San Francisco. He had spent two months reminding himself what human contact was like, and much of it had strengthened him, but some of it had made him feel strange and ungrounded. He was ready for a mental shift.

Owl. Here was the offer of shared energy, but the energy was restless and dark.

He sat back and closed his eyes, resting his hands in his lap. He drew in breath, held it, released it slowly. "I give up what my will is; I accept what you offer," he muttered three times, and opened his eyes.

He rolled the window shut, leaned over and pushed down the button locks on all the other doors, and climbed out of the car, locking the driver side door behind him. The city influence was still strong within him. He opened the tailgate and picked through a jumble of wrack until he found his favorite dowsing rod, then locked the back door and put the car keys inside the back bumper.

Sitting on ground matted with fallen pine needles, he stroked the dowsing rod, murmuring to it, "Please work with me; lead me where it is right for me to go; let us discover whatever waits for us here."

The rod pulled at his hands, and he answered the pull, rising and wandering under the pines, breathing in the scent of warm needles and pine sap, aromatic in the late afternoon sun's heat, each step of his moccasins crushing and kicking up the spice of the fallen. Following the dowsing rod's pull, he climbed up a rocky escarpment and reached a thick stand of Ponderosa pines and Doug-firs higher up the slope. The tip of the rod dipped groundward at the edge of a clearing with rocks huddled around it.

A mixture of strange energies whispered to him from the clearing. In its center blackened stones ringed a firepit; the scent of wood transformed by burning lingered in the air, blending with a rank human smell and the echo of vanished drumbeats.

Edmund stepped where the rod pointed, a place less walked on than any other spot in the clearing. At first he felt nothing from the Earth. He knelt, setting the rod aside, and pushed his fingers through the pine needles and mold into the rich soil below. I am here, he thought, I reach for you, I release you, I welcome you.

For a long moment he felt stillness, and wondered if he had misread the pull of his dowsing rod. Then he felt a sensation like the tearing of a dried leaf, and a core of energy flowed up from the Earth, green and welcoming as a cool spring on a hot day.

Edmund slipped out of his shoes and socks and worked his toes down under the layer of pine needles, then stood silent, opening himself to the green.

"Welcome," he whispered, "welcome into me, welcome through me, welcome as you leave me; I offer you these stains, I offer you what you want from me, I thank you for connecting me with the Lady." Green washed through him like warm water.

"Hey!"

So deep he was, feeling the green, opening to it, feeling it scrub away the oily psychic dirt, that he did not hear the woman's voice at first.

"Hey! Hey, what are you doing on my property?"

When she poked him with the business end of a rifle, he felt it, and brought his awareness up into his head, looking out of his eyes. Hunting energy, owl energy. He had known the green was not the only thing he would find on this mountain.

"What are you doing here? Think I don't know about you all, all you stupid men, sneaking up here, invading my space, taking without asking, think I won't do anything about it, like the other women you've known all your lives? You got another think coming!" She prodded him with her rifle. "Arms up, high!"

He lifted his arms, stretching them as high as he could. Sky energy, I salute you. The green energy was still flowing through him; he felt cleansed. Gently, with thanks, he disengaged.

He looked at the woman in front of him. She was much shorter than his own six foot three. The squint lines at the edges of her gray eyes were graven deep as the cracks in sun-baked mud. Winter-gray strands wound among the glossy brown of her tightly braided hair. Her small frame was lost in a layering of light blue workshirt, black T-shirt, green sweater tied by the arms around her waist, baggy jeans with frayed cuffs that ended above the toes of worn hiking boots.

She squinted at him. "Trying to figure out what you can get from me, bastard? Nothing. Nothing. I'm through giving anything to self-involved idiots like you."

He stretched his fingers to the sky, curled them, flexed them, waiting for the next direction.

"I know what you call me. Witch. Witch. I know you have your stupid quests. That idiot guru of yours sends you up here to face me. Make me stand for your hateful mother. Think you accomplish something coming up on my mountain, stealing a stick or a stone from me for some kind of trophy, go off and display it to your little group of yuppie warrior friends. Knew if I waited long enough I'd catch one of you bastards alone."

"People come hunting on your land without your permission?" he said.

She straightened when she heard his voice. Most people did. His best friend Julio had told him years ago that there was music in his voice, though Edmund couldn't hear it himself. She swallowed. "Not people," she said, after a moment. "Men."

"Men come on your land," he said. The well of green beneath his feet flowed full, inviting. He glanced around the clearing, realized that the stones around its edge had been placed there, that this was a place where Earth energy and human intention had met for centuries. Below the whisper of recent drumbeats and chants were older communions.

"I didn't know this was a private place," he said. "I'm sorry. Is there any way I can repay you?"

Her lips pinched, and she took a step back. "Think you're pretty cute, don't you?"

He smiled at her, turning his hands above his head, sky energy caressing his palms.

"What have you got you could give me?"

"Labor."

"What sort of work do you do?"

"Hand work, wood work, craft work, garden work," he said.

"Cooking? Cleaning? Scrubbing?" At last she smiled.

"Sure," he said, wondering if owl energy could be disarmed by housework.

"That'd be a sight," she said. "Might be payment. You have any weapons?"

He glanced down at himself. He wore a loose white cotton shirt; the tan pants were tighter and had no pockets. "I have a stick," he said, nodding toward his dowsing rod, which lay next to his moccasins and socks. An oak tree had given it to him.

"A stick," she said. Keeping the gun aimed toward him, she edged around and knelt to pick up the dowsing rod. "Ouch!" She shook her hand, leaving the rod on the ground. "That thing boobytrapped?"

"I don't know," he said, staring at the rod.

"It stung."

He rubbed his hands together over his head, then lowered his arms. "Let me look," he said, holding out a hand to her.

"Hey! Get those hands up!" She gripped the rifle with both hands. He raised his arms again.

"Start walking." She gestured toward a thin trail on the other side of the clearing.

Edmund glanced at his moccasins, then decided he was better off without barriers between himself and the Earth. He walked.

Her house backed against a slope, rocks fitted together and cemented with mud mixed with moss, the roof overlaid with branches and lichens and melting into the Earth. A stovepipe poked up from the roof. Two small dark windows showed nothing of the interior. The plank door between them bore a shiny padlock. She lowered her rifle and wrestled the lock open, then cast him a dark look. "Never used to have to lock up."

He thought of locking his car before he came up the mountain. City energy.

"You better not take anything from me."

He said, "Nothing you don't give me."

"Ha!" Her voice was bitter. She stood on the threshold of her house, staring at him from under her brows for a while. "Okay," she said at last, "you can put your arms down. But don't you try anything. I'm not afraid to hurt you."

"I understand." He didn't understand. He had never met anyone as angry as she was. He didn't spend very much time with people, though. Maybe there were a lot like her, and he just hadn't run into them yet.

"The dishes are over there," she said, pointing inside the house. "Think you can get them clean?"

He slipped past her into a close darkness that smelled of fire and sweat and decaying food.

When his eyes adjusted he saw piles of soiled ceramic and tin dishes stacked on a counter beside a large enameled basin.

"I purely hate doing dishes," said the woman.

He went to the counter. The water in the basin bore a soap scum on its surface. He dipped in a finger. The water was cold and greasy. He looked around, spotted a woodstove with a scorch-bottomed enameled coffee pot and a small pan on it. The stove was cold too.

He opened it and found a glut of ashes with a few charred sticks of stovewood on top.

He glanced around the house. What light there was came from the open door and the two small windows. A bed stood against the back wall, a frame with strips of leather nailed across it, dark blankets thrown over it, a clutter of rags scattered across the floor near it. A wooden table and a chair stood below one of the windows, the table bearing a sketchbook, some colored pencils, and books stacked beside an unlit kerosene lamp. Shelves stood against other walls, cluttered with dark things. Herbs hung from the eaves. A breath of cold damp air moved past him, and he looked toward its source, realized a rug on the back wall concealed a passage deeper into the mountain.

On the back wall opposite the door, where the late light fell full upon it, a black paper circle hung, with a paper heart the green of sour apples glued to it. Against the green glinted two small half-moons of gold. Of all the things in the room, this green heart gave off the most energy, a haze of bitter anger.

Biting his lip, Edmund opened to the other energies here, and what he felt was: under siege.

"May I start here?" he said, touching the stove.

"Sure," she said, grinning. Still hugging her rifle, she went and sat on the bed, which produced a symphony of squeaks. "Go right ahead."

"Is there a tool?"

"You got your hands, don't you?"

He looked at her a moment, then took his shirt off and laid it on the ground below the stove. Gently he pried the ashes and the skeletons of former fires out of the stove and onto his shirt, sinking a little under the surface of life so he could talk with the ashes, ask them not to jump up in clouds, listen to their tales of the wood they once had been, reassure them that they could return to soil and rise as wood again. The stove's iron spoke with him too, saying it would give up these ashes if he promised it new ones; it wanted a fire in its belly.

Something cold poked his spine. He surfaced, looked up.

"You tetched?" said the woman.

"What?"

"There's nothing left in the stove. Darned if I know how you did it, but it's washday clean inside. Won't do you any good to keep rubbing at it."

"Oh," he said. The ashes lay in a compact heap on his shirt, and the stove's interior shone. His hands were smudged and gray.

"So,—you tetched?"

Tetched. Touched. He thought of the touches he had learned to know, the caressings of energies, the gentle guidance from powers he was trying to tune in to better.

Was he touched? He nodded yes.

She sat down cross-legged on the floor a little way away, the rifle across her legs. "You aren't like my ex, are you?" She glanced up at the green heart on the wall. She fed a thin flame of anger to the heart, a sort of talismanic worship he had seen before. He realized that the gold moons were the halves of a wedding ring. She looked back at him, coming out of her brief trance. "One of those yuppie weekend warriors?"

He frowned. "I don't know what that means."

"That get out in my woods and drum and howl at the moon and yell about their warrior forefathers and their manhood and scamper around on all fours naked and painted up?"

"What?" he said, trying to imagine it, and, imagining it, unable to suppress a smile.

"You're just some fool wandered up here."

"I didn't know it was your place."

She sighed. "And all you wanted to do was stand in the fire circle like a fence post?"

"Mm-hmm."

"Nobody sent you up here to face the great Woods Witch and conquer her goddess power and her mother power and her lover power and steal the key from her to prove you're ready to go on the manhood quest?"

"Conquer?" he said.

"That's what they say. Sometimes I sneak up at night and listen."

He gathered the edges of his shirt and lifted. The ashes stayed in a neat pile. He rose. "My rod brought me here."

"What?" She sprang to her feet. "Your so-called magic wand?" She stared at his crotch, her face sour.

He laughed. "My stick, the one we left in the circle."

"A stick? A forked stick. I don't get it."

He walked out of the house, wandered to a stand of trees, knelt and spread the ashes among the pine needles. Thanks for living and dying and changing, he thought, patting the soft gray. He put his smudged shirt back on.

She had followed him. "I don't get it," she repeated.

"A dowsing rod," he said.

"Like they use to find water or oil?"

"Right." He dusted off his hands and stood. "Do you have a wood pile?" He had seen a small pile of kindling and shavings near the stove, but no logs.

"This way," she said, pointing with her rifle to a place behind her house. He followed her past a screen of trees and found a clearing she used for a wood lot, with a chopping block in the center, and stove wood piled neat between two trees, half hidden under a green-gray tarp. He gathered armfuls of wood and headed back inside.

He laid a fire in the stove, then touched the wood and invited fire to feast, just as she said, "The matches are—" and stopped. "How'd you do that?"

He smiled and closed the stove, adjusting the vent in the door to draw air. The coffee pot was empty. He took it off the stove.

"Water?" he said, lifting his eyebrows. He got the basin from the counter.

She licked her lip. Her brow furrowed. Her eyes shifted toward the rug covering the passage, then back.

Water had whispered to him on that quick breath of breeze from the mountain's heart, but he could tell she wanted to keep her spring a secret. He said, "I'll use this."

"But that's dirty."

He carried the basin outside and talked to what was in it. Sitting on a space of packed Earth where nothing grew, he thought, Everything that is not water, please come out. He tipped the basin slightly and watched as soap scum and grime gathered along the lower edge. Water, please stay. He tipped a little further and the impurities poured out. Thanks. Blessings.

He took the basin back inside, poured as much water into the coffeepot as it could hold, and set it on the stove to warm. The rest he left in the basin. "Do you have a trash can?"

She was staring at him. She had watched him playing with the dishpan, had seen something happen that she didn't understand.

"A waste basket?" he tried.

After a moment she shook her head and brought him a brown

paper grocery sack. He sat on the floor with a stack of dirty dishes in front of him and pried what caked-on food he could off them and into the bag. The light coming in the door and windows dimmed as night gathered. The woman lighted the kerosene lantern, then brought her chair closer to the stove.

When at last the water on the stove steamed, Edmund poured it into the cool water in the basin, mixing in soap flakes she offered him. He washed dishes. She sat in her chair and watched.

When he had finished, having stacked the drying dishes into a braided tower that left most of their surfaces open to air, he turned to her and said, "What else can I do for you?"

"I think that's plenty," she said. In the cool darkness the lamp light touched her hair, leaving her face in shadow.

"Are you sure?" He opened to the energies, asking if he had accomplished everything he had been sent up the mountain to do.

A scent came in the open door. A rank human scent, an aura of city wildness.

"Look," said the woman, "I was mistaken about you. A person comes up my mountain and just wants to stand on it, well, that ought to be all right. You've done more than enough for me. I can tell you got no harm in you. You go on along now."

He walked to the door and looked out into the night. Trees were dark jagged silhouettes against a lighter sky pricked with millions of stars. He reached up to the stars, opening to ages-old light, and listened.

"I'll walk you down to the road," said the woman. "Wouldn't want you to trip in the dark."

Something moved across the pine needles, the whisper of shoes. Something smelled of a violence beyond any scent the woman's rifle had produced.

Night, I am here, Edmund thought. Earth, I am here. Air, I am here. I am open to you. Lead me.

Through his bare feet he felt a gathering of mixed energies, dark blue and flame red, rising up and spreading along under his skin, rippling through all his muscles, tingling.

—It is on us it is in us it is against us—

—want it off us—

Light wavered in the house behind him, casting his own long dark shadow on the ground before him. "You got to move so I can get out," the woman said, touching his back with her bare hand for the first time.

"No," he said, his voice coming out odd, thicker and deeper—doubled, tripled, other forces augmenting it.

"What?" She sounded startled. "You need light—"

Blue-gray radiance gloved his left hand, growing steadily brighter, lighting up the clearing in front of her house.

"Something's out here," he said. "Stay behind me."

"The key. The queen keeps the key under her pillow," said a flat hissing voice out of the darkness. "I must steal the key."

The woman's hand gripped Edmund's shirt.

"To let the wild man out," said the whisper.

Edmund raised his hand like a torch. Clutching the trunk of a tree across from them stood a man dressed all in black, with black streaks painted under his eyes.

Hunting energy, night energy: owl energy.

"The queen. The witch. The bitch. Won't give me the key, won't let me find my golden ball."

A memory of Edmund's almost-normal childhood rose up to confuse him: key? ball? A list from a scavenger hunt? The front of his brain could make no other sense out of the mumblings, but the night-blue energy inside him answered, its voice deep and wild: "Your key is not here. You left it in the city."

"You lie. The witch has it." He released the tree and took two steps toward them. "The witch has it, keeps me locked up inside myself. Won't let me loose."

The woman's hand tightened on Edmund's shirt, pulling at him. "I know him," she whispered. "He used to be my husband."

"She took my wildness away and used it herself!" screamed the man in the woods.

"He took everything I had in the divorce, except the mountain," the woman muttered. "I was glad anyway, because he was getting too weird to live with."

Edmund closed his eyes and dropped into a deeper listening mode, asking: what is it you want me to remove?

—The screaming thing,— murmured the world. —House thing lives with; screaming thing presses down, caps the well.—

Edmund remembered the membrane that had sealed the green energy underground instead of letting it well up in the fire circle.

"I need my wild man," said the man, coming toward them.

Smoky red light gathered around Edmund's right hand. "Your wild man is not here," said a ragged voice from within him.

"She has him. She's eaten him. She's using him. I have to let him out of her." He stopped a few feet away and tugged at something on his belt. He freed it and held it up. Red light glowed along the metal of a knife.

"No," said Edmund and everything in him. He walked to the stranger.

The knife came up, aimed at Edmund's chest.

Metal, remember the fire that forged you? Edmund reached out with his red hand and touched the knife. It glowed red, then orange, then white hot, and melted into hissing drops that splashed on the ground between them. The man dropped the bone hilt, shaking his hand.

"Go away," Edmund said.

"Not without the key," whispered the man.

Edmund reached down into the pool of cooling metal with his red hand, plucked a key out of it. "Here it is. Threats and violence. Go home and unlock. Your wilderness is closer to home." He pressed the key into the man's hand.

"That's not right," said the man. "I can't be given it. Not by a man. I have to steal it from my mother."

—Talking does not work,—the world murmured, and flexed Edmund's muscles. He gripped the man's shoulders, one in a fire-red hand, the other in an ice-blue one. He turned the man and aimed him down the mountain, then walked, pushing the resisting man before him.

"No," the man cried, jerking his shoulders. Small smoke rose up from the one Edmund gripped in his red hand. Deep inside, Edmund felt alarm: he had never meant to hurt anyone. But he had given control of his body to these powers, who had different priorities.

The blue and red light from Edmund's hands showed them a path to follow, and they made it down to the road, where a black Lincoln Towncar was parked behind Edmund's Volvo. The man had struggled and fought all the way down the mountain, but the energies inside Edmund would not be denied; they crushed resistance. Behind him came the woman's footsteps, faint on the pine needles.

Edmund turned the man to face him, pressing his back against the car. "Listen," Edmund said in the tripled voice. "The woman does not have your wild man."

The man's face bore traces of tears. "You are the wild man," he whispered.

Mazed in a web of symbols he didn't understand, Edmund shook his head, but the others inside him spoke. "You do not come to find me in this way," said the ragged red voice. "Not with theft and deception and intending harm without need. You come to me when you are ready to listen. Then you sit and wait and invite me, and maybe I will come. Not from the woman. From the Earth."

His blue hand reached for the passenger door of the car, and it opened at his touch, its lock clicking. He pushed the man inside, shutting the door after him. He leaned both hands on the car. Energies spoke to the car: hold him safe, take him home, away from here, shaped metal that once lay inside me, energies I once cradled.

The car's engine started. Edmund straightened, letting go. The car's headlights flicked on, scything through the darkness, and it pulled out into the road and drove away.

"What," cried the woman, "what? What?"

The light faded from his hands. The energies warmed him, stroking him on the inside, before they fled out his feet. He turned toward her in the new darkness, his hands down at his sides.

"What are you?" she whispered.

"Not an easy question," he said, his voice toned down to normal.

"Voices came out of you," she whispered, "voices I've heard in dreams."

"It was the mountain talking," he said. "Night and the mountain."

"How can that be?"

He smiled down at her through the darkness, even though he knew she couldn't see his face. She would hear the smile in his voice. "That's what I'm doing now; that's all I do, is listen. Sometimes the conversation comes up inside me."

"You were listening when I first saw you." Her voice was quiet and steady.

"Yes."

"To something most people can't hear."

"Most people don't stand still long enough, I guess."

"Like Brett." She sighed. "So it had to talk in a voice he could hear." Her hand came out of the darkness and gripped his. "Thank you. Thank you. What if you hadn't been here?"

"You would have had your rifle ready."

"Yes. Thank you for being here. Are you hungry? I'm not much of a cook, but I could make some kind of soup."

He couldn't remember when he'd last eaten by mouth. Powers sometimes filled and fed him. "Sounds great," he said.

"And I got something else I need to burn," she muttered. "That heart. Maybe it's the key he was looking for. Don't want it in the house anymore." She stood in the silent darkness for a moment, then said, "Can you make your hands light up again? I left the lantern up in the house."

"Not without provocation, I don't think."

"Put your hand on my shoulder, then. I know my mountain; I'll lead you."

They were halfway to her house when she broke the silence again. "Your voices say anything about yuppie warrior scum?"

He laughed. "I don't know anything about them."

"Could you be here next full moon? That's when they come. Bet they'd scare away pretty easy."

"I'll listen," he said. "If the mountain asks me, I'll be here."

INNER CHILD

You know how you can tell a kid is creepy even before he says word one? Not from his clothes or his hair or anything like that, though those can give you clues, sometimes real obvious clues. Sometimes even kids who look perfectly normal can give out vibes that say, "Beware of Dog."

Caleb Danvers was like that.

I only saw him a couple-three times a month. He came out of the big spooky house on the corner after the sun went down. The only other person I saw enter or leave that house was a tall thin gloomy guy who wore a priest's collar and didn't talk to anyone I knew.

Caleb came out some evenings and wandered up and down our street in the summer twilight, usually drifting closer and closer to me and my second-best friend Rosalie where we were playing badminton on my house's front lawn and smacking mosquito dive-bombers before they bit us. Eventually he would wind up sitting on my lawn, watching us.

He would say stuff.

Stuff like, "Abby, this is the best time of your whole life. Appreciate it." Like I could turn appreciation on and off like a faucet.

You could tell he had never really been a kid.

Lots of people stayed out late on summer nights. Sometimes Ben Hartman sat on his front porch a couple houses away and played his banjo. Sometimes Kari Olesen took her guitar over and sat with him. Sometimes they'd play a song we knew, and if we could overcome our supreme embarrassment, we would mumble along.

Sprinklers would be wetting down lawns, scenting the air with green and the sleep smells of concrete and asphalt after sundown.

Wetherells a couple houses the other way barbecued stuff from one end of the summer to the other, always raising a luscious stink that made the rest of us regret whatever we were having for dinner.

People strolled along the street in the evening, just enjoying the cool after the sun went down; and everybody's windows and front doors were open so you could almost hear the conversations they were having through the screens, or what their TVs were saying. It was like the edges of our lives melted into one another.

I couldn't turn appreciation on and off like a faucet, but I knew somewhere inside me that this was the special country of summer, and that in winter things would change.

Across the street from my house the Brewer boys usually played catch or did some noisy boy thing with projectiles that gave them an excuse to run into the street and take their chances with traffic. Of which there was none in the evenings. Their football sailed right into Rosalie's and my badminton net a few too many times for me to feel friendly toward them.

Caleb always came toward my yard, never toward the Brewers' yard. I mean, what kind of a boy was he?

This was the year I turned fourteen. I had lost my best friend, my older brother Edmund, who moved away to I never knew where— it changed weekly. He sent me postcards with brief hellos on them, weird postmarks, and no return addresses.

Four years earlier, a dazzle of magic had fallen on him and changed him into something else. I had helped him figure out how to deal with it, and he had talked to me—just me, never the parents— about what it meant and how he felt.

And then he had left.

I'd been half-waiting for my own dazzle to come, but I didn't know anyone else that had happened to, so I had been half-expecting it never to come, too. But the waiting half was stronger, and whispered to me in dreams. Someday. Someday. Someday.

In the meantime, I was more glad than ever that Rosalie lived next door to me. She was a tanned, lean-bodied, dark-haired girl who looked like she lived for sports, with a white smile and this aura of intense energy. I had spent junior high buried in one book after another. Our paths would never have intersected if we hadn't been neighbors.

We used to argue all the time about what to do, but by that summer we had routines. I would play badminton with Rose and she would go to the movie matinees with me and not make too much fun of me for mooning over the heroes. I would listen without comment to her long tirades about how movies failed to provide us young impressionable girls with good role models. I heard the same sort of talk when I watched TV with her and her mother, only it was her mother talking then. It made media-watching more of a participatory event, and I liked it.

So Rosalie and I had each other, and no one else. And Caleb would ease over to my yard, where Rosalie and I were batting the birdie to each other, and he would try to strike up conversations with us.

He looked about ten, but he had an awfully large vocabulary. This alone was not enough to condemn him; I am fond of words myself. But he talked about stuff like spontaneity and loving yourself and expressing your rage and a lot of other stupid stuff that no kid would be caught dead talking about.

He talked about healing, and nurturing feminine energy, and he stared at Rosalie and me as though we were milkshake machines, and he could turn on a spigot and out would come the flavor of compassion he wanted. Even though this never worked.

He talked about art therapy.

He talked about affirmations and trauma and inner guides.

Spooky. Postively.

The kid was trance-channeling something from an infomercial.

Rosalie was restrained by her belief in feminism. After all, if women were going to be liberated, men ought to be too, and even a total nerd like Caleb deserved his space, even when it crowded our space a little.

I was restrained by a long history of never actually pounding anybody.

We were both influenced by the fact that Caleb mostly wasn't around except a couple-three nights a month.

Otherwise we would have smashed him flat. He really drove us nuts.

Until that one night when the Brewer boys got more than usually obnoxious.

We'd all been growing up. We'd been doing it together. The Brewer boys had been getting hairier and more muscular, which was easy to tell since they rough-housed around on their front lawn without shirts on, and Rosalie and I were sticking out in front more than we used to. Ma took me bra shopping. Talk about embarrassing: having some stranger measure your chest was pretty high on my list.

So we were changing, but no one was talking about it . . . until the night everything else changed.

It was a night with no music and too much hot. Nobody was outside but me and Rosalie and the Brewer boys, us on our side of the street, the boys on theirs. Rose and I had stopped volleying the birdy for a couple minutes to wipe sweat off our foreheads with bandannas, hers pink, mine lavender. The full moon had just popped free of the Brewer house chimney. I wondered where Caleb was. He usually showed up on nights like this.

There was this big swish sound as a football crashed into our net, and then the boys were there, on our side of the street. I picked up the football, wanting to hurl it at them. What was the matter with them? Couldn't they aim? Were they trying to break our net?

I thought about throwing the football up on our roof. Maybe that would stop them, at least for a little while. I gripped the football, my fingers over the strings. Bob Brewer was coming closer. Maybe if I threw the ball into the street he would turn around and follow it. Gosh, he was big. When did he get so big?

I held out the football to him. He took it and dropped it on the grass.

"You can't want all that titty just for yourself," Bob said, and squeezed one of my breasts.

I slapped him. He laughed, and squeezed harder. I punched at him, but it didn't stop him. He came closer and pulled me up against him. He was hot and damp and smelled like sweat and grass and something dark and musky that I didn't recognize. I yelled at him. He didn't listen. He just laughed and shoved his mouth down on mine.

Eddy went for Rosalie.

"I will never forgive you for this," Rosalie told Eddy, kicking toward his groin but not quite hitting his hot button. "You're the kind of shmuck that gives boys a bad name!"

Eddy laughed and wrestled her down on the grass, lying on top of her, pinning her arms to the ground with his elbows, and squeezing her breasts with both hands. Even though Rosalie was Sports Woman, Eddy was stronger.

It wasn't just the pain in my breast that hurt me, or the smash of Bob's mouth against mine, the taste of soured chocolate, or the grip he had me in that I couldn't get out of. Something in me lifted away from all those things, and then it was as though I looked down at the yard from someplace above, seeing people struggling there as if I weren't one of them, as if I had no body and couldn't be physically hurt; but I did hurt.

When I started crying, it was because I could feel my childhood breaking off and floating away.

Part of what I was losing was my sense that I could take care of myself. I had used that for a skeleton all my life, and now that it was gone I felt boneless and insubstantial. I lay there feeling mad and sad and horrible, with Bob holding me down and touching me, hurting me, making me feel dirty. I wished I could kill him. I wished my brother Edmund had never left—he could have made this unhappen. I wished I was a boy: things like this didn't happen to boys. At least, I had never heard of it happening to boys, but I knew it happened to girls all the time.

Then Caleb was there. He was smaller than everybody else. I don't know how he did it. He had hard shoes; I think that helped. He seemed stronger than he should have been. Out of the corner of my eye, I saw a weird red haze surrounding him. He kicked Eddy and Bob where it would really hurt them, and made them let go of us and cringe and curl up, with ugly, sad, hurt cries and gasps. "Don't you," Caleb muttered, his voice coming out low and intense, "don't you do it. Don't you ruin it for us all. Don't."

I knew it was too late.

Rosalie and I picked ourselves up and brushed off grass. I saw Caleb kick a gasping Bob in the ribs. Part of me wanted to stop him: my parents had always taught me not to hurt other people. Part of me wanted to join him. I really wanted to smash Bob and Eddy right into the ground until there was nothing left of them but bone splinters and blood. How dared they? How dared they run all our stop signs and crash into us?

I felt mad and mixed up and embarrassed and about two inches high. Rosalie and I had talked about self-defense, even tried a few things from books that her mother had. Why hadn't we been able to defend ourselves? I rubbed my eyes really hard until it hurt, wanting to hurt something and settling for myself.

Then Caleb was gripping my elbow. "Come on," he said. "Inside." And he pulled me and Rosalie right up the lawn and into my own house. He was strong and just as pushy as the Brewers, but somehow it didn't feel the same. I wasn't together enough in my head to wonder about this at the time. Later I figured it out as far as I could: the Brewers were pushy to get what they wanted, and Caleb was pushy because he was taking care of us.

Ma and Pa were watching TV in the living room, with the sound high because Pa has been losing his hearing. They didn't even notice as Caleb steered us past them and up the stairs to the big bathroom, just as though he knew the blueprint of our house, even though he'd never been here before, as far as I knew. In the bathroom he let go of us and turned on the shower, feeling the water and turning the faucet until he got a temperature that satisfied him. I stood watching this, hugging myself, my teeth chattering a little, not understanding any of it. This kid moved around like he was used to being in charge. I would have been disconcerted if I had been able to use my brain for things like that.

"I'll get you some other clothes," said Caleb. He left the shower running full blast and exited the bathroom, closing the door behind him.

Rosalie and I stood there blinking at each other as steam filled the room. After a minute I went and locked the bathroom door. Then we stripped, stuffed our clothes in the laundry hamper, and climbed into the warm water together. We were both crying.

We had been in locker rooms together before. We had nothing to hide from each other except our misery. It was strange to be in that place together, when we would have both probably liked to be alone to scrub as hard as we could and hide in our shame.

The heat and the pounding of the water washed away a lot of that, though. Somehow. "What happened?" she asked after a while. "How could we forget how to take care of ourselves?"

"It was so sudden."

"But we've thought about this before. Why weren't we prepared?"

I handed her the soap, wondering whether I would ever feel clean again; water couldn't wash off what I was feeling. I shook my head. "Because it's just the dumb boys from across the street. Who expected anything to come from that direction?"

"It's just our street," she whispered.

"Yeah," I said.

"And we live here, and so do they. What are we going to do next time we see them?"

Blind red rage filled me. I clenched my teeth so hard it hurt. "I'm going to rip the ears right off his head," I said. "I'm going to knee him in the groin so hard he can't stand up straight. I'm going to slit his throat." From now on I was going to wear the hunting knife Edmund had given me on my belt every time I went outside. Yeah.

Rosalie gave a soggy giggle. I snapped back into myself. I had never hunted anything. Never even hurt anything deliberately. All I had ever done with that knife was whittle balsa wood. Maybe I could hold it as though I would use it, though. Maybe that would make Bob keep his distance.

Maybe Bob would take it away and use it on me.

"Should we tell Mom?" Rosalie asked after a little while.

"I don't know." I didn't ever want my parents to know what had happened. Right on our front lawn. They would ask why I hadn't yelled, bit, scratched, kicked, and I wouldn't know how to answer. Rosalie's mom might understand even though I didn't understand it myself. On the other hand, maybe she would ask us why we hadn't fought better too.

Maybe there was something the law could do; but what if the law tried and it couldn't do anything? Everyone in the neighborhood would know that the Brewer boys were just boys, and Rosalie and I were wimps.

We were running out of hot water. We turned off the shower and got out and dried off. "What'd Caleb say when he left?" Rosalie asked.

"He went to get us other clothes."

"How would that little weasel know where other clothes are?"

"How did he know where the bathroom is?" I asked. "Anyway, he's not exactly a weasel. He saved us."

Rosalie kicked the bathtub, then clutched her foot and hopped around. "Saved us. Yeah," she muttered when she finished cursing.

I thought about my brother and said, "You have to take help where you find it." He had let me help him, even though I was just a little kid. He had never told me I was too little to help.

Wrapped in a towel, I went to the door and opened it a crack. There was a stack of clothes on the floor just outside, and Caleb sat on the top step of the staircase, leaning against the wall and looking small and far away. He didn't glance my way, just stared into distance and hugged his knees.

I took the clothes and shut the door again. Rosalie and I got dressed: underwear for both of us, for me my favorite jeans with the holes in the knees, my favorite tie-dyed peacock T-shirt, and for Rosalie, a sleeveless red dress I had loaned her once or twice because she had no dresses of her own.

I liked changing into my favorite things. It almost felt like nothing had happened, as if I could dress up as my old self and be her too.

But what next? Were there boys still lying on the lawn? If there weren't, where were they? Would Rosalie and I have to spend the rest of our lives hiding in the house?

We went out into the hall. Caleb stood up then and looked at us. He only came up to my shoulder, and I wasn't very tall myself. How had he turned into a whirlwind? What if he turned out to be a boy like the Brewers were boys? He was small, but he had stopped them both when Rosalie and I couldn't.

He edged past us and went into my bedroom.

I looked at Rosalie. We could leave him there and go downstairs, join my parents in our living room and let the TV noise swallow everything. We could follow Caleb into my room and see what he had to say.

She shrugged.

We went into my room.

Caleb was sitting at my desk, staring at his feet on the floor and gripping the edge of the chair.

Oh, well, I thought. First things first. "Thanks for coming to our rescue."

He flushed and looked up at me as I sat on the bed facing him. "I didn't know what else to do."

Rosalie sat beside me. She stared at Caleb with narrowed eyes. After a minute she said, "I hate it that we needed help. I'm glad someone could help us when we needed it. Thanks."

A little silence trickled by. Caleb licked his lips and said, "It's my life. Helping. I don't know how to do anything else. And I'm afraid that I don't know how to help very well, either."

"What do you mean?" I asked.

"I was so furious with those boys. I knew I had to get them to let go of you, and that you needed help to get away. But I also had such rage. I hurt them beyond the need to hurt even after my first two aims were accomplished, when what they needed was counsel. I lost control of myself."

"You expressed your rage," Rosalie said, her lips tight, her tone edged with sarcasm.

He stared at her, eyes wide.

"You're always talking about all this stuff like it's good, but you never do any of it," she said.

"I'm not a good child," he whispered.

"You're a great child. You're a parent's dream of a child."

"I make a terrible child, and not a very good adult."

"What?" I said, the word popping out of me.

"It's like everything. I know theory, but I have no idea how to apply it. I'm not a convincing child at all, am I?"

"No," I whispered. A fake child. Of course. That twisted the knob on the focus of all our encounters with Caleb, made the images sharp and clear. I could believe this, because I had seen stranger things happen to my own brother.

"Even blessed with the gift of form, I don't know what to do." He spread his hands out flat, palms up on his thighs, and stared down at them. "You never believed me for a moment."

"You talk like a grown-up," I said, "and you never did seem like a kid."

He nodded, then looked up at me. "But enough about my troubles. Where are you now?"

"What are you talking about?" Rosalie said. "We're right here in Abby's bedroom."

I looked into Caleb's eyes and said, "How do we go on? Everything looks dark now. I don't even know about leaving the house. What if they're out there waiting for us?"

He frowned and nodded. "That's what I feared."

"What?" said Rosalie, belligerent.

"That this event has cast you out of the places you've lived all your life, and you can't find a road back."

I clutched my stomach. That was just how I felt. Homesick for a place I'd never see again.

"I don't know how to get back there either," he said.

"What the hell are you talking about?" Rosalie yelled.

"Even with keys to the gate," Caleb said, looking at his small hand again, and then up into my eyes.

*

Rosalie stayed mad, and she stayed overnight, too. So did Caleb. I took him down to the kitchen and made him a milkshake, a chocolate one even though he asked for vanilla. "Taste it anyway," I said. His eyes went wide after his first sip. He gulped some more and froze the inside of his mouth. "Ow!" he said. "My head!"

"Yeah," I said, and offered him a smile.

He finished the shake and we sat up all night eating microwave popcorn and watching horror movies on Channel 5. It was summer. Ma didn't mind when I did things like that. "That's what summers are for," she had said more than once.

Caleb left just before dawn. He missed the part where Lon Chaney Jr. got killed as a wolfman and turned back into a man.

When we woke up in the afternoon and went over to Rosalie's house, we talked to her mom about what had happened, after all. She hugged us and signed us up for self-defense classes. She told us it wasn't our fault this happened, and it wasn't even our fault we didn't know how to fight back. It happened to a lot of women.

Women. Yeah, right.

She also said she'd talk to the Brewers' parents, and to everybody on Blockwatch. She would talk to one of her friends who was a cop. She wouldn't give details or name names, but she'd find out if something should be done. She didn't ever want anything like this to happen to us again, or any other girls around here.

Girls. Well.

I felt so somewhere in between.

I went down to the church on the corner and found the man I had always assumed was Caleb Danvers' father. He smiled at me a little uncertainly when I came in, then took me back to an office where we sat on folding metal chairs, facing each other with nothing between us but air.

"What bit you?" I asked him.

His grin lightened his cadaverous face. "A small angry girl. I try to speak to everyone about my faith, but I don't do it very well, apparently. She was particularly unreceptive."

I thought of a million questions I wanted to ask him. Was he always strong when he was little? What else had he noticed about his transformation? How long had this been going on? But then I figured there would be time for all these questions later, and I should say what I had come to say. "I checked the calendar. There's a full moon during the county fair next month, and the fair stays open until eleven p.m. Wanna come?"

"Oh, yes!" he said, and clapped his hands together.

I don't think Rosalie is going to get this for a while. She never had an Edmund. I'm doing it anyway. Sometimes you need to listen to that little voice inside.

HOME FOR CHRISTMAS

Matt spread the contents of the wallet on the orange shag rug in front of her, looking at each item. Three oil company charge cards; an auto club card, an auto insurance card; a driver's license which identified the wallet's owner as James Plainfield, thirty-eight, with an address bearing an apartment number in one of the buildings downtown; a gold MasterCard with a hologram of the world on it; a gold Amex card; six hundred and twenty-three dollars, mostly in fifties; a phone credit card, a laminated library card; five tan business cards with "James Plainfield, Architect" and a phone number embossed on them in brown ink; receipts from a deli, a bookstore, an art supply store; a ticket stub from a horror movie; and two scuffed color photographs, one of a smiling woman and the other of a sullen teenage girl.

The wallet, a soft camel-brown calfskin, was feeling distress. — He's lost without me,— it cried, —he needs me; he could be dead by now. Without me in his back pocket he's only half himself.—

Matt patted it and yawned. She had been planning to walk the frozen streets later that night while people were falling asleep, getting her fill of Christmas Eve dreams for another year, feeding the hunger in her that only quieted when she was so exhausted she fell asleep herself. But her feet were wet and she was tired enough to sleep now. She was going to try an experiment: this year, hole up, drink cocoa, and remember all her favorite dreams from Christmas Eves past. If that worked, maybe she could change her life style, stay someplace long enough to . . . to . . . she wasn't sure. She hadn't stayed in any one place for more than a month in years.

"We'll go find him tomorrow morning," she said to the wallet. Although tomorrow was Christmas. Maybe he would have things to do, and be hard to find.

—Now!— cried the wallet.

Matt sighed and leaned against the water heater. Her present home was the basement of somebody's house; the people were gone for the Christmas holidays and the house, lonely, had invited her in when she was looking through its garbage cans a day after its inhabitants had driven off in an overloaded station wagon.

—He'll starve,— moaned the wallet, —he'll run out of gas and be stranded. The police will stop him and arrest him because he doesn't have identification. We have to rescue him now.—

Matt had cruised town all day, listening to canned Christmas music piped to the freezing outdoors by stores, watching street-corner Santas ringing bells, cars fighting for parking spaces, shoppers whisking in and out of stores, their faces tense; occasionally she saw bright dreams, a parent imagining a child's joy at the unwrapping of the asked-for toy, a man thinking what his wife's face would look like when she saw the diamond he had bought for her, a girl finding the perfect book for her best friend. There were the dreams of despair, too: grief because five dollars would not stretch far enough, grief because the one request was impossible to fill, grief because weariness made it too hard to go on.

She had wandered, wrapped in her big olive-drab army coat, never standing still long enough for anyone to wonder or object, occasionally ducking into stores and soaking up warmth before heading out into the cold again, sometimes stalling at store windows to stare at things she had never imagined needing until she saw them, then laughing that feeling away. She didn't need anything she didn't have.

She had stumbled over the wallet on her way home. She wouldn't have found it—it had slipped down a grate—except that it was broadcasting distress. The grate gapped its bars and let her reach down to get the wallet; the grate was tired of listening to the wallet's whining.

—Now,— the wallet said again.

She loaded all the things back into the wallet, getting the gas cards in the wrong place at first, until the wallet scolded her and told her where they belonged. "So," Matt said, slipping the wallet into her army jacket pocket, "if he's lost, stranded, and starving, how are we going to find him?"

—He's probably at the Time-Out. The bartender lets him run a tab sometimes. He might not have noticed I'm gone yet.—

She knew the Time-Out, a neighborhood bar not far from the corner where James Plainfield's apartment building stood. Two miles from the suburb where her temporary basement home was. She sighed, pulled still-damp socks from their perch on a heating duct, and stuffed her freezing feet into them, then laced up the combat boots. She could always put the wallet outside for the night so she could get some sleep; but what if someone else found it? It would suffer agonies; few people understood nonhuman things the way she did, and fewer still went along with the wishes of inanimate objects.

Anyway, there was a church on the way to downtown, and she always liked to see a piece of the midnight service, when a whole bunch of people got all excited about a baby being born, believing for a little while that a thing like that could actually change the world. If she spent enough time searching this guy out, maybe she'd get to church this year.

She slipped out through the kitchen, suggesting that the back door lock itself behind her. Then she headed downtown, trying to avoid the dirty slush piles on the sidewalk.

"Hey," said the bartender as she slipped into the Time-Out. "You got I.D., kid?"

Matt shrugged. "I didn't come in to order anything." She wasn't sure how old she was, but she knew it was more than twenty-one. Her close-cut hair, mid-range voice, and slight, sexless figure led people to mistake her for a teenage boy, a notion she usually encouraged. No one had formally identified her since her senior year of high school, years and years ago. "I just came to find a James Plainfield. He here?"

A man seated at the bar looked up. He was dressed in a dark suit, but his tie was emerald green, and his brown hair was a little longer than business-length. He didn't look like his driver's license picture, but then, who did? "Whatcha want?" he said.

"Wanted to give you your wallet. I found it in the street."

"Wha?" He leaned forward, squinting at her.

She walked to the bar and set his wallet in front of him, then turned to go.

"Hey!" he said, grabbing her arm. She decided maybe architecture built up muscles more than she had suspected. "You pick my pocket, you little thief?"

"Sure, that's why I searched you out to return your wallet. Put it in your pocket, Bud. The other pocket. I think you got a hole in your regular wallet pocket. The wallet doesn't like being out in the open."

His eyes narrowed. "Just a second," he said, keeping his grip on her arm. With his free hand he opened the wallet and checked the bulging currency compartment, then looked at the credit cards. His eyebrows rose. He released her. "Thanks, kid. Sorry. I'd really be in trouble without this."

"Yeah, that's what it said."

"What do you mean?"

She shrugged, giving him a narrow grin and stuffing her hands deep into her pockets. He studied her, looking at the soaked shoulders of her jacket, glancing down at her battered boots, their laces knotted in places other than the ends.

"Hey," he said softly. "Hey. How long since you ate?"

"Lunch," she said. With all the people shopping, the trash cans in back of downtown restaurants had been full of leftovers after the lunch rush.

He frowned at his watch. "It's after nine. Does your family know where you are?"

"Not lately," she said. She yawned, covering it with her hand. Then she glanced at the wallet. "This the guy?"

—Yes, oh yes, oh yes, oh joy.—

"Good. 'Bye, Bud. Got to be getting home."

"Wait. There's a reward." He pulled out two fifties and handed them to her. "And you let me take you to dinner? And drive you home afterwards? Unless you have your own car."

She folded the fifties, slipped them into the battered leather card case she used as a wallet, and thought about this odd proposition. She squinted at the empty glass on the bar. "Which number are you?" she muttered to it, "and what were you?"

—I cradled an old-fashioned,— said the glass, —and from the taste of his lips, it was not his first.—

"You talking to my drink?" Amusement quirked the corner of his mouth.

Matt smiled, and took a peek at his dreamscape. She couldn't read thoughts, but she could usually see what people were imagining. Not with Plainfield, though. Instead of images, she saw lists and blueprints, the writing on them too small and stylized for her to read.

He said, "Look, there's a restaurant right around the corner. We can walk to it, if you're worried about my driving."

"Okay," she said.

He left some cash on the bar, waved at the bartender, and walked out, leaving Matt to follow.

The restaurant was a greasy spoon; the tables in the booths were topped with red linoleum, and the menus bore traces of previous meals. At nine on Christmas Eve, there weren't many people there, but the waitress seemed cheery when she came by with coffee mugs and silverware. Plainfield drank a whole mugful of coffee while Matt was still warming her hands. His eyes were slightly bloodshot.

"So," he said as he set his coffee mug down.

Matt added cream and sugar, lots of it, stirred, then sipped.

"So," said Plainfield again.

"So," Matt said.

"So did you learn all my deep dark secrets from my wallet? You did look through it, right?"

"Had to find out who owned it."

"What else did you find out?"

"You carry a lot of cash. Your credit's good. You're real worried about your car, and you're an architect. There's two women in your life."

"So do we have anything in common?"

"No. I got no cash—'cept what you gave me—no credit, no car, no relationships, and I don't build anything." She studied the menu. She wondered if he liked young boys. This could be a pickup, she supposed, if he was the sort of man who took advantage of chance opportunities.

The waitress came by and Matt ordered a big breakfast, two of everything, eggs, bacon, sausages, pancakes, ham slices, and biscuits in gravy. Christmas Eve dinner. What the hell. She glanced at Plainfield, saw him grimacing. She grinned, and ordered a large orange juice. Plainfield ordered a side of dry wheat toast.

"What do you want with me, anyway?" Matt asked.

He blinked. "I . . . I thought you must be an amazing person, returning a wallet like mine intact, and I wanted to find out more about you."

"Why?"

"You are a kid, aren't you?"

She stared at him, keeping her face blank.

"Sorry," he said. He looked out the window at the night street for a moment, then turned back. "My wife has my daughter this Christmas, and I . . ." He frowned. "You know how when you lose a tooth, your tongue keeps feeling the hollow space?"

"You really don't know anything about me."

"Except that you're down on your luck but still honest. That says a lot to me."

"I'm not your daughter."

He lowered his eyes to stare at his coffee mug. "I know. I know. It's just that Christmas used to be such a big deal. Corey and I, when we first got together, we decided we'd give each other the Christmases we never had as kids, and we built it all up, tree, stockings, turkey, music, cookies, toasting the year behind and the year ahead and each other. Then when we had Linda it was even better; we could plan and buy and wrap and have secrets just for her, and she loved it. Now the apartment's empty and I don't want to go home."

Matt had spent last Christmas in a shelter. She had enjoyed it. Toy drives had supplied presents for all the kids, and food drives had given everybody real food. They had been without so much for so long that they could taste how good everything was. Dreams came true, even if only for one day.

This year . . . She sat for a moment and remembered one of the dreams she'd seen a couple of years ago. A ten-year-old girl thinking about the loving she'd give a baby doll, just the perfect baby doll, if she found it under the tree tomorrow. Matt could almost feel the hugs. Mm. Still as strong a dream as when she had first collected it. Yes! She had them inside her, and they still felt fresh.

Food arrived and Matt ate, dipping her bacon in the egg yolks and the syrup, loving the citrus bite of the orange juice after the sopping, pillowy texture and maple sweetness of the pancakes. It was nice having first choice of something on a restaurant plate.

"Good appetite," said Plainfield. He picked out a grape jelly from an assortment the waitress had brought with Matt's breakfast and slathered some on his dry toast, took a bite, frowned. "Guess I'm not really hungry."

Matt smiled around a mouthful of biscuits and gravy.

"So," Plainfield said when Matt had eaten everything and was back to sipping coffee.

"So," said Matt.

"So would you come home with me?"

She peeked at his dreamscape, found herself frustrated again by graphs instead of pictures. "Exactly what did you have in mind, Bud?"

He blinked, then set his coffee cup down. His pupils flicked wide, staining his gray eyes black. "Oh. That sounds bad. What I really want, I guess, is not to be alone on Christmas, but I don't mean that in a sexual way. Didn't occur to me a kid would hear it like that."

"Hey," said Matt. Could anybody be this naive?

"You could go straight to sleep if that's what you want. What I miss most is just the sense that someone else is in the apartment while I'm falling asleep. I come from a big family, and living alone just doesn't feel right, especially on Christmas."

"Do you know how stupid this is? I could have a disease, I could be the thief of the century, I could smoke in bed and burn your play-house down. I could just be really annoying."

"I don't care," he said.

She said, "Bud, you're asking to get taken." Desperation like his was something she usually stayed away from.

"Jim. The name's Jim."

"And how am I supposed to know whether you're one of these Dahmer dudes, keep kids' heads in your fridge?" She didn't seriously consider him a risk, but she would have felt better if she could have gotten a fix on his dreams. She had met some real psychos—their dreams gave them away—and when she closed dream-eyes, they looked almost more like everybody else than everybody else did.

He stared down at his coffee mug, his shoulders slumped. "I guess there is no way to know anymore, is there?"

"Oh, what the hell," she said.

He looked at her, a slow smile surfacing. "You mean it?"

"I've done some stupid things in my time. I tell you, though . . ." she began, then touched her lips. She had been about to threaten him. She never threatened people. Relax. Give the guy a Christmas present of the appearance of trust. "Never mind. This was one great dinner. Let's go."

He dropped a big tip on the table, then headed for the cash register. She followed. "You have any . . . luggage or anything?"

"Not with me." She thought of her belongings, stowed safely in the basement two miles away.

"There's a drugstore right next to my building. We could pick up a toothbrush and whatever else you need there."

Smiling, she shook her head in disbelief. "Okay."

The drugstore was only three blocks from the restaurant; they walked. Plainfield bought Matt an expensive boar-bristle toothbrush, asking her what color she wanted. When she told him purple, he found a purple one, then said, "You want a magazine? Go take a look." Shaking her head again, she headed over to the magazine rack and watched him in the shoplifting mirror. He was sneaking around the aisles of the store looking at things. Incredible. He was going to play Santa, and buy her a present. Kee-rist. Maybe she should get him something.

She looked at school supplies, found a pen and pencil set (the best thing she could think of for someone who thought in graphs), wondered how to get them to the cash register without him seeing them. Then she realized there was a cash register at both doors, so she went to the other one.

By the time he finished skulking around she was back studying the magazines. It had been years since she had looked at magazines. There were magazines about wrestlers, about boys on skateboards, about muscle cars, about pumping iron, about house blueprints, men's fashions, skinny women. In the middle of one of the thick women's fashion magazines she found an article about a murder in a small town, and found herself sucked down into the story, another thing she hadn't experienced in a long time. She didn't read often; too many other things to look at.

"You want that one?"

"What? No." She put the magazine back, glanced at the shopping bag he was carrying. It was bulging and bigger than a breadbox. "You must of needed a lot of bathroom stuff," she said.

He nodded. "Ready?"

"Sure."

On the way into his fifth-floor apartment, she leaned against the front door and thought, —Are you friendly?—

—I do my job. I keep Our Things safe inside and keep other harmful things out.—

—I'm not really one of Our Things,— Matt thought. —I have an invitation, though.—

—I understand that.—

—If I need to leave right away, will you let me out, even if Jim doesn't want me to leave?—

The door mulled this over, then said, —All right.—

—Thanks.— She stroked the wood, then turned to look at the apartment.

She had known he had money—those gold cards, that cash. She liked the way it manifested. The air was tinted with faint scents of lemon furniture polish and evergreen. The couch was long but looked comfortable, upholstered in a geometric pattern of soft, intense lavenders, indigos, grays. The round carpet on the hardwood floor was deep and slate blue; the coffee table was old wood, scarred here and there. A black metal spiral plant-stand supported green, healthy philodendrons and Rabbit Track Marantas. Everything looked lived-in or lived-with.

To the left was a dining nook. A little Christmas tree decorated with white lights, tinsel, and paper angels stood on the dining table.

"I thought Linda was going to come," Plainfield said, looking at the tree. There were presents under it. "Corey didn't tell me until last night that they were going out of state. You like cocoa?"

"Sure," said Matt, thinking about her Christmas Eve dream, cocoa and other peoples' memories.

"Uh—what would you like me to call you?"

"Matt," said Matt.

"Matt," he said, and nodded. "Kitchen's through there." He gestured toward the dining nook. "I make instant cocoa, but it's pretty good."

Matt looked at him a moment, then headed for the kitchen.

"Be there in a sec," said Jim, heading toward a dark hallway to the right.

—Cocoa?— she thought in the kitchen. Honey-pale wooden cupboard doors wore carved wooden handles in the shape of fancy goldfish, with inlaid gem eyes. White tiles with a lavender border covered the counters; white linoleum tiles inset with random squares of sky blue, rose, and violet surfaced the floor. A pale spring green refrigerator stood by the window, and a small green card table sat near it, with three yellow-cushioned chairs around it. Just looking at the room made Matt smile.

—Who are you?— asked the refrigerator as it hummed.

—A visitor.—

—Where's the little-girl-one who stands there and holds my door open and lets my cold out?—

—I don't think she's coming,— Matt said. She wasn't sure if a refrigerator had a time sense, but decided to ask. —How often is she here?—

—Every time Man puts ice cream in my coldest part. There's ice cream there now.—

Ah ha, Matt thought. She went to the stove, found a modern aqua-enameled tea kettle. —May I use you to heat water?— she thought at it.

—Yes yes yes!— Its imagination glowed with the pleasurable anticipation of heat and simmer and expansion.

She ran water into it, greeted the stove as she set the tea kettle on the gas burner, then asked the kitchen about mugs. A cupboard creaked open. She patted the door and reached inside for two off-white crockery mugs. A drawer opened to offer her spoons. The whole kitchen was giggling to itself. It had never before occurred to the kitchen that it could move things through its own choice.

—Cocoa?— thought Matt. The cupboard above the refrigerator eased open, and she could see jars of instant coffee and a round tin of instant cocoa inside, but it was out of her reach. She glanced at one of the chairs. She could bring it over—

—Hey!— cried the cocoa tin. She looked up to see it balanced on the edge of the refrigerator. She held out her hands and it dropped heavily into them, the cupboard door closing behind it.

"What?" Jim's voice sounded startled behind her.

She turned, clutching the cocoa, wondering what would happen now. Though she couldn't be sure, she got no sense of threat from him at all, and she was still in the heightened state of awareness she thought of as Company Manners. "Cocoa," she said, displaying the tin on her palms as though it were an award.

"Yeah, but—" He looked up at the cupboard, down at her hands. "But—"

The tea kettle whistled—a warbling whistle, like a bird call. The burner turned itself off just as Jim glanced toward it. His eyes widened.

—Chill,— Matt thought at the kitchen.

—Want warmth?— A baseboard heater made clicking sounds as its knob turned clockwise and it kicked into action.

—No! I mean, stop acting on your own, please. Do you want to upset Jim?—

—But this is — !— The concept it showed her was delirious joy.
—We never knew we could do this!—

Matt sucked on her lower lip. She'd never seen a room respond to her this way. Some things were wide awake when she met them, and leading secret lives when no one was around to see. Other things woke up and discovered they could choose movement when they talked to her, but never before so joyfully or actively.

"What—" Jim said again.

Matt walked over to the counter by the stove, popped the cocoa tin's top with a spoon.

"Uh," said Matt.

"Can you—uh, make things move around without touching them?" His voice was thin.

"No," she said.

He blinked. Looked at the cupboard over the refrigerator, at the burner control, at the baseboard heater. He shook his head. "I'm seeing things?"

"No," said Matt, spooning cocoa into the mugs. She reached for the tea kettle, but before she could touch it, a pot holder jumped off a hook above the stove, gliding to land on the handle.

"Design flaw in the kettle," Jim said in a hollow voice. "Handle gets hot too."

"Oh. Thanks," she said, gripping the pot holder and the kettle and pouring hot water into the mugs. The spoon she had left in one mug lifted itself and started to stir. "Hey," she said, grabbing it.

—Let me. Let me!—

She let it go, feeling fatalistic, and the other spoon lying on the counter rattled against the tiles until she picked it up and put it in the other mug. The sight of both of them stirring in unison was almost hypnotic.

"I've been reading science fiction for years," Jim said, his voice still coming out warped, "maybe to prepare myself for this day. Tele-kinesis?"

"Huh?" said Matt as she set the tea kettle back on the stove and hung up the pot holder.

"You move things with mind power?"

"No," she said.

"But—" The spoons still danced, crushing lumps of cocoa against the sides of the mugs, making a metal and ceramic clatter.

"I'm not doing it. They are."

"What?"

"Your kitchen," she said, "is very happy."

Cupboards clapped and drawers opened and shut. Somehow the sound of it all resembled laughter.

After a moment, Jim said, "I don't understand. I'm starting to think I must be asleep on the couch and I'm dreaming all this."

—Done,— said the spoons. Matt fished them out of the cocoa and rinsed them off.

"Okay," she said to Jim, handing him a mug.

"Okay what?"

"It's only a dream." —Thanks,— she thought to the kitchen, and headed out to the living room.

Jim followed her. She found coasters stacked on a side table and laid a couple on the coffee table, set her cocoa on one, then shrugged out of her coat and sat on the couch.

"It's only a dream?" Jim said, settling beside her.

"If that makes it easier."

He sipped cocoa. "I don't want easy. I want the truth."

"On Christmas Eve?"

He raised his eyebrows. "Are you one of Santa's elves, or something?"

She laughed.

"For an elf, you look like you could use a shower," he said.

"Even for a human I could."

He fished the toothbrush out of his breast pocket and handed it to her. "Magic wand," he said.

"Thanks." She laid it on the table and drank some cocoa. She was so full from dinner that she wasn't hungry anymore, but the chocolate was enticing.

"All those things were really moving around in the kitchen, weren't they?" he said

"Yes," she said.

"Is the kitchen haunted?"

"Kind of."

"I never noticed it before."

She drank more cocoa. Didn't need other peoples' memories at the moment; making one of her own. She wasn't sure yet whether she'd want to keep this one or not.

Jim said, "Can you point to something and make it do what you want?"

"No."

"Just try it. I dare you. Point to that cane and make it dance." He waved toward a tall vase standing by the front door. It held several umbrellas and a wooden cane carved with a serpent twisting along its length.

"That's silly," she said.

"I've always, always wished I could move things around with my mind. It's been my secret dream since I was ten. Please do it."

"But I—" Frustrated, she set her mug on the table, but not before the coaster slid beneath it.

"See, look!" He lifted his mug, put it down somewhere else. His coaster didn't seem to care.

"But I—Oh, what the hell." —Cane? Do you want to dance?—

The cane quivered in the vase. Then it leapt up out of the vase and spun in the air like a propellor. It landed on the welcome mat, did some staggering spirals, flipped, then lay on the ground and rolled back and forth.

"That's so—that's so—"

She looked at him. His face was pale; his eyes sparkled.

"It's doing it because it wants to," she said.

"But it never wanted to before."

"Maybe it did, but it just didn't know it could."

He looked at the cane. It lifted itself and did some flips, then started tapdancing on the hardwood, somewhat muted by its rubber tip. "If everything knew what it could do—" he said. "Does every-thing want to do stuff like this?"

"I don't know," said Matt. "I've never seen things act like your things." She cocked her head and looked at him sideways.

With one loud tap from its head, the cane jumped back into the big vase and settled quietly among the umbrellas.

"I was wondering how you get things to stop," he whispered.

"Me too," she whispered back. "Usually things act mostly like things when I talk to them. They just act thing ways. Doors open, but they do that anyway. You know?"

"Doors open?" he said. His eyebrows rose.

She could almost see his thoughts. So: that's how this kid gets along. Doors open. She met his gaze without wavering. It had been a long time since she'd told anyone about talking to things, and other times she'd revealed it hadn't always worked out well.

"Doors open, and locks unlock," she said.

"Wow," he said.

"So," she said, "second thoughts about having me stay the night?"

"No! This is like the best Christmas wish I ever had, barring having Linda here."

Matt felt something melt in her chest, sending warmth all through her. She laughed.

He stared at her. "You're a girl," he said after a moment.

She grinned at him and set her mug on the coaster. "Could you loan me some soap and towels and stuff? I sure could use a shower now."

"You're a girl?"

"Mmm. How old do you have to be not to be a girl?"

"Eighteen," he said.

"I'm beyond girl."

"You're an elf," he said.

She grinned. "Could I borrow something clean to sleep in?"

He blinked, shook his head. "Linda's got clothes here, in her old room. She's actually a little bigger than you now." He put his mug down and stood up. "I'll show you," he said.

She grabbed her new toothbrush and followed him down the little hall. He opened a linen closet, loaded her arms with a big fluffy towel and a washrag, then led her into a bedroom.

—Hello,— she thought to the room. It smelled faintly of vanished perfume, a flowery teen scent. All the furniture was soft varnished honey wood. The built-in bed against the far wall had wide dresser drawers below it and a mini-blind-covered window above. A desk held a small portable typewriter; bookshelves cradled staggering rows of paperbacks, and a big wooden dresser with chartreuse drawers supported about twenty stuffed animals in various stages of being loved to pieces. On the wall hung a framed photographic poster of pink ballerina shoes with ribbons; another framed poster showed different kinds of owls. Ice green wall-to-wall deep pile carpet covered the floor.

—You're not the one,— said the room.

—No, I'm not. The one isn't coming tonight. May I stay here instead? I won't hurt anything.—

—You can't have his heart,— said the room.

—All right,— said Matt. This room was not happy like the kitchen. It relaxed, though.

—Thanks,— Matt thought.

Jim walked to the dresser and opened a drawer. "How do you feel about flannel?" he said, lifting out a nightgown. The drawer slammed shut, almost catching his hand, and successfully gripping the hem of the nightgown. "Hey!" he said.

—Our things,— said the room.

Matt thought about the sullen teenager she had seen in the photo in Jim's wallet. Afraid of losing things, holding them tight; Matt had learned instead to let go.

"Maybe you better put that back," she said. "I can rinse out my T-shirt."

Jim touched the drawer and it opened. He dropped the nightgown back in and the drawer snapped shut again. "I've got pajamas you can use. Actually, my girlfriend left some women's things in my closet . . . ."

"Pajamas would be good," Matt said.

He showed her the bathroom, which was spacious and handsome and spotless, black, white, and red tile, fluffy white carpet, combination whirlpool tub and shower, and a small stacked washer-dryer combination. "Wait a sec, I'll get you some pajamas. You want to do laundry?"

"Yeah," she said. "That'd be great." She wished she had the rest of her clothes with her, but they were still in the basement of that suburban house, two miles away. Oh well. You did what you could when the opportunity arrived.

He disappeared, returned with red satin pajamas and a black terrycloth robe.

"Thanks," she said, wondering what else he had in his closet. She hadn't figured him for a red satin kind of guy. She took a long hot shower without talking to anything in the bathroom, using soap and shampoo liberally and several times. The soap smelled clean; the shampoo smelled like apples. His pajamas and robe were huge on her. She hitched everything up and bound it with the robe's belt so she could walk without tripping on the pantlegs or the robe's hem. She brushed her teeth, then started a load of laundry, all her layers, except the coat, which she had left in the living room: T-shirt, long johns top and bottom, work shirt, acrylic sweater, jeans, two pair of socks, even the wide Ace bandages she bound her chest with. Leaving the mirror steamed behind her, she emerged, flushed and clean and feeling very tired but contented.

"I can't believe I ever thought you were a boy," Jim said, putting down a magazine and sitting up on the couch. Christmas carols played softly on the stereo. The mugs had disappeared.

"Very useful, that," said Matt.

"Yes," he said. She sat down at the other end of the couch from him. Sleep was waiting to welcome her; she wasn't sure how long she could keep her eyes open.

After a minute he said, "I went in the kitchen and nothing moved." Matt frowned.

"Was it a dream?"

"Was what a dream?" she asked, before she could stop herself.

"Please," he said, pain bright in his voice.

"Do you want things dancing? Drawers closing on you?"

He stared at her, then relaxed a little. "Yes," he said, "at least tonight I do."

She pulled her knees up to her chest and huddled, bare feet on the couch, all of her deep in the night clothes he had given her. She thought about it. "What happens is I talk to things," she said. "And things talk back. Like, I asked the kitchen where the cocoa was. Usually a thing would just say, this cupboard over here. In your kitchen, the cupboard opened itself and the cocoa came out. I don't know why that is, or why other people don't seem to do it."

"Like if I said, Hey, sofa, do you wanna dance?" He patted the seat cushions next to him.

—Sofa, do you want to dance?— Matt thought.

The couch laughed and said, —I'm too heavy to get around much. Floor and I like me where I am. I could . . . —And the cushions bounced up and down, bumping Matt and Jim like a trampoline.

Jim grinned and gripped the cushion he was sitting on. The couch stopped after a couple minutes. "But you did that, didn't you?" he said. "My saying it out loud didn't do anything."

"I guess not," Matt said.

"And things actually talk back to you?"

"Yeah," she said.

"Like my wallet."

"It kept whining about how you would die or at least be arrested without it. It really cares about you." She yawned against the back of her hand.

He fished his wallet out of his back pocket and stared at it for a minute, then stroked it, held it between his hands. "This is very weird," he said. "I mean, I keep this in my back pants pocket, and . . ." He flipped his wallet open and closed. He pressed it to his chest. "I have to think about this." He glanced at the clock on the VCR. "Let's go to sleep. It's already Christmas."

Matt squinted at the glowing amber digits. Yep, after midnight.

"Will you be okay in Linda's room?" Jim asked.

"As long as I don't steal your heart," Matt said and yawned again. Her eyes drifted shut.

"Steal my heart?" Jim muttered.

Matt's breathing slowed. She was perfectly comfortable on the couch, which was adjusting its cushions to fit around her and support her; but she felt Jim's arms lift her. She fell asleep before he ever let go.

She woke up and stared at a barred ceiling. —Where is this?— she asked. Then she rolled her head and glanced toward the door, saw the ballerina toe shoes picture, and remembered: Linda. Jim.

The mini-blinds at the window above the bed were angled to aim slitted daylit at the ceiling. Matt could tell it was morning by the quality of the light. She sat up amid a welter of blankets, sheets, and quilt, and stretched. When she reached skyward, the satin pajama sleeves slid down her arms to her shoulders. She wasn't sure she liked being inside such slippery stuff, but she had been comfortable enough while asleep.

She reached up for the mini-blinds' rod and twisted it until she could see out the window. Jim's apartment was on the fifth floor. Across the street stood another apartment building, brick-faced, its windows mostly shuttered with mini-blinds and curtains, keeping its secrets.

She put her hand against the wall below the window. —Building, hello.—

—Hello, Parasite,— said the building, a deeper structure that housed all the apartments, all the rooms in the apartments, all the things in the rooms, all the common areas, and all the secret systems of wiring and plumbing, heating and cooling, the skeleton of board and girders and beams, the skin of stucco and the eyes of glass-lidded windows.

Parasite, thought Matt. Not a promising opening. But the building sounded cheerful. —How are you?— she thought.

—Warm, snug inside,— thought the building. —Freezing outside. Quiet. It won't last.—

—Oh, well, just wanted to say hi,— thought Matt.

—All right,— thought the building. She felt its attention turning away from her.

—Aren't you getting up now?— asked Linda's room. It sounded grumpy. —It's Christmas morning!—

—Oh. Right.— Matt slipped out of bed, pulled the big black robe around her, and ventured out into the hall, heading for the bathroom. Not a creature was stirring. She finished in the bathroom, then crept into the living room to check the clock on the VCR; it was around 7:30 a.m., a little later than her usual waking time. She peeked at the Christmas tree on the table in the dining nook. Its white lights still twinkled, and there were a couple more presents under it.

—Coat?— she thought. It occurred to her that she had never talked to her own clothes before. Too intimate. Her clothes touched her all the time, and she wasn't comfortable talking to things that touched her anywhere but her hands and feet. If her clothes talked back, achieved self-will, could do whatever they wanted—she clutched the lapels of the black robe, keeping it closed around her. She would have to think about this. It wasn't fair to her clothes. —Coat, where are you?— she thought.

A narrow closet door in the hall slid open. Looking in, she saw that Jim had hung her coat on a hanger. She put out a hand and stroked the stained army-drab. Coat had been with her through all kinds of weather, kept her warm and dry as well as it could, hidden her from too close an inspection, carried all kinds of things for her. She felt an upwelling of gratitude. She hugged the coat, pressing her cheek against its breast, breathing its atmosphere of weather, dirt, Matt, and fried chicken (she had carried some foil-wrapped chicken in a pocket yesterday). After a moment warmth glowed from the coat; its arms slid flat and empty around her shoulders. She closed her eyes and stood for a long moment letting the coat know how much she appreciated it, and hearing from the coat that it liked her. Then she reached into the inside breast pocket and fished out the pen-and-pencil set she had bought the night before. With a final pat on its lapel, she slid out of the coat's embrace.

—Anybody know where I could find some wrapping paper and tape?— she asked the world in general.

The kitchen called to her, and she went in. A low, deep drawer near the refrigerator slid open, offering her a big selection of wrapping paper for all occasions and even some spools of fancy ribbons. Another drawer higher up opened; it held miscellaneous useful objects, including rubber bands, paperclips, pens, chewing gum, scissors, and a tape dispenser.

—Thanks,— she said. She chose a red paper covered with small green Christmas trees, sat at the card table with it and the tape, and wrapped up the writing set after she peeled the price sticker off it. Silver ribbon snaked across the floor and climbed up the table leg, then lifted its end at her and danced, until she laughed and grabbed it. It wound around her package, tied itself, formed a starburst of loops on top. She patted it and it rustled against her hand.

She put everything away and set her present under the tree, then went back to Linda's room and lay on the bed, yawning. The bed tipped up until she fell out.

—It's Christmas morning,— it said crossly as she felt the back of her head; falling, she'd bumped it, and it hurt. —The one never comes back to bed until she's opened her presents!—

—I'm not the one,— Matt thought. —Thanks for the night.— She left the room, got her coat out of the closet, and lay on the couch with her coat spread over her. The couch cradled her, shifting the cushions until her body lay comfortable and embraced. She fell asleep right away.

The smell of coffee woke her. She sighed and peered over at the VCR. It was an hour later. A white porcelain mug of coffee steamed gently on a coaster on the table. She blinked and sat up, saw Jim sitting in a chair nearby. He wore a gray robe over blue pajamas. He smiled at her. "Merry Christmas."

"Merry Christmas," Matt said. She reached for the coffee, sipped. It was full of cream and sugar, the way she'd fixed it in the restaurant the night before. "Room service," she said. "Thanks."

"Elf pick-me-up." He had a mug of his own. He drank. "What are you doing out here?"

"The room and I had a little disagreement. It said it was time for me to wake up and open presents, like Linda, and I hadn't slept long enough for me."

He gazed into the distance. "Linda's always real anxious to get to the gifts," he said slowly. "She used to wake me and Corey up around six. Of course, we always used to hide the presents until Christmas Eve. We used to get a full-sized tree and set it up over there—" he pointed to a space in a corner of the room between bookshelves on one wall and the entertainment center on the other— "and we wouldn't decorate it until after she'd gone to sleep. So it was as if everything was transformed overnight. God, that was great."

"Magic," said Matt, nodding.

Jim smiled. Matt peeked at his dreamscape, and this time she could see the tree in his imagination, tall enough to brush the ceiling, glowing with twinkling colored lights, tinsel, gleaming glass balls, and Keepsake ornaments—little animals, little Santas, little children doing Christmas things with great good cheer—and here and there, old, much-loved ornaments, each different, clearly treasures from his and Corey's pasts. Beneath the tree, mounds of presents in green, gold, red, silver foil wrap, kissed with stick-on bows. Linda, young and not sullen, walking from the hall, her face alight as she looked at the tree, all of her beaming with wonder and anticipation so that for that brief moment she was the perfect creature, excited about the next moment and expecting to be happy.

"Beautiful," Matt murmured.

"What?" Jim blinked at her and the vision vanished.

Matt sat quiet. She sipped coffee.

"Matt?" said Jim.

Matt considered. At last she said, "The way you saw it. Beautiful. Did Corey take the ornaments?"

"Matt," whispered Jim.

"The old ones, and the ones with mice stringing popcorn, and Santa riding a surfboard, and the little angel sleeping on the cloud?"

He stared at her for a long moment. He leaned back, his shoulders slumping. "She took them," he said. "She's the custodial parent. She took our past."

"It's in your brain," Matt said.

He closed his eyes, leaned his head against the seat back. "Can you see inside my brain?"

"Not usually. Just when you're looking out at stuff, like the tree.

And Linda. And I'm not sorry I saw those things, because they're great."

He opened his eyes again and peered at her, his head still back. "They are great," he said. "I didn't know I remembered in such detail. Having it in my brain isn't the same as being able to touch it, though."

"Well, of course not." She thought about all the dreams she had seen since she first woke to them years before. Sometimes people imagined worse than the worst: horrible huge monsters, horrible huge wounds and mistakes and shame. Sometimes they imagined beautiful things, a kiss, a sharing, a hundred musicians making music so thick she felt she could walk on it up to the stars, a sunset that painted the whole world the colors of fire, visions of the world very different from what she saw when she looked with her day-eyes. Sometimes they just dreamed things that had happened, or things that would happen, or things they wished would happen. Sometimes people fantasized about things that made her sick; then she was glad that she could close her dream-eyes when she liked.

All the time, people carried visions and wishes and fears with them. Somehow Matt found in that a reason to go on; her life had crystallized out of wandering without destination or purpose into a quest to watch peoples' dreams, and the dreams of things shaped by people. She never reported back to anyone about what she saw, but the hunger to see more never lessened.

She had to know. She wasn't sure what, or why.

"In a way, ideas and memories are stronger than things you can touch," she said. "For one thing, much more portable. And people can't steal them or destroy them—at least, not very easily."

"I could lose them. I'm always afraid that I'm losing memories. Like a slow leak. Others come along and displace them."

"How many do you need?"

He frowned at her.

She set down her coffee and rubbed her eyes. "I guess I'm asking myself: how many do I need? I always feel like I need more of them. I'm not even sure how to use the ones I've got. I just keep collecting."

"Like you have mine now?"

"My seeing it didn't take it away from you, though."

"No," he said. He straightened. "Actually it looked a lot clearer. I don't usually think in pictures."

"Mostly graphs and blueprints," Matt said.

He tilted his head and looked at her.

"And small print I can't read."

"Good," he said. After a moment's silence, he said, "I would rather you didn't look at what I'm thinking."

"Okay," she said. For the first time it occurred to her that what she did was spy on people. It hadn't mattered much; she almost never talked to people she dreamwatched, so it was an invasion they would never know about. "I do it to survive," she said.

"Dahmer dudes," he said, and nodded.

"Right. But I won't do it to you anymore."

"Thanks. How about a pixie dust breakfast?"

"Huh?"

"Does the kitchen know how to cook?"

She laughed and they went to the kitchen, where he produced cheese omelets, sprinking red paprika and green parsley on them in honor of Christmas. He had to open the fridge, turn on the stove, fetch the fry-pan himself, but drawers opened for Matt as she set the table, offering her silver and napkins, and a pitcher jumped out of a cupboard when she got orange juice concentrate out of the freezer, the pitcher's top opening to eat the concentrate and the cans of water. She had never before met such a cooperative and happy room. Her own grin lighted her from inside.

Jim's plates were egg-shell white ceramic with a pastel geometric border. He slid the omelets onto them and brought breakfast to the table. She poured orange juice into square red glass tumblers, fetched more coffee from the coffee-maker's half-full pot, and sat down at the green table.

"I'm so glad you're here," Jim said.

"Me too," said Matt.

"Makes a much better Christmas than me quietly moping and maybe drinking all day."

Matt smiled and ate a bite of omelet. Hot fluffy egg, cheese, spices greeted her mouth. "Great," she said after she swallowed.

Jim finished his omelet one bite behind Matt. She sat back, hands folded on her stomach, and grinned at him until he smiled back.

"Presents," she said.

"That was my line. Also I wanted to say having you here is the best present I can think of, because all my life I've wanted to see

things move without being touched. It makes me so happy I don't
have words for it."

"Did you design this kitchen?"

He glanced around, smiled. "Yeah. I don't do many interiors, but
I chose everything in here, since I like to cook. Corey did the living
room and our bedroom."

"This kitchen moves more than any other place I've ever been.
I think it was almost ready to move all by itself. I bet your buildings
would like to take a walk. I wonder if they're happy. I bet they are."

He sat back and beamed at her. Then he reached for his coffee
mug and it slid into his hand. His eyes widened. "Matt . . ."

She shook her head.

"Gosh. You are an elf." He sipped coffee, held the mug in front
of him, staring at it. He stroked his fingers along its smooth glaze. He
looked up at Matt. "It's beautiful," he said.

"Yeah," she said. "Everything is."

For a long time they stared at each other, their breathing slow and
deep. At last he put the mug down, but then curled his fingers around
it as though he couldn't bear to let go.

"Everything?" he said.

"Mmm," she said. For a moment she thought of ugly dreams,
and sad dreams, and wondered if she believed what she had just said.
Some things hurt so much she couldn't look at them for long. Still,
she wanted to see them all. Without every part, the balance was missing. Jim's image of a Christmas Linda was intensified by how much
he missed her. Cocoa tasted much better on a really cold day, and a
hug after a nightmare could save a life . . . .

After a moment, she said, "I got you something." She stood up.
He stood up too, and followed her into the dining nook. She picked
up the parcel she had wrapped that morning and offered it to him. "I
had to, uh, borrow the paper."

"How could you get me anything?" he said, perplexed. "These
are for you." He handed her three packages. "I didn't know what to
get you." He shrugged.

"Dinner, cocoa, conversation, a shower, laundry, a place to sleep,
coffee, breakfast," she said. She grinned and took her packages to the
couch, where she shoved her coat over and sat next to it. "Thanks,"
she said.

He joined her.

She opened the first present, uncovered a card with five die-cast metal micro-cars attached, all painted skateboard colors: hot rods with working wheels. Delighted, she freed them from their plastic and set them on the coffee table, where they growled and raced with each other and acted like demented traffic without ever going over the edge.

Jim sat gripping his present, watching the cars with fierce concentration. "I got them for the teenage boy," he said in a hushed voice after a moment. Two of the cars seemed to like each other; they moved in parallel courses, looping and reversing. One of the others parked. The two remaining were locked bumper to bumper, growling at each other, neither giving an inch.

Matt laughed. "They're great! They can live in my pocket." She patted her coat. "Open yours."

He touched the ribbon on his package and it shimmered with activity, then dropped off the package and slithered from his lap to the couch, where it lifted one end as if watching. Eyebrows up, he slid a fingernail under the paper, pulled off the wrapping. He grinned at the pen and pencil, which were coated with hologram diffraction grating in magenta and teal, gold and silver. "The office isn't going to know what hit it," he said. "Thanks."

"I bought 'em for the architect with a green tie. Not a whole lot of selection in that store."

"Yeah," he said, tucking them into the pocket of his robe. "Go on." He gestured toward the other two presents.

She opened the first one and found a purple knit hat. The second held a pair of black leather gloves. She slid her hands into them; they fit, and the inner lining felt soft against her palms. "Thanks," she said, her voice a little tight, her heart warm and hurt, knowing he had bought them for the homeless person. She smiled and leaned her cheek against the back of her gloved hand. "Best presents I've gotten in years."

"Me too," he said, holding out a hand to the silver ribbon. It reached up and coiled around his wrist. He breathed deep and stroked the ribbon. "God!"

Matt tucked the hat and gloves into a coat pocket, patted the coat, held out a hand to the little cars. They raced over and climbed up onto her palm. "Look," she said, turning over her coat. "Here's your new garage." She laid the coat open and lifted the inner breast pocket so darkness gaped. The cars popped wheelies off her hand and zipped into the cave. One peeked out again, then vanished. She laughed. She had laughed more in the last twelve hours than she had in a whole month.

The phone rang, and Matt jumped. Jim picked up a sleek curved tan thing from a table beside the couch and said, "Merry Christmas" into it.

Then, "Oh, hi, Corey!"

Hugging her coat to her, Matt stood up. She could go in the other room and change while he talked to his ex-wife. Jim patted the couch and smiled at her and she sat down again, curious, as ever, about the details of other peoples' lives.

"Nope. I'm not drunk. I'm not hung over. I'm fine. Missing Linda, that's all . . . okay, thanks."

He waited, his eyes staring at distance, one hand holding the phone to his ear and the other stroking the silver ribbon around the phone-hand's wrist. "Hi, Hon. Merry Christmas! You having fun?"

A moment.

"I miss you too. Don't worry, your presents are waiting. When you get home we can have a mini-Christmas. I hope you're someplace with snow in it. I know how much you like that . . . oh, you are? Great! Snow angels, of course. What'd your mom get for you?"

Matt thought about family Christmases, other peoples' and then, at last, one of her own—she hadn't visited her own memories in a long long time. Her older sister Pammy sneaking into her room before dawn, holding out a tiny wrapped parcel. "Don't tell anybody, Mattie. This is just for you," Pammy had said, and crept into bed beside her and kissed her. Matt opened the package and found inside it a heart-shaped locket. Inside, a picture of her as a baby, and a picture of Pammy. Matt had seen the locket before—Pammy had been wearing it ever since their mother gave it to her on her tenth birthday, four years earlier. Only, originally, it had had pictures of Mom and Dad in it.

"I'll never tell," Matt had whispered, pressing the locket against her heart.

"It's supposed to keep you safe," Pammy said, her voice low and tight. "That's what Mom told me. It didn't work for me but maybe it will for you. Anyway, I just want you to know . . . you have my heart."

And Matt had cried the kind of crying you do without sound but with tears, and she hadn't even known why, not until several years later.

"That's great," Jim said, smiling, his eyes misty. "That's great, Honey. Will you sing one for me when you get home? Yeah, I know it will feel funny to sing a carol after Christmas is over, but we're doing a little time warp, remember? Saving a piece of Christmas for later . . .

"Me? I thought I was going to miss you so much I wasn't going to have any fun, but I found a friend, and she gave me a couple presents. No, not Josie! She's at her folks'. I know you don't like it if she's here when you come, so we set it up before I knew you weren't . . ." He glanced at Matt and frowned, shrugged. "No, this is a kid. Actually, an elf."

He smiled again. "I wish you could have been here. She made the kitchen dance and the couch dance. I gave her these little cars, because I thought she was a boy, and she made them run all over the coffee table even though they don't have motors in them. I think she works for Santa Claus."

Matt slipped her hand into a coat pocket and touched the hat he had given her. It was soft like cashmere. Maybe he worked for Santa Claus. It had been a long time since she had had a Christmas of her own instead of borrowing other peoples', and this was the first one she could remember where she was actually really happy.

"You're too old to believe in Santa?" he said. He sighed. "I thought I was, too, but I'm not anymore." He listened, then laughed. "Okay, call me silly if you like. I'm glad you're having a good Christmas. I love you. I'll see you when you get back." He laid the phone down with a faint click.

Matt grinned at him. She liked thinking of herself as an elf and an agent of Christmas. Better than thinking she must be some kind of charity project for Jim, the way she had been at first.

Stranger still to realize she was having a no-peek Christmas, alone in her own head.

She thought of families, and, at long last, of her sister Pammy. How many years had it been? She didn't even know if Pam were still alive, still married to her first husband, if she had kids. . . .

"Can I use that?" she said. He handed the phone to her. She dialed information.

"What city?"

"Seattle," she said. "Do you have a listing for Pam Sternbach?"

There was a number. She dialed it.

"Merry Christmas," said a voice she had not heard since she had lived at home, half a life ago.

"Pam?"

"Mattie! Mattie? Omigod, I thought you were dead! Where are you? What have you been doing? Omigod! Are you all right?"

For a moment she felt very strange, fever and chills shifting back and forth through her. She had reached out to her past and now it was touching her back. She had put so much distance between it and herself. She had walked it away, stamped it into a thousand streets, shed the skin of it a thousand times, overlaid it with new thoughts and other lives and memories until she had thousands to choose from. What was she doing?

"Mattie?"

"I'm fine," she said. "How are you?"

"How am I? Good God, Mattie! Where have you been all these years?"

"Pretty much everywhere." She reached into the coat's breast pocket and fished out one of the little cars, watched it race back and forth across her palm. She was connecting to her past, but she hadn't lost her present doing it. She drew in a deep breath, let it out in a huge sigh, smiled at Jim, and snuggled down to talk.

ANGER MANAGEMENT

Something wrong?"

Terry looked up, away from the car's still-hot and oily-smelling engine, a ferocious frown on her face. The woods beside the road were freeze-frame still; not a leaf moved. "Sod it," she said to the skinny young man standing there hunched in his overlarge army jacket. Where had he come from? Not a car had driven past in the ten minutes Terry had been staring under the car's hood. Sunlight shone through the boy's pale bristly hair, scoured the green from his jacket's shoulders. Terry hauled off and kicked the tire of her mother's Nova, then yelped and jumped around, clutching her hurt toe. Never wear sandals when you want to kick a car, she told herself.

"Maybe I could help?" said the stranger in a nice, medium-range voice.

Terry stopped muttering mispronounced Latin and Greek curses long enough to say, "If you know cars."

"Some cars," he said, setting down a ragged khaki backpack and leaning over the engine.

"Gidget, gadget, gizmo, guts," Terry muttered, switching to babblespell, wondering if anybody who approached a girl and a car stranded beside a highway in the woods had good intentions. "Access powerspot sprink?" Why, oh why, had she exhausted all her power on some idiot showy spring spell in the rhododendron clearing, not keeping any in reserve at all? Not like anyone was even there to see it, except the trees, which had thanked her. What did she care what some old trees thought? She wasn't a nature child.

Ah, she knew why she did it. She had been angry. She had thought doing something with plants would calm her down, vault her to some higher awareness that it was better to be calm than get upset about every little thing, but it hadn't happened. Powersplurge; piss it away. Typical Terry. She was so tired of typical Terry.

The stranger put his hands on a big greasy thing in the middle of the mess of wires and metal and fanbelts that made up the engine. He closed his eyes and meditated, it looked like. Terry wanted to whack him with a tire iron. Just what she needed in the middle of nowhere, some nut who went into trances without excuse.

He giggled.

Even worse, a giggling nut.

He opened his eyes, grasped one thing and plugged it into some other thing, or fitted it onto some other thing, and then patted the engine.

"What?" Terry asked. "What, what?"

"I think it'll be all right now," said the stranger.

"Yeah, but what's the joke, huh?"

"Uh—never mind," he said, smiling. He had a wide smile for such a narrow foxy face. He lifted the hood up, pulled the prop out of its slot, laid it in its place, and gently let the hood drop.

Terry felt anger rising inside her. She channeled it into her power reservoir the way her mentor had taught her. It was power of a sort, after all; might as well save it for when she might need it. "Well, thanks, I think," she said in a calm voice. She went and sat in the driver's seat, tried the key. The engine roared to life.

The boy picked up his backpack and edged over into the woods, out of her way, still smiling.

Terry turned the engine off and stuck her head out the open window. "Hey, you want a ride to town, anyway?" she asked in a gruff voice.

He hesitated, then came over and climbed in. He dropped the backpack at his feet and buckled the shoulder harness immediately.

"What?" Terry said again. "Car tell you something about my driving?"

He looked at her, wide-eyed, then offered her the same cheeky grin.

"It's not my car," Terry said. "It's my mom's. We don't get along. Me and the car, I mean." She turned the engine back on and tried to change from Park to Drive without pulling the steering-wheel mounted shift toward her. "Gutsa glory!"

The stranger reached over and touched the tip of the gearshift. The car slid into drive and rabbited into the road. "Hey!" Terry yelled, then worked on steering. When she had the car in the correct lane, aimed toward town, she glared at her passenger.

Facing out the windshield, he bit his lower lip, but he still had the edge of a grin.

"So what did the car say about me?" she asked after she had channeled the adrenaline and anger into her power reservoir.

"Said you get mad a lot."

"A telling observation," she said.

"Said you're a witch," he ventured.

"Or rhymes with it," she said, turning it into what she had expected to hear. She narrowed her eyes and stared at him. "So what does that make you? You talk to cars."

He shrugged.

"So what do you do when you get mad?" she asked.

He hesitated, then said, "Figure out who hurt me. Figure if they did it on purpose. Figure how to deal with it."

"Like, how? Kill them if they did it on purpose?"

"Naw. Gotta figure what'll work. Killing never really teaches anybody anything."

"Get them back?"

He furrowed his brow. "No. Mostly what counts is what goes on in here," he said, knocking on his forehead.

She pounded the steering wheel. "Who sent you? Someone sent you out there to be a lesson to me, didn't they?"

"No," he said. The grin had disappeared.

She glared at him with slitted eyes, then faced the road again. "People are always trying to tell me stuff like that."

"Hey, you asked."

She frowned, then thought it over and relaxed into a smile. "Guess I did. What's your name?"

"Matt."

"Mine's Terry. Or did the car tell you that too?"

He grinned back at her. "That's not what it calls you."

"Oh, yeah? Enlighten me."

Matt shook his head.

Terry checked with her power reservoir. All the anger she'd been feeding into it had smoothed into non-specific power. There was enough there for a tiny tangle of truthtell. She spun a slender halo of power and dropped it over Matt, even though every time she used truthtell she heard uncomfortable things. "Come on, give," she said.

"'Engine who pushes when should pull, curses and screams at own errors as though they belong to other.'" Matt frowned. "Hey!"

"The car can frame concepts like that?" Terry asked.

"Are you a good witch or a bad witch?"

"Working on being a bad witch," she said. She waggled her eyebrows at him. "What kind of witch are you?"

"I'm not a witch."

She zapped him with truthtell again, and asked, "What kind of witch are you?"

"I'm not a witch," he said. "Stop that!"

She zapped him again and said, "What's your biggest secret?"

"I'm a girl. Stop!" This time Matt wasn't talking to Terry. The car heard Matt and pulled over and parked on the verge. Matt unbuckled her seatbelt, grabbed her backpack, and slid out of the car. "Thanks, car. Thanks." She patted the car and stepped away from it.

Terry leaned over and rolled down the passenger window. "Hey, don't—"

Matt's face had gone blank. She said, "I don't spend time with people who don't respect me."

"I'm sorry," Terry muttered. "I'm sorry!" she said louder. "I won't do it anymore. Please let me drive you to town."

"Nope. Bye, Terry." Matt turned and walked into the woods, sunlight sliding stripes across her shoulders and shorn head.

Terry watched until she had disappeared into the heat and darkness. A bird called. Sun baked the asphalt and the forest, the odor of ancient death mingling with new green life.

After a moment she rolled the window closed and sat up. She whacked the steering wheel with her palm, then grimaced and stared at her hand. Yep, another case of blaming someone else for her own messes.

"Okay," she said to the car. She studied the gearshift. The car was in park. She pulled the gearshift toward her and slid the car into drive. "Okay," she muttered, already wondering if she could summon Matt back with candlework and chickenblood, then scolding herself for considering it, then wondering again.

TREES PERPETUAL OF SLEEP

They were way too far into the woods and away from human-made things for Matt's taste. When choosing for herself, Matt called the whole world home, but she generally stayed in the parts of the world where there were cars and roads and buildings and people, things she could talk to. She wished she had never met Miss Terry Dane, teenage fashion victim and witch.

Cricket noise and stream murmur edged the forest air with sound. Sunlight was just fading from the tops of the trees around the clearing, and the intense blue of midsummer sky was staining slowly into night. Everything smelled green and wet. The marshy ground squished under Matt's army boots.

Terry laid red roses in a ring on the firescarred altar rock in the middle of the clearing and opened her backpack. She whispered words while she pulled all kinds of weird things out of her pack. She set each item carefully on the rock, blessing it and preparing it for use.

Matt wished there were somewhere to sit. If she sat on the grass she would get her jeans soaking wet. Durn Terry and her Midsummer ceremony, anyway.

The whispering tree on the far side of the rock, the only tree in the clearing, had big roots, some of them with knees and knuckles sticking up above the ground. Matt edged around the big gray altar stone and sat on one of the tree's upthrust roots.

Terry opened her big time-nibbled book and set it where she could see it, as though it were a cookbook. She made some passes with her hands and spoke some words. She lit red candles, and then she lit a piece of stick incense which she waved in a pattern, leaving little trails of thin smoke and the scent of a distant country. She stacked wood on the rock in a triangle within the circle of roses, and snapped her fingers. The wood blazed up. It was fairly impressive.

Matt pulled her knees up to her chest and leaned back against the tree's trunk. Its rough bark caught at her crewcut. She didn't know what kind of tree it was, but it sure smelled good, a little like fresh pencils at the start of a school year.

Terry spoke softly, reading from the book and touching the things she had laid on the rock, lifting water, crystal, incense, salt, and a knife. Gripping the knife in her right hand, she stood a moment, her eyes lifted to the darkening sky above, then cut across her left palm and dripped blood into the fire.

"Dedication," said the tree Matt leaned against.

"Mm," Matt murmured. She had learned to keep quiet when Terry was in the middle of something; she had talked during a summoning spell Terry was doing once, and the little wind Terry had been calling up got loose and pestered both of them for three days.

"I used to have that. Almost."

"Shh," said Matt. Golden-orange light was gathering around Terry's head and hands. She held her hands up to the sky and spoke some more words, and the light brightened around her. She closed her hands a moment. She opened them again, and red-gold light flowed from her palms, half to the sky, half to the earth. She pressed her palms together and stood silent, and the light seeped away. Everything got quiet.

Terry drew in a deep breath, let it out slowly. She shifted position, her shoulders relaxing. She blessed all her tools and stored them again, and last of all she passed her hands through the flames, which rose up and then died down.

"Discipline," said the tree.

"Shhhh!" Matt said.

"She's finished."

"Shh?" Terry said, shaking her hands and smiling at Matt. The slash on her left hand had closed clean.

"I wasn't talking to you," said Matt. "I was talking to this tree . . . this tree?"

"Thought you didn't talk to trees," Terry said.

"Not usually," Matt whispered.

"I used to have that kind of dedication and discipline," said the tree again. "Well, maybe not as intense."

"You said you only talked to man things," Terry said. "What does that mean?" She patted her backpack and floated up to sit on the high-

est part of the rock, above where she had performed her ceremony.
"I can talk to things people have messed with. I know that feeling, so we can relate."

"Hmm," said Terry. She opened the outside compartment of her backpack, fished out two granola bars, and tossed one to Matt. "But now you're talking to this tree."

Matt edged out on the root so she could look at the tree's trunk. Its bark was almost fuzzy, with shallow fissures running up and down. She placed her palm against it and felt a rough surface, but not a splintery one. "How can I talk to you?" she said. "I don't know anything about nature."

"I'm not natural," said the tree.

"Oh," said Matt. She wondered whether she should stand up. She decided she'd rather sit on an unnatural tree than try climbing on Terry's rock.

"I used to be a witch," the tree said. "Now I just watch witches come and go here at the Gateway Stone. Powerspill wakes me up sometimes."

"So what is it saying?" Terry asked.

"What happened to you?" Matt asked the tree.

"I got carried away during a spell, and it turned on me."

"Wow," said Matt, wondering if it could happen to Terry, and if she maybe wanted it to.

"Could you let me out of here?"

"What?"

"I've been thinking about it for an age. I've worked out a spell that should release me, but I need help."

"Matt," Terry said. "Talk to me." She was using her pushy voice.

"He used to be a witch until he messed up and got trapped in the tree," Matt said, not realizing until the words came out of her mouth that the tree was male. One of the things she hated most about her relationship with Terry was that Terry could just tell her to do stuff and Matt would have to do it without being able to think it over first. Terry didn't do it very often—if she had, Matt would have found some way out of the tether spell, even if it involved not surviving. "He's worked out a spell to let him go. He wants us to help."

"She coerces you?" the tree asked.

"Tether spell," mumbled Matt.

"Sympathies," said the tree. "How did that happen?"

"Uh," Matt said. She should never have stopped to fix Terry's car. The car had warned Matt that Terry was a witch, but she didn't realize it meant literally until too late.

In spite of the tether spell, Matt had liked living with Terry and her mom, at first. Lately it had begun to grate.

"Oh. Right. Not easy for you to explain when she's listening," said the tree. "Hmm. You can hear me and she cannot, eh?"

"Mm."

"Are you a witch?"

"No."

"You're not? Wait a moment. How can that be?"

"I'm just me, Matt."

"Matt," said Terry. She drummed her fingers on her knee.

"What?"

Terry frowned. "So?"

"Do you want to help him with his spell?" asked Matt.

"How good a witch is she?" the tree muttered to itself. "No, don't answer that. I have watched her work, and she's one of the best I've ever seen."

"Have him tell us the spell." Terry unzipped her backpack and pulled out the ancient book, opened it to a page near the back. She got a pen out of the backpack's outside compartment. "I'll think about it."

"She's a good witch, but is she a good witch?" the tree muttered. "Evidence: she does her solstice ceremony alone. Not a communal witch. Cast out, or alone by choice? Evidence: she tethers another to her. Hmm. Hmm. Did she tell you why she tethered you? Did you do something to her?"

"Yes. No," said Matt.

"Does he want our help or not?" Terry asked. She frowned. Matt knew by now that with Terry, irritability was the first step toward true discomfort for anybody she was around.

The tree said, "By wit and by will, I bound myself. By witchings and workings I bound myself. By wood and by water I bound myself. By one into other I bound myself. Now I am ready to release myself. Now I am ready to face my fear. Now I am ready to go to war. By wood and by water I loose myself. By witchings and workings I loose myself. By wit and by will I loose myself."

"Matt," said Terry.

"Just a second," Matt said. She put her hands on the tree trunk. It was trembling.

"Water," it whispered. Matt ran to the stream and grabbed water in her cupped hands, brought it back and splashed it on the trunk.

"Wood."

She looked around, saw the unburnt end of one of the sticks Terry had used in her little bonfire on the rock, lifted it, and touched it to the trunk.

"Will," whispered the tree.

Matt put her hands on its trunk and thought about being trapped. Terry didn't seem to know how to make friends except to manufacture them. She had a twin sister who had left on some kind of magic quest and it was driving Terry nuts, though mostly Matt knew about that because the room she stayed in was Terry's twin's room, just a closet away from Terry's room, and at night Matt could hear Terry calling and crying in her sleep. Terry also had an ex-boyfriend, and a witch teacher who wouldn't talk to her anymore. This much Matt had learned from surreptitious talks with things in Terry's room. No wonder she's lonely, Matt thought; but does that mean I have to stay tied to her like this? I might even like her if she gave me a chance.

"I will you to be free, I will you to be free, I will you to be free," Matt said, leaning on her hands on the tree, which felt warm, and still trembled against her. She spoke the words for the tree and for herself.

"Matt!" Terry cried.

The tree shook harder. With a loud crack it split open and spilled out a mushroom-pale boy.

"But we don't know who or what or—" Terry said.

The tree closed its mouth. Its bark welded back together beneath Matt's hands. She patted it and stepped away, looking at the boy, who lay shuddering and twitching on the wet grass. He was naked, his limbs wraith-thin, and his hair long and dark and tangled, a few strands still caught in the bark of the tree. His eyelids fluttered. He coughed.

"—whether he's even a good person," Terry said.

Matt stooped. "Are you cold?" she asked, pulling off her plaid flannel shirt and draping it over him. She still had her black T-shirt on.

"Thirsty," he whispered.

Matt went to the rock. "Gimme the bottle of water."

Terry raised her eyebrows, but opened the pack and fished out the water bottle, then handed it to Matt.

Matt knelt on the grass, oblivious to wet knees, and lifted the boy's head onto her thigh, tilting the bottle so water trickled into his mouth. For an instant Matt was back in an alley, helping her friend Denzel drink from a bottle in a brown paper bag, trying to talk the bullet in his gut into coming out, trying to talk the blood into staying inside him, trying to talk his clothes into binding against the wound, trying even to talk to germs, though she never had before. It was a terrible time when talk got her nowhere.

She cradled the boy's pale head, giving him water a little at a time and waiting while he swallowed, stroking his hair. His eyes were green and he smelled like the tree.

After a little while he reached up and took the bottle from her hand. He struggled and sat up, then drank the rest of the water. "Thanks," he said. "All these years of witch-traffic, and you, a non-witch, you're the first one who helped me."

Helped him . . . . That was how she had gotten into trouble with Terry. When Terry had snarled her in the tether spell, Matt had decided that in the future she should leave witches alone. Usually she kept her promises to herself.

"What's your name?" she asked.

"Lewis," he said. He stretched, first one arm toward the sky, then the other. He scratched his nose and grinned at her, showing a dimple in his left cheek.

"Matt," she said, holding out her hand.

"Pleased to meet you." He shook hands with her.

"That over there is Terry," Matt said.

"Hello," said Lewis, smiling toward Terry. She nodded without smiling, her hands resting on her knees.

"How'd you get stuck in that tree?" Matt asked after a short uncomfortable silence. "What were you trying to do?"

"I came up here to get away from the war. All the men and boys were going overseas, except the ones who had some sort of exemption or those who were too old. I thought if I changed myself, I could stay home. But I wasn't as specific about what I wanted to change into as I thought I was."

"What did you want to change into?" Terry asked.

"Well," he said, "not a tree, anyway." He pushed to his feet and leaned his back against the tree, flattening his hands on the bark. "This is still me. It's all the growing I've done." He tilted his head back, looking up the trunk into the branches. Then he closed his eyes.

Frogs chorused from the stream as the longest day of the year was swallowed by the shortest night.

"When are we?" he asked. He glanced up at the tree. "I think we grew at a tree's pace, and my tree is tall. How many years have I been here?"

Terry told him.

"Fifty years. It's fifty years later. Is there still a war?" he whispered.

"There's a war," Terry said. "There's usually a war. People don't have to go against their wills right now, though. You're a witch, and you couldn't come up with a better plan to evade the draft than this?"

In the gathering darkness Matt couldn't tell for sure, but she had the impression that Lewis was filling out, losing his starved thinness as he lay back against the tree. Above them the branches rustled, though there was no wind. Small scaled twiglets pattered down. Matt caught one. It felt dry; she rubbed her fingers over it, and it came apart, leaving behind the ghost of a scent of green.

Terry pulled three candles out of her pack and lit them with a touch of her fingers. She dripped wax and set the candles in it on the rock beside her. The flames burned straight and unflickering.

"I had a better plan," Lewis said at last. His voice had deepened, added overtones. "It just didn't work." He stepped away from the tree. He was definitely bigger. He paused, lifted one foot away from the ground, then the other. "Oh," he murmured, touching the sole of his foot. "This is so strange." He pressed his palm to his chest, then touched the bark of the tree. "I feel so naked. No wonder people wear clothes." He lifted Matt's discarded shirt and slipped it on without buttoning it. The sleeves were far too short. "Not quite right, but better than nothing."

He went to Matt, grasping her elbows from behind and lifting her to her feet. His hands were warm and strong. Her first impulse was to kick back at him and twist free, but she suppressed it. He said to Terry, "I suppose you have some sort of master plan that involves tethering this boy?"

Terry's eyebrows lifted. A moment later she shook her head. "I have no plan," she said. "I realize that sometimes things come into my life when I need them—spirit gifts—and I needed Matt."

"For what?" Lewis and Matt said together.

Terry ducked her head, her gaze on her hands, which lay nested one in the other in her lap. "You know," she said. She looked up into Matt's eyes, her own eyes catching glints from the candle flames. Light turned half her face to butter amber.

"Oh, you're such a teenager!" Matt said.

Terry brushed the hair out of her eyes and offered a brief smile.

Lewis let Matt's elbows go, touched her shoulder. "You understand her?"

"She's a power nerd," Matt said after trying to figure out what she did understand.

"Whaaat?" said Terry.

"What does that mean?" Lewis asked.

"You don't—you run out of—you don't take the time to make the—it's a shortcut." Frustrated, Matt waved her fists up and down. "To get to know people, it takes time. It's not easy. Sometimes they hurt you and you hurt them. But you, you don't have to wait. You have this power. You use it to get what you need, because hoping someone else will help you takes too long and it might not work. You can make a—a relationship happen without even listening to the other person. You never have to risk getting hurt. You just . . . force it . . . and you don't have to be scared there's anything I can do."

"No," said Terry, shaking her head. "That's not right."

"I know you're doing it because you've lost them all," Matt said. "Everybody else has gone, except your mom, and she's scared of you. It's still cheating."

"No, dammit," said Terry, slapping her thighs with open hands. "No. Shut up."

But she didn't use her pushy voice, so Matt said, "You never asked me. How do you know I would have said no?"

"Everybody I've asked lately has said no."

"You didn't ask *me*."

Terry gripped one hand with the other. The tip of her tongue touched her upper lip. "Would you be my friend?"

"Take the tether spell off."

Terry sat for a long moment with her head bowed. She zipped open her pack at last and pulled out a small dark bag, reached inside, took out something about the size of a walnut. She murmured words and held the little thing over one of the candle flames. It burned quickly and left a smell like sizzled hair behind. Matt felt a lessening of tension somewhere in the region of her stomach.

Terry brushed off her hands.

"Okay," Matt said. "Yes."

"You won't go away?"

"I will go away. Doesn't mean I stop being your friend. You have to treat me with respect, though, or to take care of myself, I'll stop being your friend."

Terry hesitated, then said, "I'm not sure I know how to do that. Will you help me?"

"Sure."

"Beautiful," said Lewis. From behind, he locked his arms around Matt's upper body. "Now that you're free . . ."

"Cut it out," said Matt, tugging at his arms. She couldn't budge them. He had certainly bulked up since the tree expelled him.

"I won't hurt you," he said.

"Then let go. Haven't you been paying attention? Forcing hurts."

He hugged her, then dropped his arms. "I've missed human contact. I've missed just being able to move around." He reached for the sky with both hands, then rolled his head back and forth, lowered his arms, and twisted his upper body. He bent over and touched his toes. He walked away from the tree, at first striding fast, then slowing as he came to the edge of the meadow. He looked back over his shoulder at the tree. "I still can't believe . . . ."

Matt edged over to the rock, and Terry grabbed her hand and pulled her up, with maybe a little lifting help from air, or whatever it was that kept Terry clean and dry amidst all this dirt and water.

"...that I can just walk away. I haven't seen the meadow from a different direction in decades." His voice faded as he ventured farther.

"Do you feel safe in the forest at night?" Matt muttered to Terry.

"Most of the time," Terry muttered back. "I respect the spirits of trees and streams and places, and they know I respect them, and we regard each other but do no harm. It's only people that scare me." She stared toward where Lewis had disappeared.

"What about big animals that eat people?"

"There aren't any around here."

"No cougars or bears? How can you know for sure?"

Terry laughed softly in the darkness. The candles were on the side of Terry away from Matt, and from Matt's viewpoint, only lit some grass and half of the tree Lewis had come out of. "If we run into any big scary animals, I have a very quick distract spell that ought to turn them away."

"Have you ever tried it? What if it doesn't work?"

Terry reached behind her for her backpack, pulled it onto her lap. "If you like, I can whip you up a ward-off-evil spell," she whispered.

"Would that work on people, too?"

"I don't know. It's another thing I haven't tested."

"I'm starting to wonder about Lewis," Matt muttered.

"I've been wondering about him from the beginning."

"Why?" Matt asked. Did Terry have some extra-sensory reason?

"Because I have a suspicious nature."

Out of the darkness, Lewis's voice said, "You know what I'd really like? A nice thick steak. And maybe a beer. Ice-cold. Yeah. There's a restaurant, Morley's Landing, where you can tie up canoes and rowboats and eat right beside the Mill Race, a lovely place of a summer's night—do you know it?"

"What town are you talking about?" asked Terry.

"Spores Ferry."

"There's no mill race in Spores Ferry," she said.

"What?"

"There's no mill race, and no Morley's Landing."

"How can that be? Oh. Time." His voice sounded sad. "Will you . . . take me to town and let me see if there are any landmarks that survive?"

Terry lifted one of her candles. Matt watched as the dividing line between light and dark moved across Terry's face. "Well, I've done my devotions," she said after a moment. The light just touched Lewis's form. He stood near the edge of the forest, like the dim dream of a god. "I'm ready to go. Matt?"

"I'm more than ready to go." The night was finally cooling, and she had given up her extra shirt. She scratched a mosquito bite on her arm.

"Jump down and I'll give you a candle."

Matt slid down off the rock. Terry said a spell over the candle she held and handed it to Matt. "It will burn steady, but not set anything else alight," she said. "Lewis? Would you like a light?"

"No."

Terry pinched one of the candles out and spelled the other one, then packed up everything except the lit candle, the roses, and the ashes. She shouldered her backpack and drifted down from the rock with the candle in her hand. She kissed the rock, then set out across the meadow.

The wax felt warm and soft inside Matt's hand, and its melting smell reassured her as though it were the essence of safety. She glanced around at the dark meadow and the star-shot sky, then trailed Terry, conscious that this time it was by choice. Matt's boots slapped sound from the marshy ground; Terry walked silently. And Lewis, when he fell in behind Matt, made no sound other than soft breathing. The back of her neck prickled.

The footing was firmer on the path. Matt listened to the path: "You are walking away from me you are walking toward me you are walking on me you are making and destroying me." She liked its song better than the unknown mutters of the forest, louder now that it was night.

The way back to the car went faster than the hike out from it had. Twigs and branches didn't grab at her as much, either. Maybe the forest was glad to see her go.

Matt crawled into the back seat of Terry's white Fiat. She stroked the seat, touched the window and the carpeting, relieved to be in the wide world of home again. "Who's that?" asked the car as Lewis climbed into it. "It tastes like change."

"Don't know," Matt muttered.

"Not sure I want it inside me."

Terry tossed her pack in back and climbed into the car, started it, and drove away.

"It doesn't feel right," Lewis said.

"What?" asked Terry.

"Not only does this car look freakish, and the dashboard looks like something from a rocketship, and the engine doesn't make half the sound it should, but this—this moving away from a place—it feels wrong."

Terry said, "Do you want me to take you back?"

They were twisting and turning down a mountain road in the darkness. Matt was leaning sleepily against the back of the seat, which had shaped itself to cradle her. She closed her eyes and waited for Lewis's answer.

"Part of me wants you to," he said after time had gone by. "Being rooted felt . . . right. All this movement is confusing me. Yet for ages and ages, I longed for nothing but freedom."

"Come down to the valley and look around. If you don't like it, I'll take you back."

"You are very kind."

"Not really," Terry said, glancing toward him. Matt saw dashboard light glinting on Terry's teeth as she smiled.

They completed the drive in silence. "First off," Terry said, as she pulled up in front of the house she shared with her mother, and for now with Matt, "you need a few more clothes. There's some things of my dad's still in the house. Could you use a shower? Though you don't really smell like a guy who's been locked in a tree for years and years."

"A shower would be great," said Lewis. "I'm not really here yet. I mean . . ."

"I know. Changing shape, it takes a while to get used to the new one," Terry said.

"You've done it?"

"Oh, sure. My sister Tasha and I used to have spell fights. I turned her a lot more often than she turned me; she wasn't a very good student. But she was really good with this one spell. She liked turning people into Pekingeses. That is, until she got religion. So I know what it's like. Before you get out of the car, would you wrap something around your waist? Our neighbors are always watching our house. They've seen enough weird things already."

Lewis shifted around and took off the shirt Matt had given him, did something with it. "Best I can do," he said.

"It's pretty dark," Terry said. She snapped her fingers, and the light over the front door went out. "Okay, door's unlocked. Go for it," she said.

Lewis dashed across the lawn and managed not to drop the shirt until he had the front door open. He ducked inside. Matt and Terry followed more sedately, at least until Terry's mother screamed.

Lights switched on across the street and next door.

"Damn!" said Terry. She snapped her fingers. "Phone lines . . . Mom, I can explain . . . ."

In the front hall, Lewis stood with his back to the wall, one hand covering his genitals, the other his mouth, his eyes wide. Terry's mother Rebecca stood backed up against the sofa, both hands over her mouth, her eyes as wide as Lewis's.

"I can explain," Terry said again, but then she burst out laughing. Terry's mom started breathing again. Her hands came down from her mouth. "Better be a good one," she said.

With effort, Terry smothered her laughter. "Well, we went up to the forest. You know why. And we found this guy, Lewis, up there, and he didn't have any clothes, so I thought maybe some of Dad's castoffs might still be in the basement and I invited him home."

"Not good enough," said Rebecca. "What was he doing up there naked in the woods?"

"He was under a wicked enchantment."

Rebecca's cheeks lost color. "Terry . . . I don't appreciate that kind of humor. I don't like the—I'm not comfortable with you bringing strangers into my house."

"I'll take him out again as soon as he showers and has some clothes, Mom. And it wasn't a joke. And I thought this was my house, too."

"She's talking about me," Matt said.

"Oh, I am not, Matt," said Rebecca, irritation in her tone. "I'm glad you're here, and I hope you stay as long as you want."

"I only want to stay as long as it's okay," Matt said.

"It's okay, dammit."

Matt sighed. "Mrs. Dane, this is my friend, Lewis. Lewis, this is Mrs. Rebecca Dane."

"Pleased to meet you, Mrs. Dane," Lewis said, red staining his cheeks. He didn't hold out a hand.

"I apologize for my lack of manners, Mr. Lewis," said Rebecca.

"I understand. It's enough to turn anyone's hair white, a naked stranger running in your front door. I didn't know there'd be anybody home."

"Well," she said. "Well . . . welcome to my home. Let me show you to the shower. And you may drop your hand. You don't have anything I haven't seen before, and if I hadn't seen it before, I wouldn't know what it was, as my grandmother used to say. Obviously the kids have already gotten an eyeful."

"I'll go hunt up some clothes," Terry said as Lewis followed Rebecca down the left-hand hallway.

"What sort of enchantment was it?" Rebecca asked.

"I was trapped inside a tree for fifty years, more or less," said Lewis as their voices faded.

*

Matt went to the kitchen while Terry searched the basement. She was starving after all those hours in the wild. Part of Terry's intense discipline involved regulating what she ate and when, and while Matt was tethered to her, Matt had followed Terry's eating habits. It had been nutritious, but not much fun. She opened her arms to the kitchen and said, "Talk to me, food."

A cupboard popped open and a bag of pretzels jumped into her arms. "Oh, thank you!" she said, and sat at the table to eat some.

Lewis stayed in the shower a long, long time. Listening to the sound of water in pipes, the three women sat in the kitchen, talking in murmurs, Rebecca and Matt sharing pretzels, Terry taking tiny sip-bites of unflavored yogurt. At last Terry said, "Matt, what the hell is he doing in there?"

Matt asked the house. "Uh oh," she said when she heard the answer.

"What is it?" asked Rebecca.

"Putting down roots."

Terry knocked on the bathroom door. "Lewis? Get your toes out of the drain or I'll turn you into a porcupine!"

"Wha-a-a-at?" His voice sounded sleepy and slow.

"Turn off the water and get out of the plumbing."

"What? Oh . . . just a minute."

Matt leaned against the wall and listened to what the house had to tell her. The invasion of its systems by this stranger had worried it, and it was glad that he was withdrawing parts of himself that had gone where people parts weren't supposed to go.

"I've got clothes for you," Terry said in a less cross voice. "Any-time you're ready."

The door opened a crack and steam billowed out, carrying scents of soap, shampoo, and—green? "I'm sorry. I don't know what got into me," said Lewis. Terry handed the clothes to him and he shut the door again.

"It's what got out of him that's interesting," Terry muttered to Matt.

The waitress brought a still-steaming steak on a platter and set it in front of Lewis. She set down Terry's lemon herbed chicken and Rebecca's garlic shrimp, and then gave Matt her hamburger. Matt picked up a French fry and bit it. It was nice to finally order just what she wanted, instead of picking the same thing Terry ordered, or something else she thought might stay in her stomach even if she got too far from Terry and felt sick. Lewis's steak smelled good. Matt wondered if she should have ordered that instead.

Lewis picked up his steak knife and fork and cut into his meat. Red welled up behind the knife, and the flesh was still pink inside, rare, the way he'd ordered it. He stared at it a moment. He lifted his fork, with the morsel of steak on it, and studied it. He licked his upper lip. He blinked several times. He paled.

He shook his head. "I can't eat this," he said, setting the fork down. He swallowed. "I can't . . . I can't even stay here. Excuse me." Jumping up, he dropped his napkin over the platter and its cargo and dashed from the restaurant.

"Nuts," said Terry.

Matt picked up her hamburger. If they were leaving, she was taking it with her.

"You want to check on him, see if he'll wait while we eat?" Terry asked Matt.

Matt sighed and put her hamburger down.

"Why don't you do it?" Rebecca said suddenly. "Why this lady-of-the-manor delegation thing? It's really getting on my nerves. Matt's not your servant."

"What?" said Terry.

"Just because you can turn people into pinecones, it doesn't give you the right to order them around as though they were less important than you are."

"Mom, what's gotten into you?"

"Nothing's gotten into me. I'm just letting a little of what was

always there out. I love you, and I'll always love you; that doesn't
mean I approve of everything you're doing. And yes, I darn well expect immunity from your powers."

Terry stared at her mother for a moment, then set her napkin beside her plate, rose, and walked out.

"That wasn't too harsh, was it?" Rebecca asked Matt.

Matt shook her head. She had never had a conversation alone
with Rebecca, and she felt shy. "If you're going to live with somebody, I guess you need rules," Matt said. "I usually move on before I
get to that stage."

"She's been walking all over you."

"People do, sometimes. Usually I leave when they start, but Terry
wouldn't let me."

Rebecca blinked. "Oh. I don't like that at all."

"Got her to let me go today."

"You're still here."

Matt nodded. "You said it was okay. Lewis is kind of my respon-
sibility, since I let him out of the tree."

"You let him out?"

"Yeah. I'm not a witch, but I talk to things."

"Ah. Yes. I noticed."

Matt smiled. "He said people had been coming to that stone
where Terry did her ceremony for years but nobody noticed him before. I haven't run into other people who can talk to things like I can.
When he was a tree, I could hear him talk, but Terry couldn't."

"Hmmm," said Rebecca. She ate a shrimp. "While watching Terry operate since I found out she was a witch, it occurred to me that it
would be very difficult to let go of all the advantages you gain when
you have these special abilities. Do you ever not talk to things?"

"Lots of times," Matt said. "I usually only ask questions when
I feel like something's coming at me. When I need help or I need to
know something to survive. I don't know anything about you, really."

Rebecca patted her mouth with her napkin and smiled. "Thanks,
Matt."

"You're welcome." Matt ate her hamburger.

"I don't know much about you, either."

"We could talk about it," Matt said.

Rebecca grinned.

"For starters, I've done a lot of traveling," said Matt.

Terry returned, subdued.

"He okay?" Matt asked.

"He wants to go back."

The four of them sat out on the back lawn at Terry and Rebecca's house, drinking lemonade and looking at city-hazed stars. Someone on the block was watering the lawn; the air carried the sound of false rain and the scent of wet grass.

"Everything," Lewis said, "everything is different. I can't eat this food, and I'm starving. Music is different. Buildings are different. People dress differently, and they use a lot of words that don't make sense. The prices on that menu scared me! I could have rented a room for two weeks for the amount of money that steak cost, and I couldn't even eat it. How can things be so expensive? There are all kinds of devices in your house that I have no idea what they do, and I don't want to find out. All these years, the witches have been the same; but everything else has changed."

"So you want to run away and hide?" Matt said.

"I don't see how I can survive here. I can't just mooch off Terry and Rebecca, can I? But how could I get a job? I don't understand anything about this new world."

Matt thought about mooching off Terry and Rebecca. She didn't want to do it much longer herself, now that she had a choice. Something in her, the wandergod part of her, longed to move on, wash her present off and start over someplace new with no complications or expectations. She had been living her life in short bright sections for more years than she bothered to count. The road was continuity enough.

"Aren't you even curious?" she asked. "Don't you even want to find out?"

His answer was a long time coming. "Maybe. In a way."

"You were a Crafter once," Terry said. "What happened to your desire to shape things?"

"Hmm," he said. "I think . . . as time passed . . . I figured out what to want. Sunlight. Rain. Snow. Dead organic matter. And freedom, and someone to talk to. Maybe I was shaping as much as I could. Or maybe I was just accepting what came. It was almost enough."

"Dead organic matter is mostly what we eat," Terry said thought-fully. "You're doing okay with the lemonade, aren't you?"

"Hmm," said Lewis, looking into his cup. "It tastes good."

"What kind of tree are you when you're a tree?" Rebecca asked.

"Something local. A cedar, I think. I'm not sure exactly."

"You could put down roots," Rebecca said slowly. "And pick them up again."

"I don't know," said Lewis. "I left my tree behind."

"You started rooting in the house."

"Huh. Yes."

"We could use some more shade in the back yard," she said. "You could just . . . stay here awhile and maybe learn some more about now."

"You could stay here for a while and then go somewhere else. Learn new things all the time, and new places. Root, uproot," Matt said. "That's how I live. Try a different place every little while. You could come with me. I could teach you." She touched her mouth after the words were out. Part of her lifeway was to be alone; to always make friends, but never to take them with her on her journey from one piece of life to the next. What had come over her?

"Matt, don't go," said Terry.

"What am I doing here?" Matt said. "I need to go."

"I could teach you to root," Lewis said. He laid his hand over hers on the lawn. His fingers plunged down into the soil, caging hers between them.

"No!" said Matt, tugging, but her hand was locked to the Earth.

"Relax," said Lewis.

"No!"

"I'll let you go in a minute. Relax."

Everything in her was twisted tight and squirming. Every lesson she had learned early in life was about getting away before the Bad Things could find her, and now she was trapped. She pulled in breaths and let them out slowly, trying to relax. At last she asked Lewis's clothing if it could strangle him for her, and it said it could do that if she wanted. She relaxed, and felt—

Her fingers aiming downward, digging into dirt, reaching deeper than their lengths, seeking and finding deep cool comfort; and a lan-guage that spoke so slow a word would take a lifetime but be worth waiting for; and things seeping into her through her fingers, things that tasted like steaming mashed potatoes drowning in butter, and hot apple cider, and chocolate ripple ice cream; and a sense of strength infinite and offering itself to her: all she had to do was stay. Warmth. Comfort. Eternity. A cradle.

The pressure on her hand went away. Her hand pulled back into its own shape, and she was sitting, bereft of contact and comfort, on the lawn again, a world away from the eternal community. Shivering started in her arms and traveled through her.

"Are you okay?" Terry asked, gripping her arm. Matt shook for a little longer. The warmth from Terry's hand felt good.

When the shaking stopped, Matt patted Terry's hand and said, "Don't do that to me without asking, Lewis. Don't."

"You would have said no. And I could never describe it."

"Don't do it like that again."

He hesitated, then said, "I won't."

Matt sipped lemonade. Half had sloshed out of her glass while she was shaking. "I'll try it again tomorrow," she said, "if you'll come to town with me and Terry."

"All right," he said. "For tonight, I'd just like to stay out here."

"Pick a spot away from the house and not under the power lines," Rebecca said.

"I will. Thanks to all of you, for everything."

Matt was brushing her teeth while Terry rubbed astringent over her face. "Pay attention to your dreams tonight," Terry said. "It's a time of pollination. Seeds get set."

"I don't want any dreams," Matt said, but her mouth was full of toothpaste and the words didn't come out.

She dreamed of Home.

HOSTILE
TAKEOVER

I'm a thirty-year-old woman who lives at home with her mother. When guys do this, I suspect it's because they can't find a woman their age who will cook and do laundry and pick up after them the way their moms do. When a woman does it, the only legitimate excuse is that Mother is feeble and needs help.

My mother refuses to be feeble. I could cast a spell on her to make her feeble, but she has a rule: no witchcraft in the house. This is why I have to have an outside office to craft the spells I sell on my website. I have broken Mom's no-magic-in-the-house rule a couple times, but she really means it when she says she'll kick me out if I do it again without permission.

I tell people I still live with my mom because she needs my rent checks. I make twice as much money with my spell business as she does at her florist job. The checks meant something to Mom while Dad was defaulting on the alimony, but now that he wants to get back together with her, he's paying regularly, so my expressed reason for living with Mom is a lie.

What I really crave is living with someone who understands me. This is a big secret. Not my biggest one, but one of the top ten. My identical twin sister and I became witches the same day, and for a while we grew into our power together. We were close before we turned into witches, but afterward, we were so tight I had trouble loosening up enough to find a boyfriend. Tasha and I went to the same witch teacher and learned the same lessons. We practiced our arts on each other . . . until I took a turn toward the dark side, and she refused to follow. She got all mystical instead, dedicated herself to the powers of Air, and left me so she could pursue her new faith. Now she travels the world practicing weird rituals that don't get her anything but good will. I can see that being a bankable asset, but only if you spend it sometimes, which Tasha never does.

Mom's the only one in town who understands me. So she's stuck with me, whether she likes me or not.

As part of my business practice, I hung out at the student union building at the local university. My regular spell customers knew to find me there, and I hooked up with new ones all the time. The right conversational opening gave people all the excuse they needed to complain. Once I knew their problems, I knew which spell to sell them.

The S.U.B. was a rambling building. There was a bowling alley/ video arcade in the basement, a food court on the ground floor, offices for university clubs and special interest groups scattered throughout, potted plants, meeting rooms, and snarls of conversational furniture everywhere. I could lurk there with impunity.

A boy witch bumped into me in the food court. I was waiting to buy a gyro, and he was heading toward a girl. In addition to side-swiping me and not apologizing, he totally dinged my witch radar. I'd encountered other witches here and there on campus, but never somebody else with such powerful vibes.

"Hey," I said, giving New Witch Boy the up-down.

He brushed past me without answering. I wasn't the most beautiful woman in the world unless I worked at it, but I had style. Short dark hair in a clean cut, and single-color tailored clothes. I passed for college age all the time. Was this guy gay?

I wandered after him, not so much offended as intrigued. Maybe he didn't have witch radar and didn't recognize me for what I was. I'd met a number of powerful people, and power made its home in them in different places; I no longer expected anyone else's power to match mine.

"Shelley," he said, catching up to a girl who was hurrying away. I was disappointed. She had that blonde cheerleader look—long, washed-out hair, big blue eyes, lush lips, and big pushy breasts—so beloved in teen-centric TV and too often in real life.

"Not now, Gareth," she said. Her voice incorporated acid. "My boyfriend's watching." She swung away, bobbing gently in front, and Gareth stood, his mouth half open in either idiocy or preparation for a remark that never made it past his teeth.

I stopped beside him. "If you're that interested in her, why don't you enchant her?"

His mouth closed and he stared at me with angry amber eyes.

"Hey, hey, I was just asking," I said.

"Get away from me," he said.

"Sheesh, you don't have to be nasty."

"Did my mother send you here to pester me?"

"No, but I'd like to meet her."

He blinked. "What?"

"If she's the type of mother who sends girls to torment her sons, she might be my kind of fun."

"Who are you?"

"My name's Terry Dane. Can I buy you a cup of coffee?"

"Terry Dane? Do you run that spell website?"

I smiled. "You've heard of me!"

He looked madder than ever. "What the hell do you think you're doing?"

I shrugged. "Making a living?"

"With those watered-down imitation spells? More like wholesale fraud."

"Come on. Have you tried them?"

"I bought the spell for studying harder. It hardly helped at all."

"Did you dissolve it in hot water?"

"What?"

"You have to use hot water to make it truly active—the hotter the better."

"Oh—I thought—"

"I include instructions with the spells for a reason. It's not my fault if you ignore them. I'm feeling generous today, so I'll give you a replacement for the last one you messed up, but this is a one-time deal." I shrugged out of my backpack and rummaged through my sample case. The spells I carried with me were stronger than the mass-produced ones I made for mail order, on the principle of intermittent conditioning, and the desired-recapture-of-the-first-time syndrome. If your first hit was really effective, you kept thinking the next one would work just as well. Every once in a while I sent out the stronger versions through the mail to keep my regular customers coming back. "Here." I held out the little gray-paper-wrapped cube that was the "increased study skills" spell. "Hot water. Tea or coffee works."

He hesitated.

"Don't use it until you're cramming for something. The effect is temporary unless you reinforce it with actual studying on a regular basis. Wait until the night before the exam; it only helps you retain things for forty-eight hours, and that's an outside estimate. Why do you need something like this, anyway?"

"What do you mean?"

"Oh, come on. You're a witch. You could make your own."

He grabbed the spell and strode away without a backward look.

"So, no coffee?" I yelled.

About fifteen people turned to look at me. Usually I kept a low profile, but at the moment I was past caring. Had I just wasted a free spell on a guy who was going to ignore me?

"Hey, Terry? You got an attract spell on you?" asked Seth, a short guy with bad teeth and too many green pieces of clothing. One of my best customers. I'd slipped him a free "see yourself as others see you and figure out how to fix your obvious errors" spell once, the permanent version, because it increased the effectiveness of all the other spells I sold him. He had learned to smile with his lips closed, but he couldn't seem to overcome his penchant for green. "There's a girl I want to impress right over there."

"Sure," I said, instead of, "Another one? What happened to the last six girls you used an impress-her spell on?" The spells had to have worked, or why was he coming back for more? Maybe it was a case of wanting something until you actually had it, or maybe the short-term effect had kicked in. If you didn't actually interest the person you attracted after two or three exposures, the spell would wear off and the relationship was over. I fished out the red-wrapped spell Seth wanted—one of my best sellers—and he handed me fifty bucks.

"Thanks." He ran off. I wondered if I should use an attract spell myself and pursue Gareth, but he'd already vanished.

The next time I saw Gareth was in the supermarket by the produce section.

Ding! Ding! Witch in the vicinity! I turned from the mountain of Minneolas I was casing and saw Gareth squeezing an avocado. I decided to stalk him, since the straightforward approach hadn't worked.

He put three avocados in a plastic bag and turned to hand the bag to a woman. Ding! Okay, that was why two dings the first time, and maybe why he could ignore me so easily—he already had a companion witch.

"Gareth, I said *four*," she said.

A testy companion witch. Twice his age.

Two girls rushed up, stair-steps, wavy brown hair, with the same tawny eyes Gareth had. "Look, Mom! Stephanie found the brown sugar!" said the taller girl, and the other one said, "Lacey got the flour!"

"Good job, girls," said the woman, smiling down at them, an edge of enchantment in her expression. For sure the kids felt loved. Cheap trick. I had that one in my repertoire, but it was so easy I rarely used it. Maybe I should try it on Gareth. He was probably used to it, and would fall faster than someone never exposed.

A slender young woman, her brown-gold hair in short curls, arrived and set a bag of raisins carefully in the cart, offering the mother witch a tight smile.

"Thank you, Rae," said the mother, her voice not so supple and graceful this time.

"What else do you need?" asked Rae.

Mom witch consulted her shopping list. "Chocolate chips."

"Why didn't you tell me before? Those were in the same aisle," said Rae. She frowned and marched away.

"Mommy, what else can we find?"

"Bread, girls," said the mother to the two girls, who jumped up and down. "Look by the back wall." She gestured toward the store bakery, and the two raced off, giggling. She held out the bag with three avocados to Gareth without a word, and he went back to the produce aisle.

I edged over to him, reached for an onion. "Okay, I get why you're allergic to witches," I muttered, "but I'm not your mother."

He jerked and dropped three avocados on the floor, started an avocado avalanche. I snapped my fingers and stopped them all from tumbling, sorted them back into a stable pile. "You've got to work on your people-sensing skills," I said. "I didn't actually sneak up on you. You could have seen me in your peripheral vision."

"Are you following me?" He stood, picked up the three fugitive avocados, and placed them carefully with the others.

"Maybe."

"Get away from me."

"Am I totally unattractive to you?" That came out more plaintive than I liked. I didn't let Helpless Me out to play in public. This guy was demoralizing me, and I should probably move away from him. Instead, I said, "I can change."

"Why are you even interested in me? I'm not sending out signals, am I?" His eyes widened. "Did I put a spell on you?"

"Simmer down. I'm just short of witch company at the moment, and you're the first likely candidate I've sensed in a while."

"I'll be interested in you if you can teach me how to stop being a witch," he whispered, just as his mother swooped down on us.

"Didn't you find another avocado yet? What's taking so long?"

"Hey, Mom. This is Terry, my new girlfriend." Whoa! I was promoted! He went on, "Terry, my mother, Sally Mathis."

She stiffened immediately, worked hard, and came up with a smile. "Nice to meet you. You won't distract him from his homework too much, will you?"

"Is schoolwork a problem for Gareth?" I asked. Did she or didn't she realize I was a witch? Maybe she was one of those instinctive practitioners who had never explored the range of powers available to her. In which case, Gareth might be completely untrained. I could turn him into whatever I wanted.

I grabbed a perfectly ripe avocado and handed it to Gareth.

"He lacks concentration," said Gareth's mother. She was being pretty bitchy about her son to someone she didn't even know.

"I can help him concentrate," I said, in my best cat-purr voice.

"Wonderful," said Sally with a sour frown. "It's a thrill and a half to meet you."

"Likewise, I'm sure."

Gareth put the avocado I'd chosen in the bag with the others and handed it to his mother. "We're going for coffee."

"But—" said Sally.

I linked arms with Gareth, smiled at his mother, and led him away. I left my half-filled basket on top of a pyramid of cans of corned beef hash.

Outside, we headed for the nearest Starbucks. We both ordered the house blend, and I paid, since I'd offered to before. We settled at one of the tiny round tables, and I hunched toward him. "So what's your new agenda?" I asked. "It's quite a distance from 'get away from me' to girlfriend."

He hooked both hands behind his neck and pulled his head down like someone getting ready to be searched by cops. "I thought you could help me figure out how not to be a witch."

"Why would you want that? Are you totally not getting what a blast this is?"

He looked up. "She wanted the girls to get the power, but they didn't. She's scared of me having it."

"Are you still living at home?" I asked.

He nodded.

"Well, there's your first mistake. Get away from her." Like I could talk. My own mom was completely ready for me to move out. I was the one who wouldn't go.

"But I don't know how to—Dad's out of the picture. He hasn't paid child support in three years. There's four of us, and—She just barely managed my college tuition, even though I have scholarships. She can't afford to pay for a dorm room for me, and I—"

Couldn't he work his way through school? I guessed it depended on his skill set. "How old are you, anyway?"

"Seventeen."

"Oh." He couldn't even vote yet. But if he'd graduated high school early and gotten scholarships, why did he need spells to help him study? "How do you use your witchcraft on a day-to-day basis?"

"I don't."

"Not at all?"

"Not on purpose," he said, and flushed.

"How about your mom? What does she do with hers?"

"Woman things," he muttered, his gaze on the table top.

"What the hell does that mean?"

"She won't tell me. She does it at home in a room with the door closed. All I know is there's stinky incense involved, and words I can't hear through the door. The craft has passed from mother to daughter in our family for generations. She hates that I got it instead of the girls."

"Gareth," I said, exasperated. Then I thought, No, he knows from rough women. I better be gentle or I'll lose him.

I started over. "Okay, listen. I can't unwitch you—I don't know how—but I can teach you how to make it work for you."

"With those stupid spells you sell? I don't know much, but I can tell they don't work very well."

"They don't have to work well to sell well. I don't want to upset the social balance by giving anyone giant advantages in any of the areas I service. That might lead to scrutiny I don't want. I can teach you how to be a much better witch, but you have to agree to help me. If I train you in the business, you can make enough money to get your own place. What do you say?"

He stared at his coffee cup so long I thought he wasn't going to answer, but at last he said, "Okay."

First I took Gareth home with me. I figured he should know what a mom was supposed to be like.

"It's mac and cheese again, Terry," Mom called from the kitchen at the back of the house as I ushered Gareth in through the front door, "unless you have other ideas."

"I have a guest, Mom." We passed through the living room and the hall into the kitchen, the heart of the house, where Mom and I spent all our together time after she got off work. The patina of a million cooked meals covered the kitchen ceiling in a yellow haze. The center of the room was a round table, often stacked with newspapers and mail, with just enough room for us to set our plates and silverware down. Sometimes we cleared the debris off, but it didn't take long to build up again. The kitchen colors weren't very inspiring, beige and brown, with a yellow fridge, all geared toward comfort and convenience. A cheese-and-boiling-pasta scent greeted us.

Mom stirred a pot on the stovetop, her silvering brown hair coming down from its neat coils around her head drift in long, limp tendrils around her face. She was flushed from the stove's heat and still wearing the white shirt, black pants, and black suspenders she wore at the florist shop. It was a weird uniform that made her look more like a waiter than a flowershop girl, but they liked that at Flowers While You Wait. "Gareth, this is my mom, Rebecca Dane. Mom, this is Gareth Mathis."

"Hi, Gareth! I hope you like mac and cheese. Terry, could you throw together a salad?"

"Sure." I checked the fridge and remembered why I'd gone to the supermarket in the first place. Produce! We were out. I sighed. "Well, I guess not, Mom. I forgot to shop."

"Frozen broccoli, then." She nodded toward the microwave. I got out the broccoli.

"Gareth, would you like something to drink?" Mom asked.

"That'd be great." He looked lost, standing in our kitchen, his hands clasped in front of his chest as though he were begging or praying, his brown-blond hair an unbrushed mess.

"Help yourself to whatever's in the fridge. Cups are in the cupboard over there."

Gareth poured himself some orange juice.

Mom asked, "Where'd you two meet?"

"At the supermarket," I said. "Gareth's a witch, but he hasn't had any training. I thought I'd get him started." I filled a glass with water and took a seat at the table.

"Really?" Mom put the lid on the mac and cheese and came to the table.

Gareth had gone red again. "Terry," he said, his voice squeaking in a surprising way.

"What?"

"Maybe he didn't want me to know he's a witch," Mom said. "It's okay, Gareth. I don't tell anybody these kinds of things. I appreciate Terry being up front about it, too. It's when she's keeping secrets that I get upset. Have a seat."

"Are you a witch, too?" he asked as he settled in a chair beside me.

"No, not at all," said Mom.

He turned to me. "So where'd you learn?"

"I had a teacher for about six years after I turned into a witch." I could take him to meet my mentor, but then I'd lose my chance to train him up to be my new twin and business partner. Besides, my mentor no longer let me cross her threshold. She was pretty strict about not dabbling in the dark arts.

"But you still live at home," he said. "And you think I should move out?"

"His mom makes him feel bad about what he is," I told my mom. "She's scared of him."

"Oh, honey," said my mom. She put her hands on Gareth's, squeezed. "So sorry you have to deal with that."

"Did Terry put a spell on you to make you say that?"

"Nope. No magic in the house," said Mom.

"He doesn't even know how to check for spells," I said. "I've got my work cut out for me."

"For once, I might actually approve of what you're doing," said my mother.

"So can I start his training here?"

Mom frowned, tapped her index finger on her mouth a couple times, and then nodded. "As long as it's just matter stuff, not spell-casting on people. For the dark stuff you have to take him somewhere else. Okay?"

"All right."

We had dinner, and afterward, Mom sat at the table with coffee and a crossword puzzle while I explained basic principles of magic to Gareth. Mom loves hearing this kind of stuff. It gives her insight not only into me but into my traveling twin, who blows home every once in a while. (I mean it about blowing, too. She brings the wind with her before she remembers to tell it to go outside and play.)

I said, "You have to perceive things to be able to affect them—or, at least, it helps. Do you ever sense things other people don't?"

"I don't know. How could I tell?"

"I knew you were a witch, and that your mom was, too. I learned it through my witch senses. Do you ever get strong feelings about people or things?"

His eyes narrowed, and he glanced past me, as though looking at something out a window, though he stared toward a wall. "I used to when I was little, but not for a long time. My mom's dresser set. Her brush. It's old. It felt like it might be able to—but she wouldn't let me touch it, after that time she found me waving it around."

"Hmm," I said. "Good news, probably. You have the senses. They're just asleep. Once we wake them up, you'll be able to do things. I'll try a spell to open your witch eyes. Wait here a sec. I have to get my kit." I ran upstairs, grabbed my traveling witch kit, and dashed back to the kitchen. I cleared newspapers off the table. "Mom, is this okay?"

"Does it hurt anybody?"

"Not physically. I don't know about the psychic consequences. It should show Gareth what he does and doesn't see."

"Gareth, are you ready for this?" Mom asked.

He laughed, with scorn in it. "Hey, I've seen her work before. I don't expect anything to happen."

Mom slanted a look at me. I smiled back at her. "Go ahead," she said.

I assembled dust of ages, scent of spring gone, sound of three high notes on a piano, and a trace of vanished sunrise. Power pooled in my palms as I bracketed my ingredients with my outstretched fingers. "Show us what he could see, and why he doesn't," I whispered, not a spell I'd ever said before. I wasn't sure if it would work. It didn't even rhyme.

The ingredients flared, mixed, and vanished, leaving a twist of smoke behind. The world shifted around us. Everything in the kitchen glowed with colored light, and streams or strings stretched between people and furniture, appliances, floor, ceiling, walls. Some pulsed, beads of light sliding along the strings between things intimately connected; some shimmered in time to the hum from the refrigerator.

In the midst of all this weaving, an overlay that didn't obscure the physical forms of things—translucent as it was pervasive—something hovered above Gareth's head. A miniature thicket of rose bushes, and trapped inside, a pair of eyes, their irises deep, shifting gray/golden/dark and shadow. The bushes had cleared from in front of them, so that they peered out, as if from a cage. They looked this way and that. Whatever they looked at deepened and intensified. They looked at me, and I felt warmth against my face as though I leaned toward a fire.

"What is this?" Gareth cried, and his extra eyes looked at Mom. She had been turning and gaping at the room, trying to take in everything at once, but now the power of the eyes' gaze focused her into concentrated Mom. She was taller, with a crescent moon in her hair—wrong symbol, I thought; Mom was hardly a virgin goddess—and a veil of golden haze surrounded her.

"What did you do?" Gareth asked, turning on me, and again I felt the warmth of his regard. I held out my hands, studied what the eyes made of me. I was cloaked in shadow so dark it made me look like a silhouette, but flashes of color rippled through my new outer skin.

"Why are you closed most of the time?" I asked.

"What are you talking about?" Gareth demanded. "What's with all these visions? Did you spike my orange juice?"

The eyes blinked, a shuttering of images—all the color left the world, then returned as the lids rose. The eyes rolled up until mostly white showed.

"Someone put a spell on you to blind you." I reached out, my hand a black spider against the green and red and dark glow of vines and flowers. "Do you want to be free?"

"Make it stop," Gareth said.

"I'm not talking to you," I muttered. With my shadowy hand, I touched the roses caging his vision, pressed this stem and that. A thorn bit my finger and I sucked in breath. Itching tingle spread from the puncture. The eyes stared at me. The shadow cloaking my outstretched hand faded as the itching tingle spread from my finger to my palm, and up my arm. My powers leached away as the shadow faded, revealing nothing but normal flesh, blood, and shirt.

Damned spell! Could it kill my witchness? I never thought anything could. In trying to save Gareth, was I dooming myself to being normal?

Before my darkness left me entirely, I murmured power words and picked more carefully through the roses, looking for help. The thorns sprouted and pricked my hands again. Weakness spread through me. Both my arms were bland.

Near the base of one of the vines, I found an aphid like a small hard bump, then another. I rested fingertips on their backs. "Small things, strengthen; change the balance. Shift the spell, let loose the sight. Sip the sap and wreck the roses; give me back my stolen might," I murmured, putting the remnants of my power into it. The aphids listened and grew strong, sucked the lifeblood out of the rose spell until it withered and fell away. They nestled in my palms, gleaming soft, fuzzy green, the size of kiwi fruits, full of the power they'd sucked from the spell.

Gareth groaned. "Stop it, Terry! Whatever you did, make it stop!"

I exchanged a glance with the eyes. They blinked again, then the lids closed, slowly, and all the extra color faded from the room.

"All right," Mom said, "what was that, Terry? Did you break a rule?"

"I just did what I said. We saw what Gareth would see if he used his witch senses."

"What, all that?" he said. "That was crazy."

"You have to get used to it." I sat in a chair at the table and rubbed one of the aphids against my cheek. So soft. It made a small, vibrating sound like a purr. I was exhausted, and a little worried: the rose had poisoned my power. My defenses were weak, now; if anything with power came at me, I could be badly hurt, though not destroyed, because of my secret protection. I needed to find a spell to restore me.

Chances were the rose spell had also poisoned Gareth's powers somehow, maybe paralyzed them. Now that it was gone, maybe he could get some joy out of his power. Maybe he'd be grateful. I hoped so. I wanted to use him in many different ways. "That's where you begin with your powers," I said. "See what you can see. Then decide how you want it to change, and work toward that."

"What does this have to do with those spells you sell?"

"I decide what the spells will do. I infuse them with power and direction. Once I craft the spells, other people can use them."

"You hypnotized me," Gareth said.

I sighed and rested my hands on the table, palms up, with the aphids in them. I wasn't sure what to do with my new friends. They solved the problem for me, sank into my palms. A flush of unfamiliar power flowed through my veins, mixed with the power the roses had sucked out of me, now come home.

I leaned back and closed my eyes, felt this foreign power move through me. It was a slivery power, like bamboo under fingernails, a power with hate in it, and strength, edged with elegance and beauty. "Tell me who you belonged to," I whispered, and learned about Gareth's mother, forced by her mother and grandmother to use her power when all she had wanted was to be normal. They put a geas on her to pass her power to her daughters, but none of her daughters had been born gifted. A boy with gifts was an abomination. When she discovered Gareth's gifts, she locked them in a hedge of roses and put them to sleep. This was a power she had to renew constantly, as his witch eyes struggled to open.

And in the meantime, with that geas on her, continually unsatisfied, she twisted up in some truly unpleasant directions.

I accepted the foreign power as part of my arsenal. Strange to meet power darker than my own. Everyone I knew in the witch community thought I was the bad guy, the unnatural one who forced people into things against their will. I was as capable as Gareth's mother of mistreating other people.

I would take joy in foiling her.

Gareth shook my shoulder. "Terry?" he said. "Terry—it's happening again."

"What is?" I asked.

"The world looks screwy!"

I straightened and rubbed my palms together as a final thank-you to the aphids. I felt not only restored after the rose's poison but augmented.

I glanced around. The room seemed normal. I studied Gareth, and realized his aura had awareness in it now. He looked all around, panicked.

"Your witch eyes are open now, Gareth. You can close them if you don't like it, but you can also open them whenever you want. What you see, you can change."

"Can I change you? You look like the Grim Reaper."

"Really? Skull and all?"

He stared at my face. "Mostly it's the dark cloak. I guess I can see your face. Are you smiling at me?"

"I am, Gareth."

"How come your mom has a moon on her head?"

"I don't understand that myself. It's not there when I look at her. Have you figured out how to close your eyes yet?"

He glanced around, looking hunted again. Mom got to her feet, shaky, and went to the coffee maker for a refill. She had some experience with weird witch effects—most of them from my sister, who was allowed to witch around the house, since she didn't hurt anyone. Mom hadn't had enough exposure to be relaxed about it, though.

"I can't—oh," said Gareth. "Oh, it's all gone again. Okay, good."

"Terry. Explanations?" asked Mom. She dumped extra sugar in her coffee and drank.

"Gareth's mom put a spell on him to close up his powers. Did you see the roses?"

"I did. Thanks, by the way, for making me part of the equation."

I couldn't tell if she was being sarcastic, but, even though I hadn't planned for her to see everything, I was glad she had. It meant she knew more about Gareth's problem. "She planted those to keep his powers asleep. She tends them constantly to make sure he's crippled. My spell messed hers up. Now his powers are awake, but he doesn't know how to use them. Can Gareth live with us, Mom? If he goes home, his mother might shut him down again."

Mom's frown was ferocious, but I knew she'd cave. She had the softest heart of anybody I knew.

"I have rules," Mom said, the start of her consent.

Gareth moved into the guest room. We went back to his house the next morning, when his mother was at work and his sisters had gone to school, to retrieve his belongings.

The house had no witch vibes. It looked like a TV sit-com house, not distinctive, not identical.

His room was a sad excuse for a boy's room. There were red roses winding in the wallpaper, and no pictures of cars, airplanes, metal bands, or things blowing up. His clothes were all neatly folded or hung on hangers—no dirty laundry on the floor or draped over the desk chair. I was more of a boy than Gareth was.

I'd brought a duffle bag for him. He put everything in it very neatly, then stuffed his backpack with a bunch of books.

On our way to the front door, I said, "So where's the room your mom uses for her rituals?"

Gareth looked over his shoulder toward a doorway I hadn't noticed before—and that disturbed me, because now that I knew where to look, the witch vibes coming from it were incredibly strong. "We're not allowed to even open the door," he said, as I grabbed the doorknob. A stinging jolt shot through my hand, the same poison Gareth's roses had carried. I jerked back, shaking my hand. Weight in my other hand made me look: I saw one of the aphids, shrunk to the size of a marble, rising from my palm. As soon as it separated from my skin, I held it near the doorknob; it leaped the gap, fastened to the protect spell, and fed.

"What is that?" Gareth whispered.

"This is what freed you yesterday." I hadn't realized they could manifest again, but I was thrilled. Spellsuckers! A staggering number of household applications occurred to me. "I found them feeding on your mother's power-suppression spell, and helped them eat faster. They broke the spell for you. I wonder if they're yours?" The aphid on the doorknob was as big as a cantaloupe. My right hand, still tingling from the spell jolt, unhosted the second aphid, and I set it to join the first.

When they were both the size of fuzzy, pale-green watermelons, the tiny scritching sound of their feeding stopped and they dropped from the doorknob. I caught one, and Gareth caught the other. "Do you want the power?" I asked.

"What?"

I cradled my aphid in both hands, and it deflated, feeding me spell power again, exquisite hate and strength, a hot syrup both burning and sweet. "Put it down if you don't want the power." My voice was hoarse as my body adjusted to this influx. I was lucky to have had a taste the day before, otherwise I could see this killing me, as poisonous as it was—or it could have killed me if I hadn't had my special protection. What if someone random touched the doorknob?

I directed the power flow into a fireproof box in my mind. I could store this power and dilute it for personal use later.

The aphid vanished into my palm again.

"It's stuck! Ouch! It burns!" Gareth tried to shake the aphid off his hand, but it clung, a gelatinous mass, and shrank. He keened, a high, mindless wail.

He didn't have the defenses to handle this. I grabbed his hands as the aphid vanished under his skin and followed floods of power along dried riverbeds inside him, places where his witch power ought to flow. I couldn't stop the rush of hot new power, but I could soften it by adding power of my own, cold power I rarely tapped. He gasped over and over, and I saw that his mother's power didn't poison him either. He had been living with the restriction spell inside him long enough to acclimate to it.

The power rushed through all his channels and reached the river's source, burst through a wall, and uncapped the spring inside. I had to let go of him then, he burned so hot.

He screamed. I covered my ears with my hands and waited it out.

Finally he collapsed, twitching, on the floor.

I went to the kitchen to get a glass of water. I wasn't sure that was the right prescription, but I figured it couldn't hurt.

When I rejoined Gareth, he sat up and took the glass from me, and my shoulders, tight as corsets, loosened. I hadn't been sure there was anything left of his mind.

"I feel sick," he whispered.

"I know." He could talk! I relaxed even more. "Do you need anything I can get you?"

"An explanation?"

I laughed, relieved he could ask. I rose and grasped the door-knob. It didn't bite this time. I turned it and pushed on the door, but the door rattled: it was locked. Mechanical protection in addition to magical. I knew a lot of unlock spells, though, and the first one I tried worked. "Let's see what we earned." I hauled Gareth to his feet. He staggered, straightened, wiped sweat from his forehead with the back of his hand.

I let go of the doorknob and stepped back, giving him the choice. He studied me, then gripped the knob and turned it.

First thing out of the room was a smell, cold and rotten, like a cave where corpses were stored. The door opened inward. Gareth pushed it and let it swing. The floor inside was painted a light-sucking, tarry black.

"God," he said. "I'm glad I never saw this before. I couldn't sleep in the same house with this again.

His mother's altar took up the whole far wall, a black freize with niches in it where tentacled god-statues lurked, some veiled with dark lace, others staring, visible and revolting. On the flat stone bench below, a large brass bowl held ashy remains of burnt things and a scattering of small charred bones. A red glass goblet was half-full of dark liquid. A scorched dagger lay between the goblet and the bowl. A carved ebony box stood on the bench, too.

One of the god-statues waved three tentacles at me. I'd had dealings with him before. For a dark god, he had a great sense of humor. I wiggle-waved back.

"Let's go," Gareth said.

"Wait. Look in there with your witch eyes. See if there's anything you need to take."

"What?"

"Look."

Along the side walls of the room—any windows had been covered over—there were shelves full of magical aids and ingredients, and a small library of hide-bound books. Gareth stepped over the threshold into the room. A shudder went through him as he stood in the heart of his mother's power. "What am I looking for?" he asked.

"Something that belongs to you."

"I've never seen any of this stuff before."

I shrugged. He examined the shelves without touching anything.

I wouldn't have touched, either. Everything looked dusty or dirty, even the ingredients I recognized.

After a tour of the room, Gareth stopped at the altar. He held his hand above the dagger, the bowl, the goblet, and finally the box. He lifted the box's latch and swung the lid up. Soft light glowed from inside. "Oh," he cried. His hand hovered, then dipped in. He lifted a fist and pressed whatever he held against his breastbone. When his hand lowered, there was nothing in it, and nothing on his shirt, either. He turned toward me. His face was alive with confused excitement.

The front door slammed open. "Who are you, and what are you doing in my house?" cried Gareth's mother. She saw the open door to her secret room, and shrieked.

"I'm the girlfriend," I said.

She stalked forward, her anger growing with every step, until her shadow towered above her, filled with lightning strikes in random directions.

"How dare you open that door?" she screamed, and then, when she saw that Gareth was in the room, she went silent, which was worse than the screams, though less ear-torturing.

At last she stepped forward, muttering words that hurt my ears. She slammed her left palm into my chest, sending a power-jolt through me that would have knocked me on my ass if I hadn't just processed a lot of her power. I was still humming with stolen strength, though, and her own power inside me shielded me from the new assault. She flicked her hand toward Gareth. A bolt of blue lightning shot out, sizzled through his shirt, scorched his chest. He staggered, straightened, planted his feet and faced her.

"Okay," he said.

She gasped.

"I got your eviction notice, Mom. I'm moving in with Terry."

"What?" She stepped toward him. She laid her hand on his chest. "You — what?" Her voice was a whisper now.

"Good-bye." He pushed past her, and her hand slid off of him.

She ran to the bench and opened the ebony box, gasped again.

By that time we had grabbed Gareth's things and were headed for the front door.

*

Mom made cocoa in the kitchen for us after Gareth had stowed his duffle and backpack in the guest room.

"He'll be able to pay rent and utilities," I said. "I'm hiring him as my assistant, so he should make plenty of money." Too bad his mother was so short-sighted. She hadn't known what a valuable asset she had. He was mine, now. Her mistake.

"Sure, sure," said Mom.

"I better protect you, Mom. His mother's really scary. She might come after us."

"Great," Mom grumbled.

"Are you okay with me spelling you a shield against her? She almost killed us."

"Terry!" Mom reached across the table and grabbed both my hands, clutched them tight. "Don't do dangerous things! How many times do I have to tell you?"

"I had to rescue him, Mom. You would have, if you saw what it was like at his house."

She softened. She reached for Gareth's hand. He ducked her, then stilled and endured her touch.

"All right," my mother said. "Protect me, Terry."

Strange, almost scary happiness shot through me. Mom didn't trust me with magic; she knew my track record. She was giving me a new and precious chance.

I so didn't want to mess this up.

"Open your witch eyes," I told Gareth, "and watch what I'm going to do. This isn't a spell I sell anywhere."

I conjured magical armor for my mother, and she sat still for it.

After we washed dishes and cleaned the kitchen for the night, I followed Mom into her bedroom, leaving Gareth to settle himself in his new space.

"Lots of changes," Mom said.

"Yeah. Thanks so much, Mom." I sat on the bed. "Sorry I had to spring this on you without warning."

"Do you actually like the boy, Terry?"

"I don't know yet. He's got a lot of garbage to get through before he'll be useful."

She ruffled my hair. "There's my girl. I wondered where you went, honey. You've been way too nice all day."

I laughed.

Mom went to her closet. "I suppose you want to play with the pretties." She pulled her jewelry box from behind a stack of shoeboxes on a shelf. Not a very secret hiding place. I had warded our house against burglars, though. She could have left the box in plain sight and it would have been safe.

I opened the box, touched the charm bracelet Mom's grandmother had left her, the pearls my father gave her on their twelfth wedding anniversary, the malachite earrings she had given to her mother, taken back after her mother died. Buried under a tangle of chains, pendants, and bracelets, some of them gifts my twin Tasha and I had given her for various birthdays and Christmases, I found my heart.

I gave Mom my heart for her forty-fifth birthday. I made it into a really ugly brooch, red enameled and gaudy, with rhinestones. It was heavy and awkward to wear. If she ever pinned it to anything, it would drag down the material.

She treasured it the way she treasured everything my twin and I ever gave her, but she never wore it, which was just as well.

I knew Mom would never break my heart the way Gareth's mother had treated his. She wouldn't use my heart as a tool to supplement her own desires. As long as I kept my heart safe and separate from my body, I could not be mortally wounded, though I could be hurt—a lot. Now that Gareth had reclaimed his heart, he would be vulnerable to kinds of assaults he had been immune to before. I could make that work for me.

I held my heart in my hand just long enough to warm it, then hid it among the rocks and metal in Mom's jewelry box. I closed the box and handed it to my mother. She tucked it away.

She kissed my cheek good-night.

HERE WE COME
A - WANDERING

Matt Black met the moss man on Christmas Eve.

She was sitting on a stone bench in a pioneer cemetery, with a wall of ivy-covered brick at her back and a brown paper bag full of past-their-expiration-date plastic-wrapped sandwiches beside her. The short cool daylight faded. Mist bred in the low spots and spread. The damp in the air smelled like winter, dead leaves, iced water, chill and no comfort. Matt was glad of her thick olive-drab army jacket.

She liked the look of the old mossy gravestones in the brushy grass, some tilted and some broken, but all mute against the wet shrubs and vanishing distance. The people who had come here to commune with the dead had all died, too; no fresh dreams troubled the stillness. This was as close to nature as she liked to get, a tamed wilderness only a short walk away from a town where she could go to find warmth and comfort after she had had her supper. Here, there were still plenty of human-made things she could talk with if she wanted conversation, but she could see a forest too, gauzed in mist and twilight.

She unwrapped one of the sandwiches and sniffed it. Roast beef and yellow cheese. It smelled fine. She took a sample bite, waited to see if her stomach would tell her anything, and then ate the rest of the sandwich. The bread was dry and the edges of the cheese hard, but it was better than a lot of other things she had eaten.

Her stomach thanked her. She opened another sandwich, ham and swiss, tested it, and ate it.

She was sitting and feeling her own comfort when she noticed there was some dreaming going on to her left, a quiet swirl of leafy images emerging from the layers-thick ivy on the wall. She wondered if she were seeing the dream of a plant. She had never seen a plant dream before, though she could see what people dreamed, and what things shaped by people dreamed. This seemed like a strange time to start understanding plants.

She turned to get a better look at the dream, and it changed. The leaves wove together into green skin, the skin smoothed and formed a man, and then a man all green stepped away from the wall, shaking his head slowly.

Some texture in the sound and smell of him told her he was no dream at all.

Matt grabbed the loose plastic wrap on the bench beside her and asked it if it would cover the man's face if she threw it. It said yes. If he came at her . . . she touched the bench she was sitting on. It was too old and sleepy to mobilize. She put her feet on the ground and tensed to run.

The man blinked. His face looked like a mannequin's, no real expression, no movement of the tiny muscles, a polished and unreal perfection to the features. He turned and stared at her.

"Who are you?" she asked after the silence had stretched.

"Edmund," he said.

"What do you want?"

"Nothing," he said.

"Nothing? Why'd you move if you don't want anything? You could of just stayed in the wall." She had never met anybody who wanted nothing.

"It was time to move," he said. Something was happening to his skin in the waning light; the green faded, left tan behind. His clothes and curly hair stayed green. She hadn't noticed the clothes until the rest of him changed. T-shirt, pants—green, mossy even; tan arms and face, hands and feet. It was freezing, but he didn't seem to feel the cold.

"Want a sandwich?" she said.

He stretched and yawned. He came closer. She had thought his expression was wooden, but now she saw it was more like ice, frozen . . . though thaw was coming. He blinked. He finally smiled. It changed her image of him completely: he looked friendly and almost goofy.

Still gripping the plastic wrap just in case, she scooted over, leaving room on the bench. He sat down.

She peered into the brown paper bag. "Looks like I got a tuna and a ham-and-cheese left. The tuna might be bad. Fish goes bad faster than cured meat."

"I'll try the ham-and-cheese," he said. "Thanks."

She gave him the sandwich. He struggled with the plastic wrap. His fingers didn't bend right yet. She grabbed the sandwich and un-wrapped it for him. "How long you been part of a wall, anyway?"

"I don't know," he said. "I wonder if my car will run." He bit the sandwich and chewed, abstracted, as though he were listening to his mouth. "Hmm."

"It's Christmas Eve," Matt said when he had finished the sand-wich and sat watching her, smiling faintly.

"Huh," he said. "Been a wall a couple months then, I guess."

She opened dream-eyes and peeked at his mental landscape. A forest clearing, with a single tree rising from the center, sunlight stroking one side of its trunk. Wind blew and the tree leaned into it as though its bark were skin, its core supple. The leaves wavered and flickered, winking diamonds of light.

Not threatening, but not clear, either. "What were you doing in the wall?"

"Standing still."

"How come?"

"That's how the spirit moved me."

"Huh?"

He shrugged. "I just wander around until something tells me to act. I happened to stop here a while back, and the wall spoke to me."

Matt felt a stir inside. She traveled far and often, and had been talking with human-made things all over the country for years. She'd never met anyone else who talked with them. "What did it say?"

"'Come here.'"

She glanced back at the wall under its cloak of ivy. —Did you say "come here" to this guy?— she asked it.

—Yes,— said the wall.

—Why?—

—I wanted him.—

Nothing ever seemed to want Matt, though lots of things enjoyed meeting her, and most of them were nice to her. —Why?—

—He's a certain kind of brick. He's hot. He makes everything fit better.—

Matt looked at Edmund. His eyebrows rose.

"You're a brick?" she said.

"A brick," he repeated, with a question in it.

"Wall says you're a brick. A hot brick."

"What?" He glanced at the wall. He reached out and placed his palm flat against it.

Seemed like he hadn't heard her conversation, then. Matt felt better. She had been talking to everything for a long time without other human beings hearing her. She didn't want to be overheard.

Edmund's arm stained brick red.

—What's he doing?— Matt asked the wall.

—Connecting,— the wall said. —Are you talking to me?— Its voice had changed slightly.

—Am I?— Matt looked at Edmund. His mouth opened slightly, and his eyebrows stayed up.

—Yes,— said the wall. "Yes," said Edmund.

Matt swallowed. —This is so strange.—

—Yes.—

Slowly he pulled his hand away from the wall. His skin faded to tan again. He held his hand out to Matt. She stared at it without touching it.

"What do you want?" he asked her. "What do you need?"

"Me? I don't need anything," she said.

"I'm here for you."

"What?"

He dropped his hand to his thigh. "I follow as the spirit leads me," he said. "It led me to you. Let me know when you figure out what you want."

"I take care of myself," she said.

"Yes," he said.

"I don't need anything else."

"All right."

"What do you want?" she asked him again.

He smiled wide. "Nothing," he said again. "Guess that makes us a match."

"I don't turn into a brick," said Matt, unnerved. She hadn't realized until this moment how much she valued being different and special, even if no one else knew just how special. She knew, and that had been enough. She didn't want this man to be anything like her.

He said, "Would you like to be a brick? I like it. It's nice being part of something so solid."

Nina Kiriki Hoffman

"No." Matt shook her head. "No, no."

"Okay," he said. He pulled his legs up, bent knees against his chest, and gripped his feet.

She watched him for a while. His feet and hands started to gray to match the stone bench, and then the dark grew too heavy for her to make out details. "Uh," she said. "I'm going back to town now. Nice to meet you."

"I'll come with you."

"I'd rather you didn't."

"Oh. All right. Thanks for the sandwich."

"You're welcome." She stood and walked away, chasing mist whenever she could.

She found a newspaper in a phone booth and scanned the page of church services, picked an early one. She liked churches on Christmas Eve, the pageantry, the carols, the candles and greenery, the warmth, the smells of hot wax and pine and incense and perfume and even mothballs from some of the fancy clothes people wore. She liked the idea that a kid born in a cave could be important.

She settled in a back pew and watched everything with interest. Children thought about presents, those opened and those still waiting, full of promises. Some of the grownups did too. Some people were thinking about the service, and some were thinking about going to sleep. Some were remembering their dinners. Some were worried because they hadn't finished wrapping things or they hadn't found the right presents, and others were happy because they had done what they could.

A woman in front of Matt kept thinking about washing a mountain of dishes. She would sigh, and start the task in her mind again, go through it dish by dish, each spoon and fork and knife; and sigh, and start again.

Matt tuned her out and focused on a child who was watching the candles and listening to the singing and thinking about the words of the songs and making the flames go in and out of focus, flames, flat disks of light, flames.

A child in another place looked at every scrap of red clothing, hoping to glimpse Santa Claus.

A man cradled a sleeping child. When he looked down at her he saw his arms full of golden light.

Another child looked at the priest and saw angels behind him. Matt wondered if the angels were really there. They had beautiful smiles and kind eyes.

The church was full. It lived and breathed, a big organism full of different cells and tissues, everything cooperating.

Matt kept an eye out for the moss man. What did he want from her? He wasn't a normal human. She couldn't guess which way he'd jump.

She didn't see him again until she left the church. She was walking through a quiet neighborhood talking to houses she passed, asking any of them if they would like some extra company tonight, and listening to their stories about the festivities they had hosted, the lighted trees they held inside, the way their humans had dressed them in jewelry of lights, when an old rust-blotched brown Volvo station wagon pulled up beside her, its engine surprisingly quiet considering its exterior, and Edmund leaned along the seat and said out the rolled-down passenger-side window, "Want a ride?"

"What?" she said.

"Want a ride?"

"No," she said. She wondered if she should run.

He pulled the car over to the curb and turned off the engine. "Want company?" he said, and got out. He had on hiking boots and a short dark jacket now.

—What's with this guy?— she asked the car.

—He won't hurt you,— the car said. Its voice was gentle and warm and somehow feminine.

—Do you know what hurts?—

—Yes,— said the car. —At least I know some of the things that hurt people. Edmund won't hurt you.—

"What do you want?" Matt asked Edmund for the third time.

He rounded the front of the car and stood near her. "I want to walk around with you. I want to take your hand. I want to make sure you're warm enough tonight, and safe."

"Why?"

"Because that's where spirit is leading me."

She reached out her gloved hand and he took it, his own warm through the leather of her glove, his grip firm without threatening. "Thank you," he said.

"I don't get it," she muttered.

"That's okay." He moved to stand beside her, still holding her hand, and said, "Would you like to walk?"

"All right."

They walked without speaking for a while. Matt watched the way their breaths misted in front of them, and the way the mist globed the orange streetlights, as though fires floated on air, or small clumsy stars dipped low. He was tall beside her, his hand warm in hers, his footsteps almost silent. It took a while for her defenses to gentle down, and then she realized that it felt good to walk with another person. She couldn't remember the last time she had done it like this—if ever.

"Sometimes I feel like I might just float away," he said presently. "I have a sister. I visit her once in a while. It keeps my feet on the ground."

"I saw my sister last spring." Matt had talked to her sister last Christmas for the first time in years. In the spring Matt had hitch-hiked across the top of the country from Ohio to Seattle, catching rides sometimes from people and sometimes from friendly trucks, who opened their back doors to her at truckstops and let her out at other truckstops when they were about to turn away from her route.

Seeing Pam had been strange and difficult. Matt and her sister had started out from the same place and gone such different directions that they had almost no common ground left. Pam and her husband had offered Matt a room to stay in, and help finding a job. Matt had fixed a broken dishwasher and repaired a reluctant vacuum cleaner and a tired clothes dryer, and then she had hugged Pam and left.

"Mostly I just wander from one place to the next," said Edmund, "waiting to be needed for something, then trying to figure out what it is."

Matt wandered too, always looking at things. Sometimes she helped people, but she didn't go around looking for people to help. "What about what you want?"

"I don't know," he said. They walked farther. "I used to do what I wanted, and then one time I did what I wanted and it was the wrong thing. Scared me. I wasn't the person I wanted to be. So I decided to be the opposite."

"And things want you?"

He nodded. "Sometimes it's nothing urgent. The cemetery wall had been falling to pieces for ages, and it could have gone on disintegrating without disturbing the integrity of the local space-time continuum." She looked up at him. He smiled. "I know, I can't believe I talk like that either. Especially when I'm not used to talking at all. The wall wanted to be pulled back together. I wasn't busy, so I melted in and helped the wall collect itself and strengthen its bonds with its pieces. Then just as I finished, there you were."

"What makes you think I'm your next project?"

"That's the way spirit works. I finish one task and then comes another."

"So what are you supposed to do about me?"

He shook his head and smiled. "Maybe nothing. I know you don't need me or anybody."

She stopped in the darkness between streetlights and stared across the street at a house draped with colored blinking lights, realizing that the lights blurred because her eyes had heated with tears. Something inside her tremored, small shakes at first, which worked their way outward to her edges and turned into big shakes.

"What is it?" he murmured.

"I—" She gripped his hand harder.

He stood beside her as she shook, and then he stepped closer and slid his arms around her. She held onto him, pressed her face into his chest, smelled his strange wood-smoke and spring skies scent, and felt the choke of sobs welling up in her throat. She fought them back down, wanting to not cry in front of this stranger or against this stranger or anywhere near this stranger. She held it all in. She had not cried in a thousand years. Especially not where anyone else could hear.

He stroked her back, a gentle rub up and down of his hand over her shoulder blade. He was warm and smelled like wool and fire.

—What? What are you doing to me?— she cried without voice.

—Just waiting,— he said.

—Stop pushing!— she screamed.

He stood quiet; his arms embraced her without force. She knew she could free herself with a step backward. He did not move except for the slow exhalations and inhalations she could feel and hear beneath her cheek and ear, and the faint bumping of his heart.

—Just waiting,— he said.

Something was pushing. Something inside her. It pushed up from her chest into her throat. It hurt! Her head felt fever-hot. Then a sob broke out of her, and another, and then they were coming out, wave after wave, and the hot heavy pushing thing eased. She shook and cried, loud gulping embarrassing sobs, her nose running, her throat bobbing open and shut, and he stood quiet and just held her.

Once she stopped trying to stop herself from crying, she felt much better; she just let the sobs and tears come out however they seemed to want to. Inside her crying, she lost track of everything else, another luxury she hadn't had in all these recent years of hyperawareness of everything around her. She worried because she didn't know how to stop crying, but somehow she let that worry rise and fade like the others.

When at last the sobs died away and all her impulse to cry was gone, she couldn't understand where she was. She was warm straight through, and lying on something hard but not flat, more bumpy and falling away at the sides. She felt as limp as an overcooked noodle. She lifted her head. There wasn't much light, but she could make out a face below her, peaceful, sleeping, smooth as a statue's face. Arms around her. A blanket over her? She wasn't sure about that part.

She listened to their breathing and realized they were someplace small.

Her arms were down at her sides. She sneaked them up until she could push away from what she was lying on. The arms around her fell away. She looked down into the face, and realized it was that guy, Edmund, realized that yes, she was lying on him, on top of a guy, something she hadn't done on purpose since the zoned years. His eyes opened. He looked at her, his face serene.

"You okay?" he asked.

She rubbed her nose on her sleeve. "I don't know. What happened? Where are we?" She looked around. They were in a small enclosed space, but she could see windows now. Car windows, all steamed over.

"We're in my car. I have a futon in the back where I sleep sometimes. It seemed like a better place for crying than the middle of the sidewalk on a freezing night."

"Let me out." She scrambled off of him and crawled over to one of the doors, frantically searching for a handle, finding one, pressing, pulling, twisting. Trapped. Everything in her screamed panic.

He was beside her. He edged his hand under hers and opened the door, and she fell out into the street. She jumped up and ran.

A block. She turned a corner. She scanned for a hiding place, saw a low fence and a dense tree, jumped the fence, hid inside the shadow the tree's branches cast. She slowed her breath and tried to catch up to herself.

Nothing followed her.

Usually she found a refuge for the night in something human-built that welcomed her, someplace warm, but tonight she curled up on the cool damp ground in the treeshadow, stilled her mind, and searched for sleep.

She lay hugging her knees to her chest for a long while, her knit cap pulled down over her ears. Her neck was cold, and her ear, with only a layer of cloth to protect it from the earth, was freezing. Cold air inched up her pantlegs past her thick socks. Usually she could shut those sensations off one by one and feel comfortable and safe, and then she could sleep.

Tonight she felt strange. Her head felt floaty. Lightness was all through her, as though she had taken an unfamiliar drug. The cold, which she knew from experience wasn't enough to kill her, kept telling her it was there. She put her gloved hands up around her neck. The smooth outsides of her gloves were cold against her bare skin, and woke her more than cold air had.

She sighed and sat up. She did her best to take good care of herself. She loved her life, even though some of it was difficult. She wanted to be warm.

She remembered how warm she had been inside Edmund's car, and how strange that warmth had felt. His arms around her, not tight, but enough to let her know she was being held. She thought of being his project and didn't like that at all. Who was his spirit to decide that he should work on her? She knew that everything had spirit—she talked to the spirit in many things—but she had never felt like spirit was ordering her around, making her decisions for her. Maybe Edmund was deluded. Maybe his spirit only applied to him.

Even if he was deluded, he had been nice to her.

She stretched and edged out from under the sheltering branches. She crossed the lawn, hopped the fence, and knelt on the sidewalk. Then she pulled off her glove and touched the cold cement. —Edmund?— she asked it. —Moss man?—

—No,— said the sidewalk.

—Do you know the one I'm talking about? Do you know where he is?—

—I'll ask.—

The thread of question rippled out around her. She sat down, waiting while cold seeped through the seat of her jeans. She had asked long-distance questions before, and gotten answers. She wasn't sure how the sidewalk would recognize Edmund when it found him, though.

The mist made the night seem quiet, almost dead. Porchlights and Chrismas lights and streetlights blurred and hazed only a short way from her. She reached out and touched the fence beside her to make sure it was still there.

She didn't even hear his steps, but she saw him come out of the mist. He knelt in front of her and smiled gently. "Hi."

She opened her arms and he edged forward and scooped her up, then rose to his feet. Carrying her, he walked for a while. She clung to him, for a moment trying to remember the last time she had been carried, had reached for the one carrying her, had leaned against his warmth and felt so safe and strange. Her mind blanked.

He stopped and loosed one of his arms to reach for the back door of his car. It opened without sound. He leaned forward and set her on the mattress. It was warm. The inside of his car smelled like mountain pine and desert sagebrush. She crawled into the shadowy hollow and he came in after her, pulling the door shut behind him.

She crept up toward the front of the car and leaned against the back of the passenger seat, tucked hat and gloves into her pockets, and waited for the warmth to thaw her edges.

"Thirsty?" he asked after a little while.

"Guess I am."

He opened what looked like a dark box and pulled out an oblong something that gurgled, then edged closer to her and held it out.

"What is it?"

"Water."

She reached out. Her hand touched his. "You're so warm," she whispered. "How do you stay so warm?"

"Spirit," he said. He shifted the bottle until she got a grip on it. It was plastic and cool.

She screwed the cap off and sipped cool fresh water. "Thanks."

"You're welcome. I'm glad you called."

"Why?" She drank more water, then capped the bottle and handed it back to him.

"I wanted to see you again."

"Why?"

"I don't know." He sounded frustrated. "I don't know. I need—I don't know what it is, but I need something."

"You need something from me? I thought spirit gave you everything."

"I thought it did too, until you left." He was quiet for a while. "There's an ache inside me now that wasn't there before."

"Oh, no. No." She remembered the void that opened within her sometimes when she left behind people she had liked. Often they invited her to stay. They showed her how she could live and be with them. She found comfort and friendship and warmth and a future, soil ripe for roots. The instant she thought of staying anyplace longer than four or five weeks, though, panic burned through her. The bottoms of her feet itched until she moved on. Distant roads called and carried her away.

Once the miles were behind her, she remembered how nice the places and people had been. She yearned for them. She mourned lost moments: orange marmalade on English muffins on someone's back porch on a summer morning; an old man reciting Robert Service poetry beside a crackling fire late one winter night; rubbing shoulders with a pack of wild dirty kids as they all hid in a hayloft together and watched confused grownups running below; sitting alone on grass and watching peoples' dreams during a concert of classical music in a park; stadium fireworks with an older couple one Fourth of July. Losing them hurt. But she never went back.

"You say no, but the ache is still there," Edmund murmured.

"I'm sorry." She reached for his hand. Held it. His fingers were warm, and gripped hers back.

"You feel it."

"Yeah," she whispered. "But I don't know what to do about it."

He slid closer to her, let go of her hand and put his arm around her shoulders. Feeling strange, she leaned against his chest. She pushed her hand down between the futon and the side of the car. —What does he want? What does he need?— she asked the car, since Edmund had never given her a straight answer.

—He needs four flat tires and no spare,— the car said.

"What!" A laugh startled out of her.

"What?" Edmund asked.

"Car says you need four flats and no spare."

He didn't say anything for a little while. Finally, he said, "Maybe I do. Do you ever feel like that's what you need?"

She shook her head. "No. No. I'd go crazy if I was stuck in one place."

"Are you sure?"

Yes. "No."

"I don't know," he said. "Maybe it's time I stopped following spirit around. Spirit's all over the place anyway. Maybe I'll stay here for a while."

"Here? A little old town in the middle of nowhere?"

"Why'd you come here if you thought that?"

"Because there's always something new and interesting every-where I go."

"Yes," he said. "Here there's a wildlife preserve that needs some preserving. I saw it this evening after we split up. Earth that needs re-vitilizing, water that wants unpoisoning, plants that need encourage-ment, animals that need better cover and more things to eat. I could work on that." He paused, then said, "You could help me."

"I don't do stuff like that." There was nothing she could talk to in a landscape like that, except maybe Edmund. She got along fine with appliances and machines; plants and animals were total mysteries.

"What do *you* want to do?"

"Right now, or tomorrow?"

"Right now."

"Go to sleep, I guess."

He laughed; she could feel it and hear it. "Merry Christmas," he said. He gripped her shoulders gently and edged her over, then eased her down onto the mattress so she was lying on her back, and she let him do it. He leaned and reached for something toward the back of the car, pulled it up over them—it was a quilt—and lay down beside her.

"Merry Christmas," she whispered.

*

During the zoned years she had awakened next to strange men as often as not, her head full of hangover, her body marked with bruises she couldn't remember how she had gotten, her psyche battered with scratches and aches that she would drink away before the next night fell. That was before things talked to her. Back then, even when people talked to her she mostly didn't care or understand what they were talking about. The important thing was to get as close to drowning as she could, because that was where oblivion lay. Everything else hurt too much.

This was the first time in the unzoned years that she opened her eyes from sleep to morning light and looked into a man's face so near hers. His eyes were closed. His breathing was slow and deep and smelled like mint.

It was also the first time she had gotten a really good look at his face. He looked . . . beautiful.

Pretty much everything looked beautiful if you studied it long enough, but he looked beautiful at first glance: clear tanned skin over clean planes of cheek and jawbone, straight narrow nose, heavy domed eyelids fringed with dark lashes, neat dark arched brows, a high clean forehead, brown curls touched with gold. His mouth smiled in his sleep.

One eye opened, the other squinting shut. His eye was green. "Hi."

"Hi," she said, and looked away. He was warm and near, but not touching.

"Did you dream?"

"I don't remember. Did you?"

"Yeah. I dreamed about when I was a kid."

"A different life," said Matt. Her mother had taken her shopping for dresses for the junior prom. "Try this one, Matilda." Matt had tried a lot of them, and every one produced a stranger in the mirror, a young woman with wavy waist-length brown hair and shaved legs and armpits, and sparkles down her front. She had looked at herself and wondered what her future would be. Would there be a prince? Would there be a glamorous job? College? Parties? Adventures?

Never in a million years had she imagined this future.

"Yes. How did you know?" Edmund sat up and stretched, his hands flattening against the roof of the car. Matt sat up, too, and turned to sit cross-legged, facing him. He said, "Before this happened to me and I had to figure out what to do about it, I had these friends. We did stuff every afternoon after school, dumb stuff like going over to someone's house and watching cartoons and eating sugar cereal straight out of the box, or riding our bikes fast down hills, just for the rush of wondering whether we'd be able to brake before hitting something at the bottom. We spent whole afternoons gluing little model airplane parts into planes. I wonder who my friends turned into. I haven't thought of them in a long time."

"You probably wouldn't know them now."

He smiled. "I think I'd know them. We were really good friends."

"Would they know you?" Matt remembered knocking on her sister's door in Seattle, having a man answer. His face had shuttered over right away. Matt had understood. It had been three states since she had been to a Laundromat, but only a few miles from the barber where she had gotten her head shaved; her last ride had been in the back of an onion truck. She had a black plastic garbage bag containing her belongings over her shoulder. Her army jacket was a map of her encounters with various kinds of dirt and grease. There were holes in her shoes.

"What is it?" the man had said in an almost kind voice.

"Is Pam home?"

"Just a minute." He closed the door. It had opened a few minutes later to reveal a heavy, long-haired woman who wore blue-rimmed glasses, and a long green dress that made her look like a queen.

"Pam?" Matt had said.

"Mattie? Is that you? Oh, Mattie!" Her sister swept her up into an embrace . . . just the way Edmund had picked her up last night. Warmth, comfort, and safety. With Pammy it had only lasted a little while. There had been too many questions afterward.

"I don't know if they'd know me," said Edmund. His smile widened. "Might be fun to find out."

"What about your preserve?"

"Maybe it's time to take a break from spirit work." A moment after he said that, his eyes widened, and he looked around at his car, at her, at the ceiling, as if waiting for a sign or a blow. Nothing happened.

"It would be hard to stop being a priest and then start again," Matt said. "Wouldn't it?"

"I don't want to stop." He sat still for a moment, staring beyond her shoulder, a worry dent between his brows. "I would try to stay in that state where I'm sensitive to signs of what needs or wants doing. But I would pick my path for a change, instead of drifting. I would ask questions because I want to know the answers, instead of to find out what I should do next. Is that all right?" He looked at the roof, at the steamed-over and frosted windows, toward the front of the car— Matt glanced forward too, and saw that the dashboard of the car was covered with dried leaves, curved driftwood, feathers, moss, acorns and seed pods, sea shells, egg shells from wild birds, a sand-dollar, a twisted silver gum wrapper, a religious medal, small rocks, some smooth and some sharp-edged, the shed skin of a snake . . .

The shed skin of a snake rose into the air.

Matt hugged herself. People had accused her of doing magic before, because when she talked to inanimate objects, they could animate themselves. She didn't consider that magic: it was a door's choice whether to unlock itself, a spoon's choice whether to stir itself in a cup of coffee. All Matt did was let things know they had those choices.

But this snakeskin wasn't moving itself. Something else moved it, something Matt didn't understand or recognize.

The skin drifted over the front seats and came to wind itself around Edmund's wrist, clinging for a moment before dropping off.

"Thanks," he said, picking up the skin and pressing it against his cheek.

"That's a yes?" asked Matt.

He smiled. "Change and growth. Merry Christmas."

"So you're going to go find your friends?"

"Yeah."

What if he found them and they didn't recognize or remember him? What if he found them and they didn't like him? What if he had changed so much they were scared of him? When she looked at him and thought of him stepping out of the wall of ivy, it was hard to connect him with a boy who watched cartoons and ate sugar cereal. What if he and his friends had no places where their edges met anymore? What if he were heading for disappointment, all on a bright winter's morning?

He was a grown man and a magician or a priest or something. He'd been on his own for years, the same way she had. He could take care of himself.

She thought of how the crying had pushed up out of her last night, a lost river from somewhere inside, dammed for who knew how long, and how Edmund had waited by the waterfall, not asking questions or making demands or talking or judging or anything.

What if he had a river like that inside him? Had he ever had someone to stand by while he let it out? Maybe his spirit took care of things like that, but maybe not. A spirit that sent you a snakeskin wasn't the same as somebody's arms around you when you were cold and sad.

"Can I come?" she said.

His smile widened. "That would be great."

That would be crazy. She'd never asked a question like that before. What did she think, she could help him?

Maybe she could.

PERMEABLE BORDERS

THE WISDOM
OF DISASTER

Irene and Naples March sat on the back porch in their natural-branch chairs, close enough to hold hands if they were so inclined.

Yellow porch light spread through the rain to the forest not too far from the back porch railing. Irene loved the night's smell. Rain on incense-cedars, ponderosas, mountain hemlocks, a spicy deep green scent. Water pattered as it fell among the needles, gushed from the bottom of the drainpipe beside the house. Was the smell enough to keep her content? No, the cold was creeping in at her sleeves and the hems of her slacks. Her fingers ached.

Their grandchild, thirteen-year-old Sara, had said good-bye to them ten minutes ago and headed off through the rain. If her mother asked her where she had been, which usually didn't happen, Sara would say the library.

Irene missed the child's presence already. Sara brought heat and love and excitement into the house.

Irene and Naples had both retired a handful of years earlier. Irene had found the time heavy since. They had never seen so much of each other in their younger lives.

Now they played cards every afternoon. They sat on the porch every evening. They had dinner and settled in front of the TV and watched movies on cable, arguing about whether they were any good, or read books, or sometimes, rarely, they got their instruments out of the cases and played music together. Why didn't they do that more often?

Sara came with questions. Sara came with complaints. Sara came, full of empty places for which Naples and Irene had the contents. Sara came, running away from home almost every day, running to a home she had only found three years earlier.

Naples and Irene had not known of Sara's existence until their son Max happened to hint about her in one of his letters from prison. They had found Sara when she was ten. Sara's mother, Christy, that drunk, wanted nothing to do with Sara's grandparents. Now Naples and Irene had a stealth relationship with Sara. It made life worth living. Sara came and Sara went. Irene wished she would stay.

For years now, before retirement and since, Naples made them both sit on the porch at five-thirty every night, no matter what the weather.

When their children, Kathleen and Max, were young, they'd gathered on the porch every evening. Naples played guitar, Irene played banjo, and they all sang. Real old-fashioned family nights. That was before Kathleen and Max turned into sullen teenagers and thought everything their parents did was stupid.

Now the kids were gone. Kathleen lived in Portland with her husband and four children. Max was in prison. It was just dumb luck that his ex-girlfriend, Christy, that drunk, lived in Marcola, close enough for Sara to run away to the grandparents' house.

Naples's porch-sitting habit was fine in the summer and fall, and maybe worth the discomfort in the spring. In the winter Irene hated the porch, even when she had a big mug of cocoa with lots of little marshmallows in it, like tonight. Her bones hurt, and her joints hurt. Anyway, the marshmallows were already gone, and they'd only been out here ten minutes.

Winter. Feh.

"I'm going inside," Irene said. She had said it before, but she never left before Naples was ready. Usually twenty minutes or a half hour of porch time was enough for him. Usually she managed to tolerate it.

"Stay," Naples said. "Just a little more."

She hitched the knitted afghan tighter around her shoulders and settled back in the chair.

A pounding sounded through the house. Irene stood up.

"What is it?" Naples didn't hear as well as he used to.

"Someone's at the door."

"Didn't hear the bell."

"Was no bell. Somebody's knocking." How many times had that happened? People couldn't see a perfectly good doorbell right there under the front porch light.

"All right, all right." Naples struggled to his feet. "I'll protect you. Let's go check it out."

He had a fear of the front door. She had learned to live with that. Easier if she answered the door before he knew anyone was there, because she could deal with the person and send them off, and Naples didn't go into a spasm of remembering every bad thing that had come in the front door, starting with the telegram announcing his father's death during World War II when he was five. If he knew someone was at the door, he always wanted to go with her or instead of her. She loved that about him, even when it irritated her.

The pounding sounded again as they crossed the kitchen and headed down the hall to the front door, loud enough that Naples could hear it now.

He grabbed a walking stick with a steel point from the umbrella stand. "Who's there?" he yelled through the solid oak door.

"Hello? Can we get some help here?" The muffled voice was male, mid-range.

"Who is it?"

"Nobody you know. I just found this girl on the street, and yours is the closest house. She's been hit by a car. I can't get any sense out of her. Would you call 9-1-1?"

Naples put his eye to the peephole, then stepped back, unchained and opened the door. Rain blew in, and air that was somehow colder than it had been out back. Kalapuya Road glimmered under a street-light a thin screen of trees away.

A tall, thin young man in a sopping tan raincoat, his pale curly hair drooping with wet, stood there, his arm around a wet, dark-haired, dark-eyed girl of about eighteen who stared past them. The girl's gaze didn't shift at all. Her mouth hung half open, and her flimsy gray top had a mud streak on the chest and shoulder.

Bad news, thought Irene. The curse of the front door. This time Naples is right.

Something in the contour of the girl's chin, the dome of her brow, seemed familiar. Where had Irene seen that before? Maybe she had had a cousin with just that shape of eyelid, long and crescent, and just that short top lip with the small puffy bulge in the center like a baby bird's beak, an invitation to a kiss. Surely some other cousin had eyes just that dark gray-blue, with the long lashes spiked by wet.

"Come in," Naples said, setting aside the stick. He took the girl's hand and tugged. She didn't move.

"I don't know if she can hear," said the man. He scooped the girl up and brought her inside. "She doesn't respond to anything I say. I was taking a walk when I saw her staggering along the road. A car sideswiped her. I don't know how badly hurt she is. I don't know if she's got ID."

"Phone's this way." Irene led him back toward the kitchen while Naples shut and locked the door. "We should warm her up. She looks like she's in shock."

"I don't know," said the man.

"I'll get the brandy," Naples said. He headed toward the living room and the liquor cabinet.

The man settled the girl in one of four yellow-backed chairs at the kitchen table. She stared at the fruit bowl in the center, at the winter oranges, South American bananas, and New Zealand apples.

The young man straightened, glanced around.

Irene dialed 9-1-1 and handed him the phone handset, then filled her chipped blue enamel teapot with water and switched the burner under it on high. No matter what happened, they would need hot drinks. "Want some tea?"

"Ambulance," said the man into the phone. Absently, he took the green dishtowel from the oven door handle and rubbed his hair with it. "Yes. I found a girl who's been in an accident on the road out here, and I brought her to this house—what's the address?" he asked Irene.

"Twenty-four Sixteen Kalapuya Road."

The man repeated it. "She doesn't seem to know who she is or where she is or what happened. She hasn't said anything since I found her . . . . She's breathing all right, but she keeps staring at nothing. She was hit by a car. Not very hard. We haven't had time to figure out where she's hurt."

He waited, the handset to his ear, his gaze on the ceiling. Rain gusted heavily against the kitchen windows, and wind rushed the eaves. A fugitive piece of popcorn burned up under the electric element on the stove, scenting the room delicious and then burnt. "No, she doesn't appear to be in any immediate danger. Okay. We'll be waiting for you. Thanks."

Naples returned with brandy, poured some into a jelly glass, and held it to the girl's slack mouth. No response. The stranger gripped the girl's head and tilted it back. Naples tipped a little brandy into her mouth.

She choked, coughed, spattered brandy over herself and the table, gagged, blinked. "Wah? Skireru nenaka?" She stared at Irene.

"Hello?" said the young man. "Are you all right? Where does it hurt?"

"Kiki klishu nenka na." Her voice was low and harsh. Irene heard pain in it. Something about the words reminded her of—

The teakettle whistled. Irene poured water into four fat brown mugs, dropped Lipton tea bags into them.

The girl rubbed the back of her hand across her lips. Her pale tongue darted out and ran along the margins of her mouth. She stared at Irene. "Ninki?"

"Not ninki," Irene said. What was that niggling at the edge of her mind? "Make sense. You're here now, not there."

"Ninki," insisted the girl.

"Ninki nix." Irene got an Oreo cookie out of the chicken-shaped cookie jar and handed it to the girl, who frowned at it, glanced up at Irene. "Geshta," Irene said.

The girl cocked her head, sniffed the cookie, then took a tiny nibble of one edge. After considering the taste, she took a bigger bite.

"Irene?" Naples said. "Irene?"

"Yes, honey?"

"What are you saying to her?"

"Excuse me?"

"You're saying strange words to this little gal. Do you speak her language?"

"No. Of course not. You've known me all my life, Naples. When did I have time to learn another language?"

"I don't know. Can't think of a single moment you were ever even interested in other languages. So what language are you speaking?"

"You're hallucinating." Irene got out teaspoons. She pressed tea from the teabags in the mugs, took the teabags out and threw them away, set a steaming mug in front of the girl. "Liltina?"

"So hai," the girl answered.

Irene went to the fridge, got out the half-and-half, poured a dollop into the girl's mug, turned to the stranger. "I made tea for you, young man. Would you like cream and sugar in it?"

"What?" He looked pale and confused. His hair, curly even when wet, was fluffing up into total blond disarray, and his cheeks were pallid.

"Are you all right?" Naples asked him. "Want some brandy?"

"Oh, no, thank you. Tea would be great. Cream and sugar, sure. Lady, who are you?"

"Who am I?" Irene added half-and-half to another mug and handed it to him, got the pink sugar bowl and held it so he could spoon out sugar. "My name's Irene March. Mrs. March. This is my husband, Naples March." She turned and dumped sugar into the remaining two mugs, handed one to Naples.

"Nice to meet you," said the young man, blinking. "I'm Jeff Silverman."

"Kishti?" Irene said to the girl.

"Kishti keka," the girl answered, holding out her mug. Irene added sugar to it, stirred. "Gitti!" The girl sipped and smiled. "Nataka nexi."

"You're welcome. What are you doing here?"

"Teka nenaka kilu obe ta—"

"Miss?" Naples interrupted.

The girl turned to him.

"Could you speak English, please?"

"Klefleh."

Naples glanced at Irene, and she stared back. "Irene. What's she saying?"

"What's she wearing?" asked Jeff. He set his tea on the counter and went to the girl. He held out a hand. The girl stared at it, then reached toward him slowly, her fingers spread wide. He slid his hand under hers, palm to palm, and raised her hand a little, leaned to look at the sleeve of her jacket.

Or was it a jacket?

Irene leaned closer too.

The dove-gray cloth with charcoal shadings formed a shirt or a jacket that clothed the girl's upper body from neck to wrists, flowed down across her chest and back to disappear, tucked into black trousers with pleated, baggy legs. The material of the shirt was slick and strange, already dry. Microfibers, Irene thought, even though she didn't know what they were. Or maybe it was vinyl, some kind of plastic. How could anyone wear plastic? Didn't it make you sweat? She touched the fabric on the girl's shoulder, felt a static shock that made a color flicker in her mind's eye: vivid blue.

"Keyaka," she muttered.

"Keyaka," agreed the girl.

"Irene!" Naples gripped her shoulder. "What did you just say?"

"Keyaka," said Irene.

"What does that mean, honey?"

"Keyaka? It means keyaka. What else could it mean?"

"I've never heard that word before."

"Naples." Irene straightened, went into the front room where they kept the dictionaries they used to work crossword puzzles and to look things up when they were having an argument about meaning, which happened every night, and was one of the sources of tension between them, though Irene thought that perhaps Naples enjoyed it, suspected that he started fights about words sometimes just for the hell of it. She brought back the paperback version of the *American Heritage Dictionary*, handed it to him. "Keyaka. Look it up."

He flipped through the Ks and stared at a page, then held it out to her. *Key, Francis Scott. Keyboard. Keycard.*

No keyaka.

Irene stared into Naples's face. Suddenly everything about him looked strange in the light of the kitchen fluorescents: his gray-blue eyes, narrowed over time from perpetually squinting at the sky. How they gleamed between the puffy, lined, lacework lids. The gray tufts of his eyebrows that peaked at the outer edges, the noble nose, the fissures that framed his mouth and chin, and the generous lower lip whose feel she knew pressed against the back of her neck when she was half asleep. All of him was known to her, and yet tonight he looked foreign, other, unknown, hewn from some material not flesh, something that had melted and would melt again into something even stranger to her.

"Honey." Naples's voice had a cough in it. The lids lifted over his eyes so she could see more of their crystal gray than she had seen in years. Was he seeing more of her, too? What did he see when he looked at her?

"Keyaka," said Jeff. He touched the girl's sleeve.

"Sei stela kishti!" She snatched her hand away.

The doorbell rang.

Naples went to answer, returned with wet paramedics in dark blue scrubs and semi-clear plastic rain jackets. They carried a stretcher.

"I'm the one who called. She seems much better now," said Jeff.

"We'll check her vitals," said the smaller of the paramedics.

"Okay, Miss, we just want to make sure you're okay." He reached for her wrist.

"Stela," Irene said. The girl looked frightened, but she let the paramedic take her pulse, look at her eyes.

"Can you tell me today's date?" he asked.

She looked at Irene, who said, "Pijala lila?"

"Nai."

"She doesn't know," said Irene.

"Nekruska ali komenta mia."

"She doesn't know what calendric system we're using here," Irene said. What a strange way to put it.

"Foreign," said the larger paramedic. "Ma'am, can you tell if she's in her right mind?" He gently ran his hand over the girl's head, maybe feeling for bumps. Irene saw the tension in her face. The girl forced herself to sit still.

Naples said, "Irene."

"What? What, Naples, what?"

"You're speaking to that girl in another language. Don't look at me as though I'm insane. Trust me."

Irene glanced at Jeff, who nodded.

"Well," Irene said, "that makes no sense whatsoever."

"Miska?" asked the girl.

"Plekora denza." Irene went to the counter, picked up her own mug of tea, and drank it just to get a strong hot taste into her mouth. That time she had heard the words drop from her tongue, words she didn't even understand. What was the matter with her?

The girl stood, came to her, laid the back of her hand on Irene's cheek. "Mashta," she whispered. "Mashta."

Mashta. What was that? The girl's hand was cold, harder than it should be, as though she were a statue come to life.

"Ma'am, can you tell us her name?" asked the larger paramedic.

Irene licked her lips and asked the girl her name, listened to her answer, turned to the paramedic. "She says it's Lilia."

"Last name?" He had a clipboard and was filling out information.

Irene spoke. The girl told Irene something, and Irene said, "Ikiltokletha."

"Can you spell that?"

"No."

"Can you repeat it?"

Irene repeated it slowly until he had written down something. "Can you tell us if she's wounded anywhere?"

Irene asked another question. The girl touched her shoulder above the mud stain on her shirt. Words flowed from her. The paramedics turned to Irene.

Irene set down her mug. What could she do but help? "Something hit her when she was walking on the road. She doesn't know what it was, only that it didn't feel like an animal. It was hard and big."

"Was it a car?"

Irene said something. The girl replied, and Irene nodded. "She doesn't know what a car is."

"That's way too weird," muttered the smaller paramedic. "How can she not know that? Is there a country in the world where they don't know about cars? If there is, how'd she get here from there?"

"Where did she come from?" asked the larger paramedic.

Irene consulted the girl, then said: "Tisilga."

"Does she want us to take her to the hospital?"

"No," said Irene.

"Is she in pain?"

"No."

"Well, we're done here, I guess," said the paramedic. "Just fill out this information for us, will you?" He handed the clipboard to Irene, who passed it to Naples. Naples did all their paperwork.

Naples looked at it and passed it back. "You need to do it, honey," he said. "I don't think I could understand her answers to these questions."

Irene accepted the form from him and actually read it. Name. Address. Phone number. Insurance number. Complaint. She looked at the girl. The clipboard dropped from her hand to the redbrick linoleum. "Naples," she whispered.

He came and put his arms around her, hugged her hard and tight. This was something she knew, and she relaxed into his embrace. He had held her this hard when her father died—she had been only nineteen then—and when her mother died, ten years ago, even though by then Irene was fifty-eight. He had held her this hard when they found out Max went to jail that first time.

"I'm sorry, ma'am," the paramedic said from behind her. "I can see you're upset. We just have to do our paperwork and then we'll be out of your hair."

Irene sniffled, resting in Naples's embrace, his scent, too long since he had changed this shirt, but that just meant it smelled more like him, a little sweaty and musky, with an overlay of Old Spice. She could be here inside his arms and forget that something strange was happening inside her, something for which she could think of no explanation, forget, perhaps, that there were strangers in the kitchen and that they weren't leaving right now.

Jeff knelt beside them, picked up the clipboard. He took it to the table and sat down beside Lilia. "You got a pen?" he asked the smaller paramedic, who unclipped one from his pocket and offered it. Jeff filled out the form quickly, consulting cards from his wallet a couple of times, and handed it over.

The blue-clad paramedics thanked him and left the house.

"I'm sorry I brought you so much trouble, Mrs. March," Jeff said.

Irene rubbed her cheek against Naples's shoulder, then straightened. Naples lowered his arms. "That's all right," she said.

Naples moved to stand beside Irene. He gripped her hand. "Young man, you said you were taking a walk when you found this girl," he said. "What were you doing walking in the rain?"

"I was—"

"You're not from around here, are you? We know our neighbors." Naples squeezed Irene's hand. In the years they'd lived here, they had watched other families come and go in the houses around them. Since retiring, Irene kept close track of everyone in the neighborhood. She had binoculars, and she kept a journal of who she saw from the front parlor window, writing down when she saw them and where they were going, if she could figure it out. It was one way she helped Naples deal with his fear of the front door. That, and getting everybody they knew to walk around to the back of the house to visit them.

"No, I—" Jeff said.

"Did you hit this girl yourself?" demanded Naples.

Jeff rose, his hands sliding into the pockets of his full-length raincoat. "I did not."

"Did you know her before? Do you know where she came from?"

"I don't," said Jeff. "I found her, just like I told you. Wandering around on the road, looking stunned and out of it."

"Tell me again what you were doing. Were you in a car?"

"No," said Jeff. Irene heard anger and frustration in his voice. "I was taking a walk."

"How did you see her in the dark?"

Jeff jerked his hand out of his left jacket pocket, whipped out something Irene thought was a pistol. Breath seized in her throat before she saw what it was. It was metal and yellow rubber—a long-stemmed flashlight. "Okay, old man?"

"Where's your hat?"

"I don't like hats. I never wear them. Okay? Will you stop with the third degree?"

"But there are too many things I don't understand," Naples said "This girl, you, why my wife can suddenly speak some language I've never heard before."

"That's pretty wild, I admit," Jeff said. "Mrs. March? Are you sure you've never studied this language? I know a little French and German, but this sure doesn't sound like either of those."

"It sounds like English to me." Irene looked at Lilia, who had sat silent since the paramedics left. She left Naples and went to the strange girl. "Lilia? Who are you? Where did you come from?"

"Tisilga."

"Well, sure, but where's that?"

"Nexar, on the Leyketh Node." The girl lifted her hand and slid her sleeve up to her elbow. The forearm above her wrist was wrapped in a flat wire mesh. Irene had never seen anything like it before.

"This," said the girl, "is what brought me here. It's phasic. I wasn't planning to come here. I didn't even know it was possible to get here, wherever here is. I was just trying to commute to my job. Do you have a jump node nearby? I should go home."

Jeff leaned closer, stared at Lilia's arm. She narrowed her eyes and covered the mesh with her sleeve, dropped her arm to her side. Jeff straightened, smiling a don't-mind-me smile, and took a step back.

"We don't have things like that," said Irene. "We don't have metal nets on our arms." She glanced at Jeff and Naples and saw they didn't understand, even though it seemed to her she was speaking English. This was so odd. She was glad she and Naples had watched all those *Star Trek* episodes over the years. "Are you from another world?" she asked. "Are you from the future?"

"I don't know," said the girl. "My sampler broke. I don't know where I am in relation to where I want to be."

"What language are we speaking right now?"

"Platonic," said Lilia.

Well, that didn't sound right. Irene looked at Naples. "What did you hear her say?"

"It all sounds like gibberish to me." He tapped his right ear, the one he was most deaf in.

"You?" she asked Jeff.

He shook his head. "I can tell there are words, but I don't recognize a single one."

"Lilia, can you understand us?" Irene asked.

"You," said Lilia. "The men are speaking noises."

Irene straightened, closed her eyes, and clutched her elbows. What had happened tonight? What had happened to her? She had more-than-ordinarily strange strangers in her kitchen, a strange language in her mouth.

Maybe it was a dream.

"Mrs. March—" Jeff said.

The back door opened a foot, letting in a gust of cold wet air and the sound of rain on the porch roof. Naples went toward the door, and Sara peeked in, her dark eyes wide and frightened. "Gramps?" she said.

Naples opened the door wider. "Come in, sweetie. What's wrong?"

"There's people here. I can go away again."

"They're just visitors. Don't worry about them. Come inside, get out of the wet. What's happened?"

Sara stumbled into the room. Her dark hair was plastered to her head and shoulders with rain, and her tennis shoes and sagging socks were mud-soaked. Her face was pale, the eyes stark and dark under her slanted lids. There was such a look of Max about her Irene's heart hurt. She was still wearing the school uniform she had had on when she had left, white shirt, plaid skirt, minus the raincoat, hat, and umbrella that had kept her dry earlier.

"Oh, honey!" Irene ran to her. "What's the matter?"

"Gramma." Sara began crying, or maybe she had been crying all along. Irene folded her into a hug: a cold, wet, stiff girl with sharp knees and elbows. Shudders traveled from Sara into Irene.

"Oh, baby. Oh, baby. Come get warm. Want some cocoa?"

"Gramma, I can't go home anymore," Sara whispered.

"That's okay. You don't have to. You can stay here with us."

216   *Nina Kiriki Hoffman*

"Mom said she'd set the police on you for kidnapping."

"What happened? What was wrong when you went home?"

"I went in just like always and took off my coat and hat and hung them up, put away the umbrella, set my schoolbag on the coffee table, and then she came out of the kitchen. She screamed at me. She screamed and screamed, and she threw couch pillows and two coffee mugs and a dictionary, said she'd been to the library and the librarian said I never went there, said she knew I was sneaking off to you and you would poison my mind against her. Said I was a horrible daughter and I didn't deserve to live. The mugs broke, Gramma. She hit me with the pillows, but she didn't hit me with the mugs. The mugs broke on the wall and pieces fell on the floor and the dictionary made a big thump when it hit the wall and ripped in half and she said I was bad and ungrateful and I'd been betraying her all this time and didn't I love my mother? What kind of child am I?"

"Oh, baby. Oh, baby." Irene held Sara and rocked back and forth.

"And I said I loved her I loved her and I don't think I really do, she scares me and I can't tell if I love her, but I said it, and she didn't believe me and she wouldn't stop screaming and I, then I just turned around and came back."

"That's all right. That's good. Don't you worry, honey. You can stay here as long as you like. We've got to get you out of these wet clothes and into a warm bath. Come upstairs with me."

"Irene," said Naples. He had closed the back door and locked it, something he didn't usually do.

Irene slowly loosened her arms from around Sara and turned to her husband.

He nodded toward the kitchen table, where Lilia and Jeff waited.

"Lilia, Jeff, this is my granddaughter Sara," Irene said. "She doesn't even have a jacket. I'm taking her upstairs to get her warm."

Jeff looked puzzled. "Mrs. March? You said something to me, but it was in the other language."

Lilia stood up. "I want to stay with you, Oma," she said.

"What?" Irene shook her head. "Never mind. Come with us if you want to. Come on, Sara."

"Gramma?" Sara, too, looked puzzled and upset. "Are you teasing me?"

"Come, sweetie." Irene took Sara by the hand and led her up the stairs. Lilia followed them.

In the upstairs bathroom, Irene ran hot water into the clawfooted tub. She got big fluffy towels from the linen cupboard. "Take off your clothes, honey. Let's get you dried off and then you can get wet all over again, only this time warm."

"But Gramma—" Sara looked past Irene to Lilia.

Lilia stood in front of the mirror. She touched the mud streak on her shirt, watched her reflection do the same, stared at the sink and fixtures, then glanced toward the tub where hot steaming water flowed from the curved tap. "Water?" she said.

Irene got a rag from the cupboard and wet it at the sink, held it out to her.

"What?" said Lilia.

"Don't you know how to do anything?" Irene pressed the wet cloth to Lilia's shirt, soaking up the dirt. It peeled off without much protest, leaving the material clean and new-looking. Irene touched it; the shirt already felt dry. "Well, look at that. That's a nice trick. Lilia, you have to stand outside the door now."

"All right, Oma. Don't disappear."

"I won't. Why would I?" Irene shooed Lilia out into the hall, then returned to strip Sara and help her into the tub. "You'll feel better when you warm up. Stay in the water for a while. I'll come back in a few minutes, okay, sweetie? I'll fetch your playclothes too."

Sara had a couple of outfits of Goodwill clothes that she and Irene had bought on their after-school afternoons. Irene left Sara soaking, fetched the clothes from the guest room closet, took them back to the bathroom to leave on the counter, then headed down the stairs with Lilia following.

In the kitchen, Jeff had taken off his raincoat to reveal that he wore an olive green sweatshirt and blue jeans underneath. He had on muddy, sopping-wet hiking boots. He sat at the table with Naples. They were drinking tea and not talking to each other.

"Have you found out what Jeff was doing out there?" Irene asked Naples. Lilia stayed beside her.

"He keeps saying walking."

"Young man, that doesn't make sense. Where did you walk from?"

"Downtown Marcola."

"That's three miles from here," Naples said. "Why would you walk all that distance on such a foul night?"

Jeff hesitated, stared at his pale hands splayed on the table's surface. "I knew something would happen," he said at last.

"You knew something would happen. What?" Irene asked.

"I didn't know what. I just knew something different and strange was about to happen over this direction, and if I walked here, I'd find it."

"Did you find it?" Irene asked.

"Of course." Jeff shifted his mug one way, then the other, glanced at Irene, then gazed at Lilia. Staring at her, he said, "I came up your street and I had this tightening in my chest and then light flared, the color of lightning, only it wasn't a streak or a bolt, more like a ball of light. Then there she was, staggering in the street. She was wavery and her mouth was open. A car was coming and she didn't even get out of the way. I couldn't reach her fast enough. It was one of those tall SUVs, and its bumper grazed her shoulder, and she stumbled backwards, and that's when I caught her and brought her here."

"You came out here to the boonies looking for a girl who had been hit by lightning, before it happened," Naples said, disbelief strong in his voice. "That's your story now?"

"That's right, old man," said Jeff.

"Oma," said Lilia, "what are they talking about?"

"We don't know how this young man came to be nearby when you arrived," said Irene. "My husband is suspicious of him."

"He helped me." Lilia went to Jeff, leaned to look into his face, glanced back over her gray-clad shoulder at Irene. "He helped me. I remember now. The Node blew out. I didn't go to Mixatla the way I meant to. A charge went through me. It's not supposed to do that. This is supposed to be a safe way to travel, absolutely safe. Even if something goes wrong you're supposed to be safe; if there's a problem, it's not supposed to work at all. A charge went through me and made me feel as though I were on fire under my skin. I fell into darkness. Something struck me." She straightened and touched her shoulder. "Then he came and pulled me away from danger. He helped me come to your home. He carried me inside. I remember."

"Irene?" Naples said.

"She says thanks to Jeff for helping her."

"She said more than that, Irene."

"Well, of course she did. She was somewhere else when this started. She was using a method of transportation she considers safe, and it broke down, and sent her here instead of where she was going. This was a confusing place to arrive, and she knows Jeff helped her."

"A method of transportation?" Jeff said.

"She calls it nodes. It has something to do with the metal on her arm. She said it was . . . phasic."

"Interesting," said Jeff.

"Say you knew something peculiar was going to happen," Naples said to Jeff. "Something like a girl being struck by lightning or falling out of nowhere. Why would you go find it?"

"That's my job."

"People pay you to go to places where weird things are about to happen?"

"They do if I pitch it right. Sometimes I find lost things for people. Sometimes the police call me in for consults. Sometimes I sell articles to the tabloids. Sometimes I just satisfy my curiosity. So far I'm not making a dime off this incident."

"Do you write for the *National Enquirer*?" Irene asked.

"Sometimes. They pay the best."

"A girl falls out of the sky. How often does that happen?" asked Naples.

"First time for that one," Jeff said. "Usually I find dead people."

"Oma?" Lilia said. She put her hand on Jeff's head, patted his now-dry blond curls.

"Yes, Lilia."

"He frightened me. He helped me, though."

"Maybe not for the best reasons."

"He has not hurt me."

Irene realized that Naples thought Jeff was up to no good. Why? Naples had bristled since Jeff came in the front door. Maybe it was the whole front door thing. Maybe it was Jeff, who had now presented a second self to them: was he some kind of psychic? Did he have a third self? Was he lying even now? If he was, what was the truth?

Naples got nervous about strange things sometimes. Often it turned out he was wrong. Every once in a while, though, he recognized something wrong she couldn't even see, like the time he pulled her back from one of the hiking trails at Shotgun Creek State Park and then a boulder rolled down the mountain, crashing through bracken and underbrush, knocking down young cedar saplings and crushing berry bushes, just where she would have been walking. She had clung to him and asked, "Why did you do that?"

"I don't know," he had said.

Now she asked Jeff, "So what do you plan to do next?"

"I don't have a plan."

"What's going to happen to Lilia?"

"I don't know. I think I was drawn to her to save her from the SUV."

"But you didn't, did you? She got hit, but she wasn't hurt bad," Naples said.

"She was shocky. Something else could have happened. She was headed for the ditch when I caught up with her. She could have fallen in and drowned, or caught pneumonia."

"You brought her to us," Irene said. "Where do you go from here? Are you planning to take her with you? You expect her to walk three miles to Marcola through the rain with you?"

"No," he said. "I guess I kinda thought she'd stay with you until you find her people."

"Why would you think that?" Naples asked. Irene realized she would probably have decided to help Lilia, only she believed there was no way for them to find Lilia's people. Lilia's people were in some other dimension. She and Naples were on a pretty tight budget now that they were retired. If they added Sara to the household, and Lilia too—

"Mrs. March is the only one who can talk to her."

"That makes her responsible?"

"Stop it, Naples. Of course it does," Irene said. "You boys play nice now. I'm going upstairs to see how Sara's doing."

"But Irene—" Naples began.

Irene turned her back on him and headed for the stairs.

Lilia stayed in the kitchen with Jeff and Naples this time.

Sara had fallen asleep in the tub, the red washrag drifted down to figleaf her, the yellow chunk of homemade soap at the bottom of the tub beside her left knee.

Irene dipped a hand into the water. It had turned lukewarm. She sat on the edge of the tub and looked down at her granddaughter in the cooling water. How thin the child was, how bruised her long-lidded eyes looked when closed; how young her body was, on the edge of womanhood, the breasts just starting to swell, knees and elbows still knobby and awkward. And yet her lips were already full of promise. How young her mind was, too; so young for thirteen, less sophisticated than many of the seventh graders Irene had known. Yet she had ages of the wrong kind of experiences. Sometimes her eyes were wise with all the dark things.

Tears had dried on Sara's face, faint rough traceries of salt on the downy cheeks.

What if Christy sued to get her back? Christy was a drunk and an unfit mother, but Irene hadn't had the energy to fight her before. Irene and Naples had come so late into Sara's life. Max had said something in a letter that made Irene actually drive a whole day to visit him in Walla Walla. He hadn't told her about Sara until she bullied it out of him.

Christy had been angry and confrontive when Irene and Naples went to meet her. "He never married me. You got no rights to my girl. Leave us alone."

Sara had been hiding in the hallway, just out of sight. When Naples and Irene left the apartment, she followed them down and introduced herself. She was ten back then. The strange confusion and love that had washed through Irene just meeting Sara, the instant feeling of connection, was still strong inside her. This was a child that wouldn't have existed without her and her husband. Blood of generations ran through Irene's veins, and Sara's too. They would always mean something to each other no matter where life took Sara. Irene loved her in a fierce way that made her want to kill anything that menaced her, and give heart's blood if that would please her.

Irene sat on the tub's edge and marveled at Sara's long elegant toes under the water. For a little longer she watched her granddaughter sleep. So strange to see peace in the child's face. At last Irene fetched a big fluffy maroon towel. "Sara," she murmured. "Honey? It's time to wake up."

Sara startled awake and slipped under water, then sat up with a gasp and a splash. "Gramma?"

"Yes, honey. You're here with me and Gramps. How you feeling?"

"Nice and warm."

"Time to dry off, get dressed, and come downstairs, unless you're ready to go right to bed. Are you hungry?"

Sara pulled the plug, stood up in the tub as the water gurgled down the drain, and accepted the towel Irene wrapped around her. "Oh, yeah, Gramma. I never got dinner." Her head tilted forward, hiding her face. "Gramma? I just remembered everything."

"Yes. It's a tough one, Sara."

Sara rubbed her hair with the towel, then dried off and stepped onto the purple bathroom rug. "Oh, Gramma." She swiped at an eye. "Gramma, Mom—"

Irene rubbed the towel against Sara's back, dried the back of her neck where the wet hair curled at the nape, reminding Irene of babies, their youth and innocence, stages Sara had passed ages ago. "Maybe things will look better in the morning."

Sara sighed and dressed. They headed downstairs together, Sara in her favorite clothes: a T-shirt with Spider-Man on it, boxy blue jeans with many pockets, and pink socks with flamingos on them, all special clothes she only wore at her grandparents' house. Now that Irene looked, she realized that the shirt was too tight, the pantslegs too short. Sara was growing; in clothes, she looked bigger and older than she had under the water.

The smell of popcorn came up the stairs. Irene's stomach growled. She realized that because of all the odd things that had happened, she and Naples had missed dinner too. What had she planned to cook tonight? Leftovers: the chuck roast in foil she had made last night, and half a loaf of pre-buttered garlic bread, which needed only fifteen minutes in a warm oven. There was a bag of salad in the crisper, including dressing and croutons and parmesan. Plenty for her and Naples. But now that there were five people—

Naples had popped a big bowl of microwave popcorn. Lilia held a double handful. She stared down at the small yellow puffs of corn and air, watched as Naples stuffed a handful into his mouth.

Sara went to the table and grabbed some popcorn. Jeff had a soggy notebook on the table in front of him, was scratching something onto lined paper with a ballpoint pen.

Irene saw Sara settled in a chair next to Lilia, within reach of popcorn, then went to the refrigerator and got out the meal she had prepared already in her head.

She put the leftover roast and garlic bread in the oven to warm and poured the salad in a bowl, added all the extras after she cut them out of their plastic bags within bags. "Did you decide anything while I was upstairs?"

"How could we, when we can't even talk to the girl?" asked Naples.

"Hello," Sara said to Lilia.

"Sigili nenka," Lilia replied.

Sara sent Irene a look of confusion. "Me Sara," she said to Lilia, tapping her chest. "Who are you?"

"Oma, what is the little one saying?" Lilia asked.

"She says her name is Sara. She wants to know your name. Why do you call me Oma, Lilia?"

"Oma is grandmother."

"Gramma." Sara pulled on Irene's hand. "What are you doing?"

"I'm talking to Lilia. That's her name, Sara. Lilia."

"Weird sounds came out of your mouth just now."

"Those are words."

"It doesn't sound like you, Gramma."

"Yes, I know. Jeff, if you're psychic, can't you give me a clue about this?"

"I never said I was—oh, well. It's not always a skill I can summon at will. Something just happens, and then I have to figure out how to process it. But I have heard of speaking in tongues—a gift of faith, as I understand it. God grants you the ability to speak some other language, but mostly it's used for testifying, and then someone else has to interpret for you. Always seemed like a wonderful opportunity for scamming to me."

"Nothing as strange as this has ever happened to me before. If God wanted to use me for something, why hasn't he gotten in touch directly? What you're talking about sounds stupid. Why would anyone think confusion was a gift?"

Jeff shrugged. "For my work, I don't have to understand things like this. I just have to figure out how to describe them. When Lilia talks about where she comes from, what does she say?"

"She said she's from Tisilga, in Nexar, on some kind of node, and she was trying to commute to work using her metal thing."

"What kind of job does she have?"

Irene asked, then wondered why. She still didn't know enough about Jeff to know whether she wanted to help him.

Lilia said, "I plisheth the kerupters."

Jeff waited for a translation, eyebrows up.

Irene shrugged, repeated what Lilia had said. "I didn't understand it either. Now, listen, everyone. Naples and I weren't expecting company for dinner. We don't have enough for everybody. We could order a pizza, or give you some toast."

"Gramma," Sara said, with tears in her voice.

"What, sweetie?"

"You keep talking funny."

Irene checked with Naples. "You said some gibberish, then you said you didn't understand it either," he said. "After that, everything you said was in Lilia language."

"I was talking about supper plans." Irene watched Sara's face, Jeff's, Naples. They nodded. "We don't have enough food on hand for everybody." She watched and they nodded again. "So we need to make some take-out plans, maybe, if everybody's hungry."

They looked confused.

"I don't need food," Lilia said.

"Do you—eat?" asked Irene.

"Yes. I have a personal food supply." She touched her shirt just below her collar bone, and a flap of the gray material lowered, showing more skin covered with metal mesh, plus a flat packet of something that looked like opaque lime green Jell-O strapped to her chest. "In an emergency, there is enough here to last me ten days." She reached for the hanging-down flap of her shirt to close it, then noticed Sara's fascinated stare. She held out a hand to Sara, who edged closer and lifted her hand to meet Lilia's. "You like this, little one?" Lilia said.

Naples slapped Sara's hand down so it was trapped on the table beneath his. "Don't touch her!"

"What?" Sara paled. "Grampa!"

"We don't know where she comes from or what she wants. Or what she can do."

Lilia's face clouded, her gaze on Naples's hand over Sara's.

Jeff tapped Lilia's shoulder, and she turned to him, her face shifting from the softer expression she had had while contemplating Sara. "May I look?" he asked, glanced at Irene, maybe in hopes of a translation.

Irene didn't translate.

Lilia kept her hand on the flap of her shirt that hung down. Jeff leaned forward to stare at her chest. She bore it for ten seconds, then touched a fingertip to his forehead. A sharp zzst sound, and Jeff and his chair lay on their backs on the floor, Jeff's arms flung out to either side. A couple things thumped to the ground in the pockets of his raincoat, which had been draped over his chair. His shoulders jerked, his hands twitched, fingers spasming, and his eyelids fluttered.

"What did you do?" Irene asked Lilia.

"He helped me. That doesn't mean he can examine me."

"Did you kill him?"

"No. Wait. I don't know. We're different, aren't we? He may not have the tolerance I expect in people I know."

Naples knelt beside Jeff and felt for a pulse. "He's still breathing," he said. "His heart's still beating. I wonder if we should call 9-1-1 again."

"Gramma," said Sara. She came to Irene beside the oven.

"Sara." Irene put an arm around her granddaughter. The kitchen smelled of chuck roast in onion soup mix and garlic bread. Dinner. How normal was that? An alien at the table, a psychic unconscious on the floor, and dinner was almost ready. Irene wondered if perhaps her head would float from her neck and bob around the room just under the ceiling. Maybe if she was lucky it would slip out of the house through the back door and float up into the rainy night sky.

"Gramma, I want to go home now."

The shock struck Irene's heart. "Baby? What's wrong?" *How can I ask her what's wrong, when everything's strange?*

"Mom throws things," Sara said, "but she—"

Irene stroked Sara's drying hair away from her face, looked down into the dark eyes.

"It's not quite as crazy as here." Sara's voice was small and fading.

Irene pressed her hand to her chest. Sadness rose in the back of her throat. How had her and Naples's regimented life, their five-thirty-every-night porch meetings, their movies on video or cable, their card games—how had all these things broken down?

She looked at Naples, who climbed to his feet and stood, dejected, beside Jeff's prostrate form.

"I'll take you home," Naples said to Sara.

"I'm so sorry, Sara," said Irene. "We'll send these people somewhere else. When you come tomorrow, they should be gone."

"Will you stop talking so I can't understand you?"

Could she promise that when she didn't even know why or how she was doing it? "I'll sure try."

"Mom'll probably be asleep by now."

"She never even called us to see if you got here all right," Irene said.

Sara closed her eyes a moment, opened them. "Maybe by tomorrow she'll forget I ran off."

"Maybe." Irene pressed a kiss to Sara's forehead. "Please remember you can always run away to us. We love you, Sara. That will never change. If you want, I'll kick these other people out of here right now so you can stay."

"No. I'll be okay at home. I think."

Lilia stood up, faced Irene. "What I did has caused you trouble. I'm sorry."

"Good," said Irene. "Don't knock people out in my house unless they're actively, and I mean putting their hands all over you, trying to attack you. Understand?"

"I'm sorry. I won't do it again unless I sense I'm in real danger."

Jeff jerked, shook, rolled off the knocked-over chair, worked himself into an upright sitting position on the floor. "Bwaaah," he said. "What happened? What was that? I feel totally weird now." He pressed his hands to his cheeks. "My head is jingling."

"Sara? Ready to go? I'll take you home," said Naples.

Sara hugged Irene, then went to her grandfather.

"Wait," said Jeff. "Are you sure? Why's she leaving? What's going on? What happened?"

"Lilia knocked you out because you were staring at her chest too hard," Irene said.

"Tell her I apologize. What's this?" He pressed his palm to his forehead, explored the place where Lilia had touched him, where there was a blue streaky burn mark. "What? It hurts, but—"

Naples opened the door from the kitchen into the garage. "I'll be back as soon as I can," he said to Irene.

Wait! They hadn't thought this through. Naples was going off with Sara and leaving Irene alone with two lunatics.

Sara felt safer with her drunken mother than with her sober grandparents. Maybe only when her grandparents were entertaining lunatics. They had to stop doing that.

Back porch, rain or shine. Cocoa with marshmallows. Arguments and snit fits, how silly could she and Naples be?

Irene said, "'Bye, Sara. Come back tomorow."

"I will, Gramma." Sara disappeared after Naples into the garage. Irene turned the oven off, though she was really hungry now. Even if Naples broke the speed limit, he wouldn't be back from taking Sara home for fifteen minutes. Besides, he should take her into the house and make sure that Christy, that drunk, was passed out and in no position to hurt Sara. Dinner would have to wait.

Meanwhile, there was still popcorn. Irene sat at the table next to Lilia. "You're not going to knock me out, are you?"

"I promised I wouldn't, unless you threaten to harm me," said Lilia.

"If you can poke people in the forehead with your finger and knock them out, I don't think you need our protection anymore."

"But—" Lilia's hands convulsed on the table. She stared down between them at the popcorn that had spilled from her hands earlier when she was showing off her food supply under her shirt. "But Oma, it's not your protection I want. It's conversation. I'm so alone. You're the only one who understands me." Lilia reached for Irene's hand.

Irene remembered Naples slapping his hand down on Sara's to prevent a contact with Lilia. His hunches had kicked into high gear. Were they right? Irene remembered that the next thing anyone knew, Lilia had knocked Jeff to the floor with a touch.

Remembered that Naples wasn't here to protect her right now.

Lilia's hand floated down over Irene's. Warmth spread from it, and a confusion of something too close and familiar.

Oma.

She had a rover unit that fitted her lower body perfectly. Sitting inside it, she could slot herself into the world's traffic pattern and go anywhere she wanted on Nexar, but what she loved best was to flow into the pattern where her granddaughter Lilia spent her off hours. They roved together. Most of the other direct connections had skipped through the nodes to different homeplaces, where the fishing was better, or the sunsets had a different palette, or you could pipe direct into the ultra-consciousness of some other species, spend your sleep time living undersea in the mind of a kracken or a shark or a kleza. Lilia and Oma had discovered they liked each other more than they cared about anything else. They had the same taste in music and passive entertainment and even food. They held structured arguments that entertained them both. They rooted in each other—

Almost thought the same thoughts—

And then one day Lilia woke, and Oma—
She was just trying to get to her job. Okay, maybe not her job.
Maybe anyplace Oma might have gone without her body. Maybe
some small part of Lilia knew how to rewire a phasic, transfer to a
different resonance that held more hope—
—Oma.
"I'll do anything you want if I can only stay with you, Oma,"
Lilia whispered.
Irene looked at the domed brow of Lilia's face, the contour of her
jaw. Even the color of her hair.
Lilia was what Sara would look like five years down the road.
"Oh, Lilia, your Oma is dead."
Lilia's face went white. Her cheekbones stood out stark above
their hollows, and the skin across her splendid brow tightened.
"You're not dead," she whispered, and, phantomlike, Irene heard be-
neath those words a repeat of some of the earliest words she had
heard Lilia say: "Kiki klishu nenka na."
"I am not your Oma." What was this hot red fire in her chest?
This heat behind her eyes?
"Kaki liklili," Lilia said. She gripped Irene's hand. Irene heard
the meaning overlay, but it was fainter now: You could be.
"I have work to do here."
"Ninki." A tear flowed from Lilia's eye. "Ninki, Oma."
Irene looked at the strange young woman sitting at her kitchen
table, at the gray shirt and black pants, mourning colors, and the flap
in the front of the girl's shirt that still hung open to the meshwork and
the food supply of someone who had prepared for a journey.
"Lilia. Niniki nix," Irene said.
Lilia broke into sobs. She rose and ran from the room to the front
hall. The front door did not open. A light flashed instead, and the air
smelled of ozone.
Irene pressed her hands over her heart. Such a short time she'd
known the girl. Why did every loss hurt so much?
Jeff stared after Lilia from where he sat on the floor. Then he
looked at Irene. "What did you tell her?"
Irene covered her face with her hands. "I told her I'm not her
grandmother. Oh, God."
"Did she think you were?"
"Sure. In a way I am. Somewhere sideways there was another me, I

guess, the one she loved most in all the world, and she used her commuter system to go sideways and find me again. But I can't go there for her. I have to be here in case Sara needs me."

Jeff sat quiet. Then he scrambled to his feet and sat at the table beside her, his scruffy notebook in front of him. "I'm not quite sure how to write this up," he said. "Maybe I shouldn't."

The garage door opened, car engine sounded from inside, garage door closed, shut off, and then Naples came into the kitchen. He glanced around. "Where did she go?"

"Home," Irene said. Or maybe not. If she could go sideways one direction, maybe she could go sideways again, until she found the Oma who would keep her.

Irene had no metal mesh against her skin. "Did Sara get home okay?"

"Yes. Christy was passed out on the couch. Lots of broken crockery up there. Irene, we have to do something about that girl."

"I know. I know." She touched the back of her hand, where Lilia's hand had pressed against hers. Somewhere an answer existed.

She just had to pull it into the here.

A Fault Against the Dead

You can't keep dead people happy all the time.

Thursday night I was walking on the beach, and about five ghosts were following me, one friendly, two whiners, one halfway on its way to somewhere else, and the last one potentially a client.

"Julia," said the friendly one, a dead guy named Roger I've known for eight of the nine years I've been a counselor to the dead (talk about a job whose rewards are intangible), "are you getting enough sleep?"

"Probably not," I said. I flumped down on the cold sand, stretched out flat on my back, and waved my arms back and forth to make a sand angel amid the footprints of people who'd come to the beach by day. The breathing hush of waves coming in and going out, the shifting grains against my back, the coolness under me, and the scent of sea, with a faint undertone of something small and dead a short distance away, combined to lull me.

Roger was right. I needed sleep. But it was exam week at community college, I had been cramming for four nights in a row, and there was more ghost activity than usual. "I won't get much tonight, either. I have an anthro exam tomorrow to cram for. Minnie and Hiram have too many complaints. Nothing I say seems to help."

Minnie and Hiram had gone, moping, down to the water, where they let wavelets wash through their ankles and stared glumly out to sea. The moon shone through them; they were translucent, like thin green jade. If there had been any way to ditch them, I would have taken it. But, though they hadn't been able to figure out what was holding them in this world and solve it so they could move on, they were startlingly resourceful when it came to tracking me down and torturing me.

"They don't want to be helped. They just like you." Roger drifted down to float above the sand near me. He had been a ghost long enough to look like someone specific. I wondered if he looked like who he had been. Some ghosts didn't. A lot of them could posthumously turn into their dream selves, select an appearance they thought suited them better than the one they had been born into. I was totally freaked out the first time I saw someone I knew die and emerge from her mouth as someone else.

Some of the people I saw weren't even dead yet, and there, other rules applied.

Roger was a good-looking ghost. Also, he wore clothes. Some of the dead acted like death was a nudist colony. I was still a little frisson about that, especially about the naked guy ghosts, when I could tell whether they liked me or didn't. They enjoyed being able to get excited by live women without the women knowing, and sometimes it took a while for them to figure out I could see them and they should mind their manners. A lot of them didn't care. I guess, why should they?

Still, if they didn't care about my feelings, I didn't take them on as clients.

With Hiram and Minnie, it was hard to tell if they cared. They whined a lot. They talked in my ears when I was trying to read my textbooks, and when Minnie went in Mother mode, she drove me crazy. Still, there were a few small flickers of what looked like affection in our relationship.

At least they wore clothes.

I stopped flopping around. Sand angels didn't give a person the same satisfaction as snow angels. You couldn't tell from the outline what a person had been trying for.

"So who are you?" I asked the fourth ghost, who looked like lavender jade and drifted in the air about a foot from my head. I couldn't tell much about her; she was too new to have distinct features. She looked small, though. A kid ghost.

I had problems with kid ghosts. It was kid ghosts who sent me to the mental hospital for five years.

She didn't say anything. She just watched me with her black olive-pit eyes in their shadowed caverns.

I sat up and shook sand out of my coat sleeves. "I can't help you if you don't give me anything to work with."

She flickered and vanished.

Whew. Another bullet dodged.

"So what's your story?" I asked Ghost Five, more a colored, internally lighted smear on the dark sky than a person.

It wavered like the Northern Lights. I heard a faint wind-chime sound, then a deep bell bong.

"Great," I muttered. The half-there ghosts were sometimes dream selves and didn't need help. As soon as their bodies woke up, they'd disappear. I wasn't sure Ghost Five was one of those. You couldn't always tell. Some of the real dead spoke other languages. I hoped there were other me's out there who could help them. I'd met one other guy, Nick, who saw almost as many ghosts as I did, but he and I didn't get along. It wasn't like we had a client referral service.

Music as a language was a big problem for me. I had a tin ear. "Roger?"

Roger went to Half-There and walked through it. He came shuddering out the other side, his face stained purple and pink, his clothes writhing. "Yech!" He flumped down onto the sand beside me and shook.

"A dreamer?"

"No, he's dead."

"What does he need?"

The stains faded from Roger's translucent face, leaving his skin his more usual light brown. "Forgiveness," he muttered. "I couldn't forgive him, though. He's polluted with the deaths of others."

God, I hated those guys. I could do it, though. The sooner the better, probably. Thin down the ghost herd and then go study.

I stood up. "Okay, ghost guy. Here's what I can do for you."

The smear wavered some more. Why couldn't he have been a dream?

"Walk into me and give me your sins. Walk out of me and leave them behind, and then you can go on. If this isn't what you want, please leave me alone. I have other things to do."

Half of him shifted up and the other half circled, rippled, pulsed. I stretched out my arms as though I were making a sky angel. The ghost flowed suddenly toward me and then into me, and then my stomach clenched. A river of blood, an orchestra of screams, sick hot excitement, the cold wracking shudders afterward, the irresistible need to find more of other people's pain to taste, oh, God, I hated these guys. My stomach churned, my forehead burned, sweat burst out all over my body. He slid out of me, washed clean and pale and confused.

I forgive you. I forgive you. I forgive you. You did it because you couldn't find anything else that worked. You learned some lesson here. It happened for a reason. (Oh, God, what reason could there be? Yet this sort of thing kept happening. If I believed there was a reason—I needed to believe there was a reason. Otherwise I'd end up back in the room where you could bounce off the walls and not hurt yourself. There had to be a reason. I just didn't know what it was.) You gave others lessons—you evil, sick fuck—no, no, focus, Julia. You are done here. You are forgiven. Please move on to your next lesson. Please be free of what hurt you in this life. Please find love and joy in the next.

He shot up into the sky.

"Is he gone?" I asked, even though I knew he was.

"He's gone," said Roger.

I screamed. I dropped to my knees and pounded on the sand. I screamed again, then lay with my face to the ground and screamed a third time, as loud as I could into the sand, vomiting up the things that ghost had done in his life, cleaning his taste out of my mouth.

Bless the purge. Thank God it worked. Mostly.

"Miss? Miss?"

Uh-oh.

I clenched my fists and pushed myself up.

"Are you all right?"

The speaker was alive. He wore a big puffy dark jacket and dark jeans and knee-high rubber boots. On his head, a pale knitted cap; on his hands, dark gloves. His face was obscured by thick glasses. Even if the light weren't solely moon and stars I don't know if I could have figured out what he looked like.

He knelt, reached for me.

I scrambled away. I had forced the last ghost's sick acts mostly out of my brain, but a residue remained, the way it always did. I could remember being the guy, or I could remember what he had done. When I remembered what he had done, I took the stance of his victims. If I remembered being the guy, I stained myself with his inescapable desire for power over something, anything, preferably something that would whimper and quiver when he poked it.

Through a haze of killer memories, I looked at this live guy and thought: Killer.

"Miss?" said this mummy-wrapped guy. "I don't mean you any harm."

What my last ghost had always said to the women he managed to separate from everything they knew or could cling to for safety. Had always meant, up until the moment he harmed his victims, because he couldn't let himself know ahead of time what he really wanted and intended to do, not and function. He had to pretend it wasn't happening, had never happened, until it did.

The other kind, the ones who had no consciences and no regrets, they must go somewhere else. I didn't have to deal with those.

Puffy guy stood slowly. "I just wanted to see if you were okay," he said in a hurt voice.

"Sure." My voice was hoarse from all the screaming. "I come down here to scream because I figure it won't bother my neighbors." I could hardly hear myself, my voice was so thin. "Thanks anyway. I'm kind of frazzled."

"Frazzled," he said, an amused note in his voice.

Roger walked through him. "Julia, get out of here."

I climbed to my feet, stood swaying. From the tone of Roger's voice, I knew this guy must be a wrong one, too. What were the odds?

What chance did I have of getting away from this guy? He was a head taller than I was, and I was exhausted from too little sleep, too much studying, too much greasy food, and too much murder.

Hiram and Minnie had drifted up from the water's edge. Minnie heard Roger and flashed between me and the stranger. "Run, Julia," she said.

Run? Fat lot of good that would do me.

Hiram streaked across the beach. "I'll rouse Nick!" he cried as he disappeared. Ghost-listener Nick might listen to Hiram. He might try to help me. We didn't like each other, so I wasn't sure that would work.

Which direction should I run?

"Frazzled," I repeated. I walked past the guy, heading toward my car. If I could get most of the way there—

If I ran, he'd bring me down. An image of a lion leaping to bite a gazelle on the neck flashed through my brain. Hah. Gazelle. As if. I glanced sideways at the guy. Lion. As if.

If I pretended I didn't know what he was up to, maybe I'd have time to collect myself and restore my energy. I pulled a granola bar out of my coat pocket, ripped off the wrapper, and took a bite. I pulled a water bottle out of my other pocket, shook sand off it, unscrewed the cap, and took a long drink. My throat felt better.

He followed, weaving beside me on the sand.

"See, what happens when you die," I said, "you suddenly stop being able to forget all the horrible things you did while you were alive. You have to live with them or find someone like me to help you ditch them. You know? When I die I don't think I'll have that problem, because as far as I know, I haven't done any horrible things to anyone else, just myself. Then again, memory is so tricky. I suppose I could have done awful things and just made myself forget."

"What are you talking about?" asked the guy.

"Julia, what are you talking about?" Roger asked at the same time. "Why aren't you running? This man has evil intentions."

"I know, but I'm too tired."

"Huh?" said stalker guy.

I ate more granola bar, washed it down with water. I was feeling better.

Minnie and Roger flanked me, Roger mixing edges with stalker guy because stalker guy was walking pretty close beside me. "Julia," Minnie said, "Julia, don't join us."

"It's not my idea, but you know, sometimes things just happen." I wished I felt as calm as I sounded.

The little lavender ghost returned, floated in front of me as I walked. Sand dragged at my feet. Breeze blew past my face, flavored with a faint whiff of woodsmoke from someone's fire. Somewhere, someone was sitting in front of a nice fire in a living room, maybe reading a book and drinking hot cocoa or some nice wine. Maybe they had slippers and a fluffy bathrobe on. Maybe there was nothing in the world that worried them.

Lavender danced as she walked, and she walked backward, her dark eye-sockets the only features in her face.

"I wish you'd tell me what you want. Maybe I can help you," I said.

"Are you nuts?" asked stalker guy.

"Certifiably. I still have my ID bracelet from the mental hospital in my keepsake box."

"Really?" He sounded intrigued.

"He killed me," said the lavender ghost. "I want to kill him."

"I understand. Of course you want to kill him. You can't, though, probably. I guess it depends on whether you're so angry your rage shifts you into power mode. That happens sometimes. Then you can drive them to hurt themselves or maybe even die, if you try hard enough. But it's a waste of energy, and it drops you into a lower mode of existence next time, as far as I know, which, I have to admit, isn't that far."

"Who are you talking to?" stalker guy asked.

"The ghost of one of your victims."

Roger groaned.

"What?" said stalker guy.

"He hurt me. He hurt me so bad. He put a dirty sock in my mouth so I couldn't cry. I cried anyway, but I couldn't make the noises. He wouldn't stop."

"I'm sorry," I said. "What's your name?"

"Hazel Mindell."

"I'm so sorry, Hazel." We were almost to the parking lot.

There were two vehicles in the parking lot: my Mazda Protege, and an overmuscled pickup truck with tall tires and a camper shell.

Sure. Closer to my car, closer to his. Here I was, making his job easy by walking myself to where he wanted me.

Stalker guy grabbed my left arm. "Hazel?" he said. For the first time, he sounded upset.

"Where'd he put you after he killed you?" I asked Hazel.

"Just over there." One arm rose, pointed toward a thick stand of shore pine to the right of the parking lot. I turned my head to look. Short squat trees hunched shoulder to shoulder in the night, their tops cropped and blown back by the constant sea wind. "I was still alive when he took me there. There's a little clear place where one of the trees died. He did things to me there. Even after I was gone."

"Hazel?" said stalker guy.

"How many have you killed?" I asked, then realized it was the wrong question in almost any social situation.

"Seven," Roger told me.

Huh. He could walk through live people and pick up that much detail? I'd seen him walk through people before, but I just assumed it was an accident. I never realized—though heck, I did something similar myself with dead people.

If I survived what was about to happen, though I didn't see how I could, I wanted to ask Roger a lot more questions. Like: could he walk through some of the guys I saw at school? Even though I was years older than most of them, thanks to the unintended detour in life I'd taken courtesy of doctors, drugs, and bad advice, I suspected some of them might like me. I never knew how to approach them, though. The risk of rejection was pretty high with live people. Dead people didn't have as many options. Most of the dead people I'd dealt with liked me. I thought. The ones I had sorted loved me. They loved everybody once I cleaned them out.

The stalker guy's hand was tight around my upper arm now, and getting tighter. It hurt. "Hey," I said. "Throttle down."

"What do you know about killing, or Hazel?"

"Only what the ghosts tell me."

"You are really weird."

"Gee. News flash."

He shook me.

I shoved my right hand into my pocket and pulled out my car keys, fisted them with some of them sticking out between my fingers, the way we'd been taught in self-defense class, though doing it one-handed was a lot harder, and raked his face with the keys. He yelped, let go of me, and staggered backward.

I ran for my car, trailed by Roger, Minnie, and Hazel. I couldn't get the key in the lock, though; I was shaking too hard. "Hurry up! Hurry up!" Roger said. "Damn it, Julia!"

"That's helping," I muttered, finally shaking loose the right key and getting it into the keyhole.

Heavy breathing and even heavier steps came up behind me, and then stalker guy crushed me against my car. "You bitch."

"Oh, that's original," I whispered. The keys, caught in the car lock, were digging into my hip. Stalker guy smelled like bad aftershave and sweat. He was bulky under his coat.

"Leave her alone!" Hazel yelled. She flashed and fluoresced and flickered into another state, standing on my car. She looked about nine, with tight braids and freckles and a ragged pink dress with blood streaks on the front. "Get away from her!"

The weight left my back. "What!" said stalker guy.

I grabbed my keys, turned the one in the lock, jerked them loose, opened the door, and dived into the car. I slammed the door and locked it. Then I sat trying to get my breath.

Minnie materialized in the passenger seat, and Roger walked through the front of the car and dropped down into me.

"Come on," he said, or I said, without meaning to. He jerked my hand up and shoved the key into the ignition, pumped the gas pedal, started the car, put it in reverse, and we drove out of there while I was still adjusting to the roils in my stomach of having another ghost inside me. I was doing an automatic sort on Roger: pulling out what was keeping him here, figuring out how to solve it, sucking his sins free of his ghost self and into me so I could process and release them.

What was keeping Roger here:

Love.

He loved me.

He knew we didn't have a future, but he couldn't get himself to let go.

"Julia!" screamed Minnie. I looked ahead of us and realized I was driving thirty-five miles an hour straight toward a tree. I swerved, got the car back on the road, headed for town, tears streaming down my face.

By the time I reached the police station, Roger was gone.

THE TROUBLE
WITH THE TRUTH

Ever since I lost my best friend Roger through a kind of workplace accident, I've been wary of ghosts. They find me anyway. Because I am Julia Mangan, twenty-two-year-old ghost magnet and counselor to the dead!

Darn. That always sounds better in my head than when I say it out loud.

Some people pick their jobs, and some have jobs thrust upon them. I so didn't pick this job. I was just getting reconciled to it—largely through Roger's efforts—when I accidentally sorted him and sent him to the Next Place. He'd hung out with me for eight years, one of my first ghosts, the one who made me kind of crazy, but stuck by me during my three-year stint in the mental hospital. He found other ghosts to help me accept my state—ghosts of psychologists, like, and one really woowoo ghost who made a lot of sense once I figured out I should believe her. They all helped me deal with my talent. Roger even brought me the ghost of a social worker who coached me on what to say to my doctor at the nut house to convince him I'd returned to sanity and was ready to leave.

Roger stuck with me as I took an active role in dealing with other ghosts. I figured out what their unfinished business was, helped them resolve it, and sent them on. Most of the time all they needed was someone who heard them. Sometimes I had to do more than that, and sometimes what I heard was so awful I needed to work through it myself afterward.

In all that time, Roger had never let me sort him. A sort is when ghosts walk through me and I hear their stories and understand everything about them. I figure out how to give them peace, and they leave. I learn whole lives that way. I have an edge over other people in my psych classes. Not many of them actually experience other people's psyches.

I finally sorted Roger because he had to walk through me to save my life. That was when I found out he loved me. Then he was gone.

So I sort of didn't want to get to know other ghosts afterward. I missed Roger a lot, and I was mad at him, too. Mad at the work, mad at the world. My mom was looking at me funny again, and I was afraid she'd recommit me. In self-defense, I decided to go away to college, even though I was already twenty-two (my years in the mental hospital took a bite out of my school career).

College wasn't like it looked in the movies, though. Ghosts followed me around. They interfered with my schoolwork and the normal course of socialization. Even my dim-bulb dorm roommate Mandy could tell something was off. One of my ghosts was an opera singer who took a negative view of all the boy band pictures Mandy plastered her side of the room with. I got blamed for all the blackened teeth, pirate eyepatches, and mustaches, but I swear I didn't do it. I didn't touch her iPod, either. I wouldn't know how to substitute Mozart for bubblegum pop. Technology has never been my strong suit; some of my ghosts are kind of poltergeistical, and they do bad things to machines. That's what I tell myself, anyway; I don't want to believe I have some kind of aura that stops watches and crashes computers, but I can't sit in the front row in my classes or the overhead projectors burn out and laser pointers go astray.

I finally sorted the opera singer out of self-defense, and after I did her, I couldn't refuse the rest of them; I was back in business and resenting it.

One of my ghosts pointed out that if I really didn't want to do what I was doing, why was I taking all these psychology courses? This ghost, Avery Garrett, had showed up after I lost Roger, but he maintained his distance. He didn't seem to want to be sorted, though he was fascinated by the process.

He was also one of the few people I knew whom I felt comfortable talking to. The other friend I had made since my college career began was a freak like I was. Okay, not exactly like I was. Omri Narula, whom I'd met in Psych 101, was a fifteen-year-old megagenius. He didn't know how to relate to the other college students either. We signed up for abnormal psychology together for our second term. We were both trying to figure out what was normal.

"I don't believe in an afterlife," Avery said as I was packing to go home for Christmas break.

I had thinned the ghost herd down to Avery and a toddler-sized smear of light. I was hoping the kid could tell me what she wanted—sorting ghosts was easier if I had some idea of who they were ahead of time, even if they couldn't articulate what they needed—but mostly she just cried and stayed purple, sad, and smeary.

As for Avery, I wasn't sure I wanted him to leave. I didn't push him or try to sort him. I liked him.

Lately my two current ghosts and I had been experiencing yet another phenomenon: flocks of tiny angels appeared at random moments. They hovered, but they didn't talk. Avery was baffled. He wanted me to explain, but I'd never run into anything like them before. I tried to sort one. It disappeared as soon as I touched it. I left them alone after that. Angel murder—it just felt so wrong.

Avery and I were temporarily alone in my dorm room. I wasn't sure where the kid had gotten to. No angels hovered. Mandy had left already for Christmas break, full of cheer and peppermints and her idea of two weeks in heaven, which involved beaches, sunshine, bikinis, and crowds of buff young strangers.

I sniffed a nightgown I'd dug out of one of my drawers, then put it in the laundry bag instead of the suitcase. I was taking both laundry and clean clothes home to Mom's for Christmas break, hoping to return with everything clean.

I didn't like wearing nightgowns, but with ghosts showing up at all hours of the day and night, I felt better covered up. Some ghosts were pretty crude. You die, you often lose your manners and inhibitions, because nobody notices you anymore, so why bother?

"No afterlife for you?" I said to Avery. "You figure if I sort you, you're gone completely? That's depressing. Dude, it's not too late to find something to believe in."

Avery's sense of self was fuzzy, so his visual aspect was too; no way could I figure out what he'd looked like in life. In death, he was a kind of shadowy charcoal smear the shape of a six-foot-tall gingerbread man, with whirling lights in the head area. This was what you got with people who didn't spend time studying themselves in mirrors.

I was pretty sure Avery used to be an educator, maybe a scientist. He was familiar with finals, and, though he wouldn't tell me any of the answers directly (he totally disapproved of cheating), he coached me in some subjects, and gave me hints to help me recall things I already knew. I would have liked having him as a teacher.

He didn't like having me as a counselor. Though I was a little old to be going to college, I was too young to tell Avery anything he didn't already know. Sucked for him, because we ghost counselors were few and far between, so he didn't have much choice. (If he had wanted counseling, I could have referred him to the only other one of us I'd met, Nick, but I didn't like Nick, who was a butthead, and just about my age, anyway.)

Avery disappeared after our first encounter. He stayed away for a couple days. He was a guy who needed theories and hypotheses, and I guess he had to work some new ones out after I spoke to him. He had been dead a while when we bumped into each other, so I was sure he had developed a whole set of hypotheses by the time I came along and disproved them.

The Kid, my other current ghost project, arrived out of nowhere a couple weeks earlier, curled up on the fuzzy brown blanket at the end of my bed, and started crying. She was about three, so I wasn't sure what her real name was, or much of anything else about her. She looked like a transparent egg full of smeary lights that changed color depending on her mood. Mostly, her mood was dark purple, accompanied by whimpers, sometimes outright sobbing. A few times, she woke me up with hair-raising screams. It was eerie and irritating. Plus, Mandy got mad, because when the Kid screamed, I woke up yelling, and that woke up Mandy, who was fanatically addicted to what she called "beauty sleep."

The Kid was my first toddler. I didn't know how to help her. She didn't have a very big vocabulary, and she didn't think like a human being yet.

I might have to walk through the Kid before I understood her. I hoped for better. It went easier on both souls involved if we found out enough about each other beforehand to know what to expect before I did the sort.

I wanted to talk to Omri about all this stuff, but I was afraid of driving him away—he was the best living friend I had. Most of the other people in class patted him on the head metaphorically (nobody really touched him, because we were all too conscious of the specter of lawsuits), but I got together with him in the cafeteria, and we talked about some of the weird things we'd found out in class. I had a feeling this was old ground for him, but I didn't call him on it, because I appreciated him dumbing things down for me.

From there, we'd progressed to reading outside of homework and trying to ick each other out with weird things we'd turned up. I had just started talking to him about ghosts, and he *hadn't* patted my head, metaphorically or otherwise, and said, "Now, now" in that patronizing tone so many people used when they found out I believed. He was totally intrigued. I told him anecdotes disguised as tales. I hadn't told him about my special ghost-ray vision or my mission re: ghost world. I was still testing the waters with him.

Should I call Omri and ask for a consult about the angels or the Kid?

We were both about to leave for the winter holidays, if he hadn't already left. What if he decided I was crazy before we left? No, I wasn't ready to lose my best living friend.

Maybe when we got back.

I sat down beside the crying Kid and glanced at Avery. "Got any theories about what to do for this one?"

"Find out—" he said, and then another infestation of tiny angels popped into the room.

They had been doing it for about a month. Sometimes there were five of them, sometimes nine, sometimes six or eight. Poof! Angels the size of humming birds hovered around my head like a cloud of too-large mosquitoes. I knew they were angels because they had feathered wings and they wore little white robes and glowed. Otherwise I would have thought they were pixies. They didn't do much except make it hard for me to study.

I waved my hand in front of my face, trying to shoo them away, but they were unshooable.

I asked a couple traditional questions, even though I had tried this before without results. "Is there anything I can do for you?" No answer. "How can I help you find comfort and rest?" No answer. They never answered. Maybe they didn't have voices.

Then they started singing, which blew the no-voices theory. Four-part harmony, like a radio turned low: human, but distant. "Angels We Have Heard on High," they sang.

"Well, that's new," I said after they'd finished the first verse.

Avery studied them. He held out a hand, lifted it under one of the angels. His hand passed through the angel, and it squeaked.

"Spiritual material," he said, "but not enough for a full encounter." He sat down on the end of the bed and laid his shadowy hand on The

Kid. She took form as a small child with light brown hair and big brown eyes. She stared up at him, her sobs stopped. "Different from what happens when I touch the kid. We can feel each other," he said, and patted the toddler's shoulder.

"How did you do that?" I asked him. The angels were singing softly enough to function as background music.

"Do what?"

"Before you touched her, she was formless. Now she looks like a kid."

"Formless?"

"Light, color, no human form."

"She's always looked like a child to me," he said.

The Kid touched Avery's knee, and he, too, took form out of the dark mist I'd seen him as before. He was younger than I had thought, mid-thirties to early forties, and he looked more like a mountain climber than a professor—muscular, with wild, gold-touched brown hair. He had a rugged face, sunbrowned, with fans of laugh wrinkles at the outer corners of his eyes. His hands were big, cabled with veins and tendons; gold hair furred the backs of his knuckles. He wore scuffed hiking boots, slightly frayed jeans, and a soft green corduroy shirt. "Whoa," I said. "She focused you, too. Weird."

"Interesting. I had no idea I was out of focus."

"I didn't think you needed to know," I said. I had been ghost-wrangling for nine years, and I learned new things all the time. Most ghosts I'd met didn't touch each other, so I hadn't observed this effect before. Some ghosts didn't even know when others were around.

I'd heard people talk about astral planes. I'd been developing my own theory, loosely based on Photoshop layers. Some ghosts were in one layer, some in another; layers could run parallel or intersect, but some never compressed into each other. Most of them had some transparency. I hadn't studied the Photoshop manual enough to see if my reality matched my metaphor. "Are you an athlete, teacher, or the ever-popular other?"

"Teacher. Anthropology. I spent my summers on digs."

"You spent your summers digging through the leftovers of other people's religions and burials, and you don't believe in an afterlife?" I asked.

He smiled and shrugged. "I don't. I know many cultures put a lot of thought and energy into their versions of an afterlife, but that doesn't mean it's real."

"Okay," I said. "Explain the angels."

"Need more data," he said, and then someone knocked on my door.

"Who is it?" I yelled.

"Omri."

The angels stopped singing the moment he spoke. They still hung in the air near my head, their wings flapping, but now they all faced the door.

"Come in."

He came in, smiling, thin and gawky in nondescript pants and shirt whose legs and sleeves were too short for the size he'd grown into since coming to college in the fall. I hoped his parents would notice the change and buy him a new wardrobe. His face was broad without being fat, but it looked childish, with a sprinkle of golden freckles across his nose. He would probably always look younger than he was, and he would probably consider that a handicap for the next twenty years. His hair looked like he hadn't brushed it since the last time he washed it, which was probably that morning. Dark bangs hung down over his caramel-brown eyes. He lifted a hand to part his hair so he could peer at me. "Thought you might have left already."

The angels stared at him. They had never reacted to anyone but Avery before. I couldn't remember if they'd been around when I'd talked to Omri last.

"Still packing," I said. "I don't have far to go, and I'd rather not get there." I had lied to Mom about when the break started so I could stay a day after the others left, and I lied about when break ended, too. I was looking forward to coming back to an empty dorm a week before everybody else got back. I was sure I'd need the rest after enduring what Mom considered a proper Christmas.

"Know what you mean," Omri said.

I smiled at him, then asked, "Did you want anything specific?"

"No." He pulled out the desk chair and sat in it. He stared at me. I glanced toward Avery and the Kid.

"He has a crush on you," Avery said.

"What?"

"I didn't say anything," said Omri.

"He has a crush on you," Avery repeated.

Omri had a sweet smile, a terrific brain, and an impish sense of humor, and I had never thought of him as a potential partner. I was seven years older than he was, for God's sake. How could he have a crush on me, and why would Avery know about it?

To get away from unwelcome thoughts, I asked, "Where are you going for break?"

"When I'm not at college, I live with my Aunt Edna and Uncle Frank," he said. "Only, Mom just got out of jail, and she'll be home this time."

The angels multiplied. There were twelve now, the most I'd ever seen. All of them stared at Omri.

"You don't want to see her?"

He ducked his head, studied his hands gripping the front edge of the chair's seat. "Four years ago, I testified in court. She went to jail because I told them—told them—"

Six more angels, then another three. Such a cloud I could barely see him. I waved my hand in front of my face, and the ones blocking my vision moved aside enough so I could keep an eye on Omri. It was the first time they'd ever responded to my gestures.

"Interesting," said Avery, studying the angels.

"I used to make up stories all the time when I was little," Omri said. He swiveled the chair back and forth. "Anytime someone asked me a question, I would come up with an answer, whether I knew the answer or not. I mean, it got more and more fun to come up with wrong answers, the wilder the better. It was like playing with my brain, the most fun I knew how to have. I had this way of looking like I was lying when I was telling the truth, too. It drove Mom crazy. Finally she said, 'Tell the truth or say nothing at all.'"

"Wow," I said.

"At that point we were living alone together, and she used to hit me if I irritated her too much. She had kind of a hair trigger, probably because she was always doing things she was afraid she'd get in trouble for and she was nervous all the time. It stopped being fun telling stories after I got beat up for it. So then, I pretty much stopped talking."

"But you got over that," I said.

"No." He chewed on his lower lip. "I don't talk."

"Omri, you talk to me all the time."

"You're the only one."

"Wow." I pulled my legs up on the bed and hugged them to me, digesting this, thinking about Omri in class—he would answer questions if the professor called on him, but mostly what Omri said was rote from the textbook (one advantage of a photographic memory)—and Omri in the company of others. Quiet. He laughed at jokes if they were funny, and he smiled at some of the other people we ran into in class and the halls, but he didn't volunteer information. He didn't initiate conversations. Except with me.

"And we don't talk about things that have to be true or not true," he said. "Just about people in books." He stared toward the wall papered with Mandy's posters of saccharin boy singers. "Julia," he whispered.

If he were a ghost, and I was sorting him to send him on, I would ask questions. So I asked. "What can I do to help?"

He looked at me instead of the wall. He stroked curled fingers down his cheeks as though scratching them. "Mom's going to be so mad at me," he whispered. "Four years in jail! Because of me! Even though I told the truth, and that's what she ordered me to do. She'll want to hurt me again. She'll force me to talk. I can't tell her the truth. So fires will start, or things will fly around and break, and . . ."

"You have a poltergeist?" I asked.

He grimaced. Nodded. "I think that's what it is. Why I've been doing all this abnormal psych reading."

"Oh."

He parted his bangs and looked at me again. "Do you think I'm crazy?"

I laughed.

Wind whipped the posters on the wall.

"Okay, stop it, Omri. I was laughing with you, not at you. I'm sitting on my bed with two ghosts and a cloud of little angels. And— guess I haven't shared this part of my personal history with you yet, either—I spent several years in a mental institution. I don't think anybody's crazy."

"Oh." He hunched his shoulders, studied my bed, then me.

I smiled. "So, you know, maybe you think *I'm* crazy. Huh?" Inside I was afraid. Would I lose him now?

He glanced toward the door, then shook his head. He looked at me sideways. In all the talking we'd done, we hadn't shared either of our truths. We hadn't checked to see whether the other would be able to weather this kind of knowledge. I watched him think about what he would say next. What he came up with was, "Why are there ghosts on your bed?"

"Because I haven't figured out how to help them yet."

"Are ghosts the same as angels?"

"I don't think so. I was just talking to Avery—he's a guy ghost—about that when you knocked. I don't think the angels are actually people, but I don't know what they are."

"They're connected to the boy," said Avery.

"How can you tell?"

"There's a flavor to their energy. That wind he fluttered the pictures with, it had the same feel. I wish I'd known things like this happened when I was alive. I'd like to develop tools to detect and measure these phenomena."

"How can I tell what?" Omri asked.

"Again, talking to Avery," I said. "He said the angels are yours."

"What?" Omri jumped up, his hands fisting. Unfelt wind flurried through the angels, scattering them until they thumped softly against the wall or the bedspread or me. The ones that hit me tingled as they melted. The wind whipped past the posters again, tugging some of them free to fall like leaves on Mandy's pink chenille bedspread.

"Omri," I said. "Calm down. You're hurting them."

"What?"

"Your angels. You're blowing them around, destroying them." I crossed the room and knelt in front of him, touched his hand as it gripped the chair edge, white-knuckled. "Maybe they were never alive. I can't tell. Anyway, you don't need them right now, because you can talk to me."

"I can talk to you," he whispered. The remaining angels winked out with small flashes.

"You can lie to me."

His eyes widened and his breathing shifted into overdrive. He trembled. "I hate you," he said.

I sat back, hit the floor with a thump.

"That was a lie. I said it out loud," he said.

Oh! That's what that was. Whew. "You did," I told Omri. I checked the room. Not an angel in sight.

"I feel inferior to everybody I meet. I love my mother. I hate school. Math is hard. My general outlook is perky and upbeat. I was born on the moon." He heaved a huge sigh and smiled at me.

"Keep it coming. You're getting better."

"I am a handsome prince and I know how to rescue people." He peered at me past his bangs, then smiled like a kid who's just told a really bad joke.

"That could be true, depending on the circumstances," I said. "Remember how you got all that data off my hard drive when I was ready to throw it away?"

"Oh, yeah." He rose, walked over to peer into the mirror above Mandy's dresser. There was a clear space surrounded by pinking-shears-edged heart-shaped pix of *Tiger Beat* boys and snapshots of Mandy and her friends blitzed at parties, making obscene gestures. (Sometimes I felt *so* old.) Omri studied what he could see of his face.

"Handsome is as handsome does," I said.

"How can anyone do anything handsome? I've never understood that phrase."

"Now that you mention it, it is kind of confusing."

He glared at his image, then smiled at me. "I can make it mean something, but I still think it's weird."

"Okay," I said.

"Anyway, I don't always do handsome things."

"Variable handsomeness."

"And you're not speaking to my need for reassurance about my appearance."

"Is that a serious concern?" I asked.

Avery said, "He has a crush on you, remember?"

"Oh," I said.

"And your hesitation leads him to believe he's not handsome."

"Whereas, if I say something to indicate otherwise, it could get me into different kinds of trouble."

"Are you talking to that man ghost?" Omri asked.

"Yep." I took a good look at Omri and realized that once he grew into his bones, he would probably look fine. At the moment he was too urchin-like.

Three angels winked into sight beside my head. They had their hands clasped in front of them, and they all looked anxious. "Now what?" I said.

"He's told you directly and indirectly what he needs," Avery said. "Why not give it to him?"

"Omri, are you really worried about how you look?"

"No," he said. Six more angels showed up. Two of them were blonde, like me: a first. All of the earlier ones had been dark-haired.

"Some of your angels came back. Are you lying now?" I asked.

"I don't think so."

The blonde angels turned toward me, where all the others were focused on Omri. One of the blondes cocked her head at me.

The angels were vocabulary. They were about Omri not being able to talk. I wondered if they were agents of his poltergeist energy. Well, wait. They hadn't been the acting force when the wind blew through the room—the wind had hurt them. Omri was at war with himself, and he had some interesting and strange ways of manifesting it. "What are you not telling me?" I asked him.

"I don't care about how I look, except how I look to you," he muttered, and three of the angels vanished. Not the blonde ones.

I felt lost. I knew what to say to ghosts, most of the time. I didn't have to sugarcoat things. They'd already gone through death, which was pretty extreme. Most of them appreciated straight talk. The living took different handling.

"I think you're cute and sweet and lovable," I said, "and I'm almost old enough to be your mother."

"You are not."

"Well, okay. I've always been able to lie," I said. "But I'm not lying about this. I love talking to you, and I like having you for a friend. In fact, you're the best alive friend I've ever had. I don't think about you in boyfriend terms, though. Is that what you wanted to know?"

"Not exactly," he said, and sighed. More of the angels disappeared, though not violently: they faded from sight. "Do you have a boyfriend?" he asked.

"Nope." I had never had anybody express an interest that I could interpret, except for one of the burlier nursing assistants at the mental hospital, and he was creepy; Roger helped me avoid him, and later helped me report that he was harassing another girl who didn't have ghosts to defend her. The administrator investigated the guy and turned up other problems he was causing. The hospital fired him. It was one of the stepping stones I used to get out of there.

I had learned not to be interested in the boys I met in school afterward. They all thought I was too weird. After Roger had gone, I had realized he was the one I wanted. By then it was too late.

"So there's still hope," Omri said.

"Not right away. You need to get older, and I need to get used to the idea."

"Both those things will happen," he said, and smiled.

"Wouldn't you rather connect to someone your own age?"

"Nobody's my age." His face looked older when he said that, and I realized that it wasn't just college age people he was talking about. Because of his intellect, he didn't fit in with people his age, and because of his age, he didn't fit in with older people.

"Okay," I said.

"You see ghosts, and I have my own ghost, or sort of ghost," he said.

"I guess we do have things in common."

"Ask him if he can produce phenomena at will," Avery said.

"Why?"

Omri knew I wasn't talking to him. "Where is the ghost?" he asked.

"Both of them are still on the bed," I said.

"One's a guy, and the other's—what?"

"A little girl."

He stared toward the bed. Angels appeared there, too. They drifted until they settled on Avery's and the little girl's head and shoulders. "Oh my god," said Omri. "There's a—there's—I can't see them, but I—"

"Odd," said Avery, smiling. "Still the same semi-solid spiritual material, but focused in a different way."

Omri put his hands over his ears. "Did he just speak?"

"He did."

"Oh my god. Oh, my god."

"He wants to investigate you, too," I said.

"And the little girl," Omri whispered.

I went to the bed and knelt in front of the child. She was distracted by the angels. She tried to catch one, but it vanished as her insubstantial fingers closed around it, and another appeared a short distance away. She tried again, with similar results. Her face clouded.

"Her name is Sadie," Avery said quietly. He tugged the child onto his lap. "She just needs love."

Omri's angels doubled around them, all silent and focused on the ghosts. "Sadie," Omri whispered. Before I could turn to him, the child burst into tears, and I knew it was time for me to sort her.

I sat down on the bed and held out my arms. Avery put the child into them. She sank through my lap into me, and I knew her story. Mother, too young, messed up, didn't know what to do with the kid, couldn't stand its crying anymore. Got in the car with the kid in the front seat, neither of them buckled in, and drove off a cliff.

No wonder Sadie cried, I thought, and hugged her inside me. "I love you," I whispered. "I love you. I love you."

In a little while, she heard me, and then she left.

"Oh my god," Omri whispered from across the room. "I felt that."

"Did you see where she went?" I asked Avery. We sat side by side on my bed, staring at a particularly heinous boy singer poster, which Sadie had walked through on her way to the light.

"Nope," said Avery. "She went through the wall and disappeared. Next time, I want to stand in front of them when they're leaving, see where they walk as they come toward me."

Next time. Avery was making plans for a future that included both of us. I smiled.

"Julia?" Omri whispered.

"Yes."

"Can I—will you let me—can I—"

"Need a few more parts of speech, Omri," I said.

"Will you teach me about ghosts?"

"Will you teach me about poltergeists?"

"If I can figure them out for myself, sure," he said.

"Nobody's more likely to. And yes, I'd love to teach you about ghosts."

Omri checked his watch. He stood up. "I guess I better get my duffle and head down to meet the airport shuttle."

"Will you be okay with your mom?"

"No," he said. "But she's not my legal guardian anymore. Aunt Edna and Uncle Frank are. Uncle Frank won't let her hit me. She said she found God in jail, but I don't believe it."

I wished I could sort Omri. "I wish I could go with you, but I don't think I better." I went to the desk and got paper and pen. "Here's my mom's phone number," I said as I wrote. "Call me if you need me. Or if the angels show up, I'll assume you need me. What's the number at your aunt and uncle's?"

He told me. I wrote it on the bottom of the piece of paper and tore the paper in half, gave him the half with Mom's number on it.

"You can practice lying when you get back," I said. I took a step toward him and gave him an awkward hug. He returned my embrace, then bolted out the door.

I sighed and checked with Avery. "What about you? Ready to move on?"

"On, to nothing? I don't think so. Too many interesting things are happening right here." He flicked a finger at an angel. It flitted away. Most of them had disappeared; three lingered.

I packed my best friend's phone number and headed home, wondering what Avery would make of Mom.

HOME

GONE TO HEAVEN SHOUTING

I've been on this quest for forty-seven years, ever since my sixteenth birthday. Every once in a while I find what I'm looking for, and the restless urge to search settles for a little while. It sleeps.

It never sleeps long.

I haven't been home in thirty years, though I've directed others there.

There are music webs in every community. Find a thread to follow and it will lead you to little knots of musicians, who will give you other threads. There's the church choir circuit, and the community choir circuit, and the big performing arts centers that play host to all kinds of different musicians, big names in classical, rock, folk, alternative; and then there are the contra dance groups, and the old time fiddlers, and the rock bands and the jazz bands and the other people who play in little night clubs and taverns and small concert halls. There are high school garage bands who know about each other.

Then there are the people who practice alone at home when no one else is around to hear, and those I can almost never track down, their threads are so short. Mostly they aren't the ones I want, but it hurts me to know that perhaps sometimes they are.

Some threads lead to more than one sort of musician, and some never cross into alien territory at all.

I never know where I'll find my people. I used to search for them in a more diffuse way, move into a town and walk its streets up and down and wait for the tug of recognition, watch for a gesture or a flash of light or a certain look around the eyes. These last few years I've gone to the music webs, tweaked threads, listened for rumors.

I'm probably missing a lot of my people. Not all of them have found their way to music.

Not all of them wish to be found.

I've caught more family fish with music as a net than I did just strolling and trolling with no bait at all.

My name is Cyrus Locke. I carry a fiddle.

Also bamboo spoons for rhythm, and a pennywhistle and some harmonicas, but those are easier to hide.

It was a December Saturday night like many they get in the Pacific Northwest, stars scattered across the dark sky, fog lying like pooled milk in roadside ditches and in low spots in the pastures. The air smelled of cold and woodsmoke. I was traveling by air, the way I do at night when people are less likely to notice. I don't go directly over the roads, where headlights might catch me, but I keep close enough not to miss the sort of buildings I want to investigate.

I had watched a Christmas parade that morning in town, paying particular attention to the various marching bands, but I hadn't seen any trace of my people, though I'd enjoyed the spectacle. Now I was just covering territory and listening. On a cold night you don't often hear music. People have got their weatherproofing up and keep their tunes inside. I would rather search than hole up, though, especially since I had just finished three cups of coffee at a diner and was wide awake.

I drifted over a small country school, slowing to look at it properly. Sometimes there are community events in a school of a Saturday night, and I specialize in community events. If someone is going to shine, that's a good place to find them.

No sign of life there, but on the air, a thread of music.

South of the school was a big old oak tree, and huddled near and beneath some of its limbs, a grange building. Light, music, parked cars. Just the sort of place I liked. I chose a shadow in the grove of oaks behind the building and slipped down into it, checking the back porch for people smoking or children playing. I used to get caught once in a while in the early days, when I hadn't learned caution. Once, getting caught led to one of my better discoveries. All in all, though, I'd rather pick my moments.

I listened to the music. Country western, swing, old tunes that I remembered hearing on radios in backwoods in the fifties, early in my questing years. I took my spoons and a D-pitch harmonica out of my knapsack and stuck them in my pants pockets, then lifted and lodged the knapsack in the high branches of one of the oak trees.

On the ground again, I opened my fiddle case and took out Lucia. She's been with me twenty-two years, ever since I rescued her from a pawn shop. If I had some of the gifts of other people in my family, I might be able to get her to talk, tell me her past history. What I know of her is that the label inside says she's a copy of a Stradivarius, like most fiddles you find, and it has the name of a German city and a date, 1897. I got out the bow and tightened the hairs, rosined it, then tuned the fiddle, listening to the music leaking out of the building, an old tune Hank Williams had covered in the early fifties, "Take These Chains from My Heart."

I put the fiddle and bow away, straightened, took a deep breath, then wandered toward the front of the grange, wondering how these people took to strangers. The windows were curtained with what looked like yellow-orange sheets, so I couldn't see in. One window, the one nearest the stage, was open to the frosty night. I caught a whiff of people: cologne, perfume, and sweat. I heard the shuffling sound of dancers on a rosined wooden floor.

There is a dream that comes to me sometimes, more often lately than I like, of all the world poisoned and empty and dead. The only colors are gray, black, brown, and ice-white. In this dream I am alive.

In life I have survived many things and anticipate surviving many more.

In the dream, I am alive, but alone.

I opened the double door into the grange hall and saw people dancing and people playing music, and I smiled the way I do every time I know my dream has not come true yet. I am so glad to see people alive, whether they are family members or not. My heart lightened. I edged to the left, where older folks were sitting on a padded bench, and murmured to a white-haired woman in a pale blue dress, "This a private party, or can anybody join?"

"Welcome, stranger," she said. "Go right on up and make yourself at home." Such a nice smile she had.

They were playing "If Teardrops Were Pennies" as I edged past couples dancing. Everyone had smiles for me. I smiled back. Sun has beaten my skin brown and folded, and age has bleached my hair oyster-shell white. I am a fraction taller than most but can still fit into clothes I find on the medium rack in thrift stores, like the scuffed loafers, faded dungarees, gray-and-white striped shirt, black leather vest, and beat-up bomber jacket I was wearing. All around the cavernous room were people who looked vaguely like me in size and age, some sitting on benches that lined the walls, some out on the dance floor, coupled and whirling. A few of them were a little more dressed up than I was—men in cowboy shirts with Southwest Indian designs on them, pearl snaps, and silver collar tips, ladies in sparkling shoes, green, red, and silver gilt Christmas brooches on their dresses. There were a few kids too, and some younger couples. My dream of destruction retreated as I looked around and felt I had found a temporary home and family.

I get this family feeling at the best of times. Sometimes it's deceptive. Often it's not, though. There are other places and people, foreign to where I stood that Saturday night, that feel even closer to home to me. Sometimes I walk into alien worlds when I open a door. Sometimes, after I've spent a little time in an alien world, it embraces me too. Not many cast me out completely.

There were three people with guitars toward the front of the room, and a woman with a string bass, two fiddlers, one white-haired fellow with a bandolier of harmonicas, a young woman with a banjo, and an older woman sitting and strumming a mandolin. Three microphones on stands amplified voice, fiddle, harmonica; cords were hidden under little throw rugs. Black instrument cases littered the stage behind the musicians, and the desks and floor near where they were playing. Some cases had instruments still in them; a rotating cast of musicians, apparently.

Not quite sure of the particular protocol of this place, I took a seat near the woman with the mandolin and held my fiddle case on my lap. She was wearing a purple sweatshirt with big furry white cats on it in puffy paint and glitter. She had red-framed glasses and a big grin, and curly dark hair shot with silver. Her earrings were silver snowflakes.

The tune ended and she smiled and nodded at me. "You new in town?"

"Yep."

"Welcome to Spruce Grange." She held out a hand and I shook it. "I'm Alma."

"Cyrus," I said.

"Care to join us?"

"Love to."

"You want to sign up for a couple tunes?" She nodded toward a yellow shopping pad sitting behind the musicians on a podium that had been shoved up against the stage. "You can just play backup if you want."

"I'll sign," I said.

One of the fiddlers stepped up to the central microphone and began "Black Velvet," an old waltz. I hadn't heard it in a long time. It was surely pretty.

I edged behind the other musicians, who made room, and picked up a chewed pencil. The sign-up sheet had twenty numbers with names listed beside them: Joe W., John I., John P., Grace, Calvin, Annie, Jim, Sharon, Lilian, Harry, Dale, Earl, Everett, fine old names with nothing strange about them. None of them sounded like names my family would use; we generally venture farther away from common when naming our babies. I wrote "21" and "Cyrus," wondering where on the list they had reached, how soon they would expect me to play.

Someone would tell me.

I set my case on the edge of the stage and opened it and got out Lucia and the bow. Tightened bow hairs, ran some rosin across 'em again, checked my tuning, glanced at the other musicians near me, got a nod and a smile from the bass player, and edged into the tune, playing melody very softly to get it back in my fingers and my head, then venturing into harmony, observing the rules of being a backup player: Listen to the leader. Never play louder than whoever was leading, and never play fancier. Follow the leader's tempo by watching his or her foot tapping even if other people are lagging behind or getting ahead. Smile.

It wasn't great music, but it was good-enough-to-dance-to music, and that was swell. People were moving to it and smiling. Near the door at the other end of the hall, three people were even boot-scooting, while nearer couples held each other and waltzed. New ways coming in, I thought, then wondered how I knew they were new. I was melding just a little. Thoughts can travel by air, and air is my sign. Join a tune, mix with it, slide under the surface, add your mite while others are adding theirs, and you can get a little tangled with the thoughtstream.

Here it was friendly for the most part. The first fiddler focused on fingering, hoping the tune would stick with her until she got through her fourth repeat of it. The second fiddler hated the sound of the banjo, but didn't hate the banjo player. One of the guitar players was annoyed at the second fiddler, thinking that the second fiddler was misbehaving by playing fancier than the first fiddler: grandstanding. Bad manners. The mandolin player was interested in me. She did think I was a good-enough musician, and so far not too musically pushy, and that was warming.

I let the thoughts go and sank into the music, which had a life of its own. The tune had its shadowy ancestry, passed from person to person, and its brief life, born at the first bowstroke, dying with the final flourish; in the middle it reached out into people's heads and planted its seeds there. With luck it would be reborn many ways—a hum, a whistle, or maybe a kid hearing it and wanting to figure out how to play it. Tunes were like benign viruses. They could sure as shooting mutate from one life to the next, too.

The first fiddler kicked up her foot to signal that she was approaching the end of the tune. She closed it down after that, nodded to the few people who applauded, turned and told us, "Chinese Breakdown," and started on her second tune.

I played twiddles that supported her tune and watched people two-step lively around the floor. It was so fine to see people enjoying themselves in the midst of music and dance. I basked in it, part of the music tapestry myself.

After a while I woke out of the moment and thought about my quest, and opened up my ears for that particular thread of sound that would tell me I had found a family member. An overtone, a harmonic that nobody else could quite produce. It was not a sound that came out of an instrument, but I could hear my own melody there in the overhead, singing about who I was and what I was doing at that moment, a tumbling tune of joy.

Faintly, faintly, masked by other sounds, there was the thread I sought. Fainter than I had ever heard it before. I tuned my listening to this trace, kept my mind on it while my hands played music along with the first fiddler.

It was a strange little melody, plaintive and constant. "Chinese Breakdown" came to a rousing finish and the dancers and listeners clapped, and still this tiny tune played on, the same notes sounding, no shift in awareness (my own tune had spun to a waiting pedal note until the next overtune would rise and it could harmonize). In the brief break between one player and the next I listened to the faint tune and recognized it. "Bright Morning Stars Are Rising," an old Christmas tune whose origins I did not know.

One of the guitar players stepped up to the mike, then turned back to face the musicians. "'Hey, Good-Looking,'" she said, "in G." She grinned at us. "Alma, play me in, okay?"

The mandolin player nodded, grinned, and struck up the tune, and pretty soon we were all flowing along the notes together. The guitar player had a nice clear voice, the bass kept good rhythm, and dancers flocked to the floor. In the middle between verses the guitar player surprised me by turning to me and lifting her brows, then nodding toward one of the mikes. I stepped up and played a verse, wondering how this would all work out in the hierarchy of musicians, that she had asked a stranger for backup before she went to the ones who were already here. Such tiny shifts and swerves in the living dynamic; everything could change, or everything could absorb change and return to its flow unimpeded.

I played well and strongly, decorated notes with flourishes, finished my verse and nodded back to her, smiling, then stepped away from the mike. "Thanks," she said, and sang the second verse. It was all right. The others still projected contentment. Polite, friendly, welcoming people.

The tiny thread of family still played, underneath it all, unchanging as the evening moved on. We played down through the list, with some people putting down instruments and going out to dance and others coming in off the floor to pick up instruments. I played two tunes, "Florida Blues" and "Kentucky Waltz."

Then the musicians took a break and most people went to the dining room for potluck desserts.

"Mighty fine, mighty fine, Cyrus," Alma said as she put her mandolin back in its hardshell case. "Hope you'll come next week. We're playing out at Ethel Creek Grange then."

"Thank you. I don't know if I'll still be in town, but I appreciate the invitation."

"Want some coffee?"

"In a couple minutes, thank you," I said.

She smiled, picked up a cane that had been lying beside her chair, and moved off after most of the others toward the dining hall.

I put my fiddle away, set the case on the stage. The mystery tune was still playing, clearer now that other ambient noise had quieted. I looked around the nearly empty room.

I glanced through the door into the next-door room and saw a combination kitchen-dining room which ran the length of the dance hall but was narrower across: cream walls, lace curtains, two rows of end-to-end long narrow tables draped with paper tablecloths, folding metal chairs lined up on both sides of them and people sitting in the chairs, talking. At the far end of the dining room was the kitchen area, with a counter spread with snacks in dishes or supermarket plastic containers. People lined up, holding paper plates, to get desserts. Some dropped a dollar in a donation coffee can on the buffet.

A few people lingered on the benches in the dance hall, talking with each other. One of the guitar players, a tall old guy named Dale, was still sitting up front and noodling on his guitar. The banjo-playing woman came back from the kitchen carrying two Styrofoam cups of steaming coffee. She set them down carefully and then sat next to Dale.

I wandered up the hall and down, pausing near the small clots of people and listening for the tune. Not there, not here, not there. I wandered toward Dale and Rose, the banjo-player. The tune was louder there, but it didn't seem to be coming from either of them.

I climbed up onto the stage.

Louder.

Was someone hiding up here? I was satisfied at this point that the tune was something other people didn't naturally hear, since no one else had responded to it. The music had that flavor of family, and it went on and on. It was hard for me to believe that some lost lonely little person would hide out on the stage or in the wings making this music when there were so many friendly people out front.

Not everybody in my family can adjust to regular people, though. Lots of them hide out entirely and never mix. There seems to be more and more of a trend toward isolation with some of my people, and I deplore it. Wonderful people are everywhere. You miss a lot if you stop looking for them.

Simple blank flats framed the stage, with a few pieces of rickety furniture against them. The back wall held a working door. I went through it, listening to the air, tasting. Bats, somewhere up above in the galleries. To the left, to the right, slender dark corridors leading to the wings. No complicated stagecraft here. I had seen grange skits before. Full of enthusiasm, nothing complicated. Occasional raw talent. Occasional trained talent.

On a table, a straw farmer's hat. A bouquet of silk flowers in rust and bronze and gold.

No sign of the tunemaker.

"What are you looking for?" asked a voice from behind me. I turned and found Alma leaning on her cane and peering at me along the backstage corridor.

That was the question, wasn't it?

Without the aid of music as a carrier, I had no idea what she was thinking.

"A tune," I said after a moment.

"You're looking for a tune behind the scenes at Spruce Grange?"

"Do you know that old Christmas carol, 'Bright Morning Stars Are Rising'?"

"Eh?" She cocked her head.

I listened to the trace of music. Here, close to its source, I heard a child's voice singing the words on top of thin fiddle notes. I lifted my voice and joined the song in mid-verse: "'Oh, where are our dear mothers? Oh, where are our dear mothers? Day is a-breaking in my soul.'"

Alma took two steps back, her face clouding, mouth drooping from its smile.

"What is it?" I asked. "I didn't mean to upset you."

"Why are you looking for that song here?" she whispered.

I opened the door in the scene and stepped out into the light on stage. She entered from the wing. I sat on a metal chair among the instrument cases, and she sat on a chair next to me and laid her cane on the floor.

"Something is singing that song," I said.

"What do you mean?" Her eyes were bleak behind her glasses.

"Do you believe in ghosts?" Some people do, I know. I believe, but then, I've met a number of them.

"No," she whispered. She looked right and left, then stared down at her feet.

"Never mind, then," I said. I patted her hand.

A thread of family here, but not really in the present time. I could come back later and search, I was pretty sure, after everybody else had left. Might as well enjoy what was left of the evening.

"When I was a little girl," she whispered, and looked up at me.

I smiled and waited.

"When I was a young girl, I was searching in the woods for scrap metal to help with the war effort. My daddy had gone off to war and I was a wild girl, a handful, roaming up and roaming down. Momma couldn't keep me home at all. Any excuse to get out would do. I was out picking blackberries before there were any ripe ones, or looking for filberts or pears or apples from trees gone wild from pioneer orchards. Scrap metal was a good excuse to wander, those years.

"It was in these woods, off away back of the grange here—that was before there were all these people in the valley; folks lived much farther apart, and the town was a lot smaller in those days—in these woods I found them."

"Who?"

"That little family. They'd raised a house out of up-and-down logs, not regular crosswise. Squatters was what they was. This all used to be part of Tim and Adeline Venture's donation land claim, but they never did log it all off, weren't enough kids in the family . . . well.

"So I was running through the woods keeping an eye out for metal, only I was so far in wasn't much chance anybody had left any metal thing out there. I thought I was walking where no man had walked before, and then I smelled smoke and came to a clearing."

She paused, her eyes staring unseeing across the hall. Below us, out on the dance floor near the microphones, Dale and Rose played a mournful old song about departed lovers and lonesome train whistles. The banjo made everything sound spunky.

"Morning glories had twined right up over the house." Her voice had dropped to a whisper. "I never saw such a thing before or since. Up-and-down logs—some still part of growing trees, Cyrus, with branches sprouting out the top. Did you ever hear of such a thing?"

"Maybe," I said quietly. If the little family she talked about had any sign of Earth people in it, with their gifts of growth and plant-talk, many things were possible.

"And a little vegetable garden up near the house," Alma murmured, looking into the past. "Sassy green leaves on those squash vines. Tall corn. Lacy carrot tops. I tell you, I felt like I had walked into a fairy tale, this snug little house in the middle of nowhere with the flowers growing all over it."

She fell silent again. I sat and listened to the child's thin voice. "Oh, where are our dear fathers? Oh, where are our dear fathers? Oh, where are our dear fathers? Da-a-ay is a-breakin' in my soul."

"I woulda run away again," said Alma presently. "Too many stories my ma told about tripping over a fairy mound and going into another land for a century or two until you come out and everything's changed, everyone you know is dead. I woulda run, but the wind changed then, and I smelled that smell, and heard the child's voice."

She was quiet a long time then. I feared the other musicians would return from the coffee-and-dessert break and the music would start and Alma would fall out of her memory into the present. Once she left this confiding mood, I would not know how to bring her back to it, and she was getting to the meat of the story now.

I touched her hand. A terrible temptation came over me to use my powers of persuasion and force the story out of her, but I waited, and the impulse passed. I could make people talk about anything; I could make them forget afterward everything they had said; but I could not make myself forget what I had done, and those memories were difficult to live with. I had enough of them already.

"The child was singing that song," Alma said. "Her voice didn't have much voice left in it, if you know what I mean. And the smell was the smell of dead things that have been lying a while in the heat."

"What happened?" I whispered.

"She wandered around the side of the house, a thin little girl in a dirty white dress that was all tatters. She was sick. Her cheeks were caved in, and her eyes sunk down in her head. Come to find out later, after the doctor saw her, she probably hadn't eaten anything in days, and there were vegetables lying on that ground just as fine as anything you see in the market. She wandered and wavered around, singing. 'Some have gone to heaven shouting.'"

I could hear her singing that verse even as Alma spoke.

"I stepped out of the woods. 'Little girl, little girl. Who are you?' I said. She didn't even look my way, just pranced away and back, singing. I went to her and caught her hands. She looked at me then, and her eyes were like a dead person's. She hummed the tune. Months afterward I couldn't get it out of my head.

"The smell was stronger. I didn't know what to do. I wasn't so old myself. 'What's the matter, little girl?' I said. She sang at me and that was all. She didn't try to pull away or anything. Just sang."

Alma's hand slipped from under mine. She put her hands over her eyes. "You know, I knew that everything had gone wrong, and I didn't know what to do. I let go of the girl. I opened the door of the house. The door, it had a carving of a man's face on it, a bearded face with leaves all around it, and it scared me some—too much like something from Ma's tales, a door that could look at you.

"I opened that door, and that horrible smell came out, stronger than before, and the buzzing of flies. Only light in the room came from it might be a hole in the roof, I didn't look long enough to figure it out; but there was the two of them in there on a bed, lying under that hard light, dead, as far as I could tell, for days maybe; covered with flies."

She lowered her hands from her face, gripped mine in both of hers. "She had to be going in and out," she whispered. "The fire was still lit. That was hard for me to know, that she would go inside with them in such a state." She shook her head.

"I didn't know what to do. I took the girl's hand and led her out of there. The grange was the closest building. I led her here. It was a Saturday, and women were quilting. I brought the girl here and they all started up like a flock of birds. Someone got the doctor. They tried to feed that child, tried to give her water, tried to get her to name herself, but she never did. Only thing she ever did was sing. She died later that night. Doctor said it was starving did it."

The hall filled with talk and commotion as people came back from their conversations and coffee. Musicians gathered around the microphones. Alma gripped my hands and finally looked up at me. "We never even knew their names," she said. The anguish she had felt more than fifty years earlier was still in her face.

"It's all right," I said. I held her hands tight, trying to give her reassurance. "I'll take care of it."

She cocked her head and stared hard at me, almost as hard as she had stared into the past. "What do you mean?" she asked.

I looked at her and wondered how much to tell her. "I believe in ghosts," I said at last. "I'll talk to her."

"Talk to her." Her voice sounded flat.

"She's here. Still singing. I'll talk to her."

"What good will that do?"

"I think she must have been a relative of mine," I said, "and in my family, we know how to care for our dead."

"Alma?" someone called from below. "You back me up on 'Your Cheatin' Heart'?"

"Sure, honey," she said in a distracted voice. She grabbed her cane, left the stage, and went to get her mandolin. We both joined in the music again. Between tunes, though, she was always looking at me.

The dance lasted until eleven, the dregs of it anyway; people packed up and left in trickles earlier, until at last only Alma and Rose and a guitar player named John and I were left, and the couple who swept the dancing dust off the floor and put away the folding metal chairs.

"Time to go home," John said, "before they kick us out."

I wiped the rosin off Lucia's strings and face with a bandana I keep in her case for that purpose. I loosened the horse hairs on my bow. John put away his guitar, Rose packed up her banjo, and Alma locked her mandolin in its case. We said good night to the caretakers and left the building amid their invitation to come back next month.

Rose and John went to their cars. Alma stood beside me in the chill night. The motion-sensitive light above the door lit us from behind, but if we stood still long enough, it would switch off again. I waited.

"You got a car, Cyrus?"

"No."

"How'd you get here?"

"Hitched a ride." On a wind.

"You want a ride somewheres else?"

I smiled at her. "I still have business here."

"You believe in ghosts," she said, and then whispered, "I've been so afraid they exist. None of those deaths was quiet, and I've never been able to stop seeing them. Poor little mite. Holding her hand was like holding twigs."

"What I need to do now is private, Alma."

"Don't tell me that," she said. "Don't you tell me to go away with this darkness still in my head. I've lived with it a long time, Cyrus. I am more than ready to let it go."

I sighed. I wondered. Even though Alma didn't want to go, I could tell her to go, and she would do it. But if the thought of these spirits was troubling her so much, how could I leave her with that darkness? "Wait here," I told Alma, and I went around back of the grange and lifted up into the tree where I had hidden my things.

Mostly I make my own rules, but there are some very strong ones almost all of us follow, and one of them concerns outsiders. I'm not supposed to reveal family secrets if I can help it.

I took my snow crystal out of my knapsack and sat on a branch, holding the crystal in both hands. "Powers and Presences, lead me and guide me," I murmured. "Help me to choose what is right for each person."

"Which are your choices?" whispered a breeze past my ear.

"Here is a spirit that needs a path, and here is a person who has a troubled mind. I would like to help them both if I can."

"Why not?" whispered the wind.

"One is not of our family."

A moment of silence slipped by, and then the whisper came: "In your hands."

I kissed the crystal, tucked it into my pocket, and shrugged into my knapsack. I climbed down the tree, and a good thing, too: Alma was on the ground below, leaning on her cane and looking up. "What were you doing up there?" she asked.

"Praying a little and getting my things," I said, hanging by my arms from the lowest limb, then dropping. I had not swung from a limb in quite that way since I was a boy, and I felt absurd.

"Your things," said Alma. She glanced from my fiddle case, still at the base of the tree, to the knapsack on my back. "Those are all your things?"

I nodded. "Just passing through."

"On your way to where?"

"Everywhere."

"Nowhere," she said.

For a moment I felt a strange sense of vertigo. My dream of the death of the planet unfolded in my mind. Fields of barren ground, dark blasted hills, ice along the edges. How bleak it would be to have no one to look for, no one to talk to, no one to jam with. Why explore when every place was gray and dead?

But this was not my reality. I blinked and looked at Alma.

"Everywhere," I said again. Everywhere there were musicians, coffee shops, radio stations, roads; crops in the field, people in cars, animals in forests, crickets and frog choruses and murmuring bees, and the slow rich sound of voices talking on a porch of a summer evening, voices murmuring in a firelit room of a winter's night.

Usually my voice wasn't among them, though. I did a lot of listening and appreciating, but not much sharing.

"Have it your own way," Alma said. "Now what?"

"I'm going back inside as soon as they close it up and leave."

"Just how do you imagine you'll get inside that building? You some kind of burglar?"

I smiled at her.

"I have a key," she said. "I'm on the planning committee. I'll let you in."

"Alma? Alma!" Voices called from the front of the building. They sounded alarmed. "You out here? You all right? Alma!"

"Oh, my car's still there," she muttered. She and her cane stumped around to the front of the building. "You go on home, Charlie and Liz. I'll lock up. I've got some thinking to do."

"All right," they said, relief in their voices. Presently a car started and drove off down the road.

"Come on, Cyrus," said Alma and we went back inside Spruce Grange through the front door.

The hall looked unfamiliar and dark with nobody in it but us. Alma went into the coat closet and flipped on banks of lights.

"Can you light the stage?" I asked.

Lights went on above the stage.

It was strange to see this empty place that minutes earlier had been alive with people and dance. My doom dream murmured in my mind.

"What next?" Alma said.

I climbed the stairs to the stage. No clutter of instrument cases and coats; even the metal chairs were folded and stood against the backdrop.

I listened.

"Some are down in the valley singing . . . ."

I knelt on the bare wood stage. I took my snow crystal from my pocket and placed it on the floor, then slid out of my knapsack and sat back on my heels, looking around.

"*Some are down in the valley singing. . . .*"
Alma leaned against the stage's edge and watched me.
"What I'm about to do may seem strange to you," I said. "It will not hurt you, but it may frighten you. Are you sure you want to watch?"
"*Some are down in the valley singing. . . .*"
"It concerns that little girl?"
"I believe it does."
She gripped her cane, hunched her shoulders. "Go ahead."
"*Da-a-a-ay is a-breakin' in my soul. . . .*"
I took a small glass plate from my knapsack. I had made it as part of my apprenticeship to the glassblower in Cielito, before I understood the limitations of my being Sign Air—fire would heed me as much as it did anybody without fire persuasions; I had no skill with it, but still, the plate was a gift of earth and fire, lopsided and thick as it was, and I smiled at it as I did every time I dug it out of its protecting silk. I set it on the stage beside my snow crystal and placed a sprig of desert sage and some dried cedar twigs on it.

I sat and gathered my mind, preparing a version of the "Things Seen and Unseen" chant that would let the invisible attain visibility if it so desired. Usually this chant revealed things whether they wanted to be shown or not, and only for a brief time. I wanted a version that would grant power to the invisible to choose the length of its interaction with light.

When I was satisfied that I had shaped the tool I wanted, I touched fire to the spices on the glass plate. They burned quickly, leaving a smudge of smoke, a signature in the air that smelled of desert starlight and night forest. I addressed Powers and Presences and spoke my chant.

The song stopped.

When I looked up, a young girl stood across from me.

She was slender and hollow-eyed and wore a white shift. She looked just like my little sister Drusilla had at ten, long dark wavy hair almost to her waist, a pale fine-featured face with large gray eyes, slender hands. She was not gaunt the way Alma had described her.

"Presence," I murmured.

Her eyes widened. She touched her chest.

I smiled at her. "Presence," I said again.

"Uncle?" she whispered.

"Cousin," I said. If she had died during World War II, at about ten—she looked perhaps ten, perhaps eleven—then she and I had been born at about the same time.

"I don't understand," whispered the girl. She blinked. She glanced around, saw Alma, who stood there staring at her. Alma dropped her cane. Her right fist pressed against her breastbone, and her left hand gripped her right. Her eyes were wide.

"Gift me a name? Mine is Cyrus Locke," I said.

"Helena Exile," said the girl, still staring at Alma.

Exile! A name taken by those who were cast out from our family, the threads binding them to us cut. She was too young to be exiled; her parents must have been the ones banished. I did not even know which clan place they had come from; it was all old news now, no doubt, though I would have to check with the Powers and other Presences about final disposition.

"Helena," I said. "This is Alma."

Alma stood unmoving, her mouth a little open.

"Alma, are you all right?"

Alma said, "How? How can she be standing there more real than life? She looks much stronger than when I saw her."

Helena's face clouded. "Cousin Cyrus," she said. "Please."

"Cousin." I lifted my hands to her even though I knew she could not touch them. "You are only halfway here. You've been halfway here a long time, fifty years or more. I offer you a chance to choose. Do you wish to go farther away? Do you wish to return?"

"I—I—My mother! My father!" She stiffened, her eyes glazing.

"They are gone too. They left before you did. They may be waiting on the other side of shadow, or they may be trapped without a proper unbinding. I will tend to them soon. Just now, let's think about you."

"I don't feel—" She reached across to me and tried to grasp my hands. Hers passed through mine. "Oh!"

Alma gasped as well. I looked at her. She was paper pale. Her eyelids fluttered and she began to sag. I bespoke the air around her to hold her up, worried even as I did so that I was going too far. Ghosts, whether she believed in them or not, were part of her everyday, a conversational coin always being spent. Solid air would be outside her experience. "Breathe deeply," I said to her, and asked air to strengthen and sustain her.

After a moment the color returned to her face. She still looked terrified.

"Alma," I said.

"You—you're one of those black magic demon sorcerers, aren't you?"

"No." I glanced at Helena, who looked down at her hands, at the glass plate and snow crystal at her feet, at me, and then at Alma. Helena might be confused, but if her parents had raised her with any knowledge of her heritage, she would be able to understand what had happened to her, given time and explanation. Alma, on the other hand—

"Demon has nothing to do with what I am," I said.

"Are you evil?"

Sometimes. Regrets still pricked me. "No."

"Let me go."

"Are you all right? You looked like you were going to fall."

"I'm fine," she said, her voice hollow as though she were trying to convince herself.

I bespoke air to be air-like again, and Alma shuddered, then bent to retrieve her cane. She limped to the double doors at the far end of the hall, never looking back. When she had closed the doors behind her, I turned to Helena.

"Little cousin," I said. "Flesh has left you. Where do you wish to go next?"

She squatted across from me and stared at me. "I have been so lost," she whispered, "so alone in the darkness."

"Your spirit tied itself to this place."

She looked around. "What is this place?"

"This is a grange hall. A community place where people get together; not usually members of our family, though. There is music here sometimes. You were singing."

"Why am I here?"

"This is where you died, Alma said."

"Alma . . ."

"Alma found you in the forest and brought you here. She was trying to help you."

"I remember a girl." Her eyes looked inward. "A tall brown girl with twigs in her hair. One of the first strangers I ever saw. I remember her and I don't remember her." She shook her head. "That was after . . . I—"

She screamed.

It was a high, huge, sad, chilling sound, a sound that might have echoed across a cold landscape of white and gray, the last sound of life on a dead world. It lasted a good while. The hair on my head and the back of my neck rose, and my skin tingled with goosebumps.

Alma looked in through the doors.

Helena screamed, first with her eyes closed, then with her eyes opened. She stared up at the ceiling and screamed.

She stopped. The ensuing silence lay like a weight on me. She stared at me.

"My parents died!" she yelled.

"Yes."

"They died and left me all alone!"

"Yes."

"I couldn't wake them! Mami! Papa! How could you leave me?"

"They couldn't help it," I said when no other answer came.

"I couldn't let them go, but they weren't there anyway."

"Yes," I said.

"They didn't come back."

"No." I held out my arms to her, wanting to hug her, but how?

Air whispered past my ears.

Air could be solid for me.

"Helena," I murmured, holding out my arms, asking air to be solid where she was in it.

She sobbed and came to me and crawled into my lap, and I put my arms around her, air and light and spirit unbreathed, unfinished. I held her and she cried. Her world had been as bleak as the dead land in my dreams, shorn as it was of all she knew of warmth.

"You don't have to be alone anymore," I told her when her sobs slowed. "You can stay with me, or you can go on and find your parents."

"How can I find them now?" She stirred and pushed away from me. It was strange. It did not feel like a child I held; she was smooth and cool and had no breath or heartbeat. I embraced a weightless stone. She pushed at my arms, and I released her.

She rose and looked at Alma, who had come back and stood against the edge of the stage again. "You were the girl who came?" Helena said.

"Yes," said Alma.

"She was the girl who found me," Helena told me, "and look at her now. She's an old woman. I couldn't even find my parents when they first left their bodies. How can I possibly find them now?"

"Where are they buried?" I asked Alma.

"At the little cemetery up the hill behind Ravensville Church. All three together we put them in the ground, under a stone with no name on it. 'Mother, Father, Child' was all it said, and the year of their death."

"May we go there now?"

"I can drive," she said.

"Would you?" I spoke to her doubts and fears. Often enough I have spent time with people who have no magic in their lives, and I have done my best to understand how that feels.

There are so many things to be afraid of.

Yet Alma had returned in the middle of Helena's scream, for me the most frightening thing that had happened tonight. It was a sound of despair that came from a place so deep I had not known whether it had an end. I had been afraid I might spend the rest of my life listening to it.

"I will," said Alma.

"Thank you." I looked at Helena. "Are you ready to leave this place? You have been here a long time."

"There's nothing here for me," she said.

I thought of the music and dance earlier that evening. When I died, I might like to haunt a place like this for such a taste of life, friendship, warmth once a month. But Helena had not been awake to any of it.

I looked at the glass plate on the stage, the dusting of gray ash left behind by cedar and sage. I thanked Powers and Presences for help, asked for more, put away my tools and climbed to my feet, picked up my knapsack and my fiddle case. Helena and I went down the stairs together to the floor below.

"I see it," Alma said, staring at us.

I glanced at Helena, then at Alma.

"You *are* related. Your nose, hers. Your eyes. How can that be? How could you know?"

"Recognition," I said. "In the music."

She frowned. Her eyebrows drew together. "Guess I don't have to understand it to see that it works," she said. "Let's go."

For a moment Helena and I hesitated in the grange's doorway. I watched her. She looked behind her at the stage, confused.

"You've woven yourself into this place," I said.

"Unbind me."

I worked it out in my head, a thread-cutting chant for ties of place. It had to be specific. I don't like unbinding work; too risky, too counter to my impulses to connect. I said this chant for Helena Exile, though, and felt the brief shock of freedom shake her.

I remembered that shock. I had cut myself free of my home place all those years ago, though I didn't realize I was doing it at the time. It had hurt.

Alma drove a big maroon sedan with well-padded white seats. Helena and I got in the back. Alma glanced over her shoulder, shook her head, started the car, and drove through the cold December night along back roads that cut through quiet fields, past houses where all the lights were out. Every once in a while Alma shook her head again.

We went through brief patches of forest, then through a little sleeping town that had a general store, a garage/gas pump, and a feed store. A little farther along we came to a white church among trees, its spire pointing to the stars.

Alma turned the car off on a dirt road past the church and we edged up a small forested hill to a graveyard. She stopped the car, turned off the engine and the headlights. We sat there in silence for a little while.

I opened the door and climbed out, my knapsack in my hand. Helena joined me.

The car engine ticked. Somewhere birds chirped and silenced. Gravestones stood in less-than-orderly rows, some new, some old, some ornate, some plain, some with fresh or plastic flowers at their foot, and some embraced by weeds.

Alma emerged. "Not really my favorite place to be at night," she said after a moment.

"There's nothing here will hurt you," I told her. Then I checked. Sometimes the energies surrounding death and the dead can get muddled and enhanced and strange. Much depends on how people relate to their dead, and what the dead plan to do next.

There was no smell of danger in this place.

Alma shuddered. She straightened her shoulders, gripped her cane in one hand and a flashlight in the other, and headed in among the stones. We followed her.

It was a plain stone, not even granite or marble: a rounded rock you might find in a river, and it said just what Alma had told us: MOTHER, FATHER, CHILD 1943.

"Oh," said Helena, holding out open hands, waving them above the ground. "I feel so strange."

I took my snow crystal from my pocket, held it in my right hand. *Powers and Presences, help us to find the right way to proceed. May we awaken those who sleep here?*

They are here and they do not sleep.

I looked up as Alma dropped her cane and gripped my arm. Two glowing shadows stood beyond the headstone, holding hands.

I said the chant I had said for Helena, "Things Seen and Unseen," modified so that those unseen could become seen for as long as they wished.

The shining shadows darkened, took on weight and hue. A broad man and a narrow woman, he in overalls and an undershirt, she in a calico dress. They had the faces of my cousins.

"Helena! Bright star!" the woman cried, reaching toward us.

"Where have you been?" cried the man, opening his arms. "We've been waiting ages!"

"Mami! Papa!" Helena gave a choked sob and ran to them, was swallowed in their embrace.

Exiles. In death, were they still separated from the rest of us?

People make such separations, something whispered past my ear. *Most of us do not.*

My dream of a wasteland: a place I had sent myself?

Helena separated from her parents, came back to me. "Cousin Cyrus," she said. "Thank you. Thank you." She rose on tiptoe and kissed my cheek, a cold hard spot of pressure and then release. "Thank you for trying to help me," she whispered to Alma, kissing her too. Alma's fingers dug even deeper into my upper arm.

Helena darted back to her parents. They smiled at us, melted into each other, glowed brighter and brighter, then vanished in a final flare.

"What . . . happened?" Alma said.

I was not alone on a dead world now. Alma's grip convinced me

I was alive and in company. "I guess they knew where they were going after all," I said, "once she came back to them." I felt a strange longing to go home myself, and see my sister and my parents and my cousins and aunts and uncles. Some of the people I had known were no doubt dead now, and some new ones had probably been born. I wanted to make sure the family was still where I had left it.

"I don't mean what happened to them, the—the ghosts—I mean what happened? What happened this whole night? Who the heck *are* you, anyway?" Alma said. "And what were you talking about when you were saying all those things in that other language?"

People make such separations. Most of us do not.

There was family, and then there was family—all over the place. "I'll buy you coffee at Shari's and we can talk about it," I said, stooping to pick up her cane.

ABOUT THE AUTHOR

Over the past thirty years, Nina Kiriki Hoffman has sold adult and YA novels and more than 250 short stories. Her works have been finalists for the World Fantasy, Mythopoeic, Sturgeon, Philip K. Dick, and Endeavour awards. Her novel The Thread that Binds the Bones *won a Stoker award, and her short story "Trophy Wives" won a Nebula Award.*

Her middle-school novel Thresholds *was published by Viking in August, 2010, and its sequel,* Meetings, *came out in August of 2011.*

Nina does production work for The Magazine of Fantasy & Science Fiction. *She also works with teen writers. She lives in Eugene, Oregon, with several cats and many strange toys and imaginary friends.*

For a list of Nina's publications, check out: http://ofearna.us/books/hoffman.html.

OTHER TITLES FROM FAIRWOOD/DARKWOOD PRESS

Brittle Innings
by Michael Bishop
trade paper: $19.99
ISBN: 978-1-933846-31-6

Unpossible
by Daryl Gregory
trade paper: $16.99
ISBN: 978-1-933846-30-9

End of an Aeon
Bridget & Marti McKenna, eds
trade paper: $16.99
ISBN: 978-1-933846-26-2

Dragon Virus
by Laura Anne Gilman
limited hardcover: $25
ISBN: 978-1-933846-25-5

The Best of Talebones
edited by Patrick Swenson
trade paper: $18.99
ISBN: 978-1-933846-24-8

A Cup of Normal
by Devon Monk
trade paper: $16.99
ISBN: 978-0-9820730-9-4

Boarding Instructions
by Ray Vukcevich
trade paper: $16.99
ISBN: 978-1-933846-3-1

Harbinger
by Jack Skillingstead
trade paper: $16.99
ISBN: 978-0-9820730-3-2

www.fairwoodpress.com
21528 104th Street Court East;
Bonney Lake, WA   98391

CPSIA information can be obtained
at www.ICGtesting.com
Printed in the USA
FSOW02n0453110915
10824FS

9 781933 846323